Caroline Bourne

Talon's Heart

Prologue

Fort Davis, Texas, March 26, 1857

The little fort, affectionately called *Painted Camp on the Limpia* by its inhabitants, basked in the afternoon sun, only slightly cooled by intermittent spurts of arid wind. Deep in a canyon, with rock wall palisades on three sides, the post looked out of her open side to a windswept prairie spreading toward the southern horizon. Lieutenant Beale's twenty-five camel survey expedition was on station, and Captain Salem George Compton, who had been at Ft. Davis since its establishment three years before, barely endured the nauseating stench washing through the open windows.

Staring critically at his reflection in the small mirror above his washstand, he hoped his daughter, Julia Rose, would not think the indelible stench emanated from him, since he had taken special care with his grooming that morning. In less than an hour, she was scheduled to arrive by Santa Fe stage, traveling west on the San Antonio-El Paso Road. He hoped to make an impression that would not scare the devil out of her. By the time of her arrival, she and her cousin, Lydia, would have spent a full and weary week of travel since leaving Boston.

The harsh Texas sun had darkened Salem's skin, the mirror reflecting a man appearing older than his actual age of thirty-five. He had grown thin and gaunt, he thought due to the distance between he and his daughter, and a scattering of gray hair had managed to sprout in his once rich chestnut waves. He worried that his Julia Rose might not immediately recognize him, though she, too, had changed. She was now a young lady, nearly sixteen, and an adored only child he hadn't seen in three long years, except through occasional photographs that had attested to her yearly change. By the accounts of her frequent and often read letters, and those of his aunt in whose care she had been left, she was quite an attraction to the lads about the fair city of Boston.

Completing his nervous primping, Salem turned from the mirror, at once facing the mocking gaze of Lieutenant Samuel Lytton. A happy-go-lucky young friend from upstate New York, he also lived in the multi-unit bachelor quarters at Fort Davis. Samuel had teased him unmercifully these past two weeks about the reunion with his daughter.

"Less than an hour, Sir, and your Miss Compton and her pretty cousin will be drawing up," Samuel laughed, throwing off the fatigue hat more often preferred by the enlisted soldiers. "Every officer inside these mighty hills is gallantly lined up outside awaiting a first glance at the comely lass...or I should say *lasses*." By each of their confessions, they had fallen in love with Julia Rose through the small, framed photograph her father kept on his bureau, and through his frequent boasting over the past three years.

Salem Compton managed the briefest of smiles. "Be forewarned, Sir," he grumbled good-naturedly, "that all you spoiled Army boys had better keep your lecherous eyes off my Julia Rose and her cousin...or I shall be forced to draw and quarter the lot of you."

Though he grumbled, he had the officers to thank for the brightly colored ribbons, procured from a post seamstress, tied around the sparse trees standing within the grounds of Fort Davis to welcome Julia. A dance would be held Saturday night, and every unmarried officer had officially signed her dance card by proxy, and that of her cousin, Miss Lydia Porter. Though he had jokingly told Sam he'd thrown the cards out with the rubbish, he certainly had no intentions of doing so. With their long-awaited and initial reunion behind them, Salem planned to press the dance cards into the hands of each of the young ladies for their coquettish enjoyment.

Still chuckling at his high-strung superior, Samuel Lytton wandered off in search of other mischief on post, his first destination the overpriced sutler's bar where off-duty soldiers converged to drink to their heart's content. He had forgotten his fatigue hat, lying against the pillow on his cot.

Salem Compton removed the framed portrait of his daughter from atop the bureau, and sat on the trunk below his bed to quietly admire it once again. Though the portrait was sepia-toned, he imagined the traveling gown and cape to be a perfect match to her exquisite blue eyes. He had mailed her the ensemble to wear on the last leg of her trip from El Paso. That she had donned it for the sitting had been a pleasant surprise.

Salem quietly relived the six years he had raised Julia alone in Boston after her mother's death, overseeing her education while maintaining a busy military career. When he had transferred to this remote Texas outpost at the beginning of its installation, he had promptly put her in the guardianship of his aunt, rather than drag her into a hostile environment that might exact a terrible toll on her youth and sweet innocence. He saw from the photograph that the refined elements of Boston had kept her pale and lovely, and her cheeks radiated with maidenly reticence. Though he was career military and gloried in his numerous battle feats over the years, he considered his beautiful, golden-haired daughter his greatest achievement.

Returning the portrait to the bureau, Salem pulled out his pocket watch and looked at the time. The hands stood at half past two and the coach was due to arrive at three. Having quietly rehearsed the words with which he would greet his daughter, he felt that nothing had sounded either appropriate or fatherly. He had simply spent too much time around men, and the harshness of military life at this desolate outpost had allayed the gentlemanly refinements he had once perfected to an art. Perhaps he should just let his heart do the talking when his lovely girl stepped down from the coach.

Aware of a silent presence, Salem turned toward his friend, again standing in the doorway. "Forgot your hat, eh, Lytton?"

"Yes, I—that's not why I've returned." His usual exuberance was muted by his troubled expression. "Lieutenant Colonel Seawell requests that you see him at HQ posthaste."

"Now?" Salem queried, annoyance as readable as his anxiety. Pivoting toward Sam, he reminded him that, "he knows

I'm expecting my daughter any minute."

"He's aware of it," Samuel replied at once, "but his adjutant said it is urgent." Stepping from the threshold, the lieutenant outstretched his hand, which was noticeably trembling. "Come, Salem, I'll walk with you."

Out of doors, a gentle wind, whining like a child lost and alone, swept down from the ragged bluffs of the Davis Mountains. Where the post had been sedate and basking in the afternoon sun just an hour ago, it now stirred with activity. The soldiers of the Ninth U.S. Cavalry had mustered to the parade field, fully armed and with mounts in full gear. Across the din of urgency, a major yelled, "Boots and saddles, soldiers!"

Then Salem noticed the flatbed wagon that had pulled up to the post infirmary. One civilian, his head wrapped in bloody bandages, arrows protruding from his right shoulder and left leg, was being helped down from the seat by a medical orderly. Flies swarmed over several corpses partially obscured by canvas in the bed of the wagon. He started to question his friend walking quietly beside him, but a sudden dread filled him so completely he couldn't think clearly, let alone utter a distinguishable syllable.

Quickening his pace to a near run, Salem entered the administration building, where he faced several high-ranking officers, including the post commanding officer, Lieutenant Colonel G. W. Seawell. All faces turned to him with profound anguish.

Captain Salem George Compton didn't have to be told what had happened.

He already knew.

One

Camp Casey,
northeast of the Huachuca Mountain Range,
Arizona Territory, 1882

Matthew Money had taken on this last official duty as a Deputy United States Marshal, only because he was destined for the little Army post anyway. He sat for a moment on the trail descending from Cimarron Bluff, rubbing the stiff leg that had forced him into retirement at just over forty years of age. Bear grass springing from the rocks partially obscured his view as he looked over sentry-like chimneys and long rows of stone buildings facing a large military parade ground. At the left of the parade ground was the military prison, the guardhouse, where he planned to make his first stop. Spurring his horse into action, he noticed more wickiups outside the grounds to the east where the families of the Apache scouts stayed to be close to their men. Approaching the main gate, the horse trailing him stalled and pulled on its lead rope, and he drew his own tired mount up. Then he turned in the saddle to issue another in a long line of warnings to his silently brooding prisoner.

But the half-breed Comanche, shackled hand and foot to a fine buckskin mare, simply glared at him from beneath a plain brown bandanna. "My horse stumbled," Talon bristled. "Want to shoot her, Marshal Money?"

Soon, they drew up to the main gate and Money, a familiar face at Camp Casey, was promptly allowed to enter. Matthew— Mattie to the soldiers who knew him—noticed the way Talon glared at the Apache scouts conducting routine drills on the parade ground. Moments later, he dismounted at the guard station and went to his prisoner's side to ease a key into the left leg shackle. "You kick me, Comanche Talon, when I remove the irons, and so help me—"

He left the silly threat dangling, and Talon recalled that he'd used exactly the same words when they had dismounted to spend the night beneath the stars. She would have escaped then, but he had fettered her right leg to a chain locked to the trunk of a Paloverde. She had obeyed his first warning, and one this morning when they'd resumed their journey. Talon hardly thought it worthwhile to try to escape from this towering almost ex-deputy U.S. Marshal now. He had promised he would do what he could to spare her from the hangman's noose the Army kept handy for Indian troublemakers. A strong sense of self-preservation compelled her to trust his word.

Mattie jabbed Talon's leg, parting her from her thoughts. "Did I kick you last night, Marshal Money, or this morning? So why would I kick you now? I told you yesterday, I don't spit, kick, kill or maim."

Mattie laughed lightly. "For a minute there, little gal, I thought you went to sleep on me." The shackles freed from her soft-booted ankles, his large hands moved to her waist.

As Talon came down from her saddle, she faced the lawman who had finally managed to capture her. Matthew Money was big and tall, darkened by the harsh climate of Arizona Territory, and dressed in drab browns. He had warm brown eyes, square, rugged features, and didn't look like a man in his forties, though he'd told her he was. He also had a gentle nature that harshly barked orders could not mask. "You could still let me go," she whispered, eliciting nothing more than another small laugh.

"If I turned my back, Comanche Talon, you'd be out of here like a firefly."

They had engaged in pleasant conversation, and even fond reminiscences of their separate lives. Since he was taking the job of civilian blacksmith at Camp Casey, he had even offered to take care of her horse *if a sad fate befalls you, little lady, despite my efforts*. Talon felt he had no cause to distrust her now. "You're just full of your own importance to think I'd waste that much energy trying to escape a worn out *old* ex-deputy marshal like you." Again, he simply laughed, and Talon, nervously laughing as well, tucked herself protectively against him. "Forgive me, Marshal Money. I'm just so scared. Promise you won't let those Army boys hang me."

Big, burly, gentle fingers crept beneath Talon's stiffly set chin. "I told you, gal, I wouldn'a brought you here if I thought they'd hang you. Let me take care of you, all right?"

His response managed to revitalize her trust, so Talon took a moment to look over the Army camp, smaller than others scattered throughout Arizona territory. On each of its long sides, the stone and mortar buildings, joined by short stretches of pole fencing at the back walls, formed a barricade to the outside world. But a small cemetery and the camp's shorter ends were wide open, with a single guard station centrally located at each. A flagpole on the parade ground proudly waved the American flag with its thirty-eight stars above the flag of Arizona Territory. Both were now lowered to half-mast, she supposed in respect of the previous commanding officer who had died suddenly a week ago.

Mattie urged her toward Major Hiram Stahl, Officer of the Guard, who had appeared from the dark interior of the guardhouse. "Confine my prisoner while I talk to Colonel Heitman."

The post had received a wire yesterday morning to expect Talon, but Stahl had yet to prepare accommodations for a female. "Sgt. Mulroney." A stout, dwarfish soldier, his uniform soiled by many days of wear, stepped from the darkness of the guardhouse. "Take this prisoner to general confinement."

As Mulroney approached. Talon instinctively pressed into Mattie. The sergeant stank of chewing tobacco, body odor and dribbled food, as offensive a man as Talon had ever encountered. "I don't need to be drugged," she protested as his fingers groped her upper arm.

The sergeant threw up his hands mockingly, backing off. To ward off the scene Talon looked prepared to make, Mattie took her into the guardhouse himself. Settled into a large confinement cell, she was surrounded by stone walls and a dozen unoccupied cots. She had heard that military prisons in this area were dark, damp, and stank of human waste, filth, and Apaches. This one was clean, with fresh bedding, floors still damp from a recent mopping, an almost antiseptic smell permeating the atmosphere.

And no smell of Apaches!

* * *

Lieutenant Colonel Paul Heitman directed his old friend to a chair at his temporary office in HQ, explaining that he needed to finish up a mailing for the late evening coach. While Paul added the final flourishes to his letter, Mattie recalled the first time he'd met this suave, efficient career Army officer who had come to the Southwest as a fresh-faced lieutenant during the Indian wars of the '50's. They'd been young then, wild, and real ambitious about fighting Indians. While Mattie had gone to Texas for a while to fight the Comanches, Paul had remained here to deal with Apaches. He had kept his slim stature through the years, wore his mix of uniform and buckskins well, but at forty-five his skin, beneath a crop of unruly, peppered hair, was as parched as the Arizona desert.

Mattie became aware of Paul's close, slightly amused scrutiny. Dead tired and in need of a good night's sleep, he could scarcely think clearly as he sat forward to speak to his old friend. "Paul, I just left the Comanche Talon Rose in your guardhouse."

The United States Army had been after the Indian outlaw for two years, but she had stayed constantly on the move and ahead of both the law and the Army. He had heard she often hid with the band of cutthroats led by Manolito Menendez. "I couldn't believe you civilian boys finally caught the thieving cow. But what the hell do you expect me to do with her?"

Beyond Talon's little arguments, she had been thoughtful and imaginative, and had actually been a pleasant talker when the mood struck her. Mattie visibly cringed at the insults Paul Heitman slung at an Indian woman who had valiantly and defiantly struggled through the hardships of her young life. "The ranchers woulda lynched her. Me an' my bossman figured she'd have a better chance here."

Paul rose, settling to the corner of his desk to look squarely down at his friend. "We hang bad Indians here, too, Mattie."

"She's ain't bad, an' she's got a real good heart. So what if she helped round up some silly steers that got herded to Mexico. Dadgum, Paul, she's desperate for family, an' them greasers—they treated her like she was one of 'em. You got a scout troop here, and she'd make a helluva scout. Since I'll be stayin' on as blacksmith, I'll help keep an eye on her, keep her straight—"

Paul glanced out the window as the Apache scouts dismounted at the corral. "You bring a renegade here—half-blood Comanche at that—who's also been stealing Army horses and supplies for two years and selling *them* below the Rio Grande, who, I might remind you, caused the death of one of my soldiers, and you want me to make a scout of her? I'd have downright mutiny among my Apaches if I did that."

"That sergeant's horse pitched him off a ridge into a ravine. Hang the dag-blasted horse for it, but you ain't goin'ta hang Talon."

He had so seldom heard Mattie raise his voice that Paul suppressed a smile. Before he took that shot in his knee, his old friend had been too busy riding Arizona dustlands rounding up troublemakers to keep up with the law. Otherwise, he'd know he didn't have authority to hang the Comanche without due process. "I'll do what I must to put a halt to this renegade's activities, no matter how unpleasant it is to you, Mattie."

Mattie was convinced that Talon had some worth, and it had only to be nurtured in a strict environment, such as a military camp. So he sat forward, ready to present the argument he had rehearsed for the past twenty hours. "Let me tell you about this little gal."

Paul reluctantly conceded, but only because Mattie was generally a good judge of character. "I'll give you the next five minutes to tell me enough about this troublemaking breed to convince me she has any value beyond food for the worms."

"I'll need only three minutes, Paul—" Mattie responded, enthusiastically launching into the life story of Talon Rose, the half-blood Comanche, orphaned child of a white captive and a village leader, traded by a vindictive Comanche squaw at age eight to a muleskinner for four horses and burro, enslaved by the Sioux for five years, and now, full grown, wanted in two territories and the State of Texas for crimes that never once included murder. Finally, he ended with, "You know what that gal was doin' when we caught her yesterday mornin'? Takin' a jackrabbit one of them greasers killed to a squatter who broke his leg in a fall. She even cooked it first, her not bein' real domestic like, so he wouldn't have to worry with it. So, Paul, I'm askin' you real polite-like to give Talon a chance." He thought of something else. "An' on top of that, she was educated by a white man from the east...speaks better English than most of us here."

His head slightly back on his chair, Paul gazed at Mattie at an angle across his cheek. "You and that annoying Texas drawl of yours just took six minutes of my time."

* * *

Private Andrew Wilson and the other guards had taken their pleasures looking at the pretty, green-eyed Indian woman from the encroaching shadows of an adjacent corridor. So, when Talon asked for a glass of water, Wilson jumped at the chance to accommodate her. "I'll be right back, ma'am."

Talon Rose wasn't sure she'd ever been called a 'ma'am' before and suppressed a small smile. When he returned with a tin cup of water, she lifted her shackled hands with feigned effort—certainly to elicit sympathy—took the cup with a softly spoken, "Thank you," and settled onto the nearest cot to sip the cool water.

Mulroney announced that the C.O. wanted to see Talon. The door unlocked, Wilson stepped aside so Talon could enter the corridor ahead of him. Minutes later they crossed the parade ground and entered HQ. When she stepped into Heitman's office, Mattie stood, Talon returning his small smile. Now she turned her attentions to the colonel, looking over documents on an untidy desk. The guard retreated, and Mattie returned to his chair.

"All right, let's get this—" Paul Heitman's sentence paused conspicuously as he looked to Talon for the first time. He had expected a dowdy, pock-faced squaw blackened by the sun and

14

stinking of filth, certainly not this stately young woman with honey-colored skin and vivid green eyes unmasking her white heritage. She was tall, slim, with a womanly shape, her light deerskin dress hugging her small waist and hanging to mid-calf. Her thick, ebony hair, plaited in a single braid, fell fully to her waistline. She hardly looked dangerous enough for the shackles confining her slim wrists, though Paul imagined, with looks like hers, she was dangerous as hell. No wonder Mattie was so taken with her.

No matter her mixed bloodline, Paul thought he had never looked so deeply into raw Indian hate. "My soft-hearted friend here believes you have redeeming qualities. I'm willing to consider a reprieve."

Before he might continue, and with a glance toward Mattie, Talon spilled forth a string of Indian words, not one of which Heitman understood—or thought might be polite.

"Talon, you ain't nothin' but a show off with all them languages you speak," Mattie fussed. "English, please."

At once annoyed by her own rash response, especially since her life was on the line, Talon resented Mattie's reprimand. He knew she spoke only Sioux and English, enough Spanish to get by south of the Rio Grande, or infantile Comanche words dredged from her childhood memories. But his insult went without retort as she concentrated on the colonel, his tall, mature frame spilled into tight buckskin trousers tucked into long boots, one of which lay carelessly across the corner of his desk. His gray flannel shirt—common military apparel of the enlisted soldiers—was partially unbuttoned and rumpled beneath his open dark blue jacket.

"I said, Sir, what are the conditions of this reprieve?" Talon half-expected Mattie to come off his chair and shake some sense into her. Why did she have to be so impulsive? Dear old Shepperd, the old school teacher with whom she had lived after escaping the Sioux, had lovingly pointed out that one fault more times than she could count. *Think, Talon...remember this man holds your fate in his hands.*

Mattie had failed to mention that the breed Comanche was

a spitfire. Paul's first instinct was to send her straight back to the guardhouse, but he had promised his friend—

"The conditions are that you'll serve the United States Army as a scout for the next two years, you will be deemed a felon who cannot leave Camp Casey except with your scout troop, and if you do, you'll be shot on sight. Is this clear so far?" Talon slightly nodded. "Infractions will result in flogging or confinement." Though he'd thrown in flogging simply to keep her in line, he smiled at the fear jumping into her glassy emerald eyes. "Any discipline will be considered administrative— without benefit of court martial. Clear so far?"

"My comprehension is intact," Talon replied somewhat glibly.

Heitman suppressed a smile. "You will not have the option to resign, nor can you be discharged." He now eased forward. "Frankly, I think you'll be a damned nuisance at this camp, young woman, but I owe Mattie a favor. You have him to thank for your life today." Concluding his narration, Heitman thrust the documents his clerk had just prepared toward Talon. "This is your official contract in triplicate. By putting your mark on this paper, you enter into a binding agreement that Mattie, in his last official capacity as a deputy U.S. Marshal, has also signed. Then you'll be turned over to the Chief of Scouts, who'll be your direct superior."

Apaches! He will put me in the hands of Apaches! I would rather eat bugs! "Direct superior or my jailer?" Talon Rose, daughter of a Comanche leader, was unwilling to be under the control of any man. When Mattie had promised to help her, she thought she'd have to make silly promises to be good, then be turned loose, not forced to scout with a bunch of traitorous Apaches. Again, she resorted to the language of the Sioux, strung together in a cortege of mindless anger. Drawing a long, steady breath to cool her outrage, she mumbled a few more words, as if she were determined to cut off any retort the colonel might have.

That she was mad enough to spit adobe bricks didn't pass Heitman's notice. "I suppose you just told me to go to hell?"

Talon waved her hand in frustration, clinking the chains between her wrists. "No, Sir, I did not. I just need to think."

"I will tell you words spoken by squaw." Chief of Scouts John Nightwing had planned to speak to the colonel about matters relating to his troop. Only the woman's nasty insults had halted a polite retreat.

"I didn't know you spoke Comanche, Nightwing."

Talon strained to see the Apache standing in the darkness of the corridor, thinking at once that he was a coward for not stepping into her view.

Since he'd been absent from training for a few minutes, Nightwing had not seen Mr. Money bring the prisoner into camp. But he'd heard all about her from one of the guards. "Squaw speak Dakota Sioux, the language of my mother. She say she chose to die than be under thumb of stinking dog-eating Apache, or serve dung-smelling Army. She also says no man will ever whip her again." Nightwing began a retreat; his business here would keep.

"Nightwing, stand by for a few minutes. We need to talk."

"I will be in corridor, Sir."

Heitman now turned his eyes to Talon. "What my chief just told me, Comanche? Is that what you said?"

That horrid Apache was trying to weave a noose around her neck by repeating her insults. "Yes, that is what I said."

Heitman called sharply, "Guard!" Without delay, Private Wilson stood ramrod straight in the doorway, awaiting his orders. "When you return this thieving renegade to confinement, inform Major Stahl he has thirty minutes to prepare her for hanging." His attentions returned to Talon. "Are you sure you prefer to hang?"

Talon thought it was just her luck an Arizona Apache understood Sioux, the language of the northern tribe that had made a slave of her for five years. She also prayed that her instincts were correct, that the colonel was not serious about the hanging. "If I must be executed, let it be by firing squad."

Heitman laughed outright. "Waste a dozen bullets and the time of twelve soldiers on one breed Comanche? Hanging takes twelve feet of strong rope, and that we can reuse on your *amigos* in the Menendez gang when we catch up to them. Now, woman, scout for the United States Army—or hang?"

A little quieter, and certainly with far less conviction, she replied, "If those are my choices, I suppose I'll have to hang."

Mattie was furious with her. "Dadgum, gal, don't you be doin' this—"

"She's made her choice," Heitman snapped, and to Private Wilson, "Take her back now and inform the post chaplain to be on hand for final rites. And Sergeant Huck that we'll need a burial detail this evening." Heitman made special note of the woman's reckless defiance, even as her eyes darkened with fear.

Private Wilson, distressed to the point of trembling, even as he didn't believe his C.O. was serious, stepped aside so Talon could skirt him into the corridor.

Suddenly, cold fear writhed in the pit of Talon's stomach. She'd have fainted if she hadn't consciously stiffened every joint in her bones. Willing herself to take a few awkward steps from the office, she faced John Nightwing's steady black eyes, the only part of him she actually saw through her fear, and paused noticeably. *What the hell am I doing? So I'll have to work with Apaches? It is far better than dying. I have never killed anyone. So, I took a few steers—an unbroken pony or two, maybe—but hardly hanging offenses. So I might have to do a little crawling...get my knees dirty...I can live with dirty knees!* Casting off her horrid thoughts, Talon pressed her mouth nervously as she politely addressed the C.O. "Colonel Heitman, Sir, perhaps I am being too hasty about that hanging. I will sign your contract."

"Too late! You have made your choice."

Shaking off the slim hand Wilson closed over her arm, Talon rushed back, halting within touching distance of Heitman. "I will be a good scout. And...I have never killed anyone." Her eyes cut pleadingly to Mattie. "Tell him...tell him I have never killed anyone."

Mattie had closed his own trembling fingers over the lower half of his face. He didn't even look at Talon.

Heitman suppressed all evidence of his heartless bluff. "You killed a good sergeant."

Surprised by the accusation, Talon Rose blinked nervously. She recalled hearing about the Army soldier who had fallen in the bluffs and died while chasing her. "I looked back from the ridge just as his horse pitched him. How can that be my fault?"

"He was chasing you."

"I did not *ask* him to chase me, Sir."

Failing to recognize the bluff, Mattie slowly began forming new arguments. He would've turned Talon loose before bringing her here to be hanged. His boss in Yuma had left her fate completely in his hands, since he didn't think she'd done anything bad enough to hang either. If she hadn't riled all those wealthy ranchers by stealing their longhorns and horses—

"Listen to her, Paul. She'd make a helluva scout."

Paul stretched back in his chair, coddling his chin thoughtfully. "I just don't know."

Talon's long, slim fingers closed over the sleeve of his jacket in gentle entreaty. She was as surprised as he was by the moment of intimacy. "Flog me, if you wish, Sir, but let me live. I swear by all things holy, I will be good."

"For Pete's sakes," he grumbled, the harshness of his tone forcing her back a pace. "Rather than see you grovel, we'll give scouting a try." Talon hopped forward, a gleeful yelp rushing from her lips. Turning in his chair, Heitman called to his clerk, "Roan, come here." Again, the contract in triplicate was shoved toward Talon. "Make your mark there."

"Would signing my name be proper procedure, Sir?"

"Sign your name then, for Pete's sake!"

Scarcely able to contain both her relief and jitters, Talon took the pen he now offered and bent to sign her name—Talon Rose—to each copy in flowing cursive. She had every intention of escaping first chance she got, but if signing these silly contracts spared her from death today, she was willing to do anything. "There, done. It is official, Sir."

The humor hiding at the corners of Heitman's mouth made a sudden and very brief appearance. "You'll have to stay in the guardhouse for a few days, until we find proper quarters. Clearly, a single female scout cannot be housed in the scout barracks with men. Apache wives would be after you with a broomstick."

Talon placed the pen down. "Nor would I wish to stay with those—"

"Gal—you hush." Mattie shook his head as a further warning.

"And I caution you—" Heitman paused while he handed the signed contracts to his clerk for proper processing, "that any disrespect of the Apaches will be dealt with strictly. They've earned the respect of each man on this post, and they'll have yours, too."

Not in my lifetime. I will be out of here within two days. Talon nodded. Heitman, believing the presence of this woman might lead to mutiny among the notoriously well-disciplined Apaches of his scout troop, now called to Nightwing. "I hope your other business can wait?" Nightwing nodded respectfully. "Chief of Scouts Nightwing, this is your new scout." And to Talon, "You'll do nothing, woman, which this man doesn't first approve or authorize. He will not only be your chief, but your father and your god."

Talon refused to look at the tall, somber Apache who had repeated her words to the colonel and almost gotten her hanged. But when he said, "Rude Comanche thief not belong in troop, Sir. Better to hang," her eyes turned boldly to him. At once surprised that an Apache was not only pleasant in appearance but didn't smell bad either, Talon saw that he was very tall and slim, firm muscles straining against the tight fabric of his shirt, and his skin almost as light as her own. His hair was waist-length, well-combed, partially plaited at the sides with interwoven rawhide, not hacked off unevenly at the shoulders like most Apaches she had seen. He wore his uniform in a much more orderly fashion than the commanding officer quietly enjoying their interaction did.

Talon was sure this Chief of Scouts was *not* full blood Apache.

Heitman smiled at Nightwing's assessment, noticing the admiration in his dark eyes as he watched the pretty half-blood. "We're not going to hang her today, Nightwing, as much as we might enjoy it. When you walk out that door with her, you and Reisner are responsible for her until this new Officer of Scouts arrives."

John Nightwing suspected Major Troy Reisner, the new camp adjutant on Monday, would not take an active role in handling this wild Comanche female. He doubted the new Officer of Scouts would either. In his experience, white officers assigned to Indian scouts were spoiled and lazy. Duty wise, Reisner had turned the physical training of the troops over to Nightwing, while he took care of the paperwork and payroll vouchers in the comfort of his well-furnished office. Reisner seldom sat a horse, and then only with great trepidation and resentment. Nightwing enjoyed the authority he had in the scout troop, and hoped the new Officer of Scouts would also direct his official duties from across a tidy desk. "This squaw be good scout," Nightwing remarked with gentle sarcasm as he swept out his hand. "Come. *Your* chief will take you to guardhouse."

"At first light, Nightwing, take her to Dora's for uniform fittings," Heitman suggested. "Roan will advise her of the appointment."

"I do not have to dress like *them,* do I?" Talon hastily protested.

"You'll dress like the other scouts."

"No, Sir! I will not wrap my legs—my body—as a man. People will think I want to be a man—which I do not!" With a halted smile, Nightwing again outstretched his hand. Talon made a very wide sweep around him as she began a reluctant withdrawal from the room, and from Mattie, who had kept his word—somewhat—to save her life. "I do not want to wear men's clothes. And you, Apache—" she growled at Nightwing, "do not *ever* call me a squaw again."

"Dadgum, Talon." Mattie's patience had worn as thin as pauper's rags. "If you don't hush that sassy mouth, I'll take you out and hang you myself."

"He should not call me a squaw," she pouted, pretty enough that Mattie regretted his absurd threat at once. "And look how the trousers cling to that Apache's legs. It is a disgrace to put a woman in those." Though she hated the idea of wearing trousers, Talon thought the scout uniforms were very handsome...for a man...dark blue fatigue jackets with four large brass buttons, an ammunition belt across the chest and over the right shoulder, crossed arrow insignias on the collars, and tan trousers with double blue stripes down each leg. The hat John Nightwing carried against his chest bore a tidy red bandanna pinned down by a Chief of Scouts' insignia, crossed arrows with a centered feather bonnet. The scouts on the parade ground had worn their bandannas against their foreheads.

Her arguments depleted, as well as the patience of both men in the room, Talon left with the Chief of Scouts. When she was out of sight, Paul snapped at Mattie, "You should have known I never had the authority to hang that female! Maybe you'll be a better blacksmith than you were a lawman. You sure didn't do much digging in law books!"

Mattie grinned. "I promise you, Paul, I'll keep a watch on Talon."

A smile raked Heitman's leathery features. "You've got a romantic eye on this breed?"

"A fatherly eye only," he assured him. "An', Paul...Talon, she's inclined to think with her mouth, an' she does things real impulsive-like—you know how women are—so you won't be lettin' these Army boys take leather to her, will ya?"

Light laughter rolled from Heitman's tight lips. "Leather to that pretty thing? I don't think so, Mattie. If she's too unruly, we'll just slap her behind bars for a few days to straighten her out." An exit door slammed just as Talon yelled at Nightwing. Though neither man in the C.O.'s office understood Sioux, she had unquestionably insulted her new chief. Nightwing's gentle laughter resonated in the warm morning air.

* * *

A few minutes later, Talon angrily threw herself to the farthest cot in general confinement. She refused to look at the

22

Apache who had accompanied her into the cell.

Nightwing assessed this beautiful, but very rude Comanche female who—among other things—had called him a *spineless Apache dog* in his mother's native tongue. Not only was he amused by her sharp tongue, but also by the fact that she considered trousers a serious threat to her womanhood. Recalling her insults beginning in Heitman's office, Nightwing remarked, "If rude thief hungry, good food tonight in scout mess tent. Fresh dog soup, tender young terrier, I think. Umm-ummm!" The tall Indian withdrew, throaty laughter rippling along the stone and mortar walls.

Talon thought they should have just hanged her.

It would be over now, and she wouldn't have to face life as a prisoner among sarcastic, black-eyed Apaches.

Two

Mattie watched Talon absently caress the small deerskin pouch containing treasures of her mother. Her tearful eyes were free of rebellion for the first time in two days, and she had curled up on the farthest cot, with her forehead against her knees. When he sat beside her, she let a full minute pass before acknowledging him. "I have been a thief and a troublemaker, Mattie, but do I owe two years of my life to those Apaches?"

"Two years is a small price to pay for the trouble you've caused, little gal. You just be good an' obey the rules. I'll be right over at the livery, an' you come to me any time. I mean that."

"Why do you care what happens to me?"

"I care, gal, 'cause Ol' Shepperd cared about you. When you run away from them Sioux that made you a slave, an' heard your ma died, you showed up in Powder Wash not quite fourteen, makin' a thievin' nuisance of yourself. Ol' Shepperd gave you a home when you needed one. Where your ma left off educatin' you in the way of white folk, Shepperd took it up. He loved you an' taught you to talk real good English, to read good, and write better'n mos' folk I know. So you straighten up and make somethin' of yourself."

In a moment of quiet reminiscence and shame, Talon remembered Jacob Shepperd, the refined, well-educated gentleman from the east who'd come to the southwest to teach at the Indian School south of Powder Wash. He had taught her English, and she remembered with a smile how he had forbidden her to use contractions in her speech. Every once in a while she had slipped up—mainly when she was angry—but for the most part she had always remembered the lessons he had taught her. Jacob Shepperd had spent years being a father to her, and winning her love and trust. Just when he managed to accomplish that insurmountable task, he became ill and died within a few weeks.

Then she took to the hills, stealing throughout the territory, both from the Army and the ranchers, befriending other bands of thieves, and taking stolen livestock into Mexico to sell it. Her reputation had earned her a five hundred dollar reward on her head, put up by a number of ranchers, and a *hang on sight* order any one of them would have been glad to carry out. The posse would never have caught her if she hadn't left Manolito's well-hidden camp to take that silly rabbit to the squatter.

"Lost in the past, eh, gal?"

Her thoughts vanished in a cloud. "What will happen to me now that I am a prisoner?"

"You ain't no prisoner. You'll be a scout. An' I reckon that's up to you. You can make the best of it, or you can make the worst of it. But whatever you do, don't make me regret stakin' my reputation on you." Drawing up, he took Talon's hand and held it warmly. "Now, you make me a promise you'll be good."

Talon crossed the fingers of her left hand against the folds of her skirt, feeling guilty at once for doing so, because this kind ex-deputy marshal trusted her. "I will be good, Mattie."

"About the scouts, gal, I ain't never seen one of 'em eat a dog. So you be nice to them."

Talon shrugged, heeding his small order, but only because it was the path of least resistance, which Old Shepperd had suggested she always take. "But that chief, Mattie."

Mattie caught the mischief remaining in her tone. "Nightwing's one of the best Indians I've ever met. Part Apache, part Sioux, an' he's got a whole lot of respect at this camp. Took the name John to honor the previous Officer of Scouts killed four years ago. That shows he's a real good man."

"I knew he was not full blood Apache," Talon replied thoughtfully, "and that explains how he knew what I said in the colonel's office."

"Will you try to get along with Nightwing, even if you don't try with the full bloods?"

"I will try to get along with them all...if I must." When Mattie stood, nearly tripping over the end of the bunk, she was glad to leave the subject of the Apaches. "Rearranging the furniture without permission, Mattie?"

"Don't you go givin' me that sass, gal," he replied, grinning. "I'll be takin' care of that horse you love, so you better be nice to me, too." Listening to Talon's sweet, sincere laughter, Mattie felt confident she would manage just fine in her new world.

* * *

Talon unconditionally loathed the Apache, who traditionally never fought unless they had an advantage, or faced a strength equal to or greater than their own. They preferred to prey on the weak and vulnerable. Their different tribes were notoriously savage and superstitious. Talon imagined that, mixed blood or not, the Chief of Scouts had no better character than his scouts did.

Character, indeed! she thought, if they were willing to work for the soldiers against their own kind. As far as she was concerned, all this scout rhetoric about *saving Apache lives by bringing them under white-eye protection,* whereas, the hostiles were intent on self-martyrdom, had the smell of a lot of bull. And now she, a half-blood Sioux-speaking Comanche, was about to betray Indians by working *with* Apaches and *for* the soldiers. Nausea rose from the pit of her stomach.

Talon half-ran to keep pace with Nightwing as they crossed to the married NCO quarters. A group of Army children stopped playing to watch them. Because Nightwing had said nothing to her since his dark eyes alone had coaxed her from her cell, she felt that she should also remember the keen sense of the Apache that ran in his blood. If she was to survive in their midst, she'd have to settle her defiance, perhaps even show a grain of humility until she found that perfect moment to escape.

Stepping onto a tidy gray porch, Talon stood quietly by while the Apache rapped on the door. Embarrassed that he had shackled her wrists, she hid them beneath her long sleeves. Presently, a lady wearing a dark green dress and white apron appeared, a smile instantly disappearing as Nightwing rudely thrust Talon toward her, uncovering the shackles. "You take those off her right now, John Nightwing."

"Shackles stay."

"I need outstretched arms for proper measurements. Take them off."

Talon thought her firm voice ill-matched to her pleasant countenance.

Nightwing reluctantly withdrew a key from the pocket of his jacket, unlocking only one shackle. "She can outstretch arms. Other iron stays on wrist."

It was a compromise of sorts. "You go on about your business, John Nightwing." Dora had looked forward to meeting the Indian woman who had ducked the Army for two years. "Leave us ladies to do what we need to do."

"Do not trust her. She run off if you turn back."

"You go on now." As Dora pushed the door to, one plump arm went around Talon. "You're not going to run off now, are you?" Before a response could be given, she added, "I'll trust you not to," and continued to hold her in a gentle embrace. "Talon Rose, is it?"

"Yes, ma'am, and please do not place too much trust in me. I most likely will if the chance is there."

"If you do run off, I can't say I'd much blame you. You're much too pretty to be tied down to a man's life for two long years."

Talon, smiling shyly, holding the loose shackle, and looked around the neat, well-kept parlor of the house Dora Huck occupied with her husband, the sergeant of the gardener's brigade. There were lace doilies on the backs and arms of chairs and divans, lace table coverings, and pretty glass figurines everywhere. Living in the villages of the Comanche and the Sioux, and then with Old Shepperd believing only in books and the basics, Talon hadn't been exposed to pretty things like this.

Accompanying Dora into a small room off the parlor, Talon faced shelves of yard goods, a treadle sewing machine, and many baskets of notions, laces, ribbons, and buttons, every conceivable thing a woman might need to sew a garment. She vaguely recalled her mother trying to teach her to sew with a bone needle, eventually giving up because she kept sticking herself badly enough to bleed. Old Shepperd didn't have much better luck teaching her this domestic task either, and usually ended up doing the mending himself.

Now that Talon was free of the scrutiny of soldiers, guards, and scouts, she relaxed and stood quietly by while Dora gathered measuring tapes and pins. Dora was a pale, pleasingly plump woman, with a pretty face, red hair gently peppered with gray twisted loosely atop her head, and lively nutmeg-colored eyes.

"Let's get you out of your pretty dress so we can get some proper measurements."

Talon dropped her eyes in a moment of shame. "I have nothing on underneath."

"Do you not now, lass?" Moving toward a narrow, open doorway, Dora stood with her hands propped on her hips. A small room, lined with shelves, held many more baskets and a number of boxes neatly labeled with their contents. Pulling a box down, she went through it hurriedly, then handed it to Talon. "I believe you'll find something suitable in here. I'll just step out while you put something on."

As soon as the door closed, the hooves of a shod horse struck the earth very close by. Talon assumed the man, whose boots now echoed across the porch, was the lady's husband. His voice mingled with Dora's at once, and Talon listened to their indistinct murmurings. Turning back to the box, she caught sight of the pistol atop a small dresser, partially hidden by a bit of fabric. Listening to the horse again, snorting in the cool darkness of morning, then looking to the pistol, instinct claimed her as completely as breathing.

Snatching up the pistol, Talon quickly scanned the still dark parade ground, climbed out the window, and was in the saddle of Sgt. Huck's horse before she'd even caught a second breath. Heeling the slight roan past the north guard station of Camp Casey, in her haste to make an escape she forgot all about her beloved horse.

The warning blurts of a bugle robbed the morning of its peace. But Talon paid little mind. Freedom awaited her just beyond this small military barricade, and nothing else mattered.

She *would not* be a slave of the Apaches.

* * *

The dark thickening of night had faded to the cool lavender of morning. Laine Taylor eased the sure-footed sorrel onto a narrow trail skirting a low valley deep in the Huachucas, feeling the stiffness of two days in the saddle that a few hours of sleep at the Mullins-Adair way station had not eradicated. Anxious to shed his buckskins and shake out the trail dust, he wanted only for these last three miles to pass into history.

His attention drawn by a shady dell and caught in a fragile stir of morning air, he turned the horse toward the stream churning over rocks a dozen yards away. Easing down the slope of a hill, he thought this mountain range was like a magical, misplaced oasis in Arizona's ancient dustlands. The horse halted at the bank of the stream, the current broken by the low branches of a Paloverde firmly rooted just the other side. As the horse pulled slack in the reins to drink from the stream, Laine climbed down, crouched, and brought a handful of the crystal clear water to his mouth.

Suddenly, he caught a sound, strangely out of place among the soft reflections of nature. The low, gentle weeping of a woman wafted around him like an all-consuming mist. Blue eyes swept the narrow dale ribboned by the stream, and among the spindly trunks of a few young ash and pine. Captured so completely by the sorrow of this unseen woman, he entered the tree line with the sorrel trailing him.

Then he spied the weathered logs of an old cabin, possibly once occupied by the men who operated the abandoned mines in this area of the Huachucas. There, folded to the crumbling remnants of a low porch, an Indian woman, her forehead pressed into a support post, wept as though her heart broke. She was very young, her dark hair partially unraveled from a single braid falling fully to her waistline. Taking a step toward her, he did not see the pistol resting in the folds of her light deerskin dress.

Talon knew she'd been foolish to run away the moment the guard's bugle had bellowed the first warning. Not only had she left Shadow Dancer in the post corral, but the sergeant's horse which she had stolen had taken off the moment she'd stepped down from the saddle.

The dry leaves blanketing the soil this early February morning crackled a dozen yards away, and the shadow of horse and man, caught by a shard of early morning light, embraced Talon as quietly as death. By sheer instinct, she spun on her knees and swept the pistol out, accidentally discharging the only bullet in the old weapon's revolving chamber. At once her fearful eyes found the tall, very surprised man clad in buckskins, with shoulder-length golden hair and treacherously narrowed eyes.

"Son-of-a-bitch," Laine ground out hoarsely.

Watching the blood spread through the upper sleeve of his shirt, a horrified Talon threw the pistol, bounding to her feet and through the stand of ash in an attempt to escape. At once the man's heavy boots were in a run, and she'd just reached the stream when his full weight was upon her. Twisting beneath him as she fell, he took her breath so completely that she couldn't scream as he straddled her hips and twisted her wrists to her back. Catching a small breath, she apologized in a frantic repetition of soft Sioux words.

Laine Taylor knew at once she wasn't speaking Apache. "Why the hell did you shoot me?" he demanded, pinning her painfully to the ground. "Or do you just hate white men?" Laine didn't know the meaning of the Indian words she'd repeated—*it was accident*—and had no reason to believe she wouldn't now produce a knife. Without pause, he locked her other wrist at her back as a safety precaution. Then his hands swept rudely down her sides and front, instinctively—boldly—pausing at the soft, womanly curves hiding no knives or other weapons. "You're wearing Army bracelets, squaw, so you must have escaped from a soldier. I suppose you shot me with his sidearm? Where'd you leave his body?" Talon was too stunned by the accusation—and too afraid—to answer. "If you move, I'll shoot you where you lay." Now feeling the intense pain traveling into his hand and shoulder, he again growled, "son-of-a-bitch," and eased across the ground half a dozen feet from her. Tearing off the jacket, he rolled up his sleeve, surveyed his wound, and tied a yellow bandanna from his hat around his arm to staunch the flow of blood. He watched Talon for a moment, noticeably trembling, her fearful, very lovely face turning to him as she slightly eased to her side on the hard ground. He felt guilty then. Women had soft, delicate curves—this one certainly did—and he might have hurt her when he handled her so roughly. She was so damned pretty he wished he was the kind of man to turn her over and take his pleasures with her, while she was unable to fight him off.

Blast it to kingdom come, he was not that kind of man.

Easing up, and pulling on his jacket, Laine returned to crouch beside her. "I suppose you took the soldier's horse, too. Where is it?" Met by silence, he snarled, "Don't you speak a single word of English, squaw?"

As he drew up, Talon allowed a response only in the harsh glare of her eyes. Then she turned fully to him—as though she had a thousand insults to sling—and the gathering morning reflected the deep, green pools of her eyes.

That startled the hell out of Laine Taylor. "You're a breed." She did not respond to the insult. "Am I to be stuck in this godawful mountain range with a murderous breed who can't speak a single word of English?" Then, emboldened by the fact that she did not speak his language, he ground out, "You're a blasted fine-looking princess—for an Indian. Too fine-looking for the hangman's noose probably waiting for you." He enjoyed the defiance in her lovely eyes. "Know what I'd like to do with you right now? Hell, we might both enjoy what I have in mind." Then he grinned, ignoring the pain pulsing through his arm and shoulder. "You shot me, princess. I deserve some pleasure for my inconvenience." Massaging his arm, he softly confessed, "Lucky for you I was raised to respect you blasted women." Nudging her in the side with his foot, he ordered, "Get up."

Talon suppressed a smile, without the smallest element of fear, and braced herself on her shoulder, trying to draw her knees beneath her so that she might stand. When she took too long in Laine's estimation, his fingers circled her arm and dragged her to her feet. "How did an Apache squaw in Army bracelets get a soldier's horse and gun?" he asked quietly, though he didn't expect an answer.

Not only had he called her a squaw, he had called her Apache. There was no greater insult. But this brute of a white man didn't deserve her heated denials, or to hear the name of her true tribe—Comanche. She would have an advantage if he thought she spoke no English.

"Get ready for a walk, squaw, because you're going back." As he nudged her toward the cabin and his waiting horse, he continued to talk to her. "Too bad I'm not a bounty hunter. There's probably a big reward on your murderous head." Talon just listened. "But I'm a commissioned officer in the United States Army, barred from collecting rewards, I'm afraid. I suppose you were being taken to Camp Casey?"

She turned to stare at him, wishing he *was* a bounty hunter rather than an Army officer. With his pale hair and blue eyes, he favored the despicable brute she'd run to first time she'd escaped from the Sioux. Only eleven years old that early winter morning she'd crept away from her cruel foster parents, she'd shivered and starved in a rain-swollen ravine for two days, then rushed toward a small Army patrol passing within a hundred paces. They were white, like her mother, and she had thought they would help her. Because the Sioux had spent three years punishing her every time she spoke her mother's first language, she couldn't remember the English words for *help* or *slave*. So when her Sioux "father" had approached the whites and explained in his own halted English that his child had run away, the officer—one who looked just like this one—had returned her to him. She'd been beaten so badly that three days passed before she could move without pain. The dreadful memory awakened the hate in her heart, only her fond remembrance of Jacob Shepperd kept her from hating all white men.

When she suddenly stalled a dozen yards from the cabin, Laine's knuckles pressed into the back of her shoulder. She stumbled once, shaking off his hand when he kept her from falling. As he pulled into his saddle, he quipped rudely, "I'm so sorry you'll have to walk, my lovely Indian princess, but I have only this one horse." Sarcasm had smothered every remnant of a sincere apology. "Walking is good for you...builds muscles, makes the legs strong. Next time—if there *is* a next time—you'll run on those long, fine golden legs and hide somewhere." Easing his horse beside her, he bent slightly from his saddle. "Ready to walk, princess? Or should I drag you at the end of a rope?"

Talon suppressed the urge to spill forth every insult he deserved...in English, so he'd understand. Hiking up her chin, she moved toward the first of several trails that would take her back to Camp Casey.

Sensing what he thought might be an escape plan forming in her brain, Laine split the air with laughter. "Don't try to pull anything, princess. If you don't head southwest, I'll know it." She looked to him then, softness in her features that almost took away his thoughts. He had never seen such an exquisite Indian woman, her skin smooth and golden, her brows refined over wide, almond-shaped eyes reflecting like emeralds, her mouth full, sensual, pouting...almost childlike. For a moment, he considered letting her ride double with him. But his arm began to throb again and he thought the walk would do her good.

Talon pivoted smartly and put distance between them, her footfalls bold and sure as she entered the path across the clearing, a short cut through the Huachucas to Camp Casey. Horse and rider stayed no less than ten feet behind her. As the distance closed, and Talon grew weary of walking, she renewed her vigor in her captor's almost constant chatter, and the naughty compliments he gave her along their journey. She smiled every time he berated himself for *being a blasted gentleman.*

By the time they reached the crest of Cimarron Bluff, with Camp Casey spread out in the valley below, the muscles of Talon's thighs felt ready to explode in pain. When they were a dozen yards from camp, she saw that Heitman, Major Stahl of the Guard, Mattie, Chief Nightwing, and another officer she did not recognize, had assembled near the guard station.

As she dropped to her knees, Laine Taylor dismounted his horse. He was at once hit by a barrage of questions from Heitman. Watching the exhausted Indian woman intently, he patiently awaited his opportunity to answer. "I'm Captain Laine Taylor, I have transfer orders to this camp, and I found her three miles from here. She was wearing Army shackles, so I brought her here. It is as simple as that." Talon's defiance held back tears. "As for the wound, I had the woman's sidearm while I mounted my horse and it discharged. Peeved by my clumsiness I threw the damned thing. Now, Sir, did I miss anything of your interrogation?"

Talon looked to him as if she couldn't quite believe her ears, only vaguely aware of Nightwing's fingers circling her arm to roughly pull her to her feet. As he half dragged her toward the guardhouse, with Major Stahl and Mattie close behind, she watched the pale-haired man until the stones of the small prison swallowed them whole.

Laine had spent those three miles watching her walk ahead of him without complaint. That she was in chains, and likely an escapee, he felt she had enough problems without him adding to it. "Now, Sir—" Laine handed Heitman a portfolio he'd taken from his saddlebag, "if you'll process my transfer papers and point out the infirmary, I'll have this aggravating wound tended to."

Heitman suspected Captain Taylor was covering for the Comanche, though he didn't believe she would deliberately shoot him. "I suggest, Sir, as new Officer of Scouts, that you handle firearms with more care in the future." He pointed out the infirmary. "That's where you can get this *self-inflicted* wound taken care of. Captain Calloway is a competent surgeon, should you require one. After your treatment, come to HQ, your transfer will be processed, and I'll have an orderly show you to your quarters. Tomorrow morning will be soon enough to properly meet Chief of Scouts Nightwing and your Apache troop."

* * *

John Nightwing removed Talon's shackles in general confinement. Mattie entered, the disappointment in his eyes compelling her to drop to the cot in tears. "He lied, Chief Nightwing, Mattie. That man who brought me back. He lied."

Nightwing had crossed his arms, the chain of the shackles

34

draped across his left sleeve. "What did he lie about, Talon?"

"I shot him."

"Christ almighty, Talon!"

Shame darkened her cheeks as she looked to Mattie, his mouth pinched in a grimace. "I swear it was an accident, Mattie. He startled me and I turned the gun on him. It was old. I did not even know there was a bullet in it. I wouldn't deliberately shoot a man, even one like *him.*"

Mattie was too angry right now to discuss the escape with her. "I'll talk to you in the intake room, Nightwing. Gal, you settle this with your chief, an' when I see you again, I want a damned explanation for you runnin' off like that."

As Mattie left, Nightwing considered telling Talon she had shot the new Officer of Scouts. But he thought she suffered enough shame for one day. "This chief proud of you to speak truth. But I angry you escape."

Talon dropped her eyes again. "I suppose the colonel will go ahead and hang me?"

"The colonel will not hang you."

"Do I still have the option to scout?"

He did not know this word *option.* "That be decided tomorrow."

"Will I be whipped?"

"I do not know."

Fear darkened her eyes to the color of far off twilight hills. "But it is possible?" Then, shrugging, "I suppose I deserve it. If it must be done, then get it over with."

This pretty half-blood would never face the whip, no matter what she did, but the fact that she thought it was possible might allay her impulsive nature. "Major Reisner and the colonel make a decision tomorrow. Since you escape this morning, the colonel said you must be in shackles when you leave guardhouse." He recalled the short argument between Heitman and Reisner just minutes before Taylor and Talon had reached the gate. A courteous, understanding man, and terribly fond of women in general, Reisner felt that Talon would behave better if she were treated better. "And you cannot be left alone."

Talon could accept that. "I lost Sgt. Huck's horse."

"It returned to camp."

"And his old pistol."

"He has another. That one belonged to dead father. The soldiers will search for it."

"Dora trusted me not to run away."

"You must take that up with her." Shoving open the iron door in his departure, Nightwing looked at her a final time. "Do you want colonel to know you shot Captain Taylor?"

"It might look bad on him if the colonel knows he lied. Can we keep this between us?"

Nightwing nodded, closed the door, and Talon listened to the clip of his boots on stone in his retreat.

Three

Private Wilson brought Talon a noonday meal, but she was much too distressed to eat more than a bite or two of sweet corn. Sleeping most of the afternoon, she awoke late in the day to the aroma of beef and potatoes drifting from a covered plate. Settling down to her meal, she knew the friendly guard had left her tray. He had also brought her brush and comb, toothbrush and small jar of cleaning powder from her saddlebags, and a book of poetry from the camp library.

The next day, the swarthy guard was on duty. Settling down to read the poetry, she tried not to let the loneliness compound the complications she had brought into her life. As another night passed, and she wondered if she'd been completely forgotten, Nightwing came to the guardhouse for her. In the intake office, she extended her wrists for the shackles she expected, but Private Wilson whispered, "Maybe he's forgotten about that, ma'am. Go on with him now."

Though Nightwing allowed her to leave the guardhouse unshackled, he had not forgotten the order. In the cool morning air, he quipped rudely, "He did not put thief in shackles. I talk to him later." Then, "The colonel said if you try to escape, I am to shoot you."

Drawing her chin in a little, her brows furrowed as she half ran to keep up with him. "Really?"

"Really." Nightwing kept a straight face. "Now...come. Scout must be measured for uniform."

"The colonel will still let me scout?"

"He *make* you honor contract. I make it clear I think you run away again."

"I do not expect you to trust me, Chief Nightwing."

"Good, because I do not." Strangely, Nightwing *did* trust her, but was determined that she would not know it. Not only did he not wish to explain the unwarranted trust, he didn't think he could.

A few minutes later, Talon stood in Dora's sewing room, where the same box of garments awaited her attention. When Dora quietly withdrew, Talon pulled the curtains across the now nailed window and shed her dress. There were a number of nice, new things, including a hip length chemise and a pair of side fastening knickers, which she chose without delay. She had just situated herself before a cheval mirror when Dora rapped, then slid the door open. "Are we decent, Miss Talon?"

So far, the lady had said nothing about her escape two days ago. Sitting in general confinement, she'd had many long hours to try to come up with an apology that hadn't sounded hollow and insincere. "I am truly sorry about the other day, ma'am, for taking Sgt. Huck's sidearm and horse. You trusted me, and I let you down."

"The horse came back, Talon. And one of the soldiers in D company returned the gun to Sgt. Huck. We won't mention it again." Though she'd spoken politely, Talon had taken full notice of the disappointment clearly defining her voice. Dora tugged on the hem of the chemise. "That is just fine, lass, though a bit tighter than most ladies like. After we finish up your measurements you take whatever you need from the box."

Talon's clothing consisted of a beaded deerskin skirt, a shawl her mother had made, both given to her when she returned to the village of the Comanche, which were in her saddlebags, and the dress she had been wearing for the past three days. Talon's "thank you" was very humble.

The measurements took only ten minutes. Talon expressed her dismay at having to wear men's clothing, and Dora offered to sew a soft, feminine lining into the trousers where they touched Talon's special areas. The trousers now didn't seem nearly so wicked.

Afterwards, they went through a number of boxes of clothing, undergarments, and other feminine necessities. Dora offered to keep the boxes for Talon until she moved to permanent quarters. Talon chose a few items to take with her this morning, including a tan overshirt and brown, calf-length skirt sewn originally for a much shorter woman. She chose to wear the shirt and skirt rather than the dusty deerskin dress she'd been in for the past five days. By the time Nightwing returned, Talon moved easily into Dora's arms for a parting hug.

As she and Nightwing crossed the parade field, he grumbled, "You fool sergeant's wife. But I know Comanche thief not be trusted."

What the hell is wrong with this Apache? One moment he makes jokes, the next he is hostile. "And I am expected to trust a Chief of Scouts who calls himself Apache, but is also Sioux and white?" Nightwing's comment had torn through her like an arrow, because she sincerely liked the sergeant's wife.

When they entered the intake office, Nightwing grabbed the box and thrust it toward Private Wilson. "Make sure she not sneak in weapon."

A reluctant Andy Wilson went through the lady's unmentionables and clothing in the box. When he looked up, crimson flushed his youthful good looks. "She has only lady's clothing articles, nothing else," he advised Nightwing, then handed the box back to Talon. His eyes alone spoke a sincere apology. Only when another guard took Talon into the corridor and toward her cell did Private Wilson speak up in her defense. "Chief Nightwing, the lady made a mistake the other day and is graciously trying to make the best of this situation. You might do the same."

"Not lady, not gracious. Rude Comanche thief! She my business. You should mind own business."

Gangly, almost girlish, with a high-pitched voice that often evoked sport among his fellow guards, Private Wilson gritted his teeth to restore his own state of control. "As long as she's confined to this guardhouse, Chief Nightwing, she *is* my business every bit as much as she is yours."

Nightwing caught a smile as he approached the exit. This young soldier of the guard, quick to speak such cross words to a man twice his size, certainly had a healthy dose of courage. "Will come for her at one in afternoon. This time, put in irons, like I told you this morning."

"Is that necessary, Chief Nightwing?"

"It is." Nightwing felt that Talon had learned her lesson and didn't think shackles were needed, but his scouts were grumbling about her being forced on them. Less damage would be done if they viewed her as a prisoner.

* * *

Any one of the Apaches would have put a knife in her back, Talon thought a little later, with one exception, a friendly, dark-skinned full blood. Smoking a Canvas Back *cigarrito*, he had introduced himself as Dako, Chief First Sergeant. He was short and stocky, with a jaw line sharp like rock outcroppings, a narrow nose, but with wide nostrils, flaring sporadically as though he fought for air. His black eyes had twinkled with laughter as he welcomed her to the scout troop.

Talon now accompanied Major Troy Reisner and Nightwing to the major's office two buildings down from Headquarters. His was a neat, well-furnished office, with imported, privately owned furniture, and bronze military sculptures sitting on well-placed stands. Talon sat before his desk, Nightwing standing quietly by. The major was an annoyingly tidy man of medium stature, regimental Army from his polished buttons to the spit-shine on his boots. "The commanding officer notified Chief Nightwing and my office that you are officially a scout." What he had actually done was agree with Reisner that if she was treated as a scout, rather than a prisoner, perhaps she would not fight their efforts to tame her. "Nightwing, remove the irons now. I don't want to see them on this scout again." Reluctance snapped his patience as he withdrew the key and unlocked the shackles, slinging them to a side chair in an expression of disapproval. Talon absently rubbed her wrists. "Next week you will be issued both a sidearm and rifle as part of your uniform," Reisner continued, "but no ammunition for the first four weeks of your service."

"That is so we be sure confused Comanche who speak Sioux tongue not shoot Apache in back," Nightwing announced soberly.

Reisner suppressed a smile. "You are also confined to

camp, and will not leave with your troop for these four weeks. You will spend those days doing chores around camp, with supervision of a guard. And, it is my sincere hope, scout, that you won't be shooting any more men." Talon's eyes alone accused Nightwing of betraying a confidence. "Nothing has been said, scout," the major assured her, "but we all suspect Captain Taylor was not entirely truthful about his *accident*. If you confessed to anyone, the colonel and I both thought it would have been Nightwing—or Mattie—when they took you to the guardhouse that morning."

Talon would not insult the major with denials. "I do not plan to shoot anyone, Sir."

"Except Apache, maybe."

Talon cut Nightwing a scathing look, but he simply returned it to her.

"My request of you, Talon," Reisner continued politely, "is that you adhere to the provisions of your contract and cooperate fully with post and troop regulations." Drawing forward, his fingers linked atop his desk. "Any questions?"

"Will I be whipped for escaping?"

A ripple of pleasant laughter was followed by, "I wouldn't imagine any man taking a whip to you, Scout Talon. What about you, Nightwing? Are you willing to whip this scout?"

"Yes," he replied, suppressing all evidence of the small lie.

Talon lifted her nose impudently. "Then I suppose I'll have to be good!"

"Not possible," Nightwing grumbled again.

"Any other questions or concerns, Scout?" She smiled vaguely, stumbling through a few thoughts and concerns that did not make it to her lips. "I'm sorry to have to bring up a private matter, but there will be those times the Apaches would prefer you confine yourself."

Talon hid an undercurrent of laughter behind her smile, not only because the major's sallow features suffused with color, but because Indian males of all tribes feared a woman's heightened power during *those* times. They believed her mere touch took a man's strength. "I am aware of Apache superstition, Major

Reisner, and willing to indulge it."

"In addition, you do not need to sit in on English lessons with the Apaches. Your chief will find other duties for you to perform during those hours."

Mockery laced Talon's response. "The Apaches attend English lessons? You'd never know it to hear them speak."

A smile danced in Reisner's warm brown eyes. "Do you not think Nightwing speaks fluent English?"

"Oh—" A shrug accompanied that one small word, "I suppose his basic English will pass if one is not paying too close attention."

Reisner turned to Nightwing with only the slightest hint of humor. "Is there anything you wish to clarify with your scout?"

"I need to know if Comanche's horse stolen property."

"She is not," Talon snapped. "I rode her from the Dakotas when I escaped the Sioux ten years ago. She was mine then. She is mine now."

"No need get mad, Comanche." Nightwing snapped back. "Next question. Is she Indian broke, or trained to left mount? If she cannot be mounted from left, you will choose another horse from post stock. Since she over ten years old, another horse better, too. We shoot old horse for dog meat."

Talon sniffed impudently. "My horse is relaxed on both sides. I'll mount her as you wish me to do so. She is only twelve, and in good health. I will *not* ride another horse. And you will *not* shoot her for dog meat! What are you planning? To fatten up your dogs for your next festival?"

He did not know this word *festival.* "You rode Army horse to escape other day."

"So I did!"

"No need for Comanche thief to be rude and sarcastic."

"I did notice, Talon," the major interrupted their bickering, "that the mare is not shod. You need to take her over to the livery."

If Talon's features were capable of a scowl, she accomplished it with erupting success. "Shadow Dancer has never worn iron on her hooves."

"It is required of all service horses in camp. Nightwing can take her, if you wish."

"I would rather take her myself." Talon spoke with faultless sincerity. "Not only so that I can apologize to Mattie personally for what I did, but so that I can explain to Shadow Dancer what is happening to her so she will not be frightened."

Her remark surprised a laugh out of Nightwing, and Talon turned cold, verdant eyes to him in warning.

Reisner thought Nightwing and his new scout were headed into a battle neither could win. "As you might be aware, Scout Talon, a new commanding officer arrives in early March. You will be expected to have trained well enough with the scouts by then to sit a horse for a full parade muster Major Harris is organizing for Major General Compton."

Something Talon couldn't quite grasp hovered at the fringes of her memory. "I will make you proud, Sir."

Nightwing commented dryly, "If rude Comanche not hanged by then."

"If I am, it is because I shot *you,* Apache."

Reisner's voice was a thin veneer of humor rioting for release. "You know, Nightwing, the way you two dig at each other, I wouldn't be surprised if you fall in love."

"I would throw myself off Rock Bluff first," Nightwing and Talon ground out simultaneously, eliciting that pent up laugh from the major taking a full minute to bring under control.

"That is all I have, Scout Talon, but I would ask you to wait a few minutes to meet the new Officer of Scouts." Looking at his pocket watch, he remarked, "He should be here by now." With nothing else to add, Major Reisner feared he might have to break up the tussle lingering in the eyes of the astute Nightwing and his new Comanche scout. So, his information became slightly nervous, and mundane. "Quarters have been found for you, but require some mending. You will be notified when they are ready, which Sgt. Huck assures me should be by Saturday."

"That will be fine, Sir. Do you think after I meet your replacement that I could visit my horse before I return to the guardhouse?"

"Of course."

Deep thought had grappled within Talon for the past few minutes. "This new commanding officer, Sir, is his first name Salem?"

"It is. Have you heard of him?"

A shrug lifted Talon's slim shoulders. "I must have overheard the guards talking."

Looking across Talon's head, Major Reisner announced, "There you are, Captain. Come in, meet your new scout."

Turning only her eyes, instant horror grabbed and pulled Talon lower into the chair. A flushed scowl on his very handsome face, his left arm bent into a loose sling, the golden-haired brute just glared at her. Instantly, she recalled the shameful things her new *Officer of Scouts* had said he would like to do to her. Absolutely nothing would be tidy in her life from this moment on.

Sporting a new haircut and fresh shave, Captain Laine Taylor had taken special care with his regulation uniform this morning. He wore the sling only because the post physician had insisted on it. Informed that he had one scout left to meet who, for reasons beyond control, had been unavailable yesterday, he had intended to present a professional appearance without useless medical devices. He had even thought it would be a scout with some rank and prestige, certainly not the female breed who had shot him in the hills. His voice was steady and slightly mocking as he spoke. "Major Reisner, don't tell me this renegade squaw is one of my scouts." But even as he spoke, his heart beat fast at the vision of her, slumped and embarrassed in the cushions of the chair.

"She is, Captain Taylor, and you are stuck with her."

"Son-of-a-bitch!" Contempt settled deeply into his favorite expletive. "No, I am *not,* Major. This squaw *will not* be a member of this scout troop."

Looking to Talon, Major Reisner lightly shrugged his shoulders. "I'm sorry," and to Nightwing, "Inform Colonel Heitman that Captain Taylor refuses the service of this woman. It is still early in the day. He has time to hang her before nightfall."

Nightwing saw by the smile Talon discreetly caught that she didn't think she had anything to worry about. Skirting Taylor, he approached the door.

Laine's hand flew up. "Wait." Nightwing paused, looking at him almost rudely. "You're saying, Major, that if I don't have this squaw in the scout troop the C.O.'s going to hang her?"

"If she doesn't scout for the Army, hanging is our only recourse. Clearly, she can't be cut loose in Arizona Territory with her reputation."

"I'm supposed to have her death on my conscience?" Cutting his eyes to Talon, her own lowered from his view, he demanded, "Look at me, squaw." She did not. "I said look at me." Then, recalling that she hadn't spoken English in the hills, he snapped at Nightwing, "Tell her to look at me."

Nightwing patiently replied, "She heard you, Sir, and defies you."

Talon lifted her chin, but did not face him. Defiance grabbed every word she spoke. "When you call me by my name, I will look. But I *am not* a squaw, and will not respond as one."

"Son-of-a-bitch!" Then, before he might halt the accusation, "You knew *everything* I said to you the other day?"

Only now did Talon allow a smile, even as her eyes remained on Major Reisner. "Everything, Sir. I have a good memory. Shall I repeat for these men what you said?"

His cheeks suffused with color. "That will not be necessary." Then, "What is your name?"

"It is Talon." Immediately, she wished she had given him her full name—*Talon Rose*. "But you may call me *Breed*, since it seems to come easy to you."

So, you are the Talon being discussed throughout camp. He had suspected as much. "Then look at me, Talon." She did so, noticing his scowl replaced by a pleasant countenance, though it likely wasn't his intention. "Give me one reason why I should accept you as a scout?"

Oh, how she despised this man! He stood there, thinking himself such a fine officer, thinking himself godlike and superior. Suddenly, she wanted to embarrass him, to make him look a fool in front of the other two men who held her fate in their hands. So, she pinched her mouth, and for lack of a suitable response—or a reason—remembered the things he'd said to her the other day. "Because, Sir, I am a blasted fine-looking princess...for an Indian...and I have a really nice pair of—"

"That's enough reason." The smallest smile claimed his mouth before he might halt it. *Yes, and how well I remember those soft, lovely curves.* "I didn't really mean that, you know."

"You mean—" she began, feigning surprise, "that white men lie? I suppose you did not mean those other things you said either?"

The embarrassment she had hoped for fluttered against his mouth. Looking across her shoulder, he said to Major Reisner, "For now, she can train with the scouts. But she's not to have loaded guns until I know she can be trusted. Good day."

"Sir, Captain Taylor, Sir." Pausing in his retreat, Laine allowed Talon's voice to linger after her words had silenced. His glaring blue eyes turned fully to her. "While you and *that* Apache are here, may I tell you why I do not wish to be addressed as a squaw?"

"Is it important?"

"Perhaps not to you, but it is to me."

"You have one minute."

Nightwing had drawn a crooked finger to his mouth to thump it with annoyance. He had watched her deliberately embarrass the new Officer of Scouts, and now, he thought she should simply have let him walk away.

"It all began when the Iroquois first met the white explorers many generations ago. The explorers tried to ask them where they could find women. The Indians did not understand, so the explorers pointed to that place below the waistline that is distinctly different from a woman. They still did not understand, so told them the Iroquois word for that part of their anatomy. That word was squaw. The white explorers thought it was the word for women, and the mistake has persisted ever since."

Thoughtful silence hung in the aftermath of Talon's

narration. Laine had watched her intently as she had spoken. "From this moment no man at this camp will address you by this insulting term. Does that meet with your approval, scout?"

"It does, Sir, and I thank you for understanding."

A dozen seconds of silence passed before Laine broke eye contact. "This scout is *your* responsibility," he informed Nightwing. "You control her, you train her, and you discipline her when she needs it. And keep her out of my way."

Talon raised a finger. "Oh, Captain Taylor, Sir." He turned to glare at her. "But what about all those things you wanted to do to me?"

Right now, she was getting even with him for *those* things. "You are out of your mind."

"Am I, Sir? Should I remind you what you said that morning?"

Continued embarrassment made him briefly catch his bottom lip between his teeth. "Don't press your luck, scout. I wield a lot of authority over you right now, and I've read your contract. Don't think I'd hesitate to have a whip laid to you." *Blasted liar, Taylor,* he mentally berated himself, retreating before she could say something else to embarrass him.

Reisner had meant to advise Taylor he would take over as Officer of Scouts tomorrow, rather than Monday. But the exterior door slammed thirty feet away, robbing him of the chance to pass on that information.

"Why do you goad new Officer of Scouts?" Nightwing demanded.

Talon smiled rebelliously, though it lasted only a few seconds. "He had no right to say those things to me the other day. He deserved it."

Reisner, too, thought Talon should show more discretion. But he was damned glad to have her here. Not only would her presence break the monotony at camp, but he liked the way Nightwing watched her, as this astute and very compassionate Apache might watch a new, as yet undiscovered species of desert flower blowing capriciously in a breeze. "Go with Nightwing to visit your horse."

Talon's heart pounded, an almost painful quiver in her shoulders that made her want to grab and hold them. As much as she despised the new Officer of Scouts, she wondered what it would be like to—

Embarrassed by her thoughts, she rose abruptly. Approaching within touching distance of John Nightwing, she deliberately brushed his arm. "Oh, rude Comanche thief apologize," she chided, denying him even the smallest smile. "Did woman diminish the chief's big, bad, manly strength?" Then she whispered, "Silly, superstitious Apache."

Nightwing's dark eyes smiled as she flowed past him. ""Do not know *diminish*," he said to Reisner when she was out of earshot, "But sound much bad. Better for all if Colonel Heitman just hang her." But even as he spoke, he remembered his silent prayers to his spirit father when he had stood outside Heitman's office the day Talon had arrived. "Good day, Sir."

Nightwing joined Talon in the corridor, at once surprised when she tucked herself against him, her hands easing to his back. Her cheek pressed lightly to his shirt, she whispered, "Though I hate Apaches—hate them, you understand—I promise I will not try to escape again. I will watch my hateful mouth, and I will try very hard to be as good as I can possibly be."

This almost sincere vow after she had called him a silly, superstitious Apache? Touched by both her contradiction and her affection, Nightwing's hand went to her back to return her embrace. But he caught himself at once, withdrawing a little roughly. "Why you cooperate now? What changed?"

With Heitman soon to leave Camp Casey, she felt vulnerable to the new Officer of Scouts. And she *had* goaded him. "Since that horrid captain has given me to your training, will you also protect me from him?"

He laughed lightly. "I do my best."

"You will not let him whip me?"

"If you are whipped, scout, it will be by me." Again, he hid all signs of his lie. "You must not worry about this. Now come, let us visit this old horse you love."

Four

Three Weeks Later

Talon dropped to the small, cozy bed in her quarters, dead tired from the past fourteen hours in the saddle. She had been allowed to engage in bivouac in the hills surrounding Camp Casey with the scouts and Company D, Fourth Cavalry, despite being a week from her month long probationary phase.

Nightwing had kept her from having much contact with Taylor since her arrival. Despite the fact that he was arrogant and spoiled, and simply had to have his own way, she felt strangely attracted to him...to the way his golden hair caught the gleam of the Arizona sun...the way his piercingly blue eyes bore holes through her every time she tried to relax. He smirked, criticized without saying a word, intimidated simply by brushing past her, and his hand instinctively fell to his sidearm each time he anticipated her backtalk.

And if he yelled *son-of-a-bitch* one more time—

Why do I waste time thinking about you?

Enough dust had settled into Talon's clothing to add a full person to her weight, but she was much too exhausted to heat water and bathe. She had looked forward all day to getting out of these horrible trousers, cleaning up, and putting on a skirt. But for a while, she lay still and listened to the now familiar night sounds of the little Army camp. Far away, men's laughter, and the snickers of horses let loose in the corral, echoed through intermittent bouts of silence.

Her private quarters had once been an icehouse, then used to store saddles and tack needing repair. Tucked into a niche between the long barracks buildings occupied by the scouts to one side and the enlisted soldiers to the other, the tiny stone house had one small window on the east side, and a single entry door accessible at the bottom of half a dozen steps on the

49

outside. Sgt. Huck's crew had scrubbed the exterior, and painted the interior stones a soft, serene blue. Dora had selected nice pieces of furniture from storage behind the quartermaster's office for the twelve-foot square room. In addition to Talon's bed, a small, round table sat in a corner, a chifforobe for her clothing was elaborate beyond military standards, and a new straight back chair afforded her a place to sit and read. Another small table held the lamp beside her bed, and a scarcely used parlor stove was well vented to the outside. Dora had sewn a pair of calico curtains for the single window, which slid on a rod, and had sent over a soft, downy quilt, blankets, and a woven oval rug.

Lieutenant Colonel Heitman almost became a friend after her unsuccessful escape, and playfully blamed his bouts of dyspepsia on her. But Talon thought that threatening to hang people surely must exact a toll on even the staunchest of personalities. Last week he had called her to his office, and they'd had a long talk, focusing on his expectations of her when the new post commander arrived. Two days later, he climbed onto a coach and departed, and Major Daniel Harris, D Company, Fourth Cavalry, a dashingly handsome, career military man, was left in charge until the new C.O. arrived.

Since she'd been at Camp Casey, she'd found the white soldiers much more agreeable than most of the Apaches, especially that demanding Chief of Scouts. His character titillated between infuriatingly opposite spectrums, though his harshness—and little insults—had grown less frequent. Some moments he was thoughtless, unyielding, and almost cruel, and the next he might patiently explain some small duty intended to make her a better scout. Once, she thought he smiled completely free of mockery, though he snapped a harsh criticism and suppressed the smile at once. He was likely a good deal more bluff than blow.

Still, she had to give him credit, because he had diplomatically kept the new Officer of Scouts from harassing her beyond her bounds of tolerance. There remained those times that she wasn't sure if Nightwing was her protector against him, or in league *with* him.

The full blood Apaches remained as intimidating as teased tarantulas. Chief First Sergeant Dako always addressed her directly, whether criticism or compliment, but the others took their complaints directly to Nightwing. Once, while leaving the corral after grooming her horse, a knife sliced a post very near her shoulder. Though Nightwing and Dako grilled the Apaches well into the night, no one admitted throwing it.

Once he'd gotten past his disappointment in her, Mattie became her best friend at camp. He had been as patient as a new mother while shoeing her skitterish mare that morning after she'd met Taylor in Reisner's office. Talon felt she could trust him as much as she had ever trusted any one man. Even then, the trust was tendered reluctantly, for Talon rebelled against this ambivalent emotion in almost all of its forms.

She loved to tease Mattie about his hard brown eyes masking a tender sweetness, and the way his smile betrayed the dimples in his cheeks. Now that he was camp "smithy," he wore a tan buckskin vest against otherwise bare skin, and a canvas apron over fringed buckskin trousers. His thick, white hair was almost always coated with soot from the fire he kept burning to heat the horseshoes, and his sun-browned skin always slick with sweat.

Then there was tomorrow's arrival of the new commanding officer, Major General Salem George Compton. She really wanted to present a good appearance during parade formation on Monday, simply because the Apaches expected her to mess up.

Leaving her thoughts, Talon listened to footfalls on the outside steps. A gentle rap announced the arrival of a visitor, and Talon sat up with a patient, "Come in."

Dora had brought her supper from her own table, and spent a few minutes, as usual, listening to her complaints about the Apaches, Nightwing, and Taylor. Dora replied, "Shame you and the captain don't get along. He's quite a gentleman really. All the unmarried ladies—some of the married ones, too—are looking forward to dancing with this fine young gentleman at the fandango on Friday."

Talon had heard about the fandango from Nightwing, who

also warned her that the scouts had never been invited to these social functions organized by the women of camp. And she certainly didn't care about Taylor's popularity with the ladies. When Dora departed a few minutes later, Talon turned the wooden latch, pulled the curtain across the window, and prepared to settle into a warm bath. But she had scarcely turned from the door before a series of short raps drew her again to it. Private Wilson had taken a step back, allowing space for the door to be opened. "Captain Taylor summons you to his office, Miss Talon."

"Why? Is Nightwing there?"

"No, ma'am, and he said you are not to dawdle."

Talon's mouth pressed defiantly. "Dawdle? Is that the word he used?"

Wilson grinned. "Yes, ma'am."

As Wilson ascended the steps, Talon turned to grab her coat, annoyed and worried about the summons. Though Nightwing had been a bear, he had prevented her from being alone with the new Officer of Scouts, and she wished he would do so now. Crossing the parade field a minute later, she tried to think of a single event today that might have prompted the summons, and the dressing down she anticipated. But it had been a routine drill, without incident. She hadn't even been sassy.

Entering the building, she approached in silence and stood outside the closed door of Taylor's office. He didn't see her in the evening darkness, and she spent a full minute just watching him, the way he half-curled his fingers under as the pen he held scratched across a sheet of paper, and the fingers of his left hand drummed lightly against his forehead. One boot was thumping the wood beneath his desk, and as it began to grate on her nerves, she stepped forward and lightly knocked, which was followed at once by his clipped, "Enter." He did not look up as she paused before his desk. "Sit, scout."

Talon kept her eyes down. "I prefer to stand, Sir, since I do not expect to be here long."

The pen slipped into its holder, and he looked to her now,

his tone commanding and rude. "You'll be here as long as I request that you be here. Do I make myself clear, scout?"

"Perfectly clear, Sir. Please, tell me why I have been summoned so that I can attend my nightly duties before I retire."

Laine spread his hands out on his desk. "I learned from Nightwing just today that your second name is Rose. I must ask that you not use it after the new commanding officer's arrival."

Somewhat taken aback by his intrusion into a matter that was none of his concern, Talon stumbled over a few disoriented thoughts before stammering, "Why...it is part of my name...what does it have to do with him?"

Laine did not hesitate to answer, "His daughter's name was Julia Rose, and she was killed by Indians. Though it was a bloodthirsty band of Comanches, and not Apaches like your people—" He did not witness her grimace as he not only referred to her as Apache once again, but cast an aspersion toward her true tribe, "it will simply awaken old wounds to hear his daughter's name attached to an Indian. Does that make sense to you?"

"No, it does not. My name was Talon Rose yesterday, it is Talon Rose today, and it will be Talon Rose after the commanding officer's arrival. No man intimidates me out of my parents' legacy, and I have little but their blood and the name they gave me together." She had stiffened so completely that pain shot through her spine. Relaxing a little, she concluded, "Now, if that is all you wanted—"

He had expected her rebellion, perhaps would even have been disappointed had she not exhibited it so thoroughly. "That is not all I have, Scout." Feeling awkward—and rude—that he continued to sit while she stood so defiantly before him, Laine got to his feet and pressed his palms to the desk. "I have been Officer of Scouts for three weeks, and I do not like the way we treat each other. What can I do to remedy the situation short of hanging you?"

"I do not know."

"Tell me exactly what you think of me. Then we can go on from there."

"Do you want the truth, or should I honey coat it?"

He propped his spotless, spit-shined boot on his chair, crossing his wrists lazily against his knee. "I expect you to be truthful."

"What I think of you is not polite."

He had been told by the Apaches that she frequently referred to him as "Jackass," and imagined that was the indignity crawling through her thoughts at this moment. "I've been insulted before. Just tell me what you think of me."

Talon crossed her arms against her waistline, thrust her chin, and eased her boots half a foot apart before she began to speak. "Before I do, Sir, could I ask you something?"

"Of course."

"Why did you lie that morning, about how you were shot?"

"I thought you had enough trouble without me adding to it. Why? Would you prefer that I tell them the truth?"

"Of course not."

"Now, tell me what you think of me."

I think you are wonderful, or I am just a fool. "I don't know why you should care, Sir, but if you insist...I think you are crude, boorish, undisciplined, tediously punitive in your methods, and offensively patronizing. You expect every person, soldier, and civilian alike, to bow and kiss your boots for the simple pleasure of being in your company. And do let me add that the only way I would ever kiss your boots is if someone shoved my dead face into them."

One pale eyebrow arched at a devilish angle. "I intended to ask if you like me, but I suppose you answered that, too." Returning his foot to the floor, he circled his desk, paused at her back and leaned into her. His voice became softly mocking. "Despite what you think of me, scout, could we manage to cease this monotonous bickering? And, pray tell me what I can change about my methods to stop being tediously punitive and offensively patronizing?"

Talon was only too aware of his nearness, the musky aroma of masculine skin ever so close to her own. "Perhaps you should confer with your chief on that."

"I don't give a damn what that Apache thinks. What could I do to make *you* like me?"

"Why should you care whether I like you?"

"Let's pretend that I do care. What could I do?"

Kiss me, so that I can slap your smirking face. "Dying might be a good start."

He laughed now. "Short of dying."

Kiss me, I said. "You could start treating me like I have got some worth."

"You haven't hushed that sassy mouth long enough for me to notice if you do."

"You have been too busy yelling and pointing out my weaknesses to notice."

"We're bickering again." Laine suddenly clutched her tense shoulders and forced her to face him. A bent finger went beneath her chin. Even as he felt compelled to steal a kiss, his voice grew hard, almost sarcastic. "Tell you what, scout. I'll treat you better, and you be more respectful of me. Obey orders without sass, and cease those damned insults behind my back."

Cool perspiration coated her skin beneath her heavy uniform. "All right. May I go now?"

His hands dropped. He stepped back, settling against his desk. "Come here, scout."

"Sir, I...if you are through with me—"

"I said come here." He was only three feet from her. Talon took a single step forward. "One more step should be close enough." She hesitated conspicuously before taking the demanded step. Laine watched her closely, her eyes darkening, leaving only a thin green circle around her pupils. Her mouth suddenly caught in a tremble. "You're afraid of me, Talon?"

"You," she replied truthfully

"Have I ever raised a hand to you?"

"Only your voice, Sir."

"When Nightwing yells at you, you generally yell back. What is the difference between Nightwing and me? That he is Indian, and I am not?"

"The difference is not skin deep, Captain Taylor."

Laine's hand went out, palm up, and he was painfully aware that Talon flinched, as if she expected him to slap her. "Lay your hand against mine." She did so, and would have withdrawn at once from the burning heat of his touch if he hadn't closed his fingers over her own. "I will open my hand if you promise not to withdraw from me." She slightly nodded. His grip relaxed, her fingers remaining lightly against his palm. "This hand will never hurt you," he promised, his other closing over hers to fold it between his own. "I don't want you to be afraid of me. When I yell at you, treat me like you do Nightwing, yell back if you think I'm wrong. But do so with some spirit of respect."

"That is a contradiction, Captain Taylor," she replied, attempting to withdraw her hand, which he would not allow. "Yelling at my superiors shows no respect."

"You know, I'm really not such a bad fellow. You might even like me if you'd give me a chance."

"I will never like you," she vowed, though she knew that wasn't quite true.

"I think you will."

"May I go now?"

Without warning, he gripped her shoulders and pulled her roughly into him. He said nothing as he watched fear churn in the hypnotic depths of her eyes. Mockery grazed his mouth as he pledged, "One day, Talon, the emotion I see in your eyes *will not* be fear." Tenderly putting space between them, he added, "Go on to your nightly ritual, whatever it may be."

Talon took several diffident steps from him, the door suddenly pressing into her back. "I would request, Captain Taylor, that should you ever summon me personally again, that you also summon my chief."

He almost snorted, "I'll do no such thing."

"I will not let you intimidate me into leaving the troop."

"Nor do I intend to do so."

"You do not seriously care if I like you, so what was this summons all about?"

She stirred the passion within him, made him feel playful and teasing. He didn't want her to leave, and was in a mood for her sass. "I hoped you might be willing to warm my blood for an hour or two tonight. Or do you prefer Apaches in matters of intimacy?"

Whether he was serious, or merely teasing her, made no difference to Talon. She would have been offended either way and her response the same. "I'd bed wolves before an Apache...or you! I do not appreciate this kind of vulgar teasing. Between an O.S. and a scout, it is inappropriate."

"I'd be willing to play the role of a wolf if you'd warm up to me tonight."

"Please, hold your breath while I make my decision!"

He strolled casually toward her. "How long will that take?"

"Long enough for you to die!"

His arms again became a vise as he imprisoned her within them. "I've seen the way you look at me, Talon, when you think I'm not looking. You want the same thing from me that I want from you. Why don't you be truthful and admit it?"

Talon broke from him so swiftly that pain shot through her arms where he had held her. He was right, of course, she had dreamed frequently—erotically—of him these past few weeks. He had also been the monster in her nightmares. "The only thing I want of you is the privilege of attending your funeral. And that cannot be soon enough for me." Placing a few awkward steps between them, she paused when he softly spoke her name.

Laine Taylor smiled when their eyes met again. Her reaction to his teasing pounded through his blood. "Trust me, Talon," he warned, "that I am relentless in my pursuits."

"And I am relentless in my resolution to hate you."

As she fled the building, his light laughter swept up behind her, and her own emotions were caught up in a dizzying storm between humor and fury. There had been some truth in his teasing—she did think of him in awkward, unexplainable ways—and he had read her heart too accurately for comfort.

* * *

Major General Salem George Compton arrived at the Mullins-Adair way station by Overland coach just before noon the following afternoon. In the comfort of a hired buggy

57

escorted to Camp Casey by Major Harris and twenty soldiers of his cavalry, he arrived on post property a few minutes past the hour of one. Met by an entourage of company officers and enlisted men, including his good friend, Captain Taylor, his pleasant smile and easy manner quickly put every man at ease.

Since the scouts were engaged in mounting drills on the parade field today in his honor, Talon got her first glimpse of the new commanding officer. He was tall, straight, and lean, his hair thick and white. His uniform, solid dark blue, with a wide gold stripe on the trousers legs, and a red lined sash at his waistline, was impeccable despite his long journey. Even from this distance, his face radiated congeniality and warmth. Though she didn't hear their voices, she knew he spoke easily with the officers and soldiers surrounding him.

With her attention so thoroughly distracted by the activities at the coach, Talon didn't hear Nightwing's order to dismount. Only when he yelled, "Scout Talon," did she realize she was the only one still in the saddle. He hovered over her the moment her boots touched solid earth. "Scout is bored with drill?" he queried in a flat, scolding tone.

"No, Sir, I was not paying attention."

His lean good looks settled into a critical frown, his voice a soft, mocking jeer. "Sir? Chief Nightwing look like officer to Scout Talon?"

"No, Chief Nightwing," Talon amended quietly, aware of dark, grinning faces all around her.

"Interested in activities at coach?"

"No, Chief. I will be more attentive."

"Scout without attention is scout with arrow—bullet—in back. Scalp hanging on enemy belt." Turning her head, Talon rolled her eyes. At once, Nightwing's steely fingers dug into her braid, causing her to cry out in the instant of pain. "If scout want to live, scout *must* pay attention." He then returned to his horse at the head of the column.

He'd not had a chance to remount the big bay when Talon whispered harshly beneath her breath, *"Si'ca wohnaye,"* then repeated the Sioux words more softly in English, "Mean bastard."

Nightwing spun toward her from a distance of twenty feet. "Parents of Nightwing married, scout, by priest at white mission." Yelling at Dako to "take over a minute," he strolled back, paused, drew a deep breath, and his fingers tunneled through her hair again, forcing her to face him. Stormy resistance sprang through Talon's vivid green eyes, her hand covering his own in an attempt to wrest its painful grip from her hair. "I admit I mean sometimes—have to be with careless scout—but I *not* bastard!" Releasing her, he politely ordered, "Put away horse, return to quarters rest of day."

"What's the problem here, Nightwing?"

Nightwing cut a scorching eye toward Laine Taylor, approaching with a riding quirt tapping lightly against his palm.

"No problem, Sir, I cannot handle. This scout dismissed from drill."

Laine looked down the neat line of uniformed Apaches. "Is she sick?"

"Not sick. Just dismissed."

"For what reason is she dismissed?"

"For reason Scout Talon and chief work out themselves."

"For what reason?" he repeated patiently.

Nightwing obviously did not intend to answer, and Talon didn't want him in trouble because of her. She had also fretted over the weekend about the things Taylor had said to her in his office Friday night. "I called him a mean bastard," she said, sarcastically slapping her palm to her forehead. "But where is my mind? I thought it was *you* I was insulting."

Laine pivoted, straight and steady, toward Talon. Holding her defiant gaze, he thought how pretty she was with her cheeks in the full bloom of anger. "Return to drill, Chief. I'll take care of her myself."

"Sir, you said I am in charge of scout—"

"Return to drill, Chief."

Nightwing walked away, reluctance strong in each step. When he was out of hearing range, Laine swept his eyes rudely over Talon, noticing the way her full, sensual mouth pressed into a defiant line. How could hate manifest so completely in such exquisite emerald eyes? "I suppose you're still mad at me, scout?" Talon refused to answer. "You know, I've got a mind to break down your resistance to me once and for all. It's grating on my nerves." What a liar he was. He loved her fire, her defiance, such a challenge in this dusty land that scourged a man's very soul. "Remove your rifle from the scabbard." When Talon did so, he slowly circled her, his voice patient and soft. "You have two choices, spend this day in my office cleaning, dusting, scrubbing and polishing, or the next hour holding this rifle over your head with both hands." Without pause—or response— Talon lifted the rifle, spreading her boots by a foot for balance. Laine smiled. "I wasn't serious about holding the rifle for an hour."

"It is the choice I have made."

"Put it down."

Talon stiffened beneath the rifle. "I will do so when the hour is up, if I last that long."

Damned stubborn woman. "Very well, scout, when your arms tremble with weakness, I shall come up behind you—"

When he halted the threat, Talon demanded, "And do what?"

He leaned into her again. "Tickle the devil out of you."

"I am *not* ticklish."

His face was scarcely more than an inch from her own, his steely blue eyes laced with humor, his mouth pressed so tightly his jaw had become a sharp line. "If you shoot me again when I walk away, I'll string you up to that flagpole over there."

"I have no bullets. Most damage I could do is club you in the head."

Leaning close, Laine whispered, "Know what I think you need?"

Talon kept the fury from her voice with great effort. "You told me when we first met, Jackass, and the other night when you summoned me to your office."

It was the first time she'd called him that to his face. "That's not at all nice."

"You are right, Sir. I insulted the jackass."

His cheek almost brushed hers as he whispered, "My opinion has not changed. You need to be loved by a really good man. That might flame the fire, but quell the sass."

"Shame a really good man is not here, Sir."

Laine smiled, and without response, retreated to his horse. He prayed she wouldn't insist on holding that heavy rifle for even ten minutes, let alone a full hour.

* * *

Major General Salem Compton was acquainting himself with his administrative staff when he first looked out the window and saw the scout standing with the rifle over her head. Occasionally, she swayed, her arms bent, and both Taylor and Nightwing, arguing between them, were quickly in front of her. Even from this distance, it seemed obvious that one or the other of them berated her for her frailty under the rifle. General Compton knew how heavy an Army issue rifle could become, and could not believe that either the Indian chief or the gentle-hearted Southern officer he had served with in Massachusetts were being so hard on her.

Most of his staff had returned to their desks. Private Roan was unpacking books when Compton asked, "What is the tribe of the scouts?"

"Chiricahua Apache, Sir, some Mescalero and Western, and I believe one Lipan, but all Apaches of one tribe or the other. The chief's mixed, some Sioux and white, I understand."

"How long has the female scout been standing that way?"

Recalling at once that Talon was half-breed Comanche, Roan saw no need to correct the information he had provided. He would simply appear muddle-brained to his new C.O. "Since you arrived, Sir," he replied, approaching the window where the general stood. "Talon's had a rough time since she's the only female. She's also feisty as hell, and Nightwing don't like her much more than Captain Taylor does. But the chief sticks up for her if things get too rough."

"He's not sticking up for her now. Take word to Taylor that she's been standing there long enough. And advise him to see me

61

in my office at four sharp, along with the Chief of Scouts." He was not speaking to Roan as he quietly added, "I will not have cruel discipline on this post—and in my Army—while I am in charge."

By the time Roan reached the parade ground, Taylor was nowhere to be seen. So he approached Nightwing. "Where is Captain Taylor, Chief?"

"He went to officer dining room for food. What you want?"

Roan relayed Compton's orders. Though Nightwing didn't approve of Taylor's harsh discipline of Talon, he resented interference of outsiders in the training of the scout troops. Nor did he approve of Talon's popularity among the soldiers. He asked Roan to name several of the male scouts, but each time he sheepishly replied that he didn't know. Now he pointed to Talon, so completely dappled in sunshine filtering through a nearby ash—the only tree within camp walls—that it briefly snatched his voice. "Why you know that scout name, but no other scout name?"

Roan suppressed a smile, since the chief's mouth was crooked with anger. "Every man on post knows Talon's name. She's pretty as a cherry blossom."

Nightwing could not argue with that observation. "That not important to being good scout."

"If you don't mind my asking, Chief, what did Talon do to be so cruelly punished?"

He had noticed that Taylor tried several times to make Talon put the rifle down, but she had refused. Her stubbornness was a challenge to the Officer of Scouts, and certainly none of this little clerk's business. "I do mind."

"General Compton might ask."

"Scout troop not his business."

Every word exchanged between the men reached Talon, but she was in too much agony to enjoy Compton's intervention. The muscles of her arms felt strained and torn, and she prayed that her chief would order her to lower the rifle. She would not do so without it, simply because she would not give him the satisfaction of her defeat.

Nightwing's anger caught with each blow of his pulse as he approached Talon. His hands clasped at his back, he slowly circled her, paused at her left shoulder, and leaned into her. His voice was a mocking drawl. "Scout Talon has friend in new commanding officer." Then, "You should pay attention to words that come from your sassy mouth, especially when new Officer of Scouts nearby."

"I understand," she said softly, a tear rolling onto her cheek.

As though he soothed a child, Nightwing casually flicked away the tear. Her eyes were deep, green pools of fury, boiling the blood in his veins in a very pleasant wave. "If Scout not put rifle down now, I tear it from hands. Then you go to quarters."

Talon's painful arms merely fell with the weight of the rifle, and had it not been for Nightwing firmly clutching her upper arm, she would have folded to the ground. Without motive, since the most he had intended to do was send her to her quarters, she tearfully vowed, "I hate your guts. I wish you were dead."

Nightwing firmly dug well-groomed nails into her face without hurting her, at once wondering how her lips would feel against his own. "No, you do not, scout. You mad with Taylor, but he *did* tell you put rifle down. You are stubborn." Releasing her, he turned and walked away. Because the new commanding officer had summoned him to his office at four, he called an end to drills for the day, ordering all troop weapons to be cleaned before nightfall. The time was just quarter past three this Friday afternoon when he mounted his horse and rode toward the corral. Usually in drill until five or six, the scouts were noticeably disoriented by the early hour of dismissal.

Five

Precisely at four, Nightwing maneuvered through a dozen boxes in various phases of unpacking to approach Compton's desk. The old white officer pressed one palm to his forehead as he looked over documents through a pair of wire-rimmed spectacles. Though his eyes saw only the papers, his ears had not deceived him. "I requested that the O.S. also attend this meeting," he stated without looking up. "Where is he?"

The few terse words he had exchanged with Taylor in relaying the general's order snapped impatiently through his thoughts. He wasn't about to get involved in a relationship between Taylor and the C.O. bordering on childish mutiny. "He request see you later."

Compton flicked a careless hand. "Typical...Take a chair and I'll be right with you."

In seven years, John Nightwing had not sat in the presence of an officer, except at meals. He wasn't about to start now, especially when the officer intended to be quarrelsome, as this one certainly did. "I stand, Sir."

The small disobedience drew Compton's eyes to the very tall Indian. Leaning back, he propped a booted foot on his knee. "To begin with, Chief of Scouts Nightwing, I should make it clear that every event at Camp Casey *is* the business of the commanding officer, including the scout troop. Can we have an understanding on that?"

Nightwing grimaced. The little soldier clerk had a very big mouth. "I do understand, Sir, but I must make clear that to have best scout troop in your Army, keep morale strong, Officer and Chief of Scouts must have final say in matters of troop. Can we have understanding on that?"

He was bold, sure; Compton liked that in a man. "We can have an understanding. One reason I've summoned you is that I'm getting wires from other military posts throughout the

64

Southwest that your people are restless. I plan to temporarily add another forty scouts to your troop. Can you handle that many?"

Again, Nightwing grimaced. "My people?"

"Don't take offense, for chrissake. Apaches with burrs in their backsides. Mean Apaches."

"Where you get new scouts to track these mean Apache?"

"Ft. Bowie in a few weeks. It'll be up to you to make room for them."

"Apache from Bowie have no discipline."

"We'll worry about it when that day arrives." Compton dropped his foot. "About the discipline of the female scout this afternoon. This can hardly build morale, or make for a well-disciplined scout. Were you responsible for it, or was Taylor?"

Nightwing would not lie, nor would he tell the truth. No matter his personal dislike of the new Officer of Scouts, he owed him a certain loyalty. He also would not tell the C.O. that Taylor had ordered Talon to lower the rifle, but she had refused. "I conduct drill today, while captain welcome you to camp. My female scout rude and undisciplined. If she be value to troop, she must learn to control angry tongue."

"I thought Apache honored and respected their women?"

"I respect Scout Talon as woman. But she must earn honor and respect as scout. For your information, she is not Apache woman."

Compton had made a point to ask Private Roan the tribe of the scout troop. With the exception of Nightwing's blended bloodline, he had not indicated a mixture in their ranks. "What is her tribe?"

"Scout Talon slave of Sioux five year, speaks tongue of Sioux. Mother had white blood...she only child of dead Comanche leader   "

Nightwing's quietly spoken statement had the same impact as a bullet. Compton scrambled to his feet. "You're saying this female is Comanche?"

Nightwing assumed he distrusted the notorious reputation of her tribe, and that was how he chose to address his concerns. "Half-blood Comanche, yes, but with discipline, she be good scout."

A pang of hard hatred pierced Compton through as he resettled in his chair. "This butcher will not remain in your troop. You get rid of her today. Does Taylor know she's Comanche?"

"I had no reason to tell him."

"So help me, if he knew and let her stay—" Compton's face continued to flush with hate. "I won't have a Comanche—female, half-blood or otherwise—at this camp."

Nightwing pressed his lips in a futile attempt to stay a moment of argument. Anger stiffened his spine. "This scout under contract. No man break it."

"We'll just see about that." Compton yelled for Private Roan, a scurrying of polished shoes closing the distance. "Bring me a copy of the contract of this scout Talon." A minute later, Compton had HQ's copy in hand and scanned it. "This is not a standard contract." Then he noticed the signature and half-screamed, "This Comanche claims *Rose* as a name? I won't have it, do you hear?"

Nightwing, having heard the name of General Compton's daughter, had expected this issue to become a problem when he found out. "It is her name, and no one can take from her. Scout Talon came to camp as prisoner. Mr. Money ask Lieutenant Colonel Heitman to put her in scout troop—"

"Who is this Money?"

"He is blacksmith now, but he was—"

"This bitch was brought here by a blacksmith?"

"*Scout Talon* brought here by deputy U.S. Marshal."

"Make up your damned mind." Nightwing did not answer, and Compton read the one page document again. "Until I find a loophole, if the bitch is unruly, you follow the provisions of this contract. Whip or confine her."

Nightwing's angry, contemptuous tone flicked rudely at the new C.O. "Scout *not* bitch. I lock her up if she deserves it, but she will *not* be whipped by *any* Apache." Silence crawled between the two men, but Nightwing mentally swore it off. "I demand to know why you hate woman because she half-blood

Comanche?"

Coming to his feet again, Compton pressed his palms to the desk and leaned toward Nightwing. His eyes became mere slits. "Twenty-five years ago, Comanches in West Texas kidnapped and murdered my daughter—my only child—so I *will not* spend my time here seeing this Comanche bitch on a daily basis." A bony finger pointed menacingly. "And don't you *ever* again make demands of me."

Nightwing, having heard the story of Julia Compton's death, suppressed the curses lingering at his mouth. "Talon not born twenty-five years ago, so you have no reason to hate her. How many Comanche did you and soldiers kill to avenge daughter's death?"

Compton clamped his teeth hard enough to cause pain. "Get rid of the bitch, Chief. And keep her out of my sight." As he'd spoken, he'd taken a pen and brutally slashed through the name *Rose* written so beautifully at the bottom of the contract.

Nightwing was almost always obedient to orders, but not when they were unreasonable. *And if he called Talon a bitch one more time.* With an explosive sigh, he swore, "*Scout Talon* will stay. If you not want to see *Scout Talon,* keep shade down at office window."

Fury hissed from Compton's watery eyes as clearly as his words. "You're a damned cocky Apache."

"Have Sioux, white blood, too. Cocky come from white blood."

"And you're a smart mouth."

"Thank you."

"Get rid of the Comanche."

"No."

"Then you've earned yourself a stay until Sunday morning in the guardhouse."

In seven years Nightwing hadn't received so much as a verbal reprimand. His perfect record would now be tarnished by a scout he had never wanted to begin with. But he had to stand his ground with this hotheaded commanding officer who hated all Comanche because of a few bad ones.

Compton again called for Private Roan. "Write out an order for my signature that Chief Nightwing will spend until Sunday morning in the guardhouse for disobedience."

Every man in camp respected Nightwing, and the excellent work he had done with the scouts. The general consensus was that only he controlled the cultural propensity for savagery in these Indians. "Sir?"

"Be quick about it," Compton snapped. The clip of Roan's boots disappeared into the front office of HQ. "When he returns, take the order to the guardhouse and check yourself in."

"I request one hour to brief scouts on duties for weekend."

"Granted. And you make sure Taylor sees me today."

"I do not have time to be messenger boy."

"That insolence will cost you until *Monday* morning in the guardhouse. On your way out, tell Roan to make the change."

Nightwing retreated, pausing in the doorway to look back on the new commanding officer. He was again looking over Talon's contract, digging, he imagined, for that loophole.

Nightwing didn't know what the hell a *loophole* was, but it sounded bad.

* * *

Talon wasn't sure why Nightwing had felt the need to go over their weekend duties this Friday evening, rather than give them their schedules on the assigned day as usual. He had said he would be out for a couple of days, but she suspected he'd told all the Apaches where he'd be. Since Captain Taylor would be busy helping his old friend, the new commanding officer, settle in to his quarters, Dako was left in charge until Monday morning.

Returning to her quarters, Talon closed herself into the absolute darkness, fumbling for the matches on the desk to light the oil lamp, and the stove to take the chill from the air. Turning from the sudden glow, she immediately faced the new commanding officer, standing at the foot of her bed.

She looked to him, noticing things he'd been too distant earlier in the day to notice, the deep lines and heavy pouches beneath his eyes, a few dark chestnut hairs clinging among the thick crop of white. A deep cleft almost divided his chin. Then she concentrated on his eyes, shockingly blue, and almost deadly as they bore down on her. This alone kept her quiet, and from questioning his reason for the visit.

Compton didn't in any way react to expressive green eyes shimmering with surprise. A natural beauty, her lips full, moist, and slightly parted, betrayed straight white teeth. Then he noticed the slightest smile—one he ruled mockingly insincere—and remembered why he had come here tonight. "Tell me something, does Taylor know you're Comanche?"

The question caught her off-guard, and she had to think for a moment. "He referred to me just yesterday as *that Apache breed.* I did not correct him, Sir."

Compton couldn't talk any sense into the bullheaded Chief of Scouts, and Taylor, by habit, defied his orders. He'd have to deal with this female himself. Despite her ruthless Comanche blood, and the fact that she was of the more willful gender, he hoped to have better luck with her. "You're to leave Camp Casey tonight. I won't allow the guards at the gate to shoot you. Take any horse you want and ride out."

Talon wondered what she had done to displease him his first day on the job, and immediately thought Taylor might be responsible for the new C.O.'s hostility toward her. She wouldn't put it past him. "Sir?"

"I will not have a Comanche butcher at this camp."

Bewilderment clustered within her. Had Taylor told him about the accidental shooting? "But, Sir, I have never even butchered a chicken."

"I will not have one of *you* here."

"But, Sir—"

"Just get off this post." His polite tone did not sustain the hatred he spoke.

"Let me assure you I am working very hard to be a good scout—"

Giving no warning, Compton drew back his hand and hit Talon very hard across the left side of her face, sending her reeling across the small room. As she folded to one knee against the wall, Mattie charged in, pinning Compton's arms painfully at his back. He had come to talk to her about Shadow Dancer. "What the hell?" Compton attempted to match gazes with the civilian behind him. "Release me immediately. I'm the commanding officer."

"I don't give a rat's ass if you're the president," Mattie swore savagely. "You just struck this gal."

Talon wiped blood from the corner of her mouth where the blow had cut her lip. "Mattie, please...let him go. He *is* the commanding officer—"

Flinging him off, Mattie swiftly stepped between Compton and Talon. "You had your say with Talon Rose, so get out."

Compton ground his teeth at the sound of Talon's second name. "I suppose you're the ass who brought this heathen here?"

"Brought no heathens, but I did bring this mighty fine young woman."

Looking around the big, burly man, Compton pointed a trembling finger toward Talon, his words spilling from tightly thinned lips. "I'll expect you to be gone by morning. If you're not, by God—"

"Talon's not going anywhere," Mattie warned. "And you'll never touch her again." As Compton straightened his jacket, Talon noticed that one of the brass buttons had popped from his uniform. She picked it up and politely handed it to him. Compton snatched it, then pivoted and left. By the time Mattie returned his attentions to Talon, she'd settled to her bed, tears spilling to her flushed cheeks. "What the hell happened, Talon?"

"I came back to my quarters and lit the lamp. When I turned, he was standing there. He called me a Comanche butcher and ordered me to leave. When I tried to talk to him, he struck me. I do not know what I did to provoke him."

"You didn't do nothin', gal." Mattie's hand swept across her shoulders and drew her to him in a light hug. "I heard his daughter was killed by Comanches twenty-five years ago."

"What does that have to do with me?"

"You're Comanche. Weren't nothin' you done personally."

Compton's brutal assault, without provocation, charged

through Talon's veins. "Except for Dako, the Apache hate me, Nightwing, Taylor, now the C.O."

Mattie roughly shook her shoulders. "Listen to me, Talon. Nightwing stuck up for you today at HQ and Compton ordered him to the guardhouse until Monday. So he don't hate you. An' I suspect Taylor likes you a lot more'n he lets on." Turning her pretty face to him he ordered, "Let me see that lip," and after he'd looked it over, "It'll be sore and bruised for a few days, maybe some swelling. You put a cool cloth on it."

Talon was quiet and tearful, and Mattie as distressed as if his own child lay against him with an illness he couldn't cure. "I'm real sorry about Compton. He give you any trouble you come to me." He'd also heard it was Taylor who disciplined Talon on the field today. "An' you got a friend in Nightwing. Can this worn out ol' ex-lawman remind you without you gettin' all riled up that you need to watch that sassy tongue?" When she shrugged her response, he withdrew to the door. "You lock this door, you hear? And bring the mare to me in the mornin', so I can check that loose shoe."

"I will." Locking the door as he'd ordered, Talon listened to his boot steps until they faded into the night. Then, her emotions shattering into a million shards, she pressed her tearful face into her pillow and cried herself to sleep.

* * *

A furious Major Daniel Harris, hearing the news about the new C.O.'s first run-ins with both Talon and Nightwing, cancelled the formal parade muster planned to officially welcome him to Casey. Told that the Fourth Cavalry and its scouts had to track hostiles southward, Compton took the affront with little more than a grumble. But he knew it was either because he'd struck the Comanche, or locked up the Chief of Scouts. He thought Taylor might be angry as well, because he hadn't seen him since Friday.

As his scouts prepared to mount their horses Monday morning, Nightwing drew Talon aside. She worried that she'd done something else, though in the past he'd not hesitated to address her faults in front of the Apaches. His fingers moved to

71

her chin, and he looked over the bruise that had mellowed to a mottled green. "This injury?"

Talon politely eased her chin from his grip. "I was clumsy and ran into a peg."

His hand fell gently to her shoulder for the moments that he spoke. "Never lie to chief. Stay away from Compton. Come to your chief if he hurt you again."

Her gaze turned to him with a new sense of admiration and trust. "I am sorry I caused you trouble with him on Friday."

Nightwing gave Talon a look that made her feel she had said something really important. "Got plenty sleep, play checkers with skinny guard." Mounting his horse, he paused to look down on her. "Taylor will not ride with us today." A smile caught within him as she let out a sigh of relief. "Forgot to give this to you," he continued, throwing an ammunition pouch down to her. "Scout need loaded weapons." A rare smile struggled onto his mouth. "Promise not to shoot nobody. Taylor, too."

Talon spoke his name again, halting his departure. His gaze settled comfortably on her. "I had no right to be disrespectful to you Friday. I will try to control my tongue."

"Good." Another rare smile caught and held longer than usual. "I not enjoy being mean bastard to you." Then he reined about and started giving orders. Five minutes later, the scout troop passed through the front gate of Camp Casey, heading into the Huachuca Mountains to the northwest, where they would pick up the trail of hostiles and possibly turn south.

No one but Nightwing knew they'd be gone two days. He thought it best to put some time and distance between his new scout and General Compton. He also needed to tell them about the addition of forty extra scouts, which this small, tightly knit band wouldn't take well. They distrusted all Apaches, sometimes even each other.

* * *

Caught in just the right mood, Captain Laine Taylor considered himself a Southern gentleman, plagued by a rare, somewhat short-tempered demeanor by nature. Right now, he felt entirely within the realms of his character, and as peeved as a bee-stung bull. He was furious that Compton had locked up Nightwing for the entire weekend and that he'd struck Talon—in her own quarters—without provocation. His old friend from Washington had thoroughly depleted what remained of his patience this morning, and he certainly didn't want him accompanying him to his quarters to discuss business. "So, what's the problem you need to discuss, Sir?"

"Don't take that tone with me, Taylor. You may have preferred a post with a balmy southern breeze, but a good Army officer should have a diversity of experiences under his belt."

Laine held his anger. "I am glad to be at this camp. Why would you think otherwise?"

"How are you getting along with the Indians?"

"They're a disciplined lot. Are *you* having trouble with them?"

Compton huffed a rude reply, "Only that smart-mouthed chief. I'd prefer a gaggle of primitive, backwoods whites, sniffing out wild Apaches above facial hair stinking of chow and chewing tobacco."

"In their behalf, I would request that you not accost any of them personally, and certainly not punish a man for speaking his mind." They entered Laine's quarters, a spacious, one-level house with a sweeping porch, nestled between two three-storied multi-unit bachelor officer's quarters. Laine had a generous supply of liqueurs he'd ordered through the sutler's store, and poured both of them a brandy. He knew the general had a fondness for it.

"I was sorry the moment I left the woman's quarters," Compton volunteered the information. "God, there's something about her...so familiar—"

Laine still did not know why he had struck Talon. Half-falling into a chair, he set his goblet on a small table. "Tell me what's on your mind? Can't be much of a problem, since you arrived only Friday." Compton habitually found trouble where none existed, and Laine kept that in mind.

Compton now settled at the end of the divan. "That female in your troop. Did you know she's Comanche?"

In the three weeks he had been here, the matter of her tribe had never been mentioned. Despite her speaking another Indian language—and openly hating the Apaches—he had assumed she was of their tribe, likely by slavery. No one—including Talon—had contradicted his references to her as such. "First time I've heard about it. Is that why you struck her?"

His angry eyes swept the younger officer. "You know how I feel about Comanches. I want her out of this camp. And the bitch has Rose for a second name, my daughter's name."

Laine had suspected he'd hear that news, and wouldn't take well to it. "It's been twenty-five years, Sir, time to let go of the past. Talon has a right to the name her parents gave her. And, Sir, she doesn't deserve to be called a bitch. She's feisty, but hardly a bitch."

"The Comanches butchered my only child and left her to rot in a ravine. I won't have my daily life here disrupted by the presence of this heathen."

Not only had Laine never encountered Compton's kind of hate, he had never encountered Talon's kind of spellbinding beauty and defiance. Hardly a moment had passed since he'd first seen her that she didn't fire his thoughts, and his loins. "If I don't keep Talon in the scout troop, someone will kill her."

"I don't want her dead. I just want to be rid of her."

"I'm inclined to give her a chance to prove her worth. Keep in mind that what a few Comanches did years ago doesn't make them all bad today."

"There's *no* room here for compromise."

"Just don't strike her again, Sir."

"She was argumentative and insubordinate."

His commanding officer had shown a substantial lack of judgment, and a very bad premonition crawled through Laine's gut. "Was she, Sir?" Compton failed to answer. "Let me take care of the scouts. I'm letting Talon stay."

Outrage crawled over Compton's features. "If you're swayed by that pretty face, Taylor, I'd suggest that your eye for females focus on the white daughters of some of these officers. You'll get a chance to meet them this week."

"That blasted fandango? If the uppity Ladies' Auxiliary doesn't welcome the scouts, then I'm not welcome," Laine replied, now sipping his brandy. "Nothing crawls over my flesh quicker than bigoted women and giggling Army coquettes in heat."

"We must attend, or we'll be seen as arrogant cavaliers too uppity for these dusty southwestern boys."

Laine would never grow accustomed to Compton's disruptive orders, and the assumption that even his off-duty hours were subject to his control. Right now he needed to prickle Compton—childish perhaps—and nothing did that more effectively than forcing him to face his past. "Has anyone questioned, Sir, why a man of your rank was assigned to this remote post?"

Compton pressed his mouth as he recalled the morning he had gone to the War Department in Washington to visit his old friend, Colonel Samuel Lytton. He had encountered a dozen delegates taking a Comanche leader, decked out in his flowing war bonnet and ceremonial wrappings, on a personal tour of Washington, showing him the *might of the Great White Father and his Government.* Outraged at the royal treatment given him, Compton had drawn his belt through his trouser loops, ripped off the Comanche's fancy trappings, and beat him several times across the face. Panicked high-ranking officers and department personnel had pulled him away from the assault. Report of the incident back in Texas had very nearly caused a war between the Comanches and the Army. The Secretary of War, also a long time personal friend, had requested his early retirement. When he refused, he had received the reassignment to Camp Casey, a dusty hellhole meant to force his retirement. "I don't believe anyone knows," he eventually replied "But every man here knows I struck your scout."

Laine wondered if Compton's thoughts had also gone to the ten years in Texas after his daughter's death, fighting almost a one-man war against the Comanches. Though he had led hundreds of men against them, the war itself had been his own. Then a lieutenant colonel, he might still have been fighting it, if not for the frightened, fleeing Comanche woman shot straight through the infant and cradleboard strapped to her back. Though Compton himself had not fired the shot, he took the blame for it when the accused junior officer, deeply grieved by the accidental killings, very nearly committed suicide. Because he had lied under oath when he took blame, he had been required to lie for the next fifteen years. He had repeated the lie so many times that he grew to believe it himself.

Thereafter, Compton had been reassigned to a post back east, gained in rank and status, and managed to salvage what had dwindled of an impeccable military career. Then the chance encounter at the War Department with the Comanche leader had brought back the hatred, flaring it to deadly heights after time had reduced it to embers.

Aware that Compton watched him intently, Laine offered, "One malfeasance should eventually be overlooked."

One, perhaps, if there had only been one. "Locking up that Chief of Scouts didn't win me any points either. You'd think that redskin was God Almighty."

Laine rose and poured another brandy. "We can smooth over these improprieties."

"Just find a way to get the heathen off this post, and I'll do what I can to rush your promotion to major."

The thoughtless inducement incensed Laine enough that pain grabbed his shoulders. "I don't need to be bribed, Sir, to soften the blow of your assignment here."

Six

After evening chow on Friday, military wives and daughters converged on the NCO and enlisted mess halls, to prepare for the welcome fandango given by the NCO Auxiliary Club. Gaudy paper lanterns were hung in and around the mess hall, and by seven the post band, requisitioned for the affair, was belting out a bawdy rendition of *Camptown Ladies,* in between visits to a heavily spiked punch bowl.

Night had fallen by the time Compton coaxed a very reluctant junior officer from the comfort of his quarters. In dress blues, with all honors and medals of his service pinned to his jacket as the general had insisted, Laine felt like a pretentious rooster, preferring his mix of buckskins, uniform, and high boots. Wanting only to have the evening over with, he accompanied Compton to the mess hall, where he had to endure one of his long-winded, overly pompous speeches. He saw by the faces of the officers and soldiers around him that Compton had, indeed, started off on the wrong foot.

Then he was required to taste dainty hors d'oeuvres, tolerate silly similes and infantile phrases, and dance with wives and daughters as clumsy as aging oxen. His patience, and the spit shine on his boots, went the way of a well-tromped barnyard.

It also didn't take long for him to get dragged into a controversy between General Compton and Major Stahl over the training of his guards. Laine diffused the situation by inviting Stahl to the other side of the hall for a "chat."

"What do you wish to discuss, Captain Taylor?"

"Nothing. I wished to spare you our C.O.'s unwavering positions, and to apologize beforehand if he said anything to insult you or any man at this post. Both age and rank have made him more extreme in his judgments."

"And for that I thank you," Major Stahl said. "How do you

77

bear the pompous ass?"

"With a great deal of patience, Sir."

"I might warn you, Captain Taylor, that he's made a considerable number of enemies in his haste to condemn the Scout Talon simply for being Comanche."

"He does have a penchant for overreacting."

"He had no cause to strike this very capable scout. Were he not the commanding officer, he would be up on charges of assault."

They spent a quarter hour talking about events at camp, during which Laine drank several goblets of brandy. When he and Hiram Stahl parted company, his head swam in the nauseating aroma of the dining hall and too much brandy. Needing fresh air, he collected his hat from a large table and went outdoors, to breathe deeply of air free of the stench of tobacco, food, and nauseatingly cheap toilet water. Drawing a long breath, he held it a dozen seconds, and quietly blew it out. A dry, gentle wind swept down from the hills to caress him in pleasant waves.

A few men and women loitered out of doors. He politely acknowledged each as he moved among them. Then a light at the post corral drew his attentions, and he sauntered lazily in that direction, enjoying the cool of evening, and a wide, purple sky painted with starlight. With some effort, he shut out the raucous sounds of the lively fandango assailing the night with its high-pitched laughter and badly played music.

Then he saw the exquisite vision of her, wrapped in the soft glow of a single lantern.

Laine watched Talon comb the mare, taking time to untangle burrs from the long, flaxen mane and tail. Occasionally, she leaned into the mare to whisper something he could not hear, and once he was sure he heard the smallest laugh. He had seen only the hard, unrelenting eyes, the hatred like a storm, and suffered only the defiant lash of her tongue. Right now, she looked like an angel. A tan shirt fell over her hips, and a rawhide band that may have held the fabric close to her waist now lay over the corral fence a few feet away. Such a pleasant contrast to the corseted, overdressed hens and bitties at the dance.

Watching Taylor approach, Talon's first impulse was to run. As he lifted the wire latch and entered the corral, she continued to groom Shadow Dancer, lifting her eyes only when he stepped into her line of vision. Then she placed the currycomb on the small stool.

He said nothing as he held his hand out to her. "Dance with me, Talon."

She immediately caught the heady whiff of brandy. "You are drunk, Sir."

"I said dance with me." His hand darted out to capture hers in a hard grip. As she pulled from him, he drew her hand to the dark fabric of his dress jacket, his eyes ever so close to her own. "How can such a pretty woman be so damned mean?"

"Men like you have made me mean, Captain Taylor." Startled by the very peculiar warmth stirring within her she again tried to break his grip. Why wasn't he dancing with the officers' daughters Dora had said were swooning over him since his arrival? "Let me go."

His strong arm moved to the small of her back and drew her even closer. "Not until I know if you dance as well as you shoot."

The musky smell of him assailed her senses, pleasant waves warming her flesh, confusing her heart. "If I had actually aimed for you, you would be quite dead now."

A lusty smile widened his full, masculine mouth. "I know it was an accident."

"I really think you should release me."

"You'll dance with me, Talon, and you'll do it now." He had not raised his voice, and yet managed to leave no room for argument.

He eased her hand outward from their bodies and into the cool night air. Talon quietly consented to the dance, his nearness moving through her like a newly lit flame. Matching his pace to the music, and surprised that the liquor had not made him clumsy, she watched his eyes, free of the hardness and anger, slightly glassy from drink, holding her as though he had known her always, and she was precious to him.

Having looked at him as a bully and a monster, Talon hated the way she saw him now, his features lean, strong, and clean-shaven, eyes, usually dark with anger, the color of a summer sky, and his freshly washed hair like the gold she had once seen sparkling in a cool mountain spring deep in the Black Hills. A smile, which he suppressed with noticeable effort, played gently at the corners of his mouth.

The music was far away, permeating the cool night air as clearly as Captain Taylor's gentle breathing mingled with her own. Neither missed a step, as though they had practiced all night for this one magical waltz. He had made life hell for her, had insulted, and demeaned her, but right now, Talon felt that she was in paradise in his arms.

Laine was surprised that a tart-mouthed Comanche was such a proficient dancer. He wanted to know everything there was to know about her. But not right now. All he cared about was the dance, holding her close, and feeling the heat of her womanly curves against the expanse of his chest.

Even as he wished the dance would never end, the music suddenly swelled in volume and ended abruptly. With a small laugh, he kept up his pace, a breeze singing through the single ash becoming his music. He was sure he felt the gentle rhythm of her heart as she, too, maintained their closeness in the sudden silence of the night. Then he stopped, drew her firmly against him, and met her gaze with wicked lust. "All those things I said when I thought you spoke no English, and the other night in my office, I meant them." His mouth dipped ever so slowly to capture hers, as he wondered if this beautiful half-blood would willingly accept his kiss—

"Captain Taylor!"

Talon whirled at once from Laine's arms, a move that startled her mare to the far side of the corral. Now that Nightwing had their full attention, he snarled at Talon, "If you finish grooming horse, go to other duties. Captain Taylor, sorry this scout disturbs you."

Talon's eyes lowered only because Nightwing's harshly

barked orders had embarrassed her in front of Taylor, not because he was Chief of Scouts and her direct superior. Before she might flee from them, Laine grabbed her arm. "I am Officer of Scouts, and will not be usurped by your chief. You will go about your duty when I tell you to do so."

Talon ripped her arm from his clutch. "I will do as I please. I am not on duty, and you are *both* usurping *my* private time." Then, ducking past Laine and Nightwing, she retrieved her grooming tools, whistled for Shadow Dancer, and fled toward the stable.

Nightwing's face darkened in disapproval. "I told you, Sir, I will take charge of scout. Since you assigned her to me, I appreciate it if you do not make job more difficult."

"As Officer of Scouts I'll confront this scout any time I choose."

"You invite trouble, Captain Taylor."

"Then it'll be my trouble." Mellowed by the alluring woman in his arms just moments ago, and his own state of intoxication, the hardness of anger abandoned his words. "She seemed to enjoy the dance. Perhaps the problem with her is that we treat her as a scout rather than a woman."

"I ask you not be social with her."

Since he'd arrived at Camp Casey, no one—not even Compton—had riled him as effectively as Nightwing. "I danced with her...once. It'll hardly become habit, Chief."

Something warned Nightwing he would grow to dislike this new Officer of Scouts immensely, and they might even become enemies. Curling his mouth into a sneer, he boldly suggested that, "You should not make job taming scout more difficult."

"She's not a wild filly to be broken to the saddle. She's a woman and needs to be treated with some kindness."

Nightwing's mouth pinched sarcastically. "Like walking her three miles back to camp with hands shackled at back? Or order her hold rifle overhead? This is how white man treats woman?"

"You know I tried to make her put the blasted thing down."

Without response, Nightwing merged into the darkness from which he had come, a thief who had stolen precious moments Laine might have spent with his troublesome scout. Left with the memory of her in his arms as the music of the post band resumed across the parade field, he headed straight for his quarters.

* * *

Later that evening, in fragments of rest descending upon her, Talon dreamed of Taylor holding her tenderly, the gleam in his rich blue eyes as they held her gaze, the way the moon shone on the waves of his hair that had defied their military order to settle softly upon his forehead. Oh, how she wished she had tunneled her fingers through those bold locks, and swept them slowly back.

The music to which they had danced rushed through her thoughts and kept her oh, so vividly aware of him in a way she had never thought possible. She was a scout, and yet for a moment, the white officer in charge of her had treated her as an equal. Talon wondered if it was possible to overlook a man's shortcomings—he had already proven that he had many—and fall in love with him through one short dance in a darkened corral.

She just couldn't sleep. Taylor filled her mind as completely as breath filled her lungs. Scarcely could she believe she had hated him so deeply these past few weeks, and perhaps would again, when he was sober, mean-spirited, remembered the first time they had met in the bluffs, and his vow that she would one day *warm his blood.* Placing her hand softly to her cheek, she recalled with humor the very first words she had heard him growl that morning in the bluffs.

* * *

"Son-of-a-bitch!" Laine had tossed and turned for so many hours he was aggravated as hell. As darkness kept its claim on Casey, he finally arose, poured a whiskey, and soothed his nerves in the predawn chill, away from his overly warm quarters. Sitting on the wide front porch, he absently swirled the whiskey that had yet to touch his lips.

For a moment, he intently watched the small stone building where Talon lived. No light filtered from the one small window,

82

noticeable only at an angle. He had enjoyed bantering with her these past few weeks, playfully making impassioned promises, and stirring her defiance with idiotic punishments.

A cool breeze wafted down from the hills, momentarily soothing the acrid odor of too many men in close confinement. Laine recalled that morning he had come upon Talon in the hills, tearful and heartbroken, horror filling her eyes as she'd realized the bullet had actually struck him. He knew very little about women, but what he did know was that they wanted to be treated differently from men. Not like scouts. Not like half-blood Comanche outlaws. But women, plain and simple.

He pledged to halt his ardent and ineffective teasing of her, but to ply her with the sincerity of his heart.

He wanted to know the soft, gentle side of Talon, because after tonight no doubt lingered that she had one. Setting aside the glass, Laine arose, his body needing sleep, even as his mind, filled with visions of one slim Comanche female who had quietly waltzed into his heart, would not allow him the pleasure this night.

* * *

The following morning, Major Daniel Harris ordered boots and saddles for Company D, Fourth Cavalry. Apache hostiles, possibly led by supporters of Geronimo, had killed some miners thirty miles to the west, and stolen cattle and sheep from several ranches in the territory. Laine was ordered to remain at camp.

In the officer's dining room that evening Laine overheard Major Reisner comment that they'd be out for a minimum of four days. He was furious that Compton had disrupted his duties as Officer of Scouts, because he should be riding with them.

With Talon.

Compton watched Laine's face for reaction to the news he, too, had overheard. Patronizing the officer's dining room was rare for him, since he preferred the privacy of his own quarters for meals. Because he felt like the fish staring at bait on a hook, Laine took special care with his mood.

"What are you thinking, Captain?"

"Hmmm?" Laine looked up now, the food on his plate

83

scarcely touched. Compton, having eaten his fill, had settled back to smoke a cigar. "Nothing."

"You left the dance early last night."

The fork Laine had absently twirled on his plate fell with a clatter. "I went outside for fresh air."

"Fresh air in the corral, Taylor?"

Laine swept a glance toward his burdensome old friend. "I was there for a moment, looking over that fine buckskin mare."

Compton's mouth contorted into a sneer, the cigar hastily ground into the ashtray. "And the fine brown Comanche bitch who rides her?"

Laine rose, rocking the large table and drawing the attention of other officers. "Excuse me, Sir, but I have matters to attend."

Compton snapped, "Sit, Taylor." Rebellion livid in his eyes, Laine reluctantly returned to his chair. Leaning across the table, Compton's quiet, spiteful tone was meant only for him. "I secured this assignment as Chief of Scouts for you because you said you'd enjoy the duty. You've been loyal to me, as both friend and officer, and I expect your loyalty to continue while you're stationed here." He paused, again leaning back. "You treat that woman as a scout, and that does not require dancing with her."

"That stupid dance why you ordered me to remain in camp during this excursion?"

Compton fidgeted with the snuffed cigar, tapping it impatiently into the ashtray. "As C.O. of this post, I can give any orders I want. You need time to place your priorities, and I'd just as soon not have you in the guardhouse while you do so."

Narrow blue eyes picked over Compton's hardened features. "I pray I never hate as deeply as you do."

"When you spend a year searching for a child, only to find her skeletal remains in a ravine, hate comes easily." Because Compton's admonishments had grown louder, the officers around them had discreetly begun leaving the dining hall. "You keep a duty association with this scout, or you'll face my wrath."

Laine rose to his full height and bent slightly across the

table toward Compton. "You've known me a number of years, Sir, and that I take any opportunity to challenge misplaced authority. If I didn't entertain the notion of getting to know this scout personally, I damned well have that notion now."

* * *

After a full day in the saddle, twenty members of the scout troop settled for the night on the shores of the San Pedro River. The other seven scouts were thirty miles away with Company D. After a supper of crackers and jackrabbit stew, cooked over a fire of mesquite wood, the Apaches played games of dice and chance. Because she was both Comanche and female—and her insult toward them never forgotten—Talon had faced a tough obstacle in her troop. Off in the distance, the haunting calls of the great horned owls slowly replaced the sounds of men laughing and gambling. Nothing remained in her memories past dark, when the light faded quickly from the hills and washes and sleep came to her. She vaguely recalled the sounds of the river, the shrill sounds of crowded wings—bats leaving their cavernous hideaways among the hills.

Waking the following morning, Talon felt well rested and ready for another day. Lying on her side, with her hand stretched outside her blankets, she opened her eyes to discover a hand-sized tarantula perched over her fingers. It wouldn't bite unless teased or threatened, so she found a short length of stick and coaxed it into a stand of brittlebush. Those crude Apaches would make sport of seeing who could blow it into the most pieces with their revolvers, and she wasn't going to give them that chance.

By the time they saddled up, a purple-red glow lit the morning sky. The troop entered the trail and followed the shaded northern ridge along the San Pedro. When they reached a small plateau to rest for lunch, Talon felt that she'd been grabbed by every whitethorn and cat-claw growing along the ridge. The rubbing alcohol she kept in her saddlebag brought instant relief to the horrid itch compelling her to scratch her legs into raw stumps.

She couldn't wait for the comfort of her quarters, her mattress, clothing not stiffened by layers of dust, and to be able

85

to take a bath. Nor could she wait to see Taylor, and hear his distinct accent, warm and lazy, perhaps again, from the effects of drink. She had heard that alcohol made monsters of men, not men of monsters.

That afternoon, the troop rode through an old saguaro forest, and by evening had reached a dry creek bed where the flora and fauna shimmered pale and dust-colored in the hazy light. A cactus wren built her nest in cholla, and Nightwing ordered their encampment a good distance away so as not to disturb her labors.

As day stirred toward its end, the songs of wrens and doves mingled with the cries of coyotes far into the steep, eroded hills. Talon sat, hugging her knees and watching the pink gold clouds settled against the deep velvet sky.

"You not eat much."

Talon looked to Nightwing, now crouching to offer her a bit of meat from the desert pig they had killed and roasted. She recalled that typical Apache males would go hungry before they cooked their own food. "I had plenty."

Masculine laughter rippled over their encampment. A group of scouts diced, and Gad had won a jackpot. He whooped and hollered, stuffed his pockets with money, and did some semblance of a war dance around the campfire. "Must tell you, Talon, new C.O. much mad about your dance with Taylor."

They had been alone, Talon recalled. "Did you tell him?"

"He saw you with own eyes. Trust me, Talon, that I would not tell him."

"One little dance with me hardly spoils him for white society."

A shot suddenly rang out, ricocheting among the rocky outcroppings where they camped. Taking cover along the ridge, the scouts waited for another shot, to determine the direction and focus their defense. Several more shots echoed among the rocks. Then Talon, spying the gleam of a rifle caught in a shaft of moonlight high above, pulled her own rifle, and fired. After a few minutes, with no return fire, Billy Haigo went up the ridge, soon returning with a painted Indian pony, and news that Talon's shot had killed a hostile Apache.

They spent several minutes discussing why a single Apache would fire on twenty scouts, then reasoned that he was either drunk or felt protected by the overhanging rocks.

Nightwing looked to Talon, flicking dust from her trousers as if she hadn't a care in the world. "That very good shot, scout." As he drew closer to her, the gleam of her tears took him by surprise. "Are you hurt, Talon?"

"No matter what you heard about me before I became a scout, I have never killed anyone."

He crouched beside her, his voice sympathetically low. "First kill hard, Talon. Next time, will not be so hard." Blinking away her tears, Talon lifted her gaze to him, quietly appreciating his assurances. "Will you take token of hostile before we bury him?"

"I want nothing from him."

"Billy said he has new Winchester rifle, and that is fine painted mare."

"Give them to Dako, if he wants them. I just want to sleep." Dropping to her back, she pulled her knees up, throwing a blanket over them at once. Nightwing suspected his only female scout would cry herself to sleep over this killing. "Wake me for guard duty, Chief Nightwing?"

He would have liked that painted mare for his mother, since her pony was growing old. But he also knew Dako was Talon's favorite among the scouts. "I take next guard duty."

"Nightwing?" Again, he halted. "About that painted mare, you keep her if you'd like. Give the rifle to Dako."

He smiled, because their souls had gently touched. As he retreated, Talon closed her eyes in the cool, dry night, swiftly entering a world of distorted, troublesome dreams.

* * *

Though she'd heard the posted guards mustering the scouts the following morning, Talon was slow in waking. By the time she opened her eyes to the day, she felt that someone had thrown mountains onto her shoulders.

At three o'clock that afternoon, the scouts met up with

Company D. They had stumbled on Apache hostiles camped in a gorge two days ago, and three soldiers were dead. One of the hostiles had escaped into the hills, while the other nine fought to the death. Talon's bullet had brought down the escaping hostile.

A little past six that Wednesday evening, they entered camp with the dead soldiers across their saddles, wrapped in their sleeping rolls and smelling strongly of death. Nightwing reported their activities to Taylor before he returned to the corral. Talon had just brushed down Shadow Dancer. "Taylor said a commendation will go in scout's record."

Couldn't Taylor himself have come to tell her? "Shooting a man should never merit a commendation." Anxious to be alone, Talon hurried through rare parting amenities and entered her quarters, where she collapsed to her waiting bed. Four days of dust bounced and settled all around her, like pale clouds in the enclosed darkness. A few minutes later, she rose, lit the lamp, and threw a few logs into the stove. Twenty minutes passed before Nightwing knocked lightly at her door, entering with a large black pot of hot water which he added to the cold water in the tin tub.

"Scouts get together at wickiups," he announced, "Will you join us?"

The Apaches got together often in their leisure—almost always after English class—but this was the first time she had been invited to join them. Though she was tired, to refuse his invitation might be construed as an insult, and another might never be offered. "Yes, I would like that."

A while later, Talon visited Mattie to pour out her heart about the shooting, and because she knew he wouldn't tease her about the tears waiting to be shed, where the Apaches certainly would. Then she joined the scouts and their families outside the grounds of Camp Casey. One of the wives invited her to join in their meal of boiled potatoes and mutton, and afterwards, she sat with the women and watched the men and children play shinny and lacrosse. As evening progressed, the laughter and play of the children dwindled as they fell asleep one by one. By the time she herself was nodding off, Nightwing offered to walk her back to her quarters.

"You sleep well, Talon, take time tomorrow, rest, read, do what you like to do. All scouts will be at little chapel for English lesson. I wish you were not such good English speaker, so you could be there with us."

Without thinking how he might react, Talon took his hand, but released it when his eyes narrowed. "Thank you for inviting me tonight, and for the hot water for my bath."

That she'd taken his hand so gently pleased Nightwing, the warmth lingering against his skin. "Scout spend too much time alone. That not good."

"It has not been my choice," she reminded him without malice.

"That change now." Then his footfalls faded into the darkness.

Talon had trouble sleeping, so sat and read a book for hours. By the time she retired to bed, the camp rooster crowed, and she slept the following day, waking sometime in the late afternoon. Joining the scouts in their mess tent just past five, she felt the change in their attitude toward her at once.

Because she had shot a man. She wasn't sure how she felt about that.

Just before ten that evening, Talon settled at her desk to read. By the time she completed the little novel Dora had lent her, she ached through her shoulders and back and the room was overly warm. Needing fresh air, she took a chair to the side of her quarters, leaned against the wall in the absolute darkness, and watched the stars. Then, with a small sigh, she closed her eyes and enjoyed the night, the gentle sounds of the post, the far away laughter of men, and the aromas of cooking food.

But most of all she just enjoyed the intermittent moments of silence, which she filled with her own quiet thoughts and memories.

Seven

Laine didn't finish the letter he'd been writing to his sister, Analisse, putting it aside when his handwriting got careless from the effects of whiskey he'd sipped from a flask. Moving into the cool night, his gaze swept the dark outlines of buildings and scattered lights. Spying John Nightwing outside the scout's quarters, he moved slowly in his direction. "Enjoying the night, chief, or do you have troubles?"

Nightwing had hoped to be alone, and his clipped sentences reflected as much. "Not troubled, Captain Taylor. Scout in barracks snore. I come outside so will not kill scout that snore."

"Good judgment. Wouldn't want to see you hanging from the end of a rope."

"I think you would," he replied, his enmity fully intended. "You have funny—what you say—accent tonight? Do not notice when you always yelling."

"Comes out when I drink," Laine laughed, "That's a plantation drawl. Don't suppose I can shake it any quicker than you can your red skin. You speak English well for an Indian."

"This red-skinned Indian speaks English, Apache, Sioux, little Spanish. How many languages you speak, Captain Taylor?"

"Got me there, Chief. Speak nothin' but English."

"We do not all have patience to learn new things."

Nestled in the narrow space between her quarters and the scout barracks, Talon thought that Nightwing was more talkative than usual, especially with a man she knew he did not like. She didn't mean to eavesdrop, but could not politely slip away without detection.

The two men briefly discussed Talon's buckskin mare, and a particularly fine roan that had come in just that week, that Laine hoped to requisition for his own use. They also discussed the strength of the troop since Nightwing became Chief of

90

Scouts, and the lack of physical duty engaged by the former Officer of Scouts. Because Nightwing felt a personal betrayal of Reisner, a man he considered a friend, he quickly changed the subject. "Your general settled down to little camp?"

"He never will, I'm afraid. You two had any more run-ins?"

"Compton had no reason to lock me up, except I not agree with him."

Nightwing's position was short and to the point. Compton's long-winded position, in which he'd accused Nightwing of every conceivable transgression, had taken up nearly an hour of his time. "I heard it was because you spoke in defense of Talon."

"He does not like this scout."

"I wouldn't underestimate his animosity toward her."

"She did not ask to be born Comanche."

"I was surprised she shot the Apache."

"Why? She shot you."

His response caught Laine off guard. "I never said that."

Nightwing allowed a moment of silence to pass. "Woman should take a husband, bear young ones, not be scout. Woman not meant *for* man's duty. Woman meant to *be* man's duty."

"You hate this woman that much?"

"I do not."

"That statement carried no earmarks of respect."

"I respect her. Respect for woman is true test of man's strength, for man must lie beneath her hand at start of life, at end of life."

Drawing up to ease a line of tension along his spine, Laine tucked his fingers into the belt at his waistline. "I hear Talon had a white mother."

Nightwing resented this sudden interest in Talon. He preferred Taylor's harshness toward her, so that she would turn to her chief for protection. "Poor mother captive of Comanche. Talon hate Comanche blood that makes hair black like storm that steals sun from sky. She hate soldiers when she first come to camp, and she hate you, Captain Taylor. Hate Apache, too. Call us stinking dog-eating Apache. She say she hate guts of Nightwing." With a rare laugh, Nightwing suggested, "Maybe she like all of me but guts."

Talon smiled at Nightwing's final comment, even as she realized he would never forget her insult. And she thought he was growing to like her much more than he let on to Captain Taylor. She was not sure, though, where he had gotten his information, because she was proud to carry her father's bloodline.

She's a real pretty woman," Laine remarked. "Real pretty."

"Eyes not dark like Indian," Nightwing calmly diminished the compliment. "Why you discuss this rude Comanche thief? You help friend the general be rid of her?"

"From now on, I'll help protect her."

Nightwing drew up, angered by Laine's vow. "You gave Comanche over to me to train, and *I* protect her." Drawing himself up, he prepared to leave. "Trust you not tell your friend the general about whiskey I drink. He already much mad with me for not getting rid of *my* Comanche."

Nightwing walked off without parting amenities, as was his usual nature.

Laine Taylor had certainly noted his personal claim to the woman now treading softly in an attempt to muffle her footfalls. Easing around the corner of the scout barracks, then across the short span of open ground to her quarters, she had just touched her foot to the top step when he softly spoke her name.

Talon curled her fingers lightly over the hitching post a foot or so from him. Even as her voice should have been softened by the memories of the dance, she kept it deliberately hard. "What do you want, Sir?"

"You were eavesdropping from the darkness?"

Talon suppressed her displeasure at the accusation. "I was sitting there before either of you walked out, minding my own business and enjoying the night. Then I was stuck, more or less." Turning toward her quarters, she added politely. "Good evening, Sir."

"Stay a minute. Let's talk."

"Is it an order, Sir?"

Capping the flask, he slipped it into the inside pocket of his open jacket. His eyes, noticeably browed by annoyance, turned boldly to her. "A request you can decline."

"I will not tolerate any more of your insults."

"No insults, let's just talk."

"Not here. I suppose, as Officer of Scouts, you have the right to come to my quarters whenever you wish."

His eyes turned fully to her now, vexation strong in the glassy pools of his eyes. "No, Talon, I do *not.* It's hardly appropriate that I, or any man, come to your quarters without your invitation. You have a right to privacy. If any man here tries to take that from you, come to me, and I'll straighten him out."

Talon smiled. "Thank you, Sir. With rare exception—" She was thinking about Compton, "the men here have respected my privacy. I must go before Nightwing catches me—"

"To hell with Nightwing. I'm Officer of Scouts, and if I want to talk to you, I will. Do I make myself clear?"

"You and the whiskey both make yourselves quite clear."

He certainly deserved that. "Talon, I apologize for being a bear. Now, tell me, is there anything I can do to make life easier for you here?"

His tone, though kept low, was like a strong wind, commanding her attention. Talon didn't face him as she lightly tossed her head, settling her thick, ebony braid onto her shoulder. "As I told you in your office last week, Sir, you could treat me like I am worth something, not just a rude Comanche with a less than elegant past. I have made mistakes, but I am willing to behave if both you and Nightwing will allow me to do so."

"I can't speak for Nightwing, but I will most certainly treat you better than I have in the past." Laine turned to face her, one elbow pressed to the hitching rail. He looked to her, too fragile to be so strong, too vulnerable right now to be so brave. His fingers went out, closed over her wrist, and gently caressed it. "One day you'll have to tell me where you learned to dance the waltz."

Dear old Jacob Shepperd. "In the arms of a man, of

course," she laughed, withdrawing her arm from the warm cover of his hand. "Really, Sir, I should not be here. My chief—"

"Hang your chief, Talon."

Sometimes I'd like to do just that. Placing a few feet of distance between them, her head turned imperceptibly, her gaze noticeably shaded by reproof. "Should you want to know anything about me in the future, Captain Taylor, please ask me, and not Nightwing. I am *very* proud of my Comanche heritage."

"Don't leave, Talon."

"I must retire."

"I don't want you to go."

"Make it an order, Sir, and I will have to remain."

"Very well, I order you to remain." Talon approached, noticeably reluctant. "Now, may I ask you one question?" Curiosity paused in her features. "Where did you get a name like Talon Rose?"

Pride lit every curve of her face. "My *ahpu* and *pia* gave it to me together. That is my father and mother." A smile touched her mouth as she vaguely remembered the Comanche leader, Toya Ruhku, her father, so kind and loving, who had called her Tui Tamu—Little Rabbit—and often told her, his only child, that she was also his favorite. "When I was just days old, my father put his finger into my hand and told my mother I had a strong grip like the talons of a hawk. So he asked her the English translation, which he liked very much. And to soften its masculine appeal, they added Rose, because—" She was about to tell him that Rose was also part of her mother's name, but for some reason thought better of it. "Because it was my mother's favorite flower. It is a good name my parents gave me?"

"A very good name, though I might have called you something different."

Talon laughed sweetly. "Nothing like Laughing Water or Morning Doe, I hope. Those dreamy appellations of western novels written by excitable Eastern greenhorns."

Her laughter made him think of a temperate breeze caressing a mellow green hill. He wanted to draw her into his arms and hold her, love her, feel her golden curves melding into his body. But because he was too drunk right then to be anything but a bully, he stepped off the boardwalk in retreat. "Actually, Talon, I was thinking something along the lines of Woman Who Shoots Mad Paleface Officer."

"Perhaps one day you will understand it really was an accident and I feel terrible about it."

"I do know that. I knew it the moment it happened."

Talon loved the way his full, masculine mouth caught in an instant smile. "Does this mean I am free to go to my quarters now?"

He pivoted, walking backward as he spoke to her, "You're dismissed, scout. And one more thing," he continued, halting in his retreat, "Where'd you get the color of your eyes? From your mother?"

She remembered her mother's clear, blue eyes, and her frequent remarks that *my daughter has her grandmother's eyes.* "You said one question, Captain Taylor. Perhaps when I see you again I will tell you all about me." A strange sensation entered Talon, her pulse quickened, and she forced herself to depart.

* * *

Crossing the parade field to his quarters, Laine whistled Dixie, a tune he had always liked. Reaching the porch, a man spoke to him from the darkness, and he found himself facing John Nightwing a second time this evening. "What is it, chief?"

"I request you not befriend Scout Talon, and make my job more difficult. I have right to control this scout. She *is* my responsibility."

Why the hell did he let Nightwing get under his skin? Laine fought for calm. "I gave you the right to train and control the scout. I did *not* give you the right to control the woman. Do we have this straight?

"If you need woman to satisfy loins, white women in camp."

Blowing out a long breath reeking of whiskey, Laine responded hotly, "If you want to fight it out, Mister Chief of Scouts John Nightwing, I'll throw off all evidence of my rank, and we can draw blood."

95

Nightwing thought that reasonable men should talk, not fight like rowdy children. "See why you taken with Scout Talon. You much alike. Fire in tongue, quick to anger."

Laine swept back his unruly hair, knocking his hat to the ground, which he instantly swept up. "That's the whiskey doing a lot of that talking. We just need to get matters straight about Talon."

"Matters straight now, Taylor. You not spend private time with her."

Laine pivoted smartly back. "I will, if I choose."

Nightwing's calm, controlled tone did not change. "I can protect scout if you not give friend the general more reason to hate her. I order you to leave her alone."

"You can't give me orders." Laine was swiftly against Nightwing, gripping one lapel of his uniform shirt. Brilliant blue eyes clashed antagonistically with black ones, and the fact that both men had been drinking tonight did nothing to quell the tension. "What's the problem with you, chief? Afraid the big, bad white officer will take your prize from you?"

Nightwing drew his pearl-handled Bowie knife and calmly pressed it to Laine's chest, his tone as polite as if he reasoned with a child. "Let go now, Taylor."

Feeling the tip of the blade against his skin, Laine tore his hand from Nightwing's lapel. "That's *Captain* Taylor, and you just threatened a superior officer with a weapon. That could land you in the guardhouse for a lot longer than two days, if I had a mind to file charges."

"Do what you need to do, *Taylor*," Nightwing growled, resheathing his knife. "But keep away from *my* rude Comanche scout. Enough trouble with her without interference of hot blooded white man."

* * *

Talon had watched Nightwing pursue Laine across the parade field. Though their voices were indistinct, they were certainly in a heated battle of words. She tried several times to enter her quarters, but their voices grew louder. Reaching them just as they might have come to blows, she stepped boldly

96

between them. "Whatever you two are arguing about, it cannot be important enough to spend time in the guardhouse."

Laine was almost too angry for words. Clenching and unclenching his fists, he wanted only to shove Talon aside, then spring and kill this interfering Indian. "Scout, saddle your horse, and the roan that came in this week. I'll give him a ride in the hills."

"I will not leave camp tonight, Captain Taylor."

His contemptuously narrowed eyes turned to her. "You will *not* disobey me, scout. Saddle the damned horses."

Talon's nervous gaze swept between the men. "Nightwing, I do not know what to do."

He was more than willing to tell her. "Scout will *not* leave camp with Taylor."

"You saddle those horses, woman, or I'll strip and flog you according to the provisions of your contract. Do you understand me?"

The vicious threat grinding into her soul, Talon fled toward the stable, quickly saddled Shadow Dancer, but the roan, trembling with nerves in his new surroundings, took longer to saddle. She feared that when she returned to the men, one or both might be dead. But they stood several feet apart, staring at each other in intimidating silence and challenge. With the roan next to him, Laine pulled into the saddle without delay. "Come with me, scout."

"I will meet you at the front gate, Sir. I must have a word with my chief."

"Make it quick."

When they were alone, Talon rose into her saddle and looked down on this very furious mixed blood Apache. "Nightwing, could I just say to you that—"

Lethally dark eyes lifted to her. "I will hear nothing from you, scout. If you whore yourself to Taylor to feel important, go, do what you need to do. No matter color of eyes, scout, you *still* Indian. Taylor will *not* want brown skinned squaw, except in blankets!"

She could have killed him. "Nightwing, you are a dirty-minded, foul-mouthed son-of-a-bitch," she uttered, then dug her soft heels into Shadow Dancer's sides.

"Mother not bitch," Nightwing growled, merging into the darkness mad as hell, and that was twice as mad as he'd just about ever been. Then he encountered Compton halfway across the parade ground, and thought he'd rather be face to face with a highly peeved rattler. Compton had two guards with him.

"Did you have cross words with Taylor, chief?"

"I did, Sir."

"Were you disrespectful to him?"

"We disrespectful to each other, Sir."

"Where is he now?"

"Left camp on horseback."

"Was he with your Comanche scout?"

"He was, Sir."

"And what was their destination?"

Nightwing met Compton's gaze, glimmering almost maniacally as a shaft of moonlight caught the surface of his spectacles. "I not ask, Sir."

"I told you, mister, to control the scout."

"I cannot control scout if *you* cannot control Taylor."

Compton summoned the guards. Private Andrew Wilson and the swarthy guard approached, awaiting his orders. "Escort the Chief of Scouts to the guardhouse. Tell the duty guard he's to be locked up until Monday morning for rudeness and insubordination toward a general officer. Surrender any weapons you have to the guard now." Nightwing immediately removed his sheath and Bowie Knife, the only weapons he wore.

Slapping the knife into Wilson's hand, Nightwing and the guards crossed the field in silence. Before entering the guardhouse, Nightwing requested, "Take message to Dako to come to guardhouse to talk to me."

The swarthy guard, Ragin Black, had made a report to Compton of the argument between Nightwing and Taylor. Wilson was mad as hell at him for getting the chief in trouble, and maybe Talon and the captain, too. "I will, Chief Nightwing. And this time—" Wilson laughed as they entered the guardhouse, where he tossed the Bowie on the sergeant's desk. "I'm gonna tear your butt off in checkers. I been practicin' with the other guards, an' they say I'm gittin' real good."

"We will see, Skinny Whirlwind." Nightwing had given him the nickname during his first stint in the guardhouse. "But if you beat me at checkers, I must cut skinny throat."

Wilson chuckled, eliciting a scornful glare from his fellow guard. "You won't see me standin' still for that, Chief."

* * *

Talon and Laine sat on the high point of Cimarron Bluff. Talon wanted to return to camp, but couldn't go against Taylor's orders. That didn't keep her from feeling like a pawn.

"I suppose you're angry, Talon?"

"You threatened to strip and flog me. Should I not be?"

"You know I wouldn't do that."

Cutting livid eyes to him, she responded curtly, "No, Sir, I do not. I think I liked you better when you hated me."

"I never hated you, Talon. Will you forgive me for being a bear?" But before she could give a response, his hand swept out lazily. "Just look at that view. Have you seen anything more beautiful?" The moon was high and clear, affording a pale glow of light over the full plain, caressing the hills and outcroppings of the Huachucas.

Talon tried mightily to cast her anger aside. "I suppose it is grand to look at, but most of Arizona is hell to travel in."

"You don't consider it God's country?"

"I have seen the sun-bleached bones of horse and rider many times on Arizona's desert floors, men who fell from thirst, heat, and exhaustion, because distance was underestimated to the next watering hole or settlement." Talon drew a long breath. "You have me out here now, so let us not speak of death. I will show you some of my favorite haunting grounds while you grow accustomed to your new horse." Turning Shadow Dancer on the wide trail, she waited for Laine to ease beside her.

Suddenly, the lyrical song of a canyon wren, a rare treat in the night, caught their attentions. Laine chose that moment to capture Talon's hand across the short space separating their

99

horses. "I'm glad you're riding with me, Talon, and this is a damned fine horse."

"I imagine he will be yours then."

One eyebrow raised slightly, humor pressing into his features. "If I'm patient enough I generally get what I want. And I plan to be patient with you, too, Talon." She gave him only a silent look. "If Nightwing comes down hard on you because of this, let me know about it."

"I can handle Nightwing, Sir, without your intervention," she replied, though she knew that was a farfetched claim. Shyly withdrawing her hand, Talon moved her horse ahead of him, and they soon descended from Cimarron Bluff into one of the little canyons creasing the Huachuca Mountain Range. As they rode, Talon told him of the places she'd been, and of her experiences with the outlaws she ran with. An hour after leaving camp, they dismounted at Moonlight Stream, the wide, clear ribbon of water where he'd slammed her to the ground and manacled her hands behind her. Dropping to a sitting position, Talon picked up a bit of straw. The last time she'd been here—before the morning she met Laine—early winter had muted the landscape to shades of brown, trees were sparse, and the grass lay dead beneath a thick blanket of leaves and pine straw. Now, in brilliant contrast, unencumbered moonlight filtered through the sparse branches of pines, and the lavender stalks of lupine and black-eyed susans splashed the hills with color.

Laine dropped to the grass beside her, noticing how the moonlight shone on her raven tresses, reflected her glassy eyes. "I've been a bear tonight, Talon. I'm real sorry. I have a helluva temper, especially when I drink."

"It may be, Sir, that you do not know any other way to be."

"Spoiled white soldier, accustomed to having his own way." When she smiled, failing to respond, he continued quietly, "That little pouch you wear. What is it?"

Talon's mood brightened as her fingers closed around her small possession. "The treasures of a child mostly. A little blue rock I picked up when I was five, a bit of gold dust from the Black Hills." Drawing a dreamy sigh, she added reminiscently,

"And something added to it just a few weeks after my father died."

"What is it?"

"I do not know. I was told my heart would speak to me when it was the right moment to look. It has been in here for fifteen years. I will not look until my heart speaks." Seeing the question in his eyes, she laughed lightly. "And yes, I have been curious, but my heart is stronger than mere curiosity. The joy in having it is the mystery. If I look, the mystery is gone."

Laine couldn't imagine any person he knew allowing such a mystery to go undisclosed for fifteen years, especially when some of those years had been spent as a child with natural driven curiosity. He thought it showed a tremendous strength of character. Propping his head on his palm, mischief eased into his voice. "Tell me something soft and sweet about Talon, the woman who lets her heart speak to her."

"Something soft and sweet about Talon," she repeated his words. "What is either soft or sweet about a Comanche renegade? My parents died, I was a slave, a troublemaker, and an outlaw. I suppose the only things soft and sweet about Talon are her memories of her parents, and the time she spent with Jacob Shepperd, a dear old codger who loved and cared for her as his own child." She looked to Laine now. "I have spent a good deal of my life hating and being hated, Captain Taylor. I suppose I would like to know that tomorrow will be soft and sweet, and a new memory to cherish."

Without warning, his hand covered her own, halting its movements with the bit of straw she had absently dragged in a small circle beside her. "I can tell you something very soft and sweet about you, strictly from my observations tonight, you understand."

"Oh? And what have you observed about this woman who shot you, and who has insulted you every chance she got?"

"That you have a sweet nature you try your damndest to cover."

Talon laughed outright. "You do not know me well enough, Captain Taylor—"

"Laine."

"Captain Taylor—"

He continued to caress her hand. "When we're alone together, I'm Laine."

"Such familiarity, Sir, will not be proper."

"Call me Laine, or I'll kiss you right here and now."

"Laine."

Now, he was the one to laugh. "That afraid of a kiss, are you?" She had not withdrawn her hand. He liked that.

"I imagine you left an anxious white lass fretting over you back in this Louisiana of yours. She might be a little miffed to know those same lips that kissed hers had also kissed this rude Comanche."

"No anxious white lasses, Talon. I've got my eye on you tonight."

Feeling uneasy now, simply because of the way her Officer of Scouts looked at her, Talon scooted a short distance from him and eased to her back on the cool grass. "See that star there? That is my special star that my mother gave to me." She eyed him warmly. "I think that very same star tamed a heart full of manly anger so you would not be so mean to me."

Laine rolled onto his stomach beside her, bracing himself on his elbows with his face very close to her own. "And if that's not a soft, sweet sentiment, Talon, Comanche scout, I don't know one when I hear it."

The glimmering depths of his sea blue eyes assailed her with quiet admiration. Giving no warning of the intimacy, Laine's softly passionate mouth eased to her own. Never had she been kissed like this, never anything more than a brief goodnight kiss or one of greeting, and never upon her mouth.

Laine drew back from her, noticing the nervous fleeting of her eyes and the sudden flush of her cheeks. "I'm sorry. Do Indian males generally ask permission before they kiss a woman?"

She wouldn't admit to him it was her first kiss ever. "I would not know. I have never been kissed by an Indian."

"And how many white men have you kissed?"

Only you. "Oh, dozens, I am sure."

"Dozens, you say?" A smile captured his mouth as he sought another kiss. Now, her hand rose to cover his shoulder, and he gently cupped her face between his palms. How sweet and innocent she was, as though she'd never been kissed before, her breath like a whisper against his cheek. Never before had he felt a rush such as now, more than just a need to feel her against him...to taste the honeyed depths of her mouth—

He wanted her, wanted to feel her flesh against his own, to trace his hands along her bare womanly curves, and surround himself with her most intimate depths. But when his hand rubbed along her thigh, she quickly ended the kiss, scooted from beneath him, and was on her feet before he could turn to his side. As he found himself alone—his body painfully aroused by her nearness—she sauntered toward the bank of the stream and crouched beside it. A full minute passed before he approached her.

"I spent my life avoiding such emotions, Cap—Laine. Distrusting every man I met and questioning his motives. In turn, I expect men to distrust me and to question my motives."

He knelt beside her, his words quietly sincere. "I can promise you now, Talon, there's nothing in the world you can do—ever—to make me distrust you. And I'm willing to earn your trust. My only motive right now is to spend time with you, get to know you, and show you that I can be trusted to trust you." As she smiled, his cheek fell in a caress to the dark, disheveled tendrils of hair that had come loose from her braid. "The first moment I saw you weeping as though your heart broke, throwing that pistol after you'd shot me, your eyes filled with horror and disbelief, you were so damned pretty that you entered my heart as swiftly as a sparrow taking to the sky. When I'd shackled your wrists behind you, there wasn't a single part of me that didn't want to turn you over, kiss the hell out of you, and take every womanly treasure you had to offer. I've been a bear to you. But, Talon, every time I've seen you my heart beat a little faster. When you were grooming your horse that night in the corral, I'd never seen such a vision. It was as if you waited for me in the soft glow of that lamp."

Her breath quickened. "I was waiting for someone, I suppose, but I did not know it would be the Officer of Scouts whose favorite words in the English language are hell, damn, and son-of-a-bitch." He would have kissed her again if the sky hadn't suddenly opened to a torrent of rain neither of them had expected. "Let us take our horses to the cabin," Talon laughed as she arose.

Within moments, they had cut through the ash and pine to the small, ramshackle cabin sitting against the rock bluff. Everyone in the region used it at one time or the other, fishers, hunters, Indians, whites, even Mexicans who came across the border to hide from the swift hand of their own laws. Leading their horses under the lean-to of the porch, Talon shook the rain from her dark hair. Laine dropped to a bench hewn from a single split log, his uniform saturated to the skin.

The sky was now a patina of swirling grays and blacks, the moon completely obscured, the stars chased away as swiftly as a rabbit fleeing the hawk. Talon sat beside Laine on the bench and gently covered his hand with her own. The move surprised him as much as it surprised herself. "Captain Taylor—Laine—when this rain ends, we must return to camp. I am in a lot of trouble with my chief."

"He probably went straight to Compton."

"No, he would not do that." But even as she spoke, Talon wondered why she trusted Nightwing. "He would not do that," she repeated, glad of the distraction when Shadow Dancer suddenly nuzzled her back.

Laine drew her into his arms, feeling her rain-dampened hair against his cheek. Though his clothing was saturated, she warmed him completely. He looked quietly to the place where she had pointed out her star, now obscured by the low-lying shades of gray and black fleeing across the Arizona night.

Eight

Monday morning, the scout troop prepared for their weekly weapons and mount inspection. Nightwing didn't seem to be in the best of moods. Taking special care with her uniform that morning, Talon had assumed her usual place at the end of the line as Nightwing did a quick assessment of his scouts. Approaching Talon, he noticed her careful appearance, the luster of her freshly washed hair, the blush of her cheeks. He hated to think that Taylor was responsible for her becoming color. Pausing, he watched the western sky as though he searched for something elusive. Then he spoke very politely. "Scout Talon excused from drill today."

His deceptively benign calm stiffened the rebellion along Talon's spine. She kept her tone as polite as his. "There is no reason for me to be excused." Facing her now, his expression carried a small degree of canniness. He reminded her of a captured animal, waiting for its chance to break from a cage.

"There is reason for you to be excused if I say there is reason. Put away horse, scout, and retire to quarters."

Talon battled her pleasant notice of him, his jet black hair carefully combed, how straight and tall he carried himself. "You cannot deny me my rightful place in the troop if I obey the rules and fully cooperate. If you persist in forcing my dismissal this morning, I will lodge a complaint with the Officer of Scouts."

"Taylor your friend now?" Nightwing's unwavering eyes held her defiant ones. He now crossed his hands against his waistline, his demeanor calm, even as his jaw sharpened to suppress his vexation. "Chief of Scouts Nightwing one who is here, scout. Leave inspection and confine yourself to quarters for day."

Talon drew a breath almost too shallow to be detectable. "Please, Chief Nightwing, let us not quarrel. I fell in for inspection in good faith, and I intend to stay."

105

"We not quarrel. You defy me. There is difference. Will you leave now, as I order?"

"No, Chief Nightwing, I am here for weapons and mount inspection. I *will* be inspected. But if you give me *valid* reason to exclude me from drill this morning, then I will comply."

He didn't know what the hell *valid* meant. "That I not want you here reason enough."

"Give me *valid* reason, or respect my right to be here."

"Do you want Chief recommend whipping?"

"If you want me whipped, Chief Nightwing, whip me later. Right now, I am having my weapons and mount inspected."

Throwing off his composure as inconsequential baggage, Nightwing wrenched the rifle from her, looked it over, and threw it to the ground. He never raised his voice. "Rifle checked. Dirty. Take to quarters. Clean."

Talon had spent the better part of last evening dismantling and cleaning her weapons down to the finest detail. She had even cleaned each individual screw holding their wooden grips. The way the rifle had landed she knew the barrel was now filled with dirt. When Nightwing began his retreat, Talon calmly withdrew her sidearm. "You have not checked my revolver, Chief."

Nightwing pivoted back, took the revolver without looking at it, and threw it to the dirt alongside her rifle. "Revolver dirty. Take quarters. Clean."

Anger had put something of a crimp in the somewhat proper English that was his pride. Withdrawing her knife, she thrust it, handle first, toward Nightwing. "You have not inspected this, or the soundness of my horse."

Snatching the knife with a dark scowl, Nightwing quickly buried the blade four inches into the soil. "Knife filthy. Take quarters...clean. One more word sassy scout face firm discipline."

"Better disciplined than ignored." she shot back, stepping forward to retrieve her weapons. "Stop being a bully and tell me what I have done to make you so damned mad?"

You rode out with Taylor Friday night. You gone many

hours. Nightwing grabbed Talon's arm with such force that she cried out in the instant of pain. Dragging her half a dozen feet from the neat line of scouts, he quickly swooped up two pebbles the size of a man's thumbnail and placed them on the ground six inches apart. "Kneel on pebbles, Scout Talon." Talon did as she was told, the pebbles instantly causing pain against the tender bones of her knees. She refused to react, even as Nightwing's hands landed on her shoulders to shove her into them. Now he crouched before her, a little calmer. "You find pebbles under knees for one hour not comfortable like blanket in desert with Taylor."

The insult registered like a blow. Talon gulped a quick breath as she looked sideways at the snickering Apaches, all except Dako, who carried a disapproving scowl. "I did *not* share a blanket with Taylor!"

Nightwing was pleased by her admission that she had not been intimate with Taylor—Indians seldom lied to other Indians—though his demeanor did not change. "Stay on knees until I tell you rise. And should you shoot me like you did Taylor, if you think this mad, you will not like how mad I get digging bullet from back. When pain is great, cry like baby. Discipline stop."

Talon lifted her eyes boldly to his black ones. "Any pain, any tears I might shed, will not compare to the hatred I have for you."

Gripping her chin firmly, Nightwing eased his mouth alongside her cheek. "I swear this to you, Talon—one day you turn to *me* for comfort. You will know in heart honor and trust exist between Indian man...woman, not between half-blood Comanche, spoiled white officer. Taylor *will* turn back on you. Your chief *never* will!"

Pulling from him so that she might see his ebony eyes, sarcasm flooded her whispers. "You think you know Taylor that well, do you, Mister Chief Know-it-All? He will *never* turn his back on me."

Rueful silence poised between them for a moment. "You will eat words you speak one day."

Talon wanted only to embarrass him as he had embarrassed her, and pressed her mouth to his, circling his lips with her tongue. Then she drew back to smile sarcastically.

As the Apaches continued to snicker, Nightwing's fingers dug into the soft flesh of her face. "Mouth—tongue of Talon sweet like honey, but better to taste in private." He drew up to brush the dirt from his knees. "Link fingers on top of head—keep there one hour." Walking away, he laughed the words in his native tongue, "The woman hot for Apache." Then he casually ordered them to submit their weapons for inspection.

Talon's efforts to embarrass him had backfired. She also had the taste of an Apache mouth against her own. "I hate you, Nightwing," she whispered. Easing her knees from the pebbles, but careful to conceal them beneath the fabric of her trousers, she began to count to sixty...again...and again, trying to keep up with the minutes until an hour had passed. By the time she had counted to sixty twenty-four times, her legs felt amputated at the knees. A knife might have been driven into the small of her back, so great was the pain tearing upward through her spine and shoulders.

* * *

The way Compton's desk was situated, he saw out the window onto the parade field, but Taylor, seated in front of him, did not. They had taken care of business for the morning, and now he was about to address him on the indiscretions he had shown the other night. Compton was pleased to see Nightwing disciplining the female scout on the parade field—though the kiss had surprised him.

Laine himself opened the controversial topic of discussion. "I'd request if I do something to displease you that you punish me and not the Chief of Scouts. I wouldn't suggest you alienate such a valuable man—"

"I sent him specific instructions that the female was to be kept apart from *all* officers on this post, except in matters of business. That includes you, Taylor."

"He's tried, and it's caused animosity between us. I'm Officer of Scouts, and Talon's superior. If you'd give her a chance, you might even realize she's not your enemy. Perhaps twenty-five years ago the Comanches left an indelible impression on you—certainly with just cause—but she is not like those Comanches."

"I've heard rumors that men believe *she's* the one who shot you." Compton was unwilling to concede that any Comanche could have endearing qualities. "I'll issue a written apology to Nightwing, if it'll appease him. And you, Sir, are smitten with the Comanche simply because she's different."

"Perhaps, but while I'm smitten, I plan to get to know her better. And—she did not shoot me. It was an accident, as I explained to Colonel Heitman."

Compton suspected there were more subtle ways to handle what he considered an unabashed breach of Taylor's loyalty. A mask of deceit quietly claimed him. "If you feel this Comanche woman has character worthy of your attention, then by all means, get to know her. You are not a child to be scolded for keeping bad company."

A sick, hollow feeling hit Laine in his gut, simply because this was completely out of character for the unrelenting Compton. "Talon is hardly bad company."

"I chose the wrong words to make my point." He rose now, leaned across the desk, and settled his palms firmly on the worn wood. His startling blue eyes did not vacillate as he spoke. "I'd like to see these qualities that have you so bewitched." Laine's suspicions remained, though he said nothing. Compton saw the pretty scout faint dead away on the parade ground, and couldn't halt his smile. "There's no reason for your assignment to this godawful outpost to be made unpleasant by my tyranny. Now—what other business do we need to discuss?"

* * *

Talon recalled the clink of weapons, the sun mounting in the morning sky, the air hot and eroding her strength, and reaching a count of forty minutes before a silent wave suddenly and rudely swiped the daylight from her. Now she was on her back against Nightwing's muscled thighs, cool water from a canteen trickling into her mouth as he spoke softly to her.

Thinking he looked worried, surely her mind was playing tricks on her, because she knew he hated her. Easing forward, she could put no distance between herself and the despicable Indian who enjoyed torturing her in the guise of *necessary* discipline.

Sweeping her into his strong arms, Nightwing moved toward her quarters across the parade field and settled her onto her cot. "When I tell you leave, you will be wise to listen." Crouching to the bed beside her, his hand very tenderly covered the side of her head. "Do what I tell you, Scout, just once." Then he stood, towered over her for a moment, and prepared to withdraw.

Talon sat forward, her arms collapsing as she tried to maintain her balance. "Are you jealous of Captain Taylor's attention toward me?"

He faced her as if she had suddenly lost all reasoning, his stare bold and rude. "Words foolish."

"Are they, Nightwing?"

His eyes narrowed, his mouth pressing for the briefest of moments. He would willingly submit to any form of torture before admitting she might be right. "Words foolish."

"All we did the other night was ride and talk, Nightwing. I enjoyed his company, and if that makes me a rotten scout unfit to stand at inspection, then I am sorry."

Nightwing would never admit to this very beautiful half-blood that she was the last vision in his mind when he sought sleep at night, and the first he saw upon waking. Nor would she know—ever—that they had often ridden green hills beneath purple Arizona skies in the most vivid dreams he'd ever had. He had been beside her, not Taylor.

"Stay in quarters, scout," he demanded, and shut the door between them. Moments later he dismissed his Apaches and gave them permission to spend the day with their families outside camp. He encountered Taylor on the parade ground, advised him of the halt to drill, and forced himself to be civil. "I have been at Camp Casey seven years. In that time I requested only three days each year to visit my camp. I went there in

January, but now I request another three days."

Right now, his Chief of Scouts was as transparent as glass. "Something bothering you, Nightwing?"

"I need time away from scouts, from soldiers—"

"And me?"

The white officer he despised was too perceptive. "From you, yes, and from my rude Comanche scout," Nightwing conceded with a shrug. "I lose patience with her."

He despised the way Nightwing personally claimed Talon. "Go then, if you must."

"I turn duties over to Scout First Sergeant Dako for three days."

Laine thought that Talon, too, needed time away from Nightwing's persistent control. "Stay longer if you wish."

A grumble deep within did not make it to Nightwing's throat. "Do not be so anxious to be rid of me, Taylor. I need only three days."

Always ready to fight, Nightwing. "Travel in civilian clothes, and don't carry military firearms with you. That blasted Geronimo hates you Apache scouts who track him to his hideouts."

Nightwing recalled Geronimo saying once that Apache had too much hatred for the Mexicans and White-Eye to hate each other, even those who worked for the Army against them. "I take care of self, Sir."

Laine's tone became patronizing, almost rude. "You're a good Chief of Scouts, Nightwing, and I hear way too often that you've earned the respect of every man here. But when you return, I won't continue to tolerate your insubordination. I'll replace you as Chief of Scouts in a heartbeat and send you to another camp. Don't force me to do it."

Nightwing's dark eyes could have cut him down. Gritting his teeth to stay any argument, Nightwing left, gave instructions to Dako for the three days he would be gone, and further instructions to keep Talon and Taylor apart as best he could. Returning to his quarters at the back of the scout barracks, he changed into fringed buckskin trousers, a cream-colored shirt, and a dyed black buckskin vest, trading his red bandanna for a white one, so that he would blend in with Apache hostiles he might meet in the hills.

Seated on his cot, he pulled out the small black hunting bow he had made for his little son many years ago. His son had stepped on it and broken it in two, and one small piece of wood was missing from the area of the break. Thereafter, his son had been given the name, Broken Bow, by his adoring Navajo mother—Nightwing's wife—and just two months later, a band of marauders—their tribe never known—had raided his camp, killed his wife, and packed off his only son. Never a day passed that Nightwing didn't think about his child, who would now be in his tenth spring.

Nightwing strapped on his civilian side arm and retrieved his rifle and a box of ammunition from the Army trunk below his cot. Making a stop by the sutler's store, he purchased a large brown bag of gumdrops and jujube paste for the children of his village. Retrieving his horse, and the painted mare Talon had given him, he was soon on his way to his camp, only a half day's journey through the Huachucas. Given no delays, he would be there by the time the sun was directly above him.

* * *

Fort Bowie's Apaches were among the most undisciplined scouts he'd ever worked with, but Laine thought he'd trust his life to any one of them before trusting it to *the civilized* John Nightwing. His guts so tied up in anger, he needed a diversion. As soon as Nightwing's big bay pranced through the northeast gate, he turned to Talon's quarters, drew a deep, calming breath, and knocked lightly at the door. By the time she appeared, he had propped his hands lazily on his hips.

As he stepped past her outstretched hand and into the room, he couldn't help noticing that she'd been crying. "What's wrong, Talon?"

"I try so hard to please Nightwing. I just hate him."

Laine settled into the chair at her desk. "He didn't hurt you, did he?" he asked, one hand moving forward to coax her to him.

"It was my fault," she replied, skirting his attempted

affection, "because I defy him. He was actually in a fair mood when drill began." Then she dropped to her knees beside Lane. "Why are you here?"

"Do I need a reason?" Then, "He got me all fired up, too. I needed a peaceful moment."

"With me?" Sarcasm grabbed those two small words. "John Nightwing thinks I have been kneeling on pebbles for almost an hour—which I haven't—but I still don't feel all that peaceful."

Laine shot to his feet, pulling her roughly up. "Nightwing did that?" When she did not respond, he growled, "I won't tolerate his cruelty toward you. Do you understand me, Talon?"

Talon flicked a humored glance at the anger in his eyes. "He did not make me stand with a heavy rifle over my head, like someone else I know."

A smirk slid from Laine's mouth. "I gave you a choice..."

"Some choice. Spend the day cleaning your office like a scrub woman, or hold my rifle over my head."

"All right. I deserve that. But in all fairness, you should admit that you're damned stubborn."

Talon shrugged lightly. "I have never denied it," and with a smile, "It is actually one of my better traits. But I do not deserve to be tortured by either of you bullies."

An open arm invited her to him, but she hesitated, took a step toward him, and hesitated again. "Blast, woman, but *you* torture me. Do you know how much I want to be with you?"

He had certainly hinted at romantic intentions, but Talon— being Comanche and very distrustful of all men—was surprised by this confession. She wasn't sure if she was ready to hear this from the Officer of Scouts, and immediately distrusted his motives.

Laine approached and put his arms around her before putting a breath of space between them. The fear in her eyes caught him off-guard. Because he wanted to dispel that fear, Laine drew a small white box from the pocket of his coat and handed it to her. "A special lady in my family gave me specific orders to present these to the prettiest damned girl I met. You are that girl."

"I hardly think you should look at this rude Comanche female as a girl. Save whatever that is for one." Without pause, he thrust the box into her hand and refused to take it when she attempted to hand it back. He stood by until she opened it. He had certainly noticed her reluctance.

Inside Talon found a pair of pearl inlaid silver combs. "These are for white women," she announced, haughty despite the occasion to be gracious. She again attempted to hand them back to him.

Burrowing his brows thoughtfully, Laine removed the combs from the box and looked them over. "Ain't that somethin' now, Talon Rose," he kept his voice softly southern, "Someone forgot to engrave *for white women only* on them." His eyes touched hers with gentle promise. "One day I'll see your hair loose from your braid and adorned by the combs, and something soft and sexy clinging to your beautiful skin. And you'll be in *my* bed when I see you like this."

Annoyance shaded Talon's cheeks. "Would you speak such vulgarity to a white woman?"

"Hell, yes, if I wanted her the way I want you." Then the weight of his body pressed her backward to the small bed. "I'm spoiled, and always get what I want." She scooted from beneath him much too quickly for him to have seen the absolute fear in her eyes. He couldn't restrain a moment of frustrated ire. "Little Indian girl still afraid of the big bad soldier?"

"I have not encouraged you," she replied nervously, a hot rush that had grown much too familiar suddenly pulsing through her abdomen. "You hardly know me well enough to—?"

"You shot me. You owe me something."

"But my body, Sir? Such a high price to pay for a slight graze?"

"I don't think so." He grinned boyishly. "It pleases me greatly that you put such a high price on your life. By the time I'm finished putting on the Southern charm, you'll beg to be my girl."

Talon laughed, and might have had a smart comeback if a knock hadn't called her to the door. Dako threw aside one of his frequent *cigarritos* as he faced her. "Scouts meet at wickiups. Talon want join?" Spying Taylor, he managed a half-cocked smile, even as he recalled Nightwing's final order to keep these two apart, which he didn't feel was one of his duty requirements. "Never mind. Scout busy."

Halting his withdrawal with a lightly placed hand, she whispered, "Nightwing is angry with me. I really should stay in my quarters."

"Nightwing not here. Went to home village...three day be gone."

This was surprising news. She must have made him very angry. "Did he?"

"He take new pony to *Shimaa*—to mother."

And to get away from me, I would imagine. Casting a furtive look toward Laine, Talon kept her voice low and playful. "When I get rid of *him*, I'll be there."

Dako liked the pretty Comanche, and the new Officer of Scouts who had taken a fancy to her. He felt, also, that his chief and longtime friend was much fonder of Talon than he let on, so felt a sense of disloyalty as he uttered, "Bring Captain Taylor if want."

Dako left and Talon turned to eye Laine coolly, simply because she thought a white officer would decline such an invitation. "I'd love to spend the evening with you at the scout's wickiups," he contradicted her unspoken assumption. Now that they were again alone, he pulled her to his arms, but she struggled for freedom "Stop it." Pausing in her efforts, her eyes lifted boldly to him. "There, that's better."

"You are Officer of Scouts. I *must* obey your orders."

"Hell, Talon..." Even as he spoke, he smiled, "you make me so mad sometimes— "

Talon needed a diversion to the heat spreading through her. "Thank you," she whispered.

"For what?"

"Accepting Dako's invitation."

"Hell, I have no family in this hellhole, except that son-of-a-bitch who thinks he's my damned father It'll be nice to spend time with families who love one another."

"Must everything be hell, damn and son-of-a-bitch?" Attempting some semblance of a dismissal, Talon reminded a man now smiling that she'd like to change into more comfortable clothing. "No, you cannot stay and watch."

"Blast my luck." He laughed as he withdrew. "I'll await you outside, Princess."

* * *

Talon chose a green calico dress Dora had given her, sat and brushed her hair until it shone, and considered wearing the beautiful combs Laine had pressed into her hand. She decided not to wear them simply because he might rethink his hastily proffered gift and she really did like them. He was a charming rogue—for a white man—and she couldn't help wondering just why he showed such interest in her, especially since he'd initially disliked her so. If Nightwing was right—that he just needed a woman to warm his blankets—why would he choose her over the fair-haired daughters of some of the officers at camp, any one of whom would be flattered by his attentions, and a not-so-discreet invitation to share his bed?

And why was she being so suspicious of his motives?

Talon knew the one word answer to that question—her own hard life, distrustful of everything and everyone, and that demonic Nightwing.

It also disturbed her a great deal that he might have left camp because of their tense encounter this morning. Nightwing always managed to tug her in opposite directions. She disliked him immensely, yet when she was in trouble, she instinctively went to him. He was clipped and sharp to the point of rudeness, and moments later, was patient, tolerant, and helpful, like a father teaching a child to snag her first fish on the bank of a wide stream. He was tall, straight, and magnificently handsome, and yet there were those moments, especially when he was hot, tired and annoyed over something that would go away if left alone for an hour, that he resembled a bear about to pounce on its supper. Sometimes she wanted to be as far from him as an ocean would allow, and others, she was relieved to catch his dark, critical

116

eyes hovering over her. She had never thought she'd feel so unsettled about any man, and especially a man who was more Apache than anything else.

Casting aside her troublesome thoughts, Talon exited her quarters into the cool morning. Laine turned from the corral, releasing the halter of the roan he had requisitioned, and started in her direction. "Nice frock," he complimented her, disappointed that she did not wear the combs. "Brings out the green of those exquisite eyes."

Talon was prepared to give him one of her flippant replies when a booming voice dispelled a moment of peace over the small military camp. She turned just as General Compton approached. "You, scout," he bellowed, "back in uniform and to your duty. You, Taylor, in my office, now."

When Compton was well out of hearing range, Laine said quietly, "Join the Apaches, Talon, and don't change. I'll be back."

Talon stood for a moment, trying to decide which man she should obey. Sensibly, it should be the general. Dako approached her back, in such silence that he startled her by speaking her name so quietly. She forgot all about the orders of both men as she turned to face him. "May I ask you something, Dako?" He nodded. "Did Nightwing leave camp because of me?"

Dako knew she was the reason Nightwing had left camp for a few days, because he had confided his feelings for her. "He take new pony to *Shimaa*. That why he left, scout."

"And because of me," she insisted.

"He need time think, too," Dako conceded with a shrug.

"Why does he hate me so, Dako?"

"He not hate. He like...that problem, Scout Talon, not hate."

Talon laughed. "Liar," she accused without malice. "You are just too kind, Dako."

Dako grinned pleasantly. "Come...Black Jake woman roast pig. You come, stuff belly like Apache."

Moments later, Talon sat among the women, engaged in small talk, and watched the pig turn slowly over a community fire. Children played, the boys and girls at their separate games, and a number of scouts had begun a rambunctious game of horseshoes, as usual, placing bets from the remnants of their last Army pay.

Hours passed, the frenzied afternoon wore down, the food slowly diminished, and children dropped in their tracks from the exhaustion of play. Talon had stopped looking for Laine to appear hours ago. The purple haze of late evening had settled over the Huachucas, and she was just about to retire to her quarters when he rode up on the roan, leading her excitable mare.

Before addressing Talon, he shouted to Dako, "Save me a plate of food. I'm taking your scout into the hills to shoot her." As Dako and several scouts laughed, he grinned down at Talon. "How about getting away from camp for an hour or so?"

"To defy the general?"

"No, because I need fresh air free of the smell of unwashed soldiers!"

Pulling into Shadow Dancer's saddle, she cut a sideways glance at him and kidded, "Woman is afraid of the dark. Will you keep her safe from predators?"

To which he replied, with a devilish grin, "All but me."

"Men are such bores," she finally managed with a small laugh. Then, "What did the general want of you this afternoon?"

Laine's mouth instinctively pressed in anger, as he recalled the time he'd sat across from the old man and allowed himself to be unmercifully reprimanded for "keeping bad company." His arguments had been cut short by threats, so he'd patiently listened, and quietly stilled the furious pounding of his heart. Then, in dismissal, he'd been ordered to finish paperwork not due for another four days. But, he wouldn't burden Talon with his problems, and forced himself to smile. "Just business. Over with for the day."

As they turned their horses toward the gate, Talon thought there had been a lot more to Laine's afternoon than *just business*.

By the time they had climbed the trail on Cimarron Bluff, the night was a randomly splashed canvas of purple and black across the line of the mountains. Laine led the way toward Moonlight Stream, occasionally pointing out areas he'd noticed that first ride through the mountains with her shackled and walking ahead of him. Talon took special delight in reminding him of the naughty things he'd said at each of those points.

In a moment of relaxation on the pleasant banks of Moonlight Stream, they lay back on a grassy hill. With Laine perched quietly over her, Talon told him of her mother, White Swan, and her father, the village leader. She told him that he had once been a great warrior and that he had died in a hunting accident when she was very young. Laine noticed that she felt much more comfortable speaking of her father than her mother, and thought it was because she had been a captive. She also assured him that her father and mother had loved each other, providing that information, he supposed, to salvage her father's reputation. He was tempted to ask her if she had known the women taken from the Santa Fe Coach along with Compton's daughter in 1857, women who might still be alive so many years later. But the chance of them ending up in her own village of the many Comanche encampments was so remote that he didn't make a fool of himself by asking.

Then, with an undisturbed moment passing between them, Talon quietly asked, "Laine, what interest do you have in me? Am I just a different kind of woman to add to your conquests?"

Since they'd had such a pleasant evening so far, he drew back, a little startled by the impeaching nature of her inquiry. "Will you believe me, Talon, when I say that I've never toyed with the emotions of a woman? In that regard, I am genuine. And in answer to your question, my interest is of a man attracted to a woman in a way he has never before been." His hand swept her cheek without actually touching her. "You're beautiful, you're wild, you're reckless...and you're sincere. I could grow to love you...if I don't already."

"Love," she repeated the small, deeply emotional word, her cheeks suddenly suffused with heat. "We haven't known each other long enough to speak of love."

"Maybe not, Talon, but in what book is the rule set? Can a

man and woman not love each other from the moment their eyes first meet?"

A sweet smile slid onto Talon's mouth. "As I recall, your first look at me was accompanied by *son-of-a-bitch.*"

"No, Talon," he argued softly. "By the time you accidentally fired that gun, you'd already stolen my heart."

"Had I truly?"

"Truly."

Laine liked these kinds of moments with her, when she was naive and innocent, and yet astute and passionate. Before she might make one of those evasive flights he'd grown accustomed to, he stole the sweetest of kisses. She just looked at him and smiled. "Not going to run from the big bad wolf?"

Talon released a dreamy sigh. "Perhaps later, Captain Taylor."

Pressing his elbows into the cool grass, he perched above her, and rubbed his lips lightly over her sensually parted ones. A cockeyed smile twisted his mouth. "Why not now, Princess?"

"Oh—" The small word was somewhat flippant. "I suppose I am just growing comfortable being with you." Wriggling beneath him to dislodge a small stone in the small of her back, Talon met his steady gaze. "I suppose I know now that you are just a big ol' bear with more growl than bite. And besides—" Talon's fingers rose, sliding through the hair at his temple. She wanted to be close to him tonight, not to fear him or distrust him, but to be with him, as a woman with a man. "I feel safe with you, Laine. For the first time in my life, I find I am trusting a man who is not a parent or guardian." A pang caught her within, for images of Nightwing charged to the forefront of her thoughts. She didn't want to admit that she trusted the devilish rogue. Before Laine might question her sudden silence, she continued quietly, "For the first time in my life, I feel that a man truly trusts me." Then, smiling, allowing her hand to drop, she added, "I like that."

Laine gazed into the emerald pools of her eyes, glistening in the afternoon light, at her mouth, sensually parted, her cheeks touched by the palest shade of pink beneath their golden depths.

Pressing his lips together for the briefest of moments, he uttered, "Just when I'm prepared to seduce a pretty Comanche princess, she says something to make me feel too guilty to try it."

Talon scooted from beneath him at once, rushing toward her mare in a wave of pleasant laughter. He was immediately at her heels, spinning her toward him just as she reached the horses. Before he might berate her for dodging him once again, she threw her arms around his shoulders and pulled him close. "Sometimes I cannot believe this, Laine...that you actually like me...that you enjoy being with me. I feel like a girl who can trust...who *will* trust..."

Laine had no doubt she would be his eventually. Right now, he thought if she insisted on a thousand years passing before that moment came, he would willingly wait. Yet, he wanted her now, this very minute, and her sweet, innocent passion flew through him like a flame out of control. With a low, deep growl, he lifted her off her feet and held her close. "You make me feel like a giddy school boy, Talon, stumbling over his own clumsy feet. Let's get back to camp...before I forget I'm a gentleman."

Almost Talon wished he *would* forget, for she had never felt such a blazing fire within.

Only later, when they had joined the scouts at the wickiups, did Laine kick himself for letting her get away so easily. He watched her interact with the Apache wives, while he lounged with the men on the other side of a huge bonfire. She glowed in the leaping flames, and every time their eyes met, he thought he saw promise in their crystalline depths. *One day, my Princess, one day soon—*

During the evening, they stuffed their bellies with succotash, roast chicken, and pemmican, and Laine smoked kinnikinnic for the first time, an Indian blend of tobacco, sumac leaves, and dogwood bark. Being a lifelong non-smoker, it made him woozy and a little sick at his stomach, eliciting laughs among the Apache. By the time he and Talon left the gathering, he was tipsy on flip, a drink made of beer, rum, and sugar, which the women liked, and he'd kindled some genuine friendships among the scouts and their families. They had extended an open invitation to him to join them any time, which he had warmly accepted.

At the steps descending to Talon's quarters, Laine boldly suggested that he spend the night. Talon laughed, kissed him quickly, and rushed alone into her quarters. Instantly, the lock clicked at her door.

Moments later, Laine entered his own darkened quarters, the clock on the mantel chiming the hour of two just as he shut the door. He had approximately three and a half hours to sleep before he met with Compton, and would certainly grumble through the day for lack of sleep, and snap off heads at the least provocation.

Throwing off his jacket and boots, he poured a brandy and settled into his chair for a moment. Moonlight washed through a pair of wide windows to his right, throwing shadows over the whitewashed walls. The brandy would continue to prepare him for sleep, settle the visions of Talon whirling through his mind, and perhaps he would get enough sleep to carry him through the day tomorrow. Quickly gulping the brandy, he set the goblet aside, and closed his eyes for a few minutes, ignoring the sticky discomfort of sweaty clothing against his cool skin. He loved that Talon's quick kiss lingered so sweetly against his mouth.

When he finally dropped to his bed, he slept a hard, dreamless sleep, waking the following morning with a manageable hangover. A bad day for it, since the scouts would be away from camp and Compton expected his company throughout the day.

But the day passed quickly into history, and he had supper alone in his quarters that night. When he heard the stir of many horses shortly before midnight, he looked out the window and watched the scouts dismount at the camp corral. Too dark to see much more than the dusky outline of horses and riders, he heard Talon's voice, soft, sweet, and tired, as she turned her unsaddled mare into the corral and left the other scouts.

So, he sought sleep as he thought of her, imagining her slipping from her uniform into a quick bath, then tossing herself to the small cot in her quarters. He was obsessed with her warm, golden flesh, long-lashed eyes, his own mindless ache for her. His thoughts so filled with her alluring vision, an hour passed before he heard the mantel clock chime for the last time. Then sleep claimed him until the morning.

Nine

Two days later, Compton needed a diversion from the drudgery of camp life. Receiving an early log of company activities, he learned that D Company would leave camp at seven, headed into the hills and the vicinity of Rock Bluff, where Apaches were reported to be gathering. Summoning his orderly, he wrote a hasty note to Major Harris, advising him he would ride with them today. A response bluntly stated that it wasn't recommended, and Compton's return missive left no room for argument. Compton ordered that a well-behaved horse be chosen for him from camp stock.

He sent his orderly to Taylor, directing that he accompany Major Sloan and a small troop of men from K Company to Powder Wash to pick up Army deserters. Chief First Sergeant Dako was contacted, Compton requesting fifteen scouts, rather than the ten scheduled for departure that day.

That the C.O. specifically named Talon worried Dako a great deal. When he took the order to her quarters, she didn't answer his knock, and he thought she might still be asleep. They'd had a hard day in the bluffs yesterday, and the night heat, the first to settle over them this season, had kept most of them awake for hours. Opening the door to her quarters, he peered into the predawn darkness. She slept soundly on her stomach, one of her hands dangling to the floor.

Dako always wore a small eagle feather beneath the knot of his bandanna, which he now removed and drew across Talon's palm several times. Her fingers moved, and the eagle feather was instantly at her mouth. As she waved it away without waking, Dako released a single sharp war whoop next to her ear. Talon shot forward as if she'd been kicked.

Dako grinned in the half-light of morning. Although the lingering odor of one of his Canvas Back *cigarittos* brought a moment of nausea, Talon couldn't halt her smile. "What do you want?" she fussed, swinging her bare feet to the floor. "A girl cannot get any privacy here."

"Mad general request to ride with D Company out to Rock Bluff. Want fifteen scouts, Talon to be there. Have ten minutes, dress, get horse, soldiers—scouts rack up, leave camp. Be gone all day."

"Oh, hell—" Talon dropped back to her bed. "Tell me this is a very bad dream, you are not really here, and it is still hours until morning."

"Not bad dream—Dako here—Talon rise—shine, dress, get on horse."

"Will Taylor ride with us?"

"Taylor ride Powder Wash with Major Sloan." The short, stocky Indian jumped playfully across a pile of her clothing on the floor.

"And Dako—" Black eyes turned steadily to her. "Thank you—all of the scouts—for making Taylor welcome last night."

His grin was dark and playful. "Like Taylor. He funny smoke kinnikinnic. But not to tell Nightwing Apache like him. He be much mad when he know I be friend with him."

"Maybe he will not care."

"Ha!" Then Dako was gone, and Talon crawled from her bed, protesting her sore muscles from yesterday's long day in the saddle.

Now fully awake, Talon took Dako's announcement to heart. Compton despised her, so why did he personally request that she ride with the scouts today? It worried her as she dressed, and began to claw at her unmercifully as she exited her quarters.

On this cool, dry Thursday morning, March 23rd, Company D, Fourth Cavalry, was mounted and in riding formation on the parade field when Talon finally pulled into the saddle. As they rode out, with Major Harris giving orders from his front position, she remained on the left side of the formation, while General Compton rode on the right. She couldn't imagine the staid old warrior making the long ride by horseback to the area of Rock Bluff. He held to his saddle as clumsily as a toddler clinging to a rocking horse.

Ten miles into the bluffs, Major Harris sent Dako and other scouts ahead of the troops. As they stirred dust in their advance to the northwest, Compton coaxed his horse beside Harris, to admonish him for the mix of his military attire. Harris, as usual, wore a blue flannel shirt, buckskin trousers tucked into long boots, and a dirty white hat bearing the insignia of his rank. He responded to Compton's criticism with typical argument that "Southwest officers have individual license in their choice of attire, Sir. This is Arizona Territory, not Washington or a gentleman's game parlor. Comfort comes first," then spurred his horse ahead.

The company had settled down to rest and eat a bite of hard tack and jerky when the scouts returned to report that the tracks of sixty barefoot ponies were only a few hours old. Harris, his first officer, and both his sergeants studied a plat of the area and the likely routes the Apaches might have taken. Shortly after high noon, Harris decided to ride forward and attempt to cut them off northwest of Rock Bluff. He suggested Compton return to camp with an escort of ten soldiers. Hotly refusing, Compton demanded another forty rounds of ammunition for his rifle and sidearm, a big fifty-caliber Civil War issue. Harris remarked that he hoped it didn't come to a slaughter, and that he wasn't prepared to be a corpse today.

Talon, sitting quietly among the scouts a dozen yards away, had listened absently to the argument of the officers. Now Major Harris approached their group and crouched. Facing Dako, the senior scout among them, he spoke with quiet annoyance. "Since the old rascal is with us today, scouts, we should turn back. He's not worth the paperwork his death out here would require."

Compton approached, silence dropping like a rock. "What's the holdup here, major?"

Daniel Harris rose to face him. "We're turning back to camp."

"The hell we are," Compton blurted with pompous indignation. "These scouts report hostiles, and we'll attempt to engage them...unless you have sound cause not to do so."

'I was thinking only of your safety," he replied with brittle impatience.

"Blast my safety to bloody kingdom come. I'm a soldier first, commanding officer second. We'll ride ahead. If you wish to retreat, do so on your own time. Let's rack these blasted flea bags and head out."

Harris looked across the faces of his scouts, noticing the humor in dark Indian eyes, and in Talon's vivid green ones. When his gaze settled on her, she half-smiled. "Let's rack these blasted flea bags and head out," she repeated Compton's words, coming slowly to her feet. Within minutes, Company D and its scouts were on a steady course for Rock Bluff, the most dangerous outcropping for miles around. Its rocky brows hung over a wide flat of earth for a hundred yards, and men, trapped inside, could be cut down from both ends and from the brows above. It had happened before, and chances were it would happen again. Harris hoped it would not happen today.

Rock Bluff was within shouting range by three-thirty. Harris halted his troops and sent several scouts ahead. When the scouts returned half an hour later to report that the Apaches had cut through Chandler's Canyon to the west of Rock Bluff, a treacherous ribbon of dry riverbed winding into Mexico—and that they were many hours ahead—Harris said they'd turn back to camp. They would never catch them before they reached the safety of the Mexican border. Compton, who didn't protest because of a chafed posterior, said he wanted to see Rock Bluff. When Harris began putting together a small troop of men to accompany him the last half mile, Compton requested a single scout...Talon.

This worried the scouts enough that Dako offered to ride with the general in her place. He insisted on Talon, and she quietly relented. Before they rode out, Daniel Harris boldly warned, "If anything happens to the scout, you, Sir, *will* be held accountable."

"Do you think I'll put a bullet in this young woman's back?" He angrily jerked his horse around and heeled to the northwest.

When they were out of sight of the troops, Talon asked, "Sir, why did you request me? I am not exactly your favorite scout."

'I told Taylor I'd give you the benefit of the doubt," he replied without hesitation. "I thought this ride might give us a chance to know each other a little better."

Talon's gaze cut between his hand and a sidearm big enough to shatter a buffalo's skull. "My chin already knows you quite well."

"And I'm sorry about that, scout. I reacted badly to a Comanche in camp. I know you're not personally responsible for the tragedies I suffered early in my Army career."

Talon mentally stumbled over a response, coming up with nothing that sounded even remotely appropriate. A few minutes later, they halted their horses fifty yards from Rock Bluff. "There it is, Sir." Pointing to the high bluffs, she continued, "Those brows there, overhanging both sides—men crouch in ambush, and no rifle on the floor of this canyon can pick them off, they are so well protected by the rock."

Compton eased his horse close to her, so that he wouldn't have to shout across the ten feet of distance she had insisted on keeping between them for the past few minutes. "Did you crouch in ambush up there with the Menendez gang?"

Indignation quickened her pulse. "No, Sir...ambushing innocents is for cowards. I stole horses and cows. I never hurt, killed, or ambushed any person."

"Glad to hear that." Then, "If you were leading a company of soldiers toward these bluffs, what would be your recommendation?"

Talon mentally prepared her response before speaking. "That they go around," she finally answered. "It would add a couple of miles either way, but would be a wise detour."

"And suppose an officer—let's say that officer was me issuing a counter-order—insisted on riding through these bluffs contrary to the advice of his scouts, what would be your reply?"

Talon drew a small breath. "Do we speak hypothetically, Sir?"

He was surprised that an Indian knew the word *hypothetically*. But then, he had heard she'd been educated by a white man. "We do."

"I would remind you what happened to Custer when he did not heed the advice of his scouts. Then I would lead you through, and pray we did not ride into an ambush. I was hired to work as a scout, but I am also expected to obey orders, which I would do without question."

"And what would you personally think of an officer who insisted on relying on his own instincts, rather than those of his scouts?"

Talon briefly hesitated. "I would think he was naive, his orders foolhardy, certainly, and would hope his instincts were correct in that event. But the final outcome is that I would obey my C.O." She looked to him now, the moisture of his blue eyes caught by the sun's rays, the animosity reflecting in them contrary to the polite softness that had echoed in his voice. "Now, tell me, Sir, why you requested that I ride here with you alone?"

Compton laughed nervously, directing his attentions again to the bluffs. "You're too suspicious, Scout Talon. As I said, Taylor and I had a long talk. He's quite taken with you, and I agreed to give you a chance. This is a suitable start, I think, and I do appreciate your refreshing candor in reply to my hypothet."

Talon scanned the bluffs all the way to their top. She had been through here many times and always expected an ambush. "Do you wish to ride through here?"

"Would you recommend it?"

She felt more relaxed now. "I would not, but would accompany you if you insisted."

"I'll heed your warning, scout." Turning his horse, he laughed hoarsely and without feeling, as though the laugh meant something else. "We should head back to camp. I haven't sat a horse this long in years, and my posterior is chafed as the dickens."

"The post physician can provide a soothing ointment," Talon said with a small laugh, turning to join him in the return ride. She allowed a closer distance to him now, thinking, perhaps, that she might learn to trust this man who had just dropped his armor, allowed her to advise him, and had treated her like a human being, rather than a Comanche butcher and his enemy.

* * *

Laine had spent an hour with Compton upon his return from Powder Wash. After relating his ride to Rock Bluff with Talon, Compton advised him of a meeting he had called for the following morning. When he announced that Talon was to attend, Laine prayed he wasn't up to something. He spent two hours alone in his quarters that evening, thinking, admonishing himself for his suspicions, and finally went to Talon to advise her of the meeting. Nightwing was also to attend if he returned to camp in time. Losing the smile with which she had greeted him, Talon's brows furrowed with worry.

"The tone of the summons was friendly," Laine assured her. "So don't worry." *I am worried enough for both of us.* "Six-thirty sharp in his office." Laine had no idea why Compton had called the meeting, but afterwards, he planned to talk to him about replacing Nightwing as Chief of Scouts. It was vital to a good scout troop that the Officer and Chief get along. Laine couldn't see that happening. Nightwing would be an asset to a scout troop elsewhere in Arizona Territory.

"What are you thinking, Laine?"

He had absently settled into the chair at her reading table, but now looked up. "Nothing, sorry, just tired." Patting his lap playfully, he invited her to him. Rather, she dropped to her knees before him. The fingers of his left hand tunneled through the dry wisps of hair not collected in her braid, an affection which she allowed. "Am I ever going to see your hair long and loose, and you, my pretty princess, wearing something not made of leather or men's fabric?

"I wore a dress to the scout get-together—"

"Ah...fabric too thick. Do you know what would look beautiful on—"

The door flew open, Laine's endearment interrupted in mid-sentence. Talon turned so quickly to face her intruder that she lost her bearing. John Nightwing stood there, his dark eyes

130

narrowed menacingly. Though he was expected tonight, neither knew he'd returned to camp. Coated in a light layer of dust, he was obviously still in his traveling clothes.

"Scout need to sleep. Taylor need to go."

Though she'd learned to expect anything from this controlling Indian, Talon was still astonished by his intrusion. Fury filled her soul as she rose from Laine to approach Nightwing. As Laine, too, came to his feet, Talon's finger jabbed into Nightwing's chest as she spoke. "You have no right to charge into my private quarters like this. And you have no right to dictate my time when I am not on duty. I am not a prisoner, and I am not your property. Why could you not have just stayed away?"

Laine instantly closed her hands over Talon's shoulders to pull her from the confrontation. "No one here is going to fight with you, Nightwing. I suggest—no—I order that you never enter Talon's quarters without knocking first. Do I make myself clear?"

Black eyes narrowed venomously. "Yes, Taylor. Now, get out. This scout need to sleep, since we must meet with your friend, the general, early in morning."

He always spoke contemptuously of his friendship with Compton. Right now, Laine was mad enough that if he challenged Nightwing, he'd likely kill him. And since he planned to discuss his replacement with Compton in the morning, he didn't want an incident between them beforehand. "Talon does need sleep. Only for that reason will I leave."

Astonished that the Officer of Scouts would give Nightwing this control over him, Talon spat, "You do not have to leave because he tells you to."

"It's late and I should be going." Then he turned Talon to him and gently kissed her angrily pressed mouth. "Things *will* get better, Talon." In his retreat, he paused beside Nightwing and said stiffly, "I told you before, it's *Captain* Taylor. And I think you've pushed me as far as I can tolerate. You and I, Mister, are about to part ways at this camp."

"You will never be rid of me, *Taylor*. I will be rid of you."

"Are you threatening me, Nightwing?"

"If I threaten you, *Taylor*, you not have to ask. I have business with this scout, so leave us."

For a minute they stared at each other in murderous silence, and Laine turned toward the door. Looking back at Talon, he said, "I'll see you in the morning," and to Nightwing, "You discuss business *only* with her—quickly—and leave." Then he ascended the steps outside, fury echoing in each footfall.

When she could no longer hear Laine's retreat, Talon ordered, "Get out...chief."

Nightwing would not be dismissed by her anger. "Be wise to remember you half-blood Indian, born Comanche, speak Sioux, work with Apache. Taylor white man. You keep company with own kind."

"My kind is hardly a culturally confused mix blood who thinks he is my personally assigned warden. I despise you. I wish you were dead."

For the second time this week she had wished him dead. Having spent many long hours in the sweat lodge, attempting to purge her from his heart and mind, he wondered if her vicious vows of hatred might eventually accomplish what a good sweat did not.

He didn't think so, nor could he blame her for her anger. They provoked each other.

Nightwing finally withdrew. Talon slumped to the bed, tears gathering before she could prevent them. She was angry, both at Nightwing for being an over-protective bully—and making her sling contemptuous words she didn't mean—and at Laine for leaving at his command.

* * *

The following morning, Compton looked up from paperwork when Laine, Troy Reisner, and Nightwing stood before his desk. "Before your Comanche scout and Major Stahl enter, I'll get right to the point. I've decided that you, Major Reisner, will return to the position of Officer of Scouts, and Captain Taylor will be the new camp adjutant. The paperwork is being processed, and the change will take effect Monday

132

morning."

Camp adjutant was a boring position, and Troy Reisner couldn't have been more pleased with Compton's decision. But he saw that Captain Taylor was explosively angry. Nightwing simply caught a smile.

"Are you responsible for this, Nightwing?"

"I can make a decision without *his* influence." Compton spat before Nightwing could voice a denial to Laine Taylor.

"I'll notify the War Department of this," Laine threatened.

"You have the right to do so, Captain Taylor."

"Is that all, General Compton?" Laine snarled.

'It is not, Sir. Chief Nightwing, summon Major Stahl and the Scout Talon to my office."

Still softly smiling, Nightwing returned before a full minute had passed.

Talon had never been in Compton's office, and thought it rather stark, without personal touches, except for a framed photograph on the mantel, turned so she couldn't see who might warrant the display. Perhaps the daughter he had lost.

Then Laine's anger drew her attention and she quickly cut her eyes to the C.O., sitting back in his chair. "I have before me a copy of this scout's contract," he stated flatly, "which contains provisions for discipline should this particular scout be guilty of infractions."

"What infractions, and when?"

"You, Taylor, are not to intrude in my discussions with these people—"

"Then why the hell am I still here?"

"Just tell me what I've done," Talon interrupted politely.

Compton directed his comments to Major Reisner. "On maneuvers near Rock Bluff yesterday, this scout openly defied my orders, issued a threat by reminding me of Custer's fate six years ago when he didn't heed the warnings of his scout, and was rude and insubordinate to me. She also said I was a fool."

Reisner turned his eyes to Talon. "Is this true, scout?"

Talon noticed that Compton's hand shook as he picked up a glass to gulp a mouthful of water. She remembered every word they'd exchanged yesterday. Though they had spoken hypothetically, he had heeded her small warnings, and even remarked that he appreciated her candor. He wasn't giving her the benefit of the doubt yesterday, but setting her up to bring these charges. And right now, some unknown force within wouldn't allow her to call him a liar in front of these men. "I will not contradict his charges."

Compton looked up sharply when she softly spoke those words.

Stahl was sure Compton was lying, and Talon protected him. Keenly aware of his hatred of the Comanches, and thus his motives, he was not sure of Talon's. "*If* the scout committed these offenses, what is your recommendation?"

"That she be disciplined according to her contract."

Stahl replied, "We would certainly expect any discipline to be reasonable."

"Or we can avoid discipline altogether," Compton suggested. "I'll lift the shoot to kill order in effect on this scout and she can voluntarily leave her service."

"With respect, Sir." Nightwing deeply regretted that this had occurred during his absence from camp. "Talon good scout, and I wish to keep her in troop. If she leave camp, she is deserter, and I *will* bring back in chains."

Talon looked to Nightwing with admiration, because his compliments were rarely given. He mentioned desertion—and chains—simply to make a point. Then she felt Laine's closeness, and his arm gently press to her own as he coaxed her gaze from Nightwing.

"I assume you don't want her confined to the guardhouse either, chief?"

"Two-three day, beyond that, I request you not confine this scout."

"Corporal punishment then?"

Each man in the room visibly reacted to Compton's suggestion. "When Colonel Heitman added this provision—" Major Reisner perched on the brink of rage. "It was meant only to keep her in line."

"You will *not* whip her without severe personal repercussions," Laine calmly threatened.

"Sir, the American military does not flog its members," Stahl interrupted. "Just last year the British passed a law prohibiting flogging in their army and navy services."

"Need I remind you this is a scout, subject only to a contract she herself signed...and that we are *not* the British?"

Stahl snapped "Perhaps we bloody well should be!"

"I also ask you not whip scout," Nightwing cut in.

"Two or three days is not adequate confinement for the charges I bring against her, chief. You left me with only this option."

Talon was annoyed that the men argued among themselves as if she wasn't here. "I appreciate your efforts, sirs, but he is not going to have me whipped. He is simply trying to force me to leave." Her gaze swept between Reisner and Nightwing, to assure them she had properly assessed Compton's motive.

Reisner calmly asked, "Scout Talon, give us your personal account of events yesterday."

"Were there any other soldiers or scouts present?" Stahl demanded. "Perhaps they should be summoned this morning. You left with Major Harris's outfit, didn't you?"

"I did, Sir. He—" She refused to speak Compton's name, "said he wanted to see Rock Bluff before we returned and requested that I ride there with him. We were alone for twenty minutes or so. I did not mean to be disrespectful, nor did I intend to threaten him. But I will not leave Camp Casey because he wishes it."

He remained curious as to her motives in not defending herself. He was also peeved to high hell by her fire and defiance, even as she had never raised her voice. He preferred to believe she would leave, which was the outcome he favored, and the outcome motivating the charges. "At sunrise on Sunday you will be whipped. Twenty-five lashes."

"Not one lash," Talon shot back. "Not one!"

Compton chose to ignore her defiance. "After maneuvers today, Chief Nightwing, take your scout to the guardhouse to have her charges and discipline logged in the daily records. She can then be released."

"You finish with scout now?"

"Yes, go on about your duties. And be apprised that forty scouts will arrive next weekend from Fort Bowie. Make room for them and add whatever bunks you need."

Talon looked to Laine, gritting his teeth so firmly his jaw was a sharp ridge. He put out a hand to her, withdrawing it the moment Compton loudly cleared his throat. When she stepped into the warm morning a few seconds later, Nightwing grabbed her arm. "Did Scout threaten general and defy orders yesterday?"

Tears threatened to unmask her resolve. "It does not matter what I did, Nightwing! His word will stand ahead of mine! Despite your words in my defense, I am furious with you about last night. You need to remember that Captain Taylor *is* the Officer of Scouts."

"He will not be on Monday. Major Reisner replaces him."

She was visibly startled. "That is a lie."

"No, it not. It because of *you* he replaced."

"You are the one who did this. What did you do? Run to Compton with lies about Laine's improprieties?"

"I did nothing. He bring on himself." Then, furiously, "He *Laine* to you now, scout? Not Captain Taylor?"

"That is right," she spat defiantly. "We have kissed and cuddled. He has touched me where no other man ever has. One day he will make love to me, like a *white* man makes love. Not an Apache shoving his woman to her knees like a dog!" Nightwing's arm shot to her back and held her tightly. He said nothing, but his dark eyes, so fiercely narrowed, spoke all his sentiments. Unable to hold back her tears, Talon broke from his grip and ran toward the stable.

* * *

Thirty miles northwest of Camp Casey, a pale-skinned, flaxen-haired woman sat in the walled garden of the Mission St. Ignacius, once again reading a favorite Wardsworth poem. Strange, she thought, that she read the poem from the small book, a gift from Brother Jeremy that she always kept in the pocket of her apron, when she had memorized the lines many, many years ago. Her father had recited them to her in those evening moments as he tucked her into bed for the night, and she had, in turn, recited them to her own sleepy child years later.

A little disheartened at the idea of turning forty soon, Julia Rose Compton enjoyed this special niche in the garden. Here she read her favorite verses, thought her special thoughts, dreamed her sweetest dreams, and prayed that, one day, she would see her beloved daughter again.

A golden-red dawn hovered over the hills surrounding St. Ignacius. Somewhere in this vast and desolate land, perhaps, her child lived free and uninhibited, perhaps in the arms of a gentle husband. Somewhere, somehow, she must feel her mother's love reaching across time and distance to wrap her in its warm embrace.

A robin settled to the ground a few feet away, disturbing her thoughts as it picked at the dirt loosened for the wild flower seeds soon to be scattered. For a moment, Julia watched the robin, oblivious to her presence, and soon, another joined it, and another. She always looked forward to the signs of spring, when the hills awakened to fresh, new colors, new life began, and clouds tumbled lazily over serene blue skies.

Then, laughing children entered the garden, and Julia quietly tucked the little book back into her pocket. As the voices of mothers stirred behind the children's feet, she arose, knowing that a busy day in the garden awaited them.

The photographer's wagon would be at the mission for a week. Brother Jeremy had requisitioned enough funds from their offerings to have all their photographs taken for posterity. It had been many years since her photograph had been taken, and she recalled the last sitting as vividly as if it had been yesterday. Her father had sent a lovely sky-blue traveling ensemble for her journey to his post in Texas, and she'd had her photograph taken so she could send it to him several weeks in advance of her arrival. All these years, she had wondered about the photograph, whether it had made it to him, and where it was now. Sometimes she wondered if her father was still alive. He had been the anchor of her girlhood and the anchor of her memories all these years.

Again interrupted in her thoughts by the laughter of the children, Julia coaxed her feet into movement and entered the garden to join the women and children.

There would be time later to dream, to remember her father, her sweet Talon—her daughter—and childishly fret about turning forty.

Ten

The Southeastern corner of Arizona Territory had been too quiet the past few months. Renegade Chiricahuas had fled to the Sonora Mountains south of the border, and local troublemakers were keeping well out of sight of the Army posts. Nightwing was tired of having to keep his scouts busy with mundane drills, when field experience was the best teacher.

At noon, the troop settled down in a grove of mesquite trees to rest their horses and heat canned beans over a campfire. Because she wasn't hungry, Talon settled against the trunk of a mesquite, to rest and think and worry. She hadn't fully understood Compton's hatred of the Comanche until this morning. That he would set her up and outright lie left her in awe. And to replace Laine as Officer of Scouts, simply because he was fond of her—

A sudden yelp drove shards of tension through Talon's back. Across the short span of ground, some of the Apaches wrestled aggressively, others gambled, filled plates, or wiped down their tired horses. Watching Nightwing approach, she anticipated an argument as he crouched before her. Rather, he surprised her with an apology. "I much sorry, Talon that I goad you to anger, and to say things you do not mean. I am not sorry that Taylor is replaced as Officer of Scouts, but I much sorry I blamed you."

Stubbornness kept her from issuing an apology for her crude remark this morning, though she knew she eventually would. "If you did not go to Compton, Nightwing, then it is my fault."

His eyes dropped. He picked up a length of stick and dragged it absently through the dirt. "Things said about being intimate with Taylor...did you mean them?" He had asked Reisner what *intimate* meant, and did not like the answer.

"I do not wish to discuss it, Nightwing. And before you

criticize me, I believe that I love him."

He looked up now. "You believe? You do not know?" When she did not respond, he asked, "Taylor believe he loves you?"

"He implied it," she replied, hastily adding, "in a way."

"Did he speak words of love?"

Talon shrugged. "He mentioned love. But even if he had not, I would know it by his treatment of me."

"He treat you badly, Talon. When that change?"

She looked squarely to him now. "As silly as it sounds, that night we danced in the corral. It changed then. And I love the way he makes me feel, Nightwing. Can you understand that, even a little?" Then, "Why does my relationship with Laine concern you? It does not affect my duties as a scout, nor will it ever."

Because, Talon, you are strongly in this Apache heart. Rather than respond as his heart urged, Nightwing wrapped his fingers gently around hers, caressing them for the moments that he spoke. "I do not want you hurt, Talon. White men hurt Indian. No bond like this between white man—Indian woman ever good."

"That is not true, Nightwing," she replied, gently removing her hand from him. "My mother and father loved each other. They would still be together if he had not died."

"You do not know that."

"I will not argue with you about this, Nightwing. I will follow my heart."

Follow it to me, wild Comanche thief. He wanted to tell her how important she was to him, how he had grown to care for her as he hadn't cared for any woman since the murder of his wife. But the light shining within her was for Taylor, and he thought he should change the subject before he got angry and said something against the white man to whom she had turned her eyes. "I afraid for you, scout. Did Compton tell truth? No Apache want see you hurt, but if you said bad things to him, it his right to punish you."

"Please trust that I have my reasons not to contradict him.

And he will not have me whipped. I know that in my heart. He was trying to frighten me."

"Tell me these reasons, scout...do not trust old white general."

She really didn't know the reasons, but they were there, lurking just beyond the fringes of her memory. "Because, Nightwing, I will not make his life here more difficult by calling him a liar. He vents his anger and hatred of the Comanche through me. He must have loved his daughter very much, and that salvages something of his character, don't you think?" Nightwing was sullen and thoughtful. He did not know this word *salvages*. "I am sorry I called you an Apache dog."

He smiled. "I did not know you meant *this* Apache."

Talon shrugged gently. "I did not." Then, "Please promise me an incident like last night will never happen again. If Taylor does not care that I am Indian, neither should you."

His eyes turned fully to her, admonishing, almost critical. "Do not trust Taylor, Talon. Do not trust *any* white man." He rose swiftly, pivoted, and put distance between them.

This from an Apache who took a dead white man's given name to honor him? Nothing about Nightwing made sense to her these days.

Just before nightfall they entered camp and drew their horses up to the corral. Talon unsaddled her mare, threw a bucket of water over her, and rubbed her down without the usual patience and care. Moments later, the mare claimed her place at the long trough where buckets of sweet feed and hay had been deposited, and Talon turned toward her quarters, pausing when Nightwing called crossly, "I accompany you to guardhouse, Talon. Wait until I come for you."

She had almost forgotten that Compton had ordered her to the guardhouse. An hour later, with quiet darkness descended, Talon sat on the stoop outside her door and waited for Nightwing. Across the parade field, lights went off in Compton's quarters above HQ, and a minute or two later the light at his office window illuminated. Pushing up, she started across the parade field.

Salem George Compton heard the front door open, expecting Taylor to appear with another protest. But Talon entered his office. The slim woman was such a vision that for a moment his voice was swept away by an emotion he didn't quite understand—not of a man beholding a beautiful, sensual woman, but deeper, more familial, more fatherly. Strangely, his daughter's features popped into his thoughts, though the fleeting vision did not halt his cruel demand. "What the hell do you want?"

"Before we get into my dilemma, is it true you dismissed Captain Taylor as Officer of Scouts because of me?"

"I did. Now...what else do you want?"

"Return him to his position, and I will leave Camp Casey without protest."

Salem George Compton wanted her to be selfish—inconsiderate of every other living being—to agree to leave Camp Casey to spare her own worthless hide from the lash. He did not want her to show this gentle caring and concern for a white Army officer, to consider his military career important enough to personally speak up in his behalf. He was suddenly furious that she went against the grain of character, as he had assessed in her. "Who the hell do you think you are, attempting to countermand my reassignments? I will not be blackmailed by a butchering Comanche."

Talon, who had noticed the fury quietly grip him, stepped up to his desk. "I was not even born when my tribe tore out your heart. I have done nothing, except respect who—what—you are."

Compton averted his gaze, and Talon quietly demanded, "Look at me, Sir." When he lifted his eyes, she thrust out her hands. "Do these look like the hands of a butcher?"

They were slim, pretty hands, fingernails well groomed and buffed to a shine, despite the hard work she was required to do as a scout. But his mind's eye saw only a Comanche dagger clutched in those slim fingers. Rising swiftly, he approached the mantel, snatched the framed photograph of his daughter, and turned it to Talon. "Your tribe stole a child I loved more than life itself. She wasn't allowed to grow and mature as you did, scout." The face was so familiar to Talon that the doorway to a thousand childhood memories opened in her heart. *White Swan*! A light brush of tears gathering among her lower lashes, her fingers moved instinctively toward the photograph. But Compton angrily withdrew the likeness before she might touch it. Then a shadow encroached upon the corridor wall, and Nightwing stepped into the light. "Escort your scout to the guardhouse for processing," Compton yelled. "Have them hold her until I send further orders."

Talon followed Compton's movements as he returned the photograph to the mantel. Having no voice as he turned his cold blue gaze to her, she saw him in a whole different light. Nightwing's fingers circled her arm, and she half stumbled from a room swirling in colorless shades. Had they not reached a slight breeze outside, Talon was almost sure she would have fainted. Moments later, she paused beneath the ash and pressed her fingers to her glassy eyes.

Only later, when she sat in general confinement, did she recall Nightwing's anger that she had gone to Compton's office. She vaguely recalled an argument he had with Mulroney at the intake desk, and Major Stahl making an appearance to diffuse a situation she was sure involved her. Nightwing had said he would talk to her before he left the guardhouse, but half an hour had passed and he had yet to come. Then, when she thought he had forgotten about her—that she wouldn't be able to make a request of him before she lost the nerve to do so—Mulroney unlocked the door and allowed Nightwing to enter.

"I spoke to Major Stahl moments ago. He say you be released from guardhouse tonight. Do you need anything until then?"

"No, Nightwing." When he started to leave, Talon's fingers closed over his arm, halting him. "I need to tell you something, Nightwing." He turned fiercely dark, yet comforting eyes to her. But she couldn't speak the words *General Compton is my grandfather* because she didn't want to believe it herself. But she had seen the photograph...she had seen her mother's face—the same face that Compton had grieved for all these years, the face of a woman he had believed murdered by the Comanche twenty-five years ago. When she met Nightwing's dark eyes, she quietly said, "Never mind, it is not important."

"Trust that I take care of you, Talon. No leather will touch flesh."

"I do trust you, Nightwing. But I do know that he is bluffing."

Nightwing did not know this word *bluffing*.

He remembered how they had treated each other the first afternoon she had been brought to camp in chains. That she now claimed to trust him stirred a deep, profound fire in him. He quietly retreated, pausing as the metal door closed behind him.

Alone now, Talon caressed the small rawhide pouch she had worn for the past fifteen years. Recalling her mother's words, *your heart will tell you when the time is right,* Talon knew that here and now was the right time. Her heart warned her of what she might find. Slipping the rawhide string from her neck, she held it for a moment, thinking about her mother and the years she had spent with her in the village. Had she ever mentioned the name of her white family? She must have, for that first day in Major Reisner's office she had asked him if the general's first name was Salem. She didn't need to look at her unseen treasure to know that Compton was her grandfather.

In the semi-darkness of the cell, Talon widened the drawstrings and turned the pouch up, her hand first accepting the little blue rock she had picked up at the edge of a pond, then a few grains of glimmer she had swooped from a stream in the Black Hills. The soft lock of her mother's hair—yellowed with age—touched her hand. She hated the memory flooding her now, of a day after her father's death that his sister and another woman had shorn her mother's beautiful hair, because she *needed to express mourning for her dead husband.* Before the scattered locks were swept away, Talon had hidden one among her few possessions.

Tipping the pouch again, a tarnished chain came into view,

attached to a silver locket in a frame of filigree. The pouch contained nothing else, and whatever her mother had wanted her to know when she listened to her heart was inside the locket. She opened it with trembling fingers, a small, faded portrait—possibly of her mother, though the features were worn away by time—falling to the leg of her trousers. Inside the locket were two fragile squares of paper, folded to the size of a thumbnail. Talon took the one to the right, carefully unfolded it, and read the faded words written in a woman's delicate hand: *Happy 6th birthday to my darling baby, always your mother—Sarah (nee Ravenscroft) May 27, 1848.*

Smiling as she returned the bit of paper to its niche, she took the other and unfolded it, her fingers still trembling. *To Julia Rose, my sunshine and my future, on her 6th birthday.*

The tremor increased as she lowered the age-worn fragment and quietly read: *From your devoted and loving father—*

Talon couldn't bear to read her grandfather's name, though it flashed menacingly through her thoughts...*Salem George Compton.*

Only a fear of being caught in an emotional state kept Talon from weeping.

Over the span of a dozen minutes that she spent alone, she tried to remember a single instance that her mother had spoken ill of her father, but could only remember love in those moments she'd shared her memories. She couldn't imagine that Salem Compton had ever been gentle, kind, and loving...those qualities so frequently whispered from her mother's lips.

When Laine was allowed into the cell, she was glad to leave her painful thoughts, acknowledging him with a lightly spoken apology. "I am sorry you were replaced as Officer of Scouts. I tried to speak to Compton about it, but he would not listen."

"So I was told." His tone was almost rude. "My replacement as O.S. is the least of my concerns right now, Talon." Anger sparkled from the blue depths of slightly narrowed eyes. "Why didn't you defend yourself in that lying bastard's office this morning?"

Talon's soft-soled boots slid onto the stone floor. "What defense did I have?" she replied, scarcely able to contain a moment of ire. "Let us just get past this with some small shred of dignity."

"Corporal punishment is prohibited by military law. I am sending a telegram to the War Department in Washington."

"He is not going to have me whipped, Laine. Trust me on that."

Laine pulled her into his arms. "I hate that son-of-a-bitch." His mouth pressed lightly to her dark hair. "Did he lie about Rock Bluff?"

Knowing now that Compton was her grandfather, Talon couldn't bear Laine's animosity toward him, nor could she tell him the truth about Rock Bluff without tarnishing his character. Some of what he'd said had been the truth, though he'd managed to twist it and obscure its original meaning. "I will not contradict him."

"Why do you protect him when his mission is to persecute and punish you?"

"Do not be angry with him," she pleaded, closing herself more intimately into his arms. "If you think about what he lost to my father's people, you should try to understand. Do not make more trouble for yourself."

His slim, trembling fingers raked through his rangy locks. "Talon, I—" He'd been about to say *I love you.*

Though he hadn't spoken the words, she had heard them. She smiled, pressing her cheek to his shirt.

"And what about the next time he brings charges, Talon? And the next time, and the next time? He won't stop until you're gone."

She turned from him, her words abrupt. "There will be no next time, Laine." When he roughly pulled her to him, she enjoyed the stir of his passion, rising above his firmly set anger. "How can I be so fond of a man I hated so deeply?"

"You never hated me. If you had, you wouldn't have let me get away with saying all those naughty things to you that first day—"

Sergeant Mulroney appeared at the door, slipping a key into the lock as he spoke. "The C.O. just sent word that until she's released this prisoner's to have no visitors he don't personally approve. An' you ain't got that approval...Sir."

* * *

An hour after Laine had been made to leave her, Compton stood just outside the door to general confinement. He watched Talon, half in the shadows, her hands curled together and resting lightly against her chin. Again, she reminded him of his sweet, flaxen-haired girl thirty years ago, her little hands curled against her chin in just that fashion.

Talon watched Compton from the early evening shadows claiming the corner where she lay. She was curious, since she knew now that he was her grandfather. *Ironic that he hated her because of her heritage, and yet the blood of his own family flowed in her veins.*

He approached, and she swept her feet to the floor. "You know what I expect, scout?"

"You expect me to leave my service to the Army," she hurried her response in a moment of bravado. "Since you would not allow me to bargain for Captain Taylor's assignment, I shall remain in the scout troop no matter what you do to me."

Her bold indictment of his character had little effect on him. "Have you ever seen the result of a flogging, scout?"

"Only to my own body, Sir, when I was a child slave of the Sioux."

He visibly flinched, his startling blue eyes narrowed. "Since you were brought here as a prisoner, why do you insist on staying?"

"Because it is my right and contractual duty to do so."

"I suggest you leave this camp without delay." With two quick strides, Compton hovered intimidatingly over her. Though he despised her, a Comanche, his dreaded and hated enemy, he was very curious about her. "Tell me about your bloodline, scout," he demanded. "Your parents, who are they? Where are they?"

Talon didn't want to discuss her personal life with him, but

147

could not disrespect him by refusing to answer. "My father was Chief Toya Ruhku of the Noconi Comanche of West Texas. He died in a hunting accident when I was seven. My mother died of illness."

"When?"

"I am not sure exactly. Years ago."

Compton snapped, "You do not know when your mother died?"

"Indians don't keep up with such things. When I escaped the Sioux and returned home, I was told she had died."

"And your mother carried white blood?"

She was your daughter. "She did, Sir."

Salem Compton noticed that Talon protectively held a small rawhide pouch hanging from a cord at her neck. He wondered what an Indian woman might treasure enough to keep so close to her. "It's just as well she died," he said, refocusing his thoughts. "No respectable white woman who would bed an Indian is suitable for civilized society."

Talon winced at his insult toward her mother—toward a daughter he had professed to love more than life itself. "Her husband not only loved her," Talon argued softly, "but respected her, which is something you don't often see in your suitable *civilized* society." Infused with a quiet strength, she asked, "Could I know something of you, Sir?"

"What would you want to know of me, scout?"

"Suppose your daughter had lived, married a Comanche, and I was actually your granddaughter. How would you feel toward me then?"

He spun toward her, drawing back his hand as though he would strike her. Instead, his fist tightened against his trousers leg. "My daughter would *never* have lain with a stinking Comanche heathen—unless against her will. How dare you cast this vile aspersion against my dead child." Calling crossly, "Guard," he yelled at Talon, "Within the hour you'll be released, and I suggest you opt to leave, Comanche, because if you do not—" The door unlocked, he stormed out, the threat unfinished.

Stunned by his brutal reply, Talon dropped to the small cot

and stretched herself along its length. As the sun began to set beyond the row of small windows high above the cots, she placed her bent arm against her ear and tried to shut out the resounding echo of the words he had spoken. But their cruelty resonated like cannon fire.

Night was just falling when she was told she could leave. Nightwing waited in the front office. Exiting into the cool night air, Talon admitted to him that she didn't know what to do about the discipline. Should she leave? Or should she stay?

"You want be Army scout?" he inquired, his dark eyes narrowed thoughtfully.

"I do."

"You prefer lash than not be scout?"

"He will not put me under the lash," she replied, though the verity of her response held on by a thin thread. "But I want to know what you think I should do."

"I do not want you to leave. I do not want you hurt."

"If you do not want me to leave, that is all I need to hear." Soon they stood outside her quarters. Customarily, Nightwing walked off without parting amenities, but now took Talon's hand, held it gently, and ventured a comment. "In this Apache heart, I believe general lied. And you protect him, Talon." Bitterness now flooded his voice. "I do not know why you protect him. It make Nightwing much mad. Apache mad, too. Say will kill Compton if he hurt you."

A note of urgency entered Talon's voice. This was not just an embittered C.O. with a vendetta, but her grandfather. "They must not hurt him."

Perplexity hugged Nightwing's dark brow. "Why you care for this man? He does not care for you."

"Please, Nightwing, let us not argue." Rather than descend the steps to her quarters, Talon stepped off the boardwalk. "If you are through lecturing me, I shall go to the stable and groom my horse, perhaps give her a little sweet feed."

"Go. I am finished with lecture." Worry chased away his small smile. "Maybe horse you love talk sense to you."

Moving into the shade of early evening, Talon smiled.

"You never know, Chief." She gave him a haughty and slightly mocking salute as she retreated.

A few minutes later, Talon slipped through the great corridor of the livery, toward the room where Mattie spent most of his time. He sat at a small table, straightening horseshoe nails with a hammer and very large pair of pliers. Dropping to her knees beside him, Talon placed her damp palms on her thighs. "What you doing, Mattie?"

"Playin' tiddlie-winks on a horse's knee," he replied with a grin. "What you think I'm doin', girl? Some of these nails might be goin' into that mare's hooves. You want 'em straight an' easy on her, don'cha?"

Grabbing subjects for small talk, Talon asked, "Why are you content to be a blacksmith, Mattie? Wasn't being a lawman much more exciting?"

He kept working, cutting her occasional glances as he did so. "Learned blacksmithin' beside my old man when I was belly high to a squat-legged duck. Spent only seven years as a lawman before I took the bullet in this dadgum knee. No, girl, blacksmithin' comes easier to me, especially now. An' besides, you need somebody to be watchin' out for you. Hear you been spendin' a lot of time with Taylor. You got a thing for the fella, Talon?"

She laughed lightly. "I think he has a thing for me, but I do not know what it is."

Mattie's hands stilled, big, gentle fingers easing beneath her chin. "I sure see what it is, gal. Yep, I sure do."

Though Talon kept her shoulders straight, she discreetly moved his fingers so that she could lower her eyes. "I suppose you heard I am in a bit of trouble?"

The tools and nails dropped, and Mattie's fingers were under her chin again, forcing her to face him. "I have a real strong feelin', girl, this trouble ain't of your makin'. Why don't you tell Mattie what happened out there at Rock Bluff?"

She had refused to tell Nightwing, Laine, and the majors, but trusted Mattie, though not enough to tell him Compton was her grandfather. He had cared enough about her to plead for her life when they first came to Casey, so she told him the truth about Rock Bluff, repeating her conversation with Compton, verbatim as best she could recall it. "And that's the way the biscuit crumbled, Mattie. You're the only person I've told the truth, and I trust you not to repeat it. I don't believe he will whip me.""

"Remember that ol' sayin', what goes around comes around. He'll get paid back for his lie. But I got to agree with you...he ain't a'gonna lay the lash to you, gal."

Talon wrapped her fingers through his calloused ones, pressing her cheek to his knee. "I wish I'd known you two years ago, Mattie...maybe I would've been too scared of disappointing you to get into so much trouble." Talon stood, flicking dust from her trousers. "I better see to Shadow Dancer's grooming before nightfall."

"That night's done fell, gal. Take that lantern from over there on the peg."

Minutes later, Talon set a pail of sweet feed on the ground at Shadow Dancer's head. She had brought her currycomb, and apologized to the mare at once for not giving her the usual brush down when she returned this afternoon. "I have had a lot on my mind, good girl." As her fingers rummaged between the mare's ears to untangle a knot in her mane, she began to worry about the Apaches taking some kind of action against Compton. To ease the hostility toward him, she had to confess to his charges. It wasn't her first choice, but there was little else she could do. He wasn't just a vicious, lying C.O. who hated Comanches. He was her grandfather.

Alone except for an occasional guard passing on rounds, Talon focused on Shadow Dancer, noticing that she was slimming down with the warm weather. Half an hour later, a clean, well-groomed mare pranced behind her as she entered the stables.

A hand covered her mouth from behind, snatching her thoughts. She tumbled into the hay in an empty stable, managing to scoot to her back so that she might snap a harsh reprimand for the attack. A smiling Laine Taylor unclamped her mouth. "And I thought Indians were always on their toes. I could've had my way with you before you ever knew what hit you."

Sweetly returning his smile, she said, "You make it so difficult for me to hate you."

"Shooting a man indentures you to him forever." His mouth brushed her own, his cheek settling against her warm one for several seconds before he spoke again. "Compton threatened to have me locked up for disobedience, but I had to see you."

Talon loved the weight of him against her, his fingers linking among hers...the lock of wayward hair settling against his forehead. With the tiniest smile, she invited his lips to hers, relishing the warmth of his kiss and the heat of his tall frame ignoring the threads of their clothing to touch her deeply. "Why do I feel this way when you are near me?"

He drew back, a slightly mocking laugh affecting his mellow voice. "Confessions, my lady? You *do* care for me, no matter your devil-may-care attitude?"

"Our very souls are guided by that bright star to the east of the moon."

Warm, masculine hands cupped her face, his mouth claiming hers. He pulled Talon to him as he rolled to his back. "You know, we ought to just get married."

"Premature sentiments, Laine."

"You know what I want right now, Talon?" A small "hmmm?" was her only response. "To make love to you." His hand eased beneath the fabric at her shoulder, pulling it down so that he might feel her warm, bare skin. Her eyes lifted to him, softly seductive, almost giving him permission. He did not see the usual caste of fear. As his mouth passionately covered hers, his hand was still beneath her shirt, moving slowly inward. Before she might halt the seduction, he settled his palm against the fiery peak of her breast. Talon rose seductively against him, her hand pressing his more firmly to her.

Her legs spread apart against the hay, so that he might settle between them. But her body and her mind spoke different languages. "Not here, Laine, not like this—"

"Why the hell not? Who's going to come out here?"

"I am, Sir," Private Wilson announced. "Looking for you, Captain Taylor."

Boots shuffled a short distance away. Withdrawing his hand, Laine sheepishly rolled from Talon. Sitting forward, he was aggravated as hell at the interruption. His voice was husky and scolding. "Private Wilson. What is it?"

"I'm sorry, Captain, to disturb your private moments, but the general issued a summary order that you be placed under arrest."

"On what charges?

"Willful disobedience of a direct order."

"Willful disobedience of what direct order?" he asked, as if he didn't already know.

"He said you're aware of it, Sir. Will you come with me without incident?" Private Wilson hesitated to raise his rifle, because he liked Captain Taylor, and was terribly fond of Talon. "Sir, I implore you, don't force me to summon Private Black for assistance. He waits just outside."

Climbing to his feet, Laine brushed hay from his uniform and swept back his hair. He pulled Talon into his arms and held her until Wilson cleared his throat. When Laine turned to accompany him, the young fellow produced a pair of shackles. "What the hell?"

"I apologize, Sir, but he ordered you to be shackled."

"Son-of-a-bitch," Laine retorted hotly, thrusting his hands forward.

As Wilson locked the shackles onto Laine's wrists, Talon looked to the only guard she had befriended. "You take good care of him, Andy," she ordered, and to Laine, "I am sorry about this. I hope he does not keep you locked up."

Laine smiled and promised, "We'll take this up where we left off next time we're alone."

Eleven

Talon dropped to the hay in the corner of the empty stable, drew up her knees, and buried her face furiously into her curled arms. She wasn't sure how long she lay there, but by the time Nightwing came upon her, the oil in the lamp Mattie had given her had burned down and absolute darkness lay over the post. Had Nightwing not carried a lantern, he might never have discovered her crouching silently in the corner. She knew by the anger in his dark eyes that he was aware she'd been with Taylor. "Before you yell at me, Nightwing, he came to me."

Nightwing took her hand to pull her up. "It does not matter who came first, Talon. If you stay away from him, he will not stay in trouble." His hand lifted to her shoulder, half-shoving her forward. "Go to quarters, scout. Do not think about *him*."

Talon was suffused by a wave of defiance. "I suppose I shall be prohibited from riding with the scouts tomorrow?"

A brief interlude of thought coddled Nightwing's pleasant brown features. He would much rather have her with the scouts than to know she could go to Taylor. "You *will* be on horse with scouts!"

Moments later, Talon locked herself in her quarters. She had caused nothing but trouble for Laine since they had met, and wondered if she was doing the right thing by not leaving. Compton's unrelenting persecution had thrown her into a whirlwind, and had trapped Laine in its treacherous storm as well.

Rather than dwell on the harm she had done him, Talon settled at her desk and gathered writing papers to her. There was the matter of Compton's unpopularity on post, and she was, through his hatred of her tribe, directly responsible. Life and duty would be easier on him if she confessed to her grandfather's spurious charges.

For a moment, she stirred her pen in the inkwell and began

to compose her confession. It flowed smoothly, and she didn't have to start over, even once, before blotting the ink, reading over her words, and folding the paper in thirds. Tucking it into an envelope, she wrote on its face, *To Major Hiram Stahl, Major Troy Reisner, Commanding Officer Salem G. Compton, March 29, 1882.*

Now she locked the door, covered the one tiny window, and took a long, cool bath.

* * *

Before dawn the following morning, Talon moved unobtrusively toward the guardhouse. Encountering no one in the guardroom, she approached the door to Major Stahl's office and looked in on him, busy at his paperwork, for a few seconds before he detected her presence. She approached his desk and handed him the document she had written with such great care the night before. "I am not following chain of command, Sir, since I did not give this first to Chief Nightwing. I confess that everything General Compton stated against me is true."

Stahl drew a deep breath to relax his surprise. His eyes were angry, though his words were soft. "I realize he struck you without provocation, Scout, but I'm disappointed you were insubordinate to a general officer, as Major Reisner will be."

Talon caught her trembling lip. She had never taken chastisement well, especially when it was undeserved. "He is our C.O, Sir. My confession might allow him to be viewed as a fair man."

"He's hardly fair." Then, "You do understand this document will go in your service record, and that you will forfeit a month's pay?" Talon simply nodded. "It is necessary to bring in a civilian for this flogging, so you should be prepared for that."

"That will not be necessary," Talon replied in her same quiet tone. "My—the general will not have me flogged."

"How can you be so sure?"

"I am so sure, Sir, that I would wager a whole year's pay. He will not have me flogged. It is an empty threat...because he wishes only that I leave camp. He thinks the threat of a flogging will send me running into the hills, but that will not happen, Sir."

155

Talon dropped her eyes, but took a step back, her voice ever so soft as she requested, "Please, Sir, might I see the captain for a moment?"

"Compton prohibits it." He knew how much Taylor cared for Talon; he also knew how much Nightwing cared for her. The disappointment in her eyes clearly reflected that she cared a great deal for Taylor. Sometimes he scarcely believed the circumstances that had brought the two of them together. Picking up a folder of papers, he spun his chair around. "I wouldn't suggest, young lady, that you take advantage of my turned back to sneak to general confinement to see him."

Talon smiled and politely withdrew.

* * *

Laine had slept fitfully, so when his name was whispered, he came fully awake. He rose from the cot, momentarily linking his fingers among Talon's through the bars of the door. "You are as dear to me as my memories," she whispered to him.

"Talon...Talon, you *are* my memories. I think of nothing but you." For the longest moment, Laine absently smoothed those loose, disheveled tendrils that had come loose from her braid, savoring the quiet essence of her.

"I had to see you, Laine, but I must go before I am caught." The first crow of the camp rooster drifted in from the dark morning, and Talon started to withdraw. She turned back to add with some hesitation, "I have confessed in writing to all Compton's charges. One day I might explain why, but not right now." She withdrew before he could ground out an interrogation, and minutes later, slipped into the waking morning. Hurrying to her quarters, she encountered a scornful Nightwing, his arms crossed and his boots apart as he blocked her path to the steps.

"Where you go?" and before she had time to respond, "to Taylor?"

"So what if I did." Her scalding tone instantly softened. "And I do not want you to criticize me for it." Because he had been so supportive of her—and had spoken in her defense before the officers—Talon forced away her anger. "Please, let us not fight. I will retrieve my weapons, and come to the stable to ready my horse." Pivoting from him, she entered her quarters, snapped up her gun belt and holster, retrieved her rifle, and returned to him. He hadn't moved, his arms crossed at his chest, a brooding displeasure hanging from his brow. Easing past him, she stepped onto the earth and headed toward the stable, taking several steps before his longer strides caught up to her.

"You would be wise to remember Taylor always in trouble because of you."

"I am *not* going to fight with you, Nightwing."

A warm, golden haze had just settled over the rooflines, a familiar prelude to sunrise, as she entered the stable and led Shadow Dancer from her stall.

It was a long day of tedious silence between Talon and Nightwing, and when the scouts returned to camp Talon retired to her quarters without supper. She didn't feel well and sleep did not come easily.

* * *

The following dawn, Talon curled up on her bunk and drew her legs beneath her skirts. Hearing the snicker of horses across the distance, she knew the scouts, always the earliest risers, were mounting up. Nightwing planned to take them through the bluffs, look for recent Apache encampments, and report their findings to Major Daniel Harris.

A small knock at the door preceded Nightwing's entry. He stood against the encroaching dawn and looked down at Talon, still in her loose sleeping gown and hugging a small pillow to her abdomen. "You not saddle up with scouts today?"

"No," was her curt response.

His tone reflected only concern. "Why?"

"You and your superstitious bucks made the rules when I first came here."

Seeing that she appeared pale and unwell, Nightwing crouched to the bed beside her. "Otherwise, are you sick, Talon?" His hand dropped to her forehead, which was warm and moist. "Should I bring tonic to make you feel better?"

"It is a passing sickness." Her eyes smiled at him, even as

157

her mouth did not. "Are you afraid I might take your manly strength?"

His hand turned over on her forehead, moving gently down the side of her face. "If you need Apache's strength, I honored to give it." Withdrawing to the door, he looked back at her, searching for words.

Talon swung her feet to the floor. "Whatever is on your mind, Nightwing, just say it."

He returned to sit beside her, staring at the floor for a dozen seconds before he spoke. "My heart tumbles like rock down hill, Talon. It tells me you must leave camp. Then it tells me you must stay." Tears moistened his eyes as he drew her hand to his smooth brown cheek.

She had never known Apaches were capable of tears. His affection caught her off-guard, nerves stealing into her voice. "Why, big ol' bad Chief of Scouts John Nightwing," she whispered. "I would almost think you like this rude Comanche thief."

Much more than like, Talon. "To see you hurt—break my heart." Then he drew her into his arms and softly kissed her mouth. He rose without delay, the intimacy which he had not planned embarrassing him a great deal. He did not look back when he reached the door. "I send word to Mrs. Huck—bring you meal at noon."

Before he closed the door, Talon assured him, "There will be no flogging, Nightwing. You need to stop worrying about that." He drew a breath as he left. Talon heard quiet words spoken to a guard, followed by Nightwing's abruptly shouted orders. Hardly a minute later, scout ponies headed out. Drawing her fingers to her lips, she felt the lingering warmth of Nightwing's unexpected kiss.

* * *

Early Wednesday morning, Compton had just exited his quarters on the upper floor of the administration building when a murmur of voices drifted from his office. His orderly, now in the last day of his weekly assignment, met him at the base of the stairs. "Sir, every unit officer on post awaits you in your office."

158

"Do they?" Compton queried. "Stand by to deliver messages in camp." Entering his office, Compton faced Major Reisner, Major Stahl, each of his six company officers, the payroll, commissary and public relations officers, the judicial officer, and the officer in charge of the gardening brigade. John Nightwing stood with Reisner. "What is your pleasure this morning, gentlemen?" *As if I bloody well don't know.*

Each officer handed a folder to Major Reisner, who approached and laid them before Compton. "We present these petitions of protest, and also this document from Scout Talon. She confesses to every complaint lodged against her."

Startled, Compton overlooked the petitions and snatched up Talon's document. Throwing on his spectacles, he read the single, neatly written sheet.

"The Comanche herself wrote this document?"

"The *Comanche* writes as well as she speaks. Do you think another's hand signed the contract you have scrutinized to death?"

Compton ignored Reisner's thick smear of sarcasm.

When Major Stahl gave him the confession just this morning, Reisner had gotten so angry he could have flogged Talon himself. He'd been required to spend a few minutes calming down before joining these men for the meeting. "Regardless of the scout's confession," Reisner said coldly, "these petitions have been signed by every soldier and civilian at Camp Casey requesting leniency. We again ask you not to whip this scout."

"Talon made a mistake, but is disciplined scout most of the time. Perhaps you should think if she was your child, would you want her whipped?"

Compton bloated with temper at Nightwing's comment. "My only child is dead at the hands of Comanches, so I don't have to consider that. And you told me the first time we met that the female is rude and defiant, so don't feed me this bull about her pristine character now."

His retort darkened Nightwing's mood even more, and he thought he should leave before his calm facade went the way of a fading day. He also didn't know what the hell *pristine* meant. "If you excuse me, I have day to spend with *loyal* Army scouts."

All officers recognized the uncharacteristic sarcasm as Nightwing, now leaving, uttered those final words.

Major Daniel Harris recalled that Compton had insisted on Talon accompanying him to Rock Bluff. "It's because of your unconditional hatred of the Comanche that this scout is being punished. Show some compassion. The power is in your hands."

His mouth set tightly, Compton exhaled a long breath. "Very well. I'll amend the punishment to confinement for six months."

"That does *not* meet with our approval."

Compton glared rudely at Stahl. "Your approval, major?"

Reisner thwarted any further argument. "Consider the petitions. That's all we ask."

Compton could banter fresh argument back and forth all day, and it would be a waste of all their time. "Captain Taylor has wired a complaint to the War Department. I'll abide by their recommendations."

Major Reisner's sigh of relief was almost visible. "The War Department will *never* allow this beating. You must know that."

Compton actually snarled at Reisner. He didn't know Talon's motive in confessing. And—blast it all—there was no way in hell that he would ever have a leather strap laid to that woman. What made him so angry was that he suspected she knew it. "All of you, get the hell out of my office."

* * *

Talon was back in the saddle by Saturday. Nightwing called an end to drills at midday, just as the thick aroma of beef stew drifted toward them in heady waves. After they had eaten, the scouts and their families gathered at the south side of their barracks for relaxation. Talon didn't want to be alone, so joined them in stories of their conquests, and the lurid jokes of their eldest member, Gad. But Gad's stories lasted only half an hour before he looked kindly to Talon and spoke an ancient, very beautiful, prayer in flawless English.

That afternoon, her chair against the barracks, Talon began

160

drifting off to sleep. Then Nightwing's fingers wrapped around her wrist and yanked her up, one of those rare smiles playing at his mouth. "You must join in lacrosse game."

Women did not play lacrosse, something Nightwing was very aware of, so she was flattered that he had asked her. However, the Indian game could become brutally physical, and she wasn't sure she wanted to end the day bruised and bounced about by rambunctious Apaches. Nightwing insisted, so she reluctantly entered the level ground between the scout barracks and the corral, where large net goals had been placed at opposite ends of the field. Entering the team pool, she was the first chosen by Nightwing to play on his side. Within minutes, net stick in hand, she was mindlessly engaged in the heated sport of lacrosse. The laughter and shouting, the shoving and fighting, and the cheers and jeers of wives and soldiers observing from the sidelines, lasted throughout the afternoon. When the game ended in a win for the opposite team, Talon was flat on her back, a group of sweating scouts standing over her with fingers pointed in fun.

"Comanche like old squaw," Dako laughed. "She eat too much dog soup. Ha!" His legs were suddenly swept from under him, all the Apaches erupting into laughter as he landed firmly on his buttocks beside her.

"The Comanche has endurance," Talon argued without feeling, slapping Dako's shoulder as she sat forward. John Nightwing pulled her to her feet, and they congratulated each other on a game well played. Only then did Talon notice Compton beneath the ash in the late afternoon shadows. Nightwing remarked that he had watched their game all afternoon.

When sunlight withdrew from the day, Talon entered her quarters, lit the lamp on the table, and put logs into the stove to heat water for a bath. Gentle thoughts of Laine stirred within her as she shed her dusty clothing, bathed, and donned her white cotton gown. She lay quietly on her bed for an hour or so. The morning would come soon enough.

* * *

Just before dawn, a sleepless Talon felt the chill of the room hug her. The brightly colored shawl her mother had made years ago, given to her when she returned to her village, lay across the back of the chair, but she couldn't muster enough discomfort to fetch it. After brushing her hair until it shone, she settled at the small desk to read. Her mother had often recited several of the poems in the book she chose, and they were especially precious to her.

A series of raps interrupted the predawn quiet, hollow and distant, as if reaching her from the depths of a dream. Talon snapped, "Come in," much more harshly than she'd intended. When Laine entered, she hurried into his arms, noticing his paleness, and his anger. She questioned him about it at once.

One hand rubbed absently along her arm as he spoke. "I went to the telegraph office to see if I'd received a response from Washington. That sorry son-of-a-bitch at HQ pulled the wire before it was sent. Since I was in the guardhouse all week, I didn't have time to organize a mutiny in camp."

"And if you had," she bristled, stiffening against his light caress, "I would *never* have forgiven you."

His eyes narrowed, wrathful at first, softening with the love he felt for this strong, vivacious Indian woman. "I hope you're right about Compton. But I don't trust him." His tone was both somber and filled with annoyance. He pulled her close, his trembling fingers tunneling through her hair before roughly cupping her face to lift it to his own. When he kissed her, a single tear dropped to his cheek, but he turned abruptly and swept it away. He simply did not trust Compton and was worried about Talon. She pretended not to notice the tear.

Pivoting, his mood restored for the moment, he settled onto the bed beside her. Knowing full well he would get the same argument from her as he'd gotten last week, he was so exasperated he could hardly bring himself to speak. "You're not telling me something important, Talon...something that compels you to continue taking Compton's abuse."

"I cannot believe you sat in the guardhouse for a week brooding about this." Her fervor made him face her, and his instant agony compelled her into his arms. That she had tasted his kisses and felt his powerful embrace should have no bearing, and she felt that their mutual feelings were a complication and a hindrance.

Laine firmly believed Talon had an agenda motivating her to take Compton's abuses, but he was damned if he could figure out what it was. Taking her hand, he held it to his mouth, dry with anger, and trembling with worry for her. "I won't argue with you further, Talon." His arm swept across her shoulder, his forehead pressing to her own. "Want me to stay until time?"

"Until what time?"

"The flogging."

"For heaven's sake, Laine, he is not going to have me flogged!"

He pulled her into his arms, his hands tunneling again through the silken masses of her hair. "I hope you're right!" Only then did he notice her hair free of its braid. "I knew your hair would be beautiful, Talon," he whispered, dipping his mouth to her own.

By the time he stepped away from her, Talon felt that all the air had rushed from her lungs. "You should report to Compton before he assumes you are with me." His boot steps echoed across the stone floor. Dawn glimmered to the east. Stepping from her, his emotions a thin veneer apt to crack and peel any minute now, he closed the door between them.

* * *

The pale glow in Compton's office caught Laine's immediate attention. He entered the darkened building a minute later and knocked at Compton's office door, removing his hat as he faced him. Compton didn't look up from the stack of petitions he had received on Wednesday. "If you want to thank me for authorizing your release, do it and go about your business."

Laine would hardly thank the bastard for releasing him from a confinement he hadn't deserved. The only thing accomplished by his solitude was settling his heart about one thing, the love he felt for Talon. "Since my wire to the War Department was rudely intercepted, I hope that Talon is right.

163

You will not have her flogged."

Compton looked up now, noticing Laine's impeccable dress, free of his usual rough, rebellious accessories. "She should not presume to know me!" Then, "Should I have her clean the stables for a few weeks, captain? Is this what you have in mind for your Comanche?" Scattering the petitions, fury glazed his eyes. "If I pay no heed to these, I'll pay no heed to a sexually depraved Army officer who wants this woman simply to annoy his commanding officer."

"That is *not* true. And you punish her because she's Comanche...because your daughter is dead." A barely perceptible tick grabbed at Compton's mouth. "Admit that you will not be so cruel to a woman, out of your tremendous sense of justice!" Laine had not suppressed the sarcasm as he uttered those last few words.

A man with a murdered daughter has no sense of justice. Blue eyes glimmered, catching the glow of his lamp. The pen Compton had been using slipped back into the silver inkstand. He refused to admit that Talon was right—he was not so cruel as to lay leather to a woman's back, even if she was Comanche. "A good whipping might improve her character."

"A whipping *never* improves character! She's being punished because your daughter is dead," he repeated the accusation. "And because she won't leave as you ordered. Big, bad major general...challenged by a Comanche female!"

Compton shot forward, his palms pressing solidly against the blotter atop his desk. His clerk, who had quietly entered, stepped back. When Compton cut scathing eyes to him, he quietly backed from the office. Compton now looked to Laine. "If you stayed out of this heathen's filthy, flea-infested bed, you wouldn't be her damned champion."

Laine instinctively fisted his right hand. "I have not been in Talon's *clean* bed...Sir...and *that* has been *her* choice, not mine." He hated Compton, hated his bigotry and his smugness. "There's nothing I can say then to change your mind?"

"Only that the bitch is leaving." When Laine turned his back to him, something he had never done before without a respectful nod, Compton ordered, "Face me, Captain." Laine hesitated slightly before turning back. "You *will* be on the field this morning to witness her discipline."

"She doesn't believe you will flog her. God only knows why she trusts you."

A single knock announced a visitor. Nightwing stepped in, he and Laine staring at each other somewhat rudely before he spoke. "I wish to speak to *your* General Compton."

Two stints in the guardhouse had made Compton unpopular with this tall, intimidating Indian. "Stay a minute, Taylor," Compton ordered, simply because he had grown fearful of the Indians at Camp Casey. Laine closed the door and approached the desk. Nightwing hesitated. "Out with it, man. I have a busy day."

Nightwing drew a shallow breath. "She will not leave camp to avoid brutality, Sir." The few steps Nightwing took in retreat echoed fury. Then he turned to face Compton. "For many generation, white man call Indian savage. But Indian respect woman, who is giver of life. If Indian is savage, what that make white man who give order to bare—whip woman in front of many men?" Then he quietly walked away.

Despite his utter dislike for Nightwing, Laine greatly respected the bold statement he had made to Compton, who had paled visibly.

* * *

As usual, the camp rooster crowed well before morning reveille. Hearing footfalls on the steps outside, Talon turned just as Nightwing stood in the doorway, a tall, dark outline against the encroaching dawn. No matter that she had confessed, Nightwing was sick at heart, and Talon saw right through him. "Why do you all think the general will carry through with this ridiculous flogging?" Twisting her hair up and securing it with the silver combs Laine had given her, Talon snatched up her jacket and moved past him. "I will put a halt to this once and for all. All you silly men! Listen to the woman for once!"

"I will go with you."

"No! I plan to see the general and I will see him alone."

165

"You will not!"

"I will!"

Talon entered the parade field, aware that Nightwing moved several paces behind her.

She was aware of the murmurings as she moved among the men, many of whom she'd befriended and who now wore very long faces. Laine stood a foot or two from Compton, and even in the half-light, she noticed the older man's hooded eyes narrow as they swept over her. His features flushed, and perspiration popped onto his forehead, despite a rare morning chill.

Laine looked to Talon with quiet admiration. This morning he had argued with an outrageously stubborn Comanche scout, fidgeting nervously with her red bandanna. Now, she stood in the midst of the men, the rich fullness of her hair a bit carelessly coiffed and held up by the pair of matching silver combs he had given her.

Talon approached Compton without hesitation. "Sir, I respectfully request that you and I talk for a moment in private."

Compton muttered, "What the hell could you possibly have to say to me?"

That I am your granddaughter. No, she could never tell him that in view of his hatred. He would never believe her. "In your office, Sir?

Compton breathed deeply, the gold buttons of his double-breasted uniform jacket straining against the labor. "Very well." Then, "You men...keep your positions."

She did not walk beside him into HQ, but kept several paces behind. His hands were trembling, and she couldn't help but wonder why. Surely he was not afraid of her? Soon, she stood in his office, her arms crossed and booted feet slightly apart. She did not react as he growled, "Damned Comanche whore! Do you plan to beg for leniency?"

The insult, so viciously spewed by the commanding officer, stung mightily. That he was also her grandfather tore at her heart. This was not the same man her mother had spoken so fondly of on those long dark nights in their tipi, a man whose love and gentleness she had related to a youthful Talon, in awe of a white grandfather she had never known. Defiance rose within her, even as her voice remained soft and polite. "For your information, this Comanche *whore* remains a virgin."

He pulled in a shallow breath, attempting to still the tremor within. "I shouldn't have called you that," he said, short of issuing an apology. "It was neither professional nor gentlemanly."

"You have hardly been either since you arrived here." She faced him fully...boldly...sadly. "One day you will regret you have been so vicious to me. You will be all alone in the misery you have brought on yourself."

I regret it now. I feel alone in my misery now. Compton turned his glazed eyes to her vivid green ones, her softly spoken vow lingering after her words had silenced, her Comanche blood stirring the hatred he had carried like a vial of poison all these years. "Why would you confess in writing to something you did not do?"

Talon's voice remained polite, and a little sad. ""I wish someone else was in this office to hear you make this confession." Then, "One day you might know." When he made a half-turn from her, Talon quietly—respectfully—spoke his name. He paused, but did not face her. "You have no intentions of having me flogged. You feel you have backed yourself into a corner and now you do not know how to hold up your head at this camp without carrying through with the threat. I know I am nothing to you—just an Indian scout, not worth a dime in your estimation—but I have earned the respect of the men at this camp, simply by accepting and doing the job I was thrust into against my will. You, too, can have their respect—by allowing me to do my job, without this punishment you would inflict on me." He had faced her now, his hands still trembling, the slight tick at the corner of his mouth betraying his nervousness, or perhaps his deep hatred. She wished he wouldn't feel that way toward her. She turned to face the portrait of her beautiful, youthful mother on the fireplace mantel. "Send your clerk out to the field to tell the men to disperse. Please Sir, not just for me, but for yourself."

Compton's voice became rueful. "Get on your horse, scout, and leave. That is all I want."

Turning to face him, she replied defiantly, "I will stay."

"Scout—" His voice lowered, hoarse with emotion he could not suppress. "For reasons I don't know, you lied to protect my reputation at this camp. Riding away now will serve the same purpose."

She was angry with this man—her grandfather—for his unrelenting hatred, and angrier with herself for engaging in a futile challenge of wills with him. "I believe you hate this war between us as much as I do." When he turned from her, Talon clamped her fingers boldly over his arm, halting his withdrawal. "Call your clerk. Have the field cleared."

He had been so sure she would leave. "You're right, Talon Rose, I never had any intentions of having you whipped." He almost placed his hand over hers, but withdrew it before slinging her slim fingers away from his sleeve. "I simply want you to leave." He hadn't even realized he'd called her by her full name. Then he called, "Roan! Get in here at once." Roan had been nearby, possibly listening to their every word. The general turned to face him. "Tell the men to clear the field. There will be no flogging today."

Roan was scarcely able to stifle the smile turning up his mouth. "Yes, Sir."

Pivoting on the heel of his spit-shined boots, he barked at Talon, "Get out," then retreated to his quarters on the second floor.

Twelve

Hardly a soul lingered on the parade field that Sunday. Talon remained alone in her quarters, and sometime around mid-morning heard the humble words of a hymn drifting toward her from the camp chapel. Nightwing brought her a meal at noon, and before he withdrew, she said to him, "I really do not hate you, or wish you dead."

"I know." He returned to her, his strong fingers gently squeezing her shoulder. "Eat meal, Scout. Keep strong. Tomorrow we have much riding to do." Then he was gone, and Talon, strangely, wished he had stayed just a little longer.

The afternoon slid by like a hawk in gentle flight above the mountains, her thoughts flooding back through the years, to a time when a sudden rainfall on a cool April morning in her father's village had chased away the harsh, dry wind of the Texas plains. Her mother had wrapped her within her arms in their tipi, and they had talked for a very long time. Each word her mother had spoken that morning resounded through Talon's memories, each show of affection, each warning and assurance that she was loved as much as any little girl had ever been loved. She especially remembered the softness of her mother's voice as she had told her about her grandfather—her *toko*—and of her own childhood being cared for and loved by this kind, gentle man. Talon remembered that she had pictured him, pictured a kind face, and eyes as blue as her mother's glowing with love and pride, had imagined his voice as clearly as if she had heard it herself. She had known him as well as her mother knew him then, had always hoped that one day they would meet...and he would love her as he had loved his own little girl—

She suddenly thought of Nightwing. He had told her that Laine Taylor—or *Taylor*, as he always referred to him—had ridden out with a company of men to meet Major Tam MacGregor and his Apache scouts. He was not scheduled to

169

return until well past midnight. Talon joined the scouts for their evening meal, took Mrs. Huck up on her offer of a nice warm bath at her housing, and retired to her quarters for the night, determined that she would sleep a dreamless sleep and awaken well rested in the morning. She had not seen the General all day, but then, she had not left her quarters until this evening. She had just slipped into a comfortable sleeping gown and snuffed the lantern when the door to her quarters suddenly opened. She hated it when Nightwing entered without knocking, but as she was unexpectedly shoved onto her cot by a rough hand, her face pressed into her pillow, she knew this was not Nightwing. As a strong hand circled her neck and held her firm, she was unable to scream at the sudden assault. A heavy knee pressed into the small of her back and her gown was ripped down the back. She struggled, trying to free her mouth from the pillow so that she might scream, but he was too strong. She was not prepared for the lash that landed heavily against the tender flesh of her back. Tears filled her eyes as the pain seared into the very core of her heart. Instinctively struggling to free herself from this brutal assault, curling her hands tightly as she braced for the bite of the lash, Talon tried to hold her breath as another half dozen lashes burned across her skin. The subsequent lashes drove the breath from Talon's lungs in frantic rushes, and the pain was like liquid fire snaking across her flesh. Her body recoiled instinctively from the brutal assault of the whip, and she tried mightily to mentally prepare, to gain strength from her thoughts of Laine.

Only when she stopped struggling did the lashes stop, the hand withdrew from her neck, and heavy boot steps quickly retreated up the steps from her quarters. She gasped air in tiny rushes, tears flooding her cheeks as she tried to turn but could not. She was on fire and wanted only to sink into a cool spring somewhere in the Huachucas...then darkness came over her and all the strength left her body. She could only whisper, "Nightwing...help me—"

* * *

General Compton had left HQ to enjoy the fresh air and one of his expensive cigars. The night was cool, a purple haze washing over the horizon. An owl suddenly dipped from the ash to capture a small creature—perhaps a mouse—then flew off over the walls of Camp Casey with its prize. His gaze now turned to the small building where Talon's quarters were located, and he was surprised to see a dark shadow emerge from the steps and disappear into the night. It angered him that the female scout entertained men at all hours of the night, and, snuffing his cigar and throwing it to the ground, he moved on a deliberate course toward her quarters to issue a warning about her morals! *Virgin, indeed!* Descending the steps, he knocked on the door. She did not answer. The door was slightly ajar, so he pushed it open and saw at once the outline of her on the small cot. She had gone to sleep very quickly after her *guest* had departed. He thought that there was nothing he had to say to her that could not wait until morning. He turned, spying at once the whip curled on the steps, which he absently swooped up and carried back to HQ. The woman left strange things lying about!

Talon had opened her eyes for the briefest of moments. She had seen the General in silhouette against the pale night, standing just outside her door with the whip coiled around his hand. Scarcely hanging onto consciousness, she whispered with the last of her strength, "*Himeetu, Toko*?"

Why, Grandfather?

* * *

Nightwing, too, was taking in the coolness of the night when he saw the General leave Talon's quarters. What could he have had to say to Talon this time of night? He did not see a light at her window and had a sudden sense of dread. As mad as she often made him, Nightwing couldn't deny his special fondness for her, and that alone stirred his boot steps toward her quarters. Descending the steps, he found her door open, and saw the outline of her slim body on its side, her back pressed against the stones at the back of her cot. He knelt beside her, touched her forehead, and thought she felt warm. As his hand circled her shoulder to stir her to wakefulness, he felt wetness at his fingertips. Withdrawing his hand, he saw that his fingers were covered in blood. Then her body fell forward, and the light of the moon, suddenly uncovered by a thin line of clouds, glistened against the bloody welts across her back. As he took her in his arms, he thought how light she was, like a feather the soaring eagle might lose to the wind. She must have taken this whipping in silence, for surely her cries would have been heard. With his full concentration on Talon as he moved toward the infirmary, he didn't see the little pouch she always wore fall to the ground. She did not stir against him as he cradled her in his arms. Entering the infirmary, his foot banged against the chair where the camp physician, Captain Calloway, was snoozing.

"Now," Nightwing ordered. "Scout injured." Talon came to as he settled her onto a cot in the infirmary. With tears flooding her eyes, she whispered, "I am sorry, Nightwing. I am sorry. I should have left, but I could not leave Laine—" Darkness claimed her again, and if he had responded, she would not have been aware of his words.

The words she had spoken, *I could not leave Laine,* plummeted into the depths of his soul. His animosity toward Laine turned to hatred then, and he knew this camp would never be big enough for the two of them.

Talon stirred several times as Captain Calloway cleaned the wounds. Nightwing stood silently by, watching her face contort as the pain grabbed her, her slim fingers with their well-groomed nails curling now and then into the tender flesh of her palms. In one of those lucid moments, Talon whispered, "Why, Nightwing...why did he do this?"

He did not approach her, but continued to stand several feet away, his arms crossed, and his feet slightly apart. "Why did who do this, Scout?" She did not respond right away, and became aware that Captain Calloway's movements had ceased as he also awaited her answer. Nightwing moved a step closer, repeating, "Why did who do this?"

A tear streaming over the smooth contour of her cheek, she whispered, "General Compton. It was General Compton."

* * *

Major Tam MacGregor and his first sergeant had spent long, harrowing hours traveling from Fort Bowie with his troop of reluctant Apaches, who had agreed to the temporary reassignment only because they'd grown to respect Taylor the few months he was among them. Taylor's men had joined him high in the Huachucas, and now, as they approached Camp Casey, MacGregor noticed the activity of men, unusual for this late hour. He turned to his sergeant with a very tired, "Looks like these Army boys are engaging in night maneuvers." Ten minutes later, the troops entered camp, drew up to the post corral, and the major asked the nearest soldier, "What's going on here, corporal?"

"Someone injured a scout, Sir."

"All this fuss over an injured scout?"

Laine stirred his horse to the front of the men. "Which scout?"

"It was Scout Talon, Sir. She is at the infirmary."

Laine turned his horse immediately toward the infirmary. Major MacGregor asked, "The scout was shot?"

"No Sir. I understand she was whipped."

"She?"

"Yes Sir. The scout is a she-male."

"Your commanding officer allowed this whipping?"

"The rumors are, Sir, that he's the one that whipped her." Then, as if he felt he had to explain, "He had a daughter killed by Comanches back in the 50's. Talon's a half-blood Comanche."

The major, coated in dust, grime, sweat, and a very short temper, climbed down from his big gray. "Is this the same Comanche Talon who had a standing execution order and a posted reward in two territories and the State of Texas?"

"That's our girl, major."

"She would probably have been better off hanging." Allowing the corporal to take the reins of his horse, he grumbled, "I thought we were arriving at a United States Army camp, not Spain of the Fifteenth Century. What's the name of the grand inquisitor here?"

"That would be Old Iron Ass...Major General Salem George Compton."

The chief scout, Bayani, wearing native Apache garb like the rest of his scouts, eased his horse beside the white major they all respected. His people didn't like the Comanche, and had even killed a few, but even they deserved the swiftness of a bullet or arrow to this kind of treatment. "Apache no take beat of whip. Leave first. Go back to Bowie."

"Your scouts certainly won't be whipped, Chief Bayani," the major assured him, "and I'll make that clear with Taylor at this damned little hell hole." Then he yelled, "Dismount, scouts," and his tired, disgruntled Apaches crawling down from equally tired horses.

* * *

Coated in trail dust and exhausted to the point of collapse, Laine rushed into the infirmary. Before he could approach the cot where Captain Calloway was tending to Talon's wounds, Nightwing grabbed his arm, halting him. "You not Officer of Scouts. I responsible for Scout. You stay away!" Laine Taylor savagely tore his arm from Nightwing and dropped beside the cot. His fingers moved tenderly, cautiously, under Talon's chin as he spoke her name. Her eyes opened. "Who did this, Talon?"

When she did not respond, Nightwing growled, "*Your general*. She said it him."

Laine cringed at the sight of the wounds criss-crossing her back. How many times had his hands moved over its smoothness as he held her to him? He arose, his jaw so taut he thought his bones would break. "I'll be back." Storming from the infirmary, he quickly found General Compton in his office, his booted feet propped on the corner of his desk. He appeared to be asleep at first, but when Laine entered, he opened his eyes. Then Laine saw the whip thrown carelessly to a side chair and a streak of dried blood on Compton's right hand. "You must be so proud of yourself. I'll never forgive you for this." Before Compton could question him, or Laine halt his rash action, his fist flew out from his side and struck Compton squarely on the chin.

Compton shot to his feet. "What is the meaning of this?"

"You whipped Talon!"

Surprise—and outrage at the accusation—darkened his

features. "I did no such thing!"

Laine grabbed up the whip. "You lying bastard! What is this? And whose blood is on your hand?"

Only then did Compton notice the thin streak of blood. "I— God Almighty, I *did not* whip that scout—I would *never* have whipped that scout!" He spoke uncommonly quiet for a man just assaulted by a junior officer. "Captain Taylor, you are under arrest." Summoning Private Wilson, who had followed the angry junior officer into HQ simply because he anticipated trouble, he ordered, "Take this man to confinement."

"No," Laine protested. "Damn you, let me be with her."

"If she has been hurt, she has *Indians*—her own kind—to be with her. You'll go to confinement while I find out who assaulted her," Compton ordered. "Now!" And to Wilson, "If this hotheaded officer bolts, private, you cut him down."

Wilson responded quietly, "Bloody unlikely, Sir." Standing ahead of the guard's rifle, Laine pivoted toward the guardhouse. As they closed the distance, Andy said, "Bully for you, Sir. I wish I'd struck the old bastard."

* * *

Talon was like a rag doll, tossed and hugged until it was limp and discarded. After Calloway retired for the night, leaving Talon to sleep, Nightwing rested his cheek against her dark hair and whispered, "I take care of you, my rude Comanche thief." She stirred against him, her combs loosened so that her hair cascaded, drawing his fingers into their rich depths...soft hair, like a white woman's, that he normally saw disguised in the twist of a single Indian braid. He drew her into his arms and held her gently.

Talon knew at once she was in Nightwing's embrace. She had been there before, and remembered his pleasant, musky scent. Moving her cheek ever so slightly against him, she whispered, "Do you care for me, Nightwing?"

He wanted to say *I love you, Talon. Want you to be my woman*. Rather, he replied, "I care for all scouts. It might be that I care for you much more. You strong woman with brave heart."

As merciful darkness reclaimed her, Talon knew

175

Nightwing's words were the greatest compliment he could give a woman...and a Comanche.

* * *

Compton stood on the parade field in the early morning hours. Just for a moment, Laine's assault allayed the grief he felt at knowing someone had brutally whipped the scout. It seemed that every damned soldier in camp was up and about, simply because the *female* had been hurt. Something about her tugged unmercifully at him. Across the field the scouts from Bowie were settling their horses, and soldiers wandered into the camp chapel. Occasionally, a soldier stopped to glare at him, his animosity transparent and mocking. Though he despised what Talon was—a Comanche—he admired her pride and indomitable courage.

Another man stood just out of his line of vision, Compton turned to the young soldier who'd escorted Laine to the guardhouse and snapped. "I suppose you got a whip waiting to bite into me?"

Andy Wilson hated what this man had done to the pretty Talon, and now to the captain who cared for her. It was all he could do to keep a civil tongue. "The major needs the formal nature of the captain's charges for his daily log."

"Assault on a ranking officer," Compton commented acridly. "That should suffice for the time being? I'll decide on court-martial later."

Wilson turned from him, paused, sucked a small breath between his teeth, and turned slowly back. "Can I be so bold, Sir, as to tell you to your face you are the cruelest man I ever met? You can whip me for telling the truth, but every man here feels likewise. I wouldn't want to be in your boots."

It had taken only five weeks for his reputation to slither among the outhouse muck. "I'm aware that my popularity has waned, Private."

"Your popularity is nonexistent, Sir."

Compton froze his vexation. "What's your name, private?"

Nervous ticks assailed a face too young for a straight razor, though he kept his voice strong and defiant. "Private Andrew

176

William Wilson. My friends call me Andy, but you can call me Private Wilson."

"I'd suggest if you plan to make the Army your career—Private Wilson—that you show more respect for your superiors in the future."

"If a superior deserves my respect, he'll sure get it." Wilson now retreated.

Turning toward his office, Compton spied the small pouch lying on the ground and picked it up. He recalled the hand sewn deerskin hugging Talon's chest in the guardhouse, and wondered what a Comanche half-breed considered important enough to keep so close to her? Trinkets and baubles—and charms to ward off evil? Though she carried white blood, she was still Indian, with an Indian's superstitions. What did he care about crow's feet, herbs, and wampum beads?

Crushing the pouch between his fingers, Compton felt its small contents through the leather. When he entered his office a few minutes later, he threw it among the clutter in the bottom drawer, the only one in his office that was not orderly to the point of obsession. But he removed it at once, dropped to his chair, and caressed it between his fingers. Why did thoughts of Talon touch him so deeply? Why, when he saw her, did he think of his daughter? Simply because she was Comanche, and of the tribe that had robbed him of his life's blood?

No, it went far beyond that.

She brought warmth and familiarity to his very thoughts. He heard Julia's voice when Talon spoke, remembered the last time his daughter had whispered, *I'm so happy, papa.* How was it possible two women so vastly different existed as one within him? Angry and frustrated by his thoughts, Compton again threw the pouch into the drawer. Then he dropped his face into his hands and quietly wept.

* * *

Waking every few minutes, Talon had a vague recollection of Nightwing carrying her back to her quarters and settling her onto her cot. She had heard his parting words, though she couldn't recall exactly what they were. That they were strangely

177

and uncharacteristically gentle echoed softly in her thoughts. As she sought sleep, morning light disappeared from the windows as a storm rolled over the post. Just before noon, the thunder came, distant at first, then all around her, a disruptive clamor shivering through her spine.

At some point in her sleep, Talon was vaguely aware of an annoying click...click, pause, shuffle...click, pause, shuffle, accompanied by very bright explosions of light and a noise that jarred her, though not enough to release her from the darkness holding her in its merciful embrace.

After the photographer sent by Major Stahl had departed, Nightwing sat very still in the straight back chair by the single window. Talon's small, childlike sobs stirred him to tears. The post physician had sent him with an ointment for the wounds, but he had brought an Indian poultice of yarrow and boiled anemone roots that he felt would be more effective in relieving her pain and hastening the healing. Not wishing to disturb her sleep, the best anesthetic for pain, he waited patiently for her to awaken.

He would no longer fight his longings. He wanted Talon, and he'd be damned if Taylor got her. He'd kill him, if he had to. Crossing the floor he placed his fingertips to her temple to check for fever. Talon stirred, and he withdrew his touch.

"Laine?"

Nightwing's breath caught conspicuously. He watched over Talon, and it was Taylor's name she whispered in her dreams. But his resentment passed at once, for Nightwing knew he had treated her only as a scout. Taylor had treated her as a woman when she most needed it, even if it had been a silly dance in a lamp-lit corral.

The tiniest moan escaped Talon's lips. Stirring to wakefulness, she would soon feel the bite of her wounds. "I bring poultice for you," he whispered. "You will not hurt so much." Moving the chair from its place by the window, he settled it next to the cot. The stone bowl with the poultice, covered by a square of damp cotton, sat on a table. He now removed the pan of water he had set on the stove and brought it to her. He eased the fabric and gauze from her wounds. Suddenly, she turned, one sleeve falling down her arm, offering him a full view of her firm, youthful breasts. Then she resettled and the vision was taken from him.

He forced himself to concentrate on her wounds. The whipping was bad, but he was confident it would not leave heavy scars, and any redness would fade over time. As he dampened the cloth and dabbed the wounds, Talon drew her arms beneath her chest to brace against the pain. She felt that shards of glass had been driven into her flesh, and the warm cloth, though gently applied, was considerably brutal. Then, giving no warning, she turned, tucked herself into Nightwing's arms and held him closely. Tears pressed from her pain-filled eyes. "Please don't hurt me anymore, Nightwing...please—"

He dropped the cloth into the bowl, his fingers spreading over the back of her dark, tousled hair. "The physician said wounds must be cleaned." He drew a deep breath, filling himself with her fragrance, and her sorrow. "Rest back on your pillow, sweet one, let me do what I must. I try not hurt you much."

Talon pulled from him just enough to see his eyes, to see the warmth, the compassion...and something else she'd never noticed before. The deepest sense of trust she'd felt—ever— filled her as completely as her pain. "All right, John." Again tucking her arms beneath her chest, she settled the right side of her face against the pillow. Nightwing's fingers lightly brushed her cheek, replaced very soon by the pressure of his full, masculine mouth in a comforting caress.

The unspoken affection swept through Talon like a prairie fire, and when his hands returned to her wounds, she felt only the wild, merciless pounding of her heart. Minutes later, when he patted the poultice of anemone and yarrow onto the cleaned wounds the pain stretching over her skin slowly subsided.

Flustered by the way his nearness stirred this alien trust and warmth within her, when they had been at odds from the beginning, Talon reached for a diversion. "Where is Taylor, Nightwing? Has he come to see me?" But even as she uttered the inquiry, a vague picture formed in her mind of Laine coming to her, asking her who had done this. Or had it been a dream?

Silence filled the space between them. He could tell Talon that Taylor was in the guardhouse, and unable to come to her. But was he willing to do that? He didn't feel that he was. "I not see Taylor after I bring you here."

Her heart could have stilled then. "Did he not return to camp?"

"He did—but he not come here." Then, "Talon, what means *Himeetu, Toko*? You speak words two times during night." Horrified to hear the Comanche words, *Why Grandfather*, Talon lost her voice. Nightwing did not pressure her for an answer. "I will know truth about Rock Bluff one day," he promised.

His persistence flared her temper, even as she felt too weak to nurture it to fruition. "I will not argue with you, Nightwing."

He finished applying the poultice, leaving her shirt unbuttoned so that the open air might hasten the healing. "Wounds not hurt so much now?"

"Not so much," she responded, her thoughts on the general. Easing to her left side, Talon tucked her bent arm beneath her head, looking softly to Nightwing. "I know nursing a mere female does not come easily to an Indian male, so I deeply thank you for helping me."

"Do not know this word *mere*, Talon. You must know I am not like most Apache."

"I do know that."

Nightwing sat very still for a moment, content to look at her. Rising to his full, impressive height, he met the quiet agony of her eyes, wishing they were black like his own, rather than a betrayal of her white blood. But he would always see her as Indian, her courage without equal. When Talon's fingers eased toward the pain of her right shoulder, Nightwing took her hand, halting her movements. "Let wounds heal. I leave you to rest. Later I bring food."

"No salt pork, no food—I will not want it."

"Sergeant's wife make big pot of soup. You need food to get strong and heal."

"No dog soup, Nightwing." She didn't see his smile as the

door closed, but instantly heard men's voices muffled among the claps of thunder, coming to her in waves. Whatever they said eluded her. All she wanted was sleep, and for time to pass away.

All she wanted was Laine Taylor.

Instinctively, Talon reached for the pouch containing the treasures of her mother. When she didn't find it, she thought that Nightwing must have removed it. Knowing it was precious to her, he would surely have put it in a safe place. So, she closed her eyes, believing her treasure secure with him. The storm continued, but its fury slowly faded as the darkness of sleep claimed her once again.

* * *

Nightwing had just stepped off the boardwalk when Major Stahl approached. An umbrella pointed to the sky above the major's head, an attire of the white officers Nightwing had always found amusing. Stahl moved toward Talon's quarters, so he blocked his path. Nightwing's size and stature, and now his bold refusal to allow a superior officer to step around him, halted the major at once. "Do not disturb scout."

Stahl settled his boots into the mud. He hated that Nightwing's commanding presence intimidated him, even after the years they had served together at this camp. "Did the photographer come as I instructed?"

"He come one hour ago. Why you want pictures of scout wounds?"

"In case we need them, Nightwing." Then, "I wish to give a report to Captain Taylor on your scout's condition."

Straight-eyed and tough, Nightwing paid little heed to the rain dripping from his own slick black hair. "Indian take care of Indian. Taylor not concern himself."

Stahl didn't need Nightwing's negation to realize he wouldn't be allowed to personally look in on the scout. The field had become slick in the rare torrent of rain. In a hurry now, Major Stahl slipped as he progressed toward the guardhouse, but did not lose his footing. One day he would find the courage to stand up to Nightwing.

But not today.

Thirteen

The Jesuit Mission of St. Ignacius, forty miles southwest of Rock Bluff, had long ago lost contact with its Roman Catholic mother church. One of its final missives from its organizers in Paris was that the mission was being dismantled and its priests recalled. The active rebellion that followed, as the mission refused to disband, resulted in official denouncement by Rome.

In the twenty years since, the brothers had stayed on, expanded the mission, and continued its missionary work, developing a good rapport with the Indian tribes with whom they traded garden vegetables and grain for venison and cured rawhide. The mission had suffered no deaths due to hostilities in the past four years. That Camp Casey was within a day's ride also offered some assurances that peaceful times would continue.

Brother Jeremy watched the flurry of activity in the garden. Exhaling a small sigh, he pulled his brown hood over his head as he prepared to enter. Though it was a little early for their spring planting of vegetables, several of the women had taken advantage of the first fairly warm day to till fresh manure into the rows, while their children scampered around them.

The women seldom recognized Sunday as an official day of rest, which the brothers had grown to accept without quarrel. He sought out one woman in particular, and on seeing her, hurried in her direction. On her knees with her bonnet cast off, she broke the ground in a particularly hard spot with a small hand trowel, one gloved hand rising to brush hair from her cheek.

"There you are." He bent slightly to scrutinize her work.

She smiled tiredly. "Have you come to help, Brother?"

"Ask me again tomorrow."

Her eyes lifted, reflecting a melancholy Jeremy had grown to recognize. "No work on Sunday, Brother Jeremy?"

Holding out his hands, he laughed, "No, it is just that I

cleaned my fingernails and don't want to dirty them again so soon."

Julia Rose Compton smoothed out the white apron that had done little to guard her dress against the dirt as she arose, and looked toward her benefactor. Brother Jeremy was a tall, square-jawed man who walked haltingly, due to an arrow taken in his knee many years ago. Despite the handicap, he was strong and nervously energetic. "What can I do for you, Brother?"

As they walked through the garden, Jeremy thought again how pretty she was, her skin pale, with her flashing blue eyes, flaxen hair, and willowy movements. When he had seen her for the first time—ten years ago—she had been half-dead, her hair hacked off very near her skull, and not expected to live more than a few weeks at most. He—all the brothers—knew that her determination to see her daughter again had kept her alive then.

It kept her alive now.

"What are you thinking, brother?"

Jeremy cast off his thoughts at once. "You seem a bit sad this morning."

"Just an uneasy feeling I've had since waking."

"About your daughter?"

"A mother's intuition, I suppose."

"One day you'll see your child again." Jeremy patted her hand, then instantly began filling her in on the present situation. "A Comanche at the gate said soldiers are after him and requests sanctuary at the mission. He claims he doesn't understand our meaning when we ask him about the crimes that set the soldiers on his heels. Will you talk to him?"

Julia's fingers closed instinctively over her gloves, which hid the tattoos of her abductors many years ago. "I hardly think a Comanche would request sanctuary among the Jesuits." Her footfalls now progressed with less enthusiasm. "Did he say he was Comanche?"

"He wears the bandanna of the Comanche."

The thought that a Comanche was just a wall away stirred the horrid memories Julia had tried for years to suppress. The years after she lost her child had taken their toll on her physically and spiritually. Then came the day the women of the village had thought she was dead, and two old men took her to be buried in the hills. They had dug the hole before discovering she was still alive. Rather than return her to the village where her sister-in-law, Spotted Face, would have continued to torment her, they had taken her thirty miles to a camp of mining wagons. The sympathetic miners had kept her with them as they moved northwest across New Mexico territory. When they reached Arizona Territory, and with her health little improved, she was left at the Jesuit Mission of St. Ignacius to die.

"You're deep in thought, Julia."

Her hand moved over Brother Jeremy's wrist in sweet affection. "And you know me well enough, Brother, that Talon is always the thought I'm so deeply into."

Jeremy dropped his eyes. He had heard just recently that Julia's father, Salem Compton, was the new commanding officer at Camp Casey, something he had wanted to pass on to Julia. But she had told him years ago she could never return to her father, who would never understand her marriage to a Comanche she had truly loved, and that she didn't want him to know she was alive. It had troubled him all those years ago when they'd first talked, and it troubled him today, simply because he'd always thought that her father would be able to find her daughter for her.

Moments later, Julia spoke to the Indian. The Apache youth who claimed he had ridden across the Arizona desert from its border with California, had taken the Comanche bandanna from an arrow-riddled corpse on the desert. Julia reported their conversation to Brother Jeremy. "He has no family, and he certainly isn't Comanche. May I suggest that you offer him sanctuary for two weeks, and if he's cooperative that you send him with Michael Whitecloud to work the sheep on the Patterson ranch? Nettie Patterson has more lambs this year than expected, and could use an extra man to protect the herd at night. The cattle ranchers are giving her a bad time, though the sheep never graze off Nettie's land. Jessie complains a good bit about his foot, so hasn't been able to help much."

"That's the Indian boy Nettie found abandoned in the bluffs about eight years ago? What is he now, ten—eleven?" Julia simply nodded. "And Nettie's consumption is under control?"

"For the time being. But she is still very ill."

"We should all pray for this good woman." Then, "Your suggestion is a very good one. Thank you once again."

Brother Jeremy retreated to his prayers, and Julia returned to the garden, where she toiled with her Indian sisters until the dinnertime bell peeled across evening twilight. For a moment after stilling her labors, she looked to her special star, the bright, twinkling one just to the east of the moon.

Talon's star.

* * *

Talon didn't stir when Compton approached her bed.

As the clouds suddenly parted outside the high window, a shaft of light fell on the weals across her slender back. How could any man at this camp think he had personally done this? The horror caused him to retreat, and he settled into the chair by a small table, where a kerosene lamp burned low. His attention captured by the tidy row of books along the rear of the table, he looked at them absently, surprised to see one opened to a poem by Wardsworth he had often read to Julia. He thought about the afternoon at Camp Davis, as he had nervously awaited the Santa Fe Stage. Samuel Lytton had teased him for his anxiety, and somberly walked with him just half an hour later to the administration building where he learned of the attack on the coach. An elderly female passenger and two male passengers had been killed and horribly mutilated. The driver had been shot several times before crawling into the foothills with his revolver and a pair of rifles to fend off the attack. His daughter, her cousin from Boston, and a third woman whose name he had never known, had been carried away by the Comanche marauders.

Talon's hand suddenly moved toward a small table. Struggling to grasp a tin cup, she managed only to spill its contents to the floor. Just yesterday she had run with the Apaches in a rambunctious game of lacrosse. Now she hadn't even the strength to hold a cup of water to her lips. Without hesitation, Compton rose and refilled the cup from a small pitcher, and his fingers moved beneath her chin to hold her head up. Her hand moved over his in an instinctive effort to hold the cup herself.

Talon took several sips of water before her hand fell away, and her eyes lifted to his in the dark shadows. "Thank you, *Toko*."

The small, unknown word caught him off guard. A pet name for her chief, perhaps? Said with such gentle affection that she stirred a rare warmth in his heart. His hand went out, halting just short of smoothing the damp tendrils of hair against her forehead. How pretty she was...how she trembled...

This was his fault...he had made her hurt...if he had not ordered the flogging, the madman who did this would not have thought of it...

Then, just as he might have fallen to his knees to beg her forgiveness for his cruelties, his hatred, never more than a heartbeat away, returned with brutal force. Talon was Comanche, of the people who had robbed him of his most prized treasure...his flaxen-haired daughter just fifteen years old...a dear girl who had entered eternity without ever having known what it was like to be in the full bloom of womanhood. Withdrawing into the stormy night, so many emotions struggled within him he could scarcely breathe.

* * *

Andy Wilson was half nodding off at the duty desk later that night. When a slow-moving shadow caressed the semi-darkened wall outside the guard room, he rose and approached the door. Talon, her fingers embracing the bars at the door of general confinement, folded gently to the floor. By the time Wilson reached her, she had dropped her forehead to her arm, content to sit there, as close to Lainé Taylor as she could possibly get. The captain, asleep at the far side of the cell, had not stirred.

"Miss Talon, what're you doin' here?" Her eyes were so filled with pain as she looked to him that Wilson was moved to tears.

"He didn't come to me today...he must be locked up again."

Helping Talon to her feet, he unlocked and held the door for her. "You go to him if that's what you want." Andy didn't care that he would be subject to disciplinary action if caught. Talon had found the strength to follow her heart to Captain Taylor, and he wouldn't stand in her way.

Talon's steps were as quiet as falling feathers, so that she closed the distance to the cot, and eased along Laine's length just as he stirred to wakefulness. Her hand eased softly beneath the fabric of his open shirt and settled on his chest just as he detected her.

Laine instantly pressed a kiss to her warm, moist forehead. "My poor little girl," he whispered, his fingers covering hers atop his chest. Her breathing was slow and pained, and so wispy against his cheek that he hardly felt it. Small moans escaped her lips every now and then.

He held her for a long while, the silence broken by the silken stir of her breath. Very gently he vowed, "I love you, Talon, more than I could ever have imagined. One day, if you will have me, I want you to be my wife." She had heard his words, and she smiled. But before she might respond, a harsh, familiar voice resonated, answered by Andy Wilson's softer, more patient one, and the light tred of boot steps paused conspicuously just beyond his line of sight. The tall, overbearing shadow of John Nightwing held the corridor wall outside the cell for a few minutes. He was angry, no doubt, and here to take Talon from him. Laine's palm sweeping to her flushed cheek, he pressed the softest kiss to her hairline.

Talon stirred ever so slightly against him, her cheek brushing his as she whispered vows of love against his ear in a language he understood only through her soft sincerity.

Then Andy Wilson unlocked the cell door.

* * *

The Sioux words Talon had spoken to Taylor roused strong emotion in Nightwing. He pressed to the shadows, cursing her sentiments, and hating the white officer to whom she had spoken

187

them. Drawing a deep breath to calm his anger, he approached the cot and looked down on them, his hard, dark gaze meeting Taylor's quiet one. His tone was graveled and harsh. "I take Scout back to quarters now."

Laine was reluctant to let her go. "She said something to me while you were nearby. Tell me what she said."

Because he wanted Talon for his own, he wouldn't admit to his rival the endearments she had spoken. "Talon said she much trouble, that you better not be with her. She said after this night, you will not see each other again, except as duty calls."

The mantel of Laine's strength crumbled. "I don't believe she said that."

"Truth sometime hurt, Taylor. I am sorry, but I speak her words." Talon stirred, and Nightwing slipped his arms beneath her knees and the small of her back, easily lifting her away from Laine. Her dark, loose hair fell softly against his shoulder.

"No, Nightwing, let me stay with him." But she had no strength to struggle from his arms.

Sweeping his boots to the floor, anger sharpened Laine's words. "And you say she doesn't want to be with me? You lying, redskin son-of-a-bitch."

Nightwing left then, and Wilson, fearing that the captain might go after him, hastily locked the door. Laine wasn't sure how long he would be confined, but he thought Nightwing could do a lot of damage to his relationship with Talon, if he had a mind to. He had just proven he had that mind.

Laine tried to impress the Sioux words Talon had spoken to him into his brain, but they were as mixed up as his thoughts right now. Strangled by rage, he shot to his feet, his fingers ripping through the hair at his temples. He wanted out of this blasted cell.

* * *

Talon slept around the clock for the next three and a half days, but was always aware of Nightwing's presence. She remembered calling for Laine, and Nightwing's cross words she couldn't now recall echoing behind his name. Finally, late Wednesday evening, she stirred to full wakefulness, with a

188

sleep-induced headache and a starving stomach. The small lamp at her reading table had been left lit, and Dora half-nodded at the table. "Dora?" She looked toward Talon, smiling at once. "I think I am going to live," Talon managed with a smile, and her friend came to her. "General Compton, is he all right?"

Dora thought she must be delirious to be asking about the dreadful man who was responsible for these injuries. "None of us should care about him. It's poor Captain Taylor we should worry about, locked in the guardhouse since he struck the old coot." Talon did not at once remember going to Laine in the guardhouse, and recalled the times she'd asked Nightwing about him these past three days, because he had not come to her. She was suddenly furious with him. "Forty Apache scouts arrived from Fort Bowie Sunday," Dora continued with mundane camp news. "Seven are in the guardhouse for drunk and disorderly, shooting off their pistols, and hitting Major Harris's walleyed mare. The Indian only grazed it, a slight flank wound, but Major Harris is furious."

She'd have preferred any number of other news items to a grazed horse and unruly Apaches, but allowed Dora to catch her up to date on events at camp. She spoke largely about Nightwing, and his loyalty to her these past few days.

She was grateful for his care, but Talon didn't want to hear anything about Nightwing right now.

Between the anxious chatter, Talon spent the better part of an hour convincing Dora that she needed time alone. After a while, she consented. When she was alone, Talon sat up, noticing that the last bits of wood glowed in the stove. Crossing the floor, her legs were so completely without strength she supported herself on the furniture. Finally she refreshed the stove.

Now she fetched her brush from atop the small bureau, making a cursory search for her pouch as she did so. Failing to locate it, she made a mental note to ask Nightwing about it, because losing her mother's treasures worried her immensely. As a diversion, Talon sat at the table and tried to brush her hair, but the wounds halted her efforts. Wearing a loose white gown that stank of perspiration, she searched for something clean from the bureau, slipping the bolt at the top of her door to ensure a few private moments while she was nude. She brought the bowl to her bed and gently bathed her skin before drying off and pulling on a fresh gown.

Talon watched the late afternoon sun gently sink, leaving a gray pall visible through the small window. She wasn't sure what day it was, but her stomach grumbled with hunger. Burying herself in a sweet little novel by Elizabeth Phelps, the hours eased into the late evening. She had propped open the door for fresh air, but not so much as a breeze moved behind the remnants of a storm she only vaguely recalled.

Footfalls on the steps outside drew her attention.

* * *

Laine lay flat on his back, one wrist lying across his forehead and his boots crossed at the ankles. He had thought only of Talon...her raven tresses and sea green eyes...her full, moist lips slightly parting as she fought one of those funny little smiles. He wanted to feel the warmth of her skin, enjoy the rise of her womanly curves against his chest, to hear the echo of her laughter, or even a little fire flaring from her defiant mouth. He wanted to tell her again how much he loved her, just in case she hadn't believed him the first time.

Then, amidst the bawdy laughter of the Bowie Apaches confined in another cell, he was suddenly aware of another person.

Compton cleared his throat, making his presence known. Easing one eyelid open Laine peered from beneath his wrist, then drew to a seated position and to his feet. With one hand tucked into his beltline, he said nothing. He could not see Compton's eyes, which were masked in shadows.

"I believe you owe me an apology, Captain."

"Do I, Sir?" He noticed Compton's still swollen chin and fading bruise.

"You do...if you're interested in avoiding a court-martial, which would certainly be a black mark on a military career that has, until this camp, been impeccable."

"In addition to my apology, what other conditions do you set?"

"First is that your promotion to major is suspended indefinitely."

"That's a relief. I thought you'd have me flogged."

The sarcasm pricked unmercifully at Compton's mood. "For your information, I did not whip that scout. Yes, I picked up the whip on the step, but I did not whip her."

"She said that you did."

"She is mistaken. Whoever is responsible must have fled before I got to her door."

"And why were you at her door?"

Compton growled, "That is none of your concern," and refused to admit that he intended to speak to her about her morals. "I will find out who did this to the scout." Compton settled to a cot several feet away. "There are other conditions to be considered before I release you."

"I suppose I must keep my distance from the savage Comanche?"

Compton was torn. There was something about Talon that he wanted to admire, even to care for...but she was of the hated Comanche tribe, and he wanted her gone from Camp Casey for that reason alone. "I prefer that you not see her again...except as duty calls."

Laine's fingers twisted through the bars, his eyes narrowed thoughtfully. "I don't suppose you knew Talon was the child of a white captive whose choices were taken from her, just as they would have been taken from your daughter had she lived?"

Surprise jumped into Compton's ruddy features. "I knew her mother had white blood, but no, I didn't know she was a captive. I thought a voluntary union produced the heathen child "

"The *heathen child* is the *only* person at this camp who would put her own life on the line for you. God only knows why."

"The woman is Comanche, and her savage tribe killed my daughter. She'd hardly put her life on the line for me...or for any white man!" Compton was troubled by the widespread discord among the soldiers here, and the immense popularity of the scout Talon. Since Sunday night, after a death threat was slipped beneath the door of HQ, two guards had been assigned to his quarters.

Laine continued, "You told me once that your wife died weeks after injuries sustained by falling from her horse, and that your daughter was injured in the same fall. You loved your wife, and yet you do not hate all horses. Why, then, hate all Comanches?"

Compton stood, stepping out of the partial shade so that his ruddy features were in full view to Laine. The glaze of unshed tears, held back only by hatred, flickered across his eyes. "A horse does not set out to deliberately kill. A Comanche does. I'll hear no more of my wife and daughter from you." Turning from Laine, his tone mellowed. "Will you apologize for striking me and abide by my conditions in exchange for leniency?"

"I'm sorry I struck you, Sir." If another lie would win his freedom, he was willing to resort to it. "I'll keep my distance from the savage, butchering Comanche for the time being."

Damned sarcasm. "Your apology is accepted. And you'll keep your distance, not just tomorrow, or the day after that, but permanently, until I can find a way to get the young woman off this post."

"How do you know I won't go to her when I'm free?"

"Because, Sir, I have hired a civilian to kill her if you do." Though he had spoken to the muleskinner hanging around the camp, that he had hired him to kill Talon was an absolute lie. But he could tell by the sudden fear in Laine's eyes that he believed him.

"Son-of-a-bitch! Even *you* wouldn't be so heartless."

"Trust me, I am that heartless." Then, "Will you go to her, captain?"

"No, of course not, you bastard."

Compton harshly snapped, "Duty Sergeant, unlock this door." Laine pulled on his boots and picked up his uniform jacket, which he slung across his shoulder. He was instantly aware that the stench of alcohol and filth emanating from

Mulroney was stronger than usual. An ugly sneer—as though he knew something no one else knew—marred his pocked face. Outside the guardhouse moments later, Laine parted company with Compton without words.

As Compton merged into the cover of dark, Laine entered his quarters, finding the parlor stove lit and the large room much too warm on this balmy night. Someone—most likely Compton's orderly—had prepared a hot bath. Compton had known he would want out of the guardhouse badly enough to agree to keep away from Talon. He had agreed only because of the death threat. He no longer knew what Compton was capable of.

The old man had never been so controlling. It had been years since he'd had an opportunity to persecute a Comanche on a daily basis, and to make an innocent life hell.

Shedding his clothing, Laine sank into the tub. Briskly scrubbing his skin with a bar of lye soap, he cursed Compton's unreasonable hatred, this threat to keep him apart from Talon, and wished the old bastard would return to Washington.

* * *

That Nightwing had not answered her questions about Laine filled Talon with tremendous resentment. Recalling a vague dream in which she'd gone to him in the guardhouse, she almost felt his arms around her, felt the touch of his mouth against her damp forehead. How could Nightwing have denied her even the gentle sound of his name, and assurances that only his arrest had kept him from her?

Just then, Nightwing knocked lightly, entered her quarters, and placed a covered bowl on the table where she sat. Never would he have left her this afternoon if he hadn't been in need of sleep. After Dora's brief visit, he'd cleaned and detailed his weapons in these few hours he had respected Talon's right to the privacy Dora said she needed. "Soup from sergeant's wife," he announced, "Eat while still hot."

"Thank you," she replied, her voice ruefully quiet as she uncovered the bowl and set the spoon into the steaming liquid. "I can never repay you for taking care of me."

"Get better will be repay enough. Need scout back in

193

troop." He watched as she absently twirled the spoon in the soup without eating. "Something trouble you, Scout? Soup not good?"

Talon's movements stilled, the soup remaining untouched as she looked to him. "You should have told me Taylor was locked up, Nightwing. I asked about him a number of times and you let me wonder why he did not come to me."

So. She did not remember going to him—or her vow— *With every shred of my being, every beat of my heart, the fullest depths of my soul, I love you.* Words he wanted Talon to speak to him, and not that pampered white bastard. "Wounds need to heal," he replied soberly. "If I remind you about guardhouse, you would worry about him and take longer to heal."

His explanation made sense, she supposed, though she still felt he had betrayed her trust. Rather than argue—or flaunt a lack of appreciation for his care—she willfully changed the subject. "Where did you put the pouch I always wear, Nightwing? I looked but could not find it."

He didn't know where it was, or remember seeing it around her neck when he took her back to her quarters after the doctor took care of her at the infirmary. Discovering it lost would upset her, and he thought her health a much more important issue. "Cord come loose. Put in pocket, left in quarters. Do not worry." Lying came easily to him now, and he thought Taylor was certainly responsible for that uncharacteristic flaw.

Believing the pouch safe, Talon returned her attentions to her hunger. "I hope this is not dog soup."

Without a smile, Nightwing flicked his index finger at the bowl. "Not dog. Poor murdered cow." Bowing to his persistence, Talon sipped the soothing liquid, avoiding the small pieces of beef, and when she settled the spoon into the bowl minutes later felt much better, and even a little stronger. Nightwing now brought up another subject. "About Dako, much upset that general hurt you. Dako much drunk, say he go to Compton's quarters...kill him. I lock him in storeroom and give daily reports to him. He like you, Talon...worry much, too."

An extended hand invited Nightwing to her side, her fingers lightly covering his wrist. "Bring Dako to me this evening."

Nightwing dropped to one knee before her, drawing her into his arms. His affection surprised Talon yet again. "When you first come to camp, I say you rude Comanche thief, you be much trouble, better for Colonel Heitman to hang you. I not mean it. You are treasure, Talon Rose. I knew that even then." Then he stood in one easy move and turned his back to her as he prepared to retreat. "I bring Dako later."

Out of doors, Nightwing paused to pull in a deep breath, to still the rapid pace of his heart that her nearness had stirred. Every day he wanted her more, and every day his hatred for the white officer who had her heart grew stronger.

Turning his concentration to Talon's pouch, he thought only of pleasing her. If it had fallen when he took her to the infirmary, it might still be there, blending unobtrusively into the earth.

* * *

Laine stood on the covered porch of his quarters, appeasing his anger in a shot of brandy. Was Compton serious when he said he'd have Talon killed? Looking to the scout's quarters, partially obscured from his view by the single ash tree, he noticed a shard of light emerge as Nightwing left Talon's quarters. Setting his brandy glass aside, he stepped off the porch to go after him.

Nightwing had merged into the darkness. Laine found him, palms on his knees as he carefully searched the ground, lit only by the pale glow of lamps emitting from the officers' quarters. "You've lost something, Chief?"

John Nightwing drew up abruptly. "I thought you in guardhouse, Taylor."

Though he disliked Nightwing immensely, his deceptive nature, and was perturbed that he refused to address him by rank, softness entered Laine's voice. "How is Talon?"

"Talon not your business," he responded rudely. "She not wish to see you again."

"That's a damned lie, Nightwing. I love Talon, and I believe she loves me. You know that, too, or you wouldn't have lied

195

about what she said the other night."

"I tell truth. You do not like truth."

"I won't argue with a blatant liar." Then, "What were you looking for just now?"

"Why you care, Taylor?" Every inflection in Nightwing's tone betrayed his hatred for Taylor. Not only had he called him a liar, but he was a *blatant* one, and he didn't know what the hell kind of liar that made him. "If any of your business, something lost. Thought it might be here."

A guard passing on his rounds halted abruptly. "I don't mean to eavesdrop, Chief Nightwing, but late Sunday night I saw Old Iron, uh, the general pick up a little thing attached to a cord."

"The pouch Talon wears," Laine reasoned at once. "Is that what you're looking for?"

"I am," Nightwing replied, a grumble settling into his tone. "It important to her."

The guard continued his rounds.

"I know you and I have our differences," Laine kept his tone polite with great effort, "and you don't want me with Talon. But if you have any decency, Nightwing, tell her if Compton found the pouch, I'll get it back for her. And tell her—" No, he wouldn't let Nightwing know about the threat, and chance the disclosure getting back to Compton.

Nightwing nodded his response, turning toward his quarters. He really wasn't in a mood to give Taylor the time of day, let alone take his messages to the woman he was determined to keep from him.

Fourteen

At his quarters, Nightwing made sure he hadn't absently slipped Talon's pouch into the pocket of the uniform he had been wearing Sunday morning. He hadn't, so Compton must have it. Now, he passed through the cots of his sleeping scouts, toward the small storage room where Dako had been locked these past three days. Dako squatted against the wall with his eyes closed, his wrists across his bent knees. He had not touched the supper Nightwing had brought him earlier in the evening. Crouching before him, Nightwing allowed a quiet moment to pass until Dako acknowledged him only by opening his eyes. Anger at being confined was still strong within him. "Talon ask to see you."

The dark-skinned Apache looked swiftly to Nightwing, speaking his first words in three days. "Talon—she not mad with me—that I want kill general?"

"She will tell you that herself."

The short, muscular Indian eased up the wall and stepped around Nightwing. "We go now." Moments later, when they stood at the bottom of the steps to Talon's quarters, Dako expressed his reluctance to enter. "If she hate me, I do not want to hear."

Nightwing had pushed open the door when Talon called, "Come in," and now stood aside for Dako. Seeing Dako, Talon's eyes brightened and her hands went out to him. She was only too aware of his hesitation as he crossed the chamber to ease his hands into hers. He stared at the floor, too ashamed to meet her eyes.

"Dako, do you have any idea how dear you are to me?"

Tears moistened his black eyes. "I get drunk...say will kill general. You not hate Dako?"

A warm laugh slid from her mouth. "I could *never* hate you. You did not mean what you said. You were just upset because of what the general did."

Dako pressed Talon's fingers to his forehead, holding them there while he spoke. He did mean it—he still meant it. "All scout love Talon like *shilah*—like sister. Have much respect, much trust." As he drew himself up, he lowered her hands to gently squeeze them.

"That means more to me than you will ever know. Now...may I ask a small favor?"

"Will do anything for Talon."

"Promise you will not ever hurt General Compton."

Wanting the white bastard dead—and determined he would find a way to accomplish it—Dako didn't want to make this promise. Thus, his reply was very reluctant. "Dako promise." Turning to Nightwing, he smiled for the first time in days. "Not have lock me up no more. Go back barracks, sleep, be on horse tomorrow. I keep promise to Comanche."

Nightwing was proud of the words Talon had spoken to his childhood friend. His hand swept out, Dako left, and another moment passed before he spoke. "You take rest of week to get strong." Talon would've been back on her horse tomorrow if he'd required it. She was glad he didn't, simply because she preferred not to mingle with the new scouts until she'd regained her strength. "I check wounds now."

Talon turned in the chair and scooted the fabric down her arms.

Nightwing noticed again how slim and pretty were her shoulders as she freed her back of the thick masses of her hair, and how she modestly clutched the blouse to her breasts. He wouldn't tell her he had already seen them, that he had found them beautiful and womanly. The wounds were dry, without redness, and the scabs thin. Though the marks would slowly fade, he didn't believe she'd have permanent scars. Closing his hands over her arms, he paused before drawing the fabric up. "Wounds fine. Heal quick."

Though she had not found Nightwing's caress unpleasant, his were not the hands she wanted to touch her. "I can never thank you enough for your attention to me, Nightwing, and for the way you have cared."

"I find way for you to thank," he replied, then withdrew into the noiseless night.

* * *

Two days later, Laine decided to end Compton's tyranny, even if it cost him his military career. He remained at his desk in the adjutant's office for an hour past his usual quitting time of six, then arose, straightened his jacket, drew in a breath of grit and determination, and entered Compton's office. He slouched at his desk, his right index finger bent against his mouth in thoughtful silence. Since he had learned to read the rebellion in Laine's boot falls, he didn't bother to look around. "What is it, Taylor?"

Laine clasped the back of a chair with nervous vexation, grabbing at diversions before posing the subject that had brought him here. "You picked up something last Sunday morning belonging to Talon. She wants it back."

A tense moment passed between them. "Have you seen her contrary to my orders?"

"I have not seen her."

"Then I don't know what the hell you're talking about."

"One of the guards saw you pick up her pouch on the parade ground Sunday night."

"Oh, that." Whipping a condemning glance toward Taylor, he asked, "Was it hers?"

"It *is* hers."

"You have dropped the formality of addressing your commanding officer as sir?" And before Laine might respond, "She should've taken better care to protect it."

"She was hurt—hardly the time to guard her valuables."

The frequency of Taylor's sarcasm, especially now that he thought they had settled this particular problem, grated miserably on his nerves. "Gone to the burn pile."

"Don't punish her further by keeping it from her." He waited a few seconds for Compton's response, but when none came approached the window and looked out on the descending day. "I've had time to think these past few days," Laine reflected

199

thoughtfully, his back still to Compton, "I won't obey your edict to keep away from Talon. I love her and plan to marry her if she'll have me. I'll request a transfer from here so you won't have to see her again."

"I told you what would happen if you don't leave her alone."

Laine spun toward him now. "I don't believe you would kill Talon. I've known you a number of years. You've always been a kind, considerate man—as long as one isn't unfortunate enough to be born Comanche. So I don't believe you're so heartless as to cause an innocent woman's death simply to keep me away from her."

Compton turned his chair. "Roan!" At once, his young clerk stepped from the darkened corridor. "Take word to the man at the Conestoga outside camp to see me posthaste." When Roan retreated, Compton cut a measured look toward a man who had shown nothing but contempt toward him for weeks. "Sit. Make yourself comfortable."

"I prefer to stand." The childish disobedience gave him some small ration of control. In the few minutes that passed, Compton's mood was like dynamite waiting to explode, Laine deliberately fueling it with his silence. Now a door opened, and Roan's voice sifted through the stillness. In a dozen seconds, a large man in filthy, ragged brown clothing, barely recognizable as a human being through massive facial hair, filled the open doorway. His eyes, bloodshot from drink, carried only a trace hint of gray color.

Compton swiveled in his chair. "I told you about Captain Taylor when we spoke yesterday, did I not?" As the man entered, the stench of decay and filth saturated the confined air. He merely nodded. "Tell my adjutant here the deal we made."

"You tol' me, Sir, if the adjutant at this camp and the female scout is seen together, I'm to cut her throat while she sleeps."

"Son-of-a-bitch!" Laine's expletive commanded the attention of both men.

But Teakle grinned, enjoying the young officer's moment

of stunned rage. "I'm plannin' to love on the sweet brown filly first," Teakle said, grinning. "Them Injuns—they sure hot in all the right places." Laine tensed noticeably, Teakle grinning again.

As Teakle turned his back to him, Laine pulled his revolver. "You...muleskinner." Teakle turned to face the pointed weapon without as much as a flinch. "You should also leave instructions for your burial, because if you go near Talon, I'll kill you."

"You better be ready to fire that thing, cap'n," Teakle returned the threat, quickly pulling what he fondly called his "Arkansas toothpick" from his beltline. The tip of the black handled Bowie, thrown with precision, caught Laine's revolver. Tearing it from his fingers, the pain of the assault hurled from Laine's mouth in a string of curses. "Next time, I won't aim for y'er gun. Got any arguments, Cap'n Taylor?"

"Only a fool argues with a skunk or a muleskinner and you are both." Laine held a hand trembling with pain against his waistline. "Every man at this camp cares for Talon, and despises that smug bastard sitting there. When I spread word he's hired you to kill Talon, you won't have time to say your prayers."

"Not that I do a lot of prayin' anyway, Cap'n Taylor, an' I'll deny any such hirin' took place." Teakle grinned again, revealing surprisingly straight white teeth. His menacing opaque eyes slightly narrowed as he approached to retrieve his favorite knife from the floor, politely handing Laine's revolver back to him. "I watch my back jes' fine."

Compton had risen sometime in the past half minute and now got between the two men. Teakle approached the door and Compton snapped, "Stay, Teakle. Taylor, *you* leave." Laine reholstered his revolver with his left hand, his furious eyes holding Compton as he withdrew. When he was sure Laine was out of hearing range, Compton warned, "Don't you *ever* again threaten Captain Taylor with a weapon." He approached and slid the window open to allow fresh air into the room. A slight stir of dry, warm air did not dissipate Teakle's stench. "As I told you yesterday when we spoke, my warning still stands. If you go near Scout Talon, or hurt her in any way, not only will you not get paid, but I'll kill you myself. Taylor will only stay away from her if he thinks she's in danger."

"Yeah, so you tol' me. Said you had a special feelin' for her, but don't rightly know what it is." He dug food from his teeth with a long, dirty fingernail. "I seen her...an' I know what it is. Them long brown legs goin' all the way up—"

Compton spun toward him, his features ruddy with surprise and rage. "I have *no* such feelings for the Comanche, you filthy-minded bastard."

"Whatever you say, Sir." Then, "When I leave here camp I want them twenty half eagles you promised me for lyin' to the cap'n. None of that worthless paper."

Compton opened a drawer and flung a small sack with the eagles inside. Teakle swooped it up. "You're dismissed."

"Ain't your servant. I'll politely leave so you won't have to dismiss me like one."

"And don't cause any trouble at this camp while you're here."

"Fact is I got me a drinkin' chum works over in the guardhouse. So this filthy-minded bastard'll just mosey over to the sutler's bar, have some tarantula juice, an' stay out'a trouble."

Tarantula juice. The term for whiskey was regional, and scurrilous. "You just let me know if Taylor goes near the Comanche."

Teakle flipped a dirty hat back from his forehead. "Nice doin' business with you."

* * *

Later that evening, Nightwing stepped up to the porch of Taylor's quarters. Lightly knocking, he waited a full minute for the door to open. The ex-Officer of Scouts reeked of brandy. His uniform shirt was unbuttoned, outside the waist of his trousers, and heavily soiled by perspiration. He also had a carelessly bandaged right hand. "It Friday, Taylor. You not send word you speak to general about Talon's pouch."

Laine turned, retrieved his brandy from a small table, and quietly gulped the amber liquid. "Compton said he threw it away."

Nightwing stepping into the large, sparsely furnished room. "You think he did?"

This blasted Indian was possibly the last person on earth Laine wanted to be talking to right now. He imagined Talon had not received the message he'd asked him to relay Wednesday night. "He keeps it from her simply to be spiteful." Approaching a small credenza, he poured another drink.

"You barely stand up now, Taylor," Nightwing reminded him. "Do you need that?"

Fury was like a torch in Laine's eyes as they turned to Nightwing. "I won't be lectured by you on my drinking habits. The pot calling the kettle black."

Nightwing wasn't sure what pots and kettles had to do with drinking whiskey.

Laine dropped to the chair, the glass tumbling, spilling the liquid to the floor. As the Indian withdrew, Laine politely spoke his name, halting his retreat. "Keep a close watch on Talon. I can't give you the details, but she's in danger."

Silence rippled between them for half a dozen seconds before Nightwing spoke. "No man at camp harm Talon. Why I believe what you tell me?"

"Yes, Nightwing...there is one." Laine sat forward now. "Protect her, and stop being an argumentative ass. Can't you see we're on the same side here?"

Strangely, Nightwing *did* believe him, and silently admonished himself for placing even this small degree of trust in him. "I keep scout safe." He withdrew, stood on the porch of Laine's quarters and quieted the tremble within. A minute later, he knocked at Talon's quarters, where she read at the small table. She was almost too pretty this evening, her hair free and full, settled over her shoulders like thunderclouds. She wore the loose white gown that was much too big for her.

As she looked to him, he paused to collect his thoughts. Bending to one knee before her, he crossed his arms on his raised knee. "I did not pick up pouch, leave at quarters and forget to bring to you. Compton picked it up Sunday night. Taylor said he threw it away."

Fear twisted through her, rushing to her eyes like a raging fire. "I do not want to lose my mother's things, but would rather believe he threw it away. If he kept it, he might one day—" He saw panic in her features.

Confusion darkened Nightwing's strong, lean features. He couldn't believe she bordered on such a strong emotion over a missing pouch. "True treasures of mother—memories—always be yours. No one take from you."

Tears glistened, and when Nightwing's finger gently rose to flick them away, she pressed affectionately against his touch. "My life has turned so topsy-turvy. How will I survive?"

"Do not know this funny word *topsy-turvy*...you survive, Talon Rose."

Talon met his warm, dark eyes. "Did he say why he hasn't come to me?"

"Taylor?" She nodded. "He much upset." That Taylor might have confessed his love for Talon had intensified Nightwing's hatred for him. "He said things to you in guardhouse he did not mean. He say he not love you, but care that you hurt by bad man."

"Oh...I see," was all she could manage. New tears made it necessary for her to explain that, "I'm upset about the pouch."

And to think that Taylor does not love you," Nightwing thought.

She now had to deal with not only her lost keepsakes, but Laine's false confession of love for her. All his little remarks, promising that she would be his girl and that he loved her and wanted to marry her. He had played games with her all along.

As hurt as she felt right now, the pouch caused her a great deal more distress. She thought of the years, traveling north with the muleskinner, and then in the village of the Sioux, that she had so carefully guarded it against discovery. Then to have lost it here, for her own hate-filled grandfather to pick up. "Did Taylor believe Compton threw it away?"

"He said he not sure."

She knew by the way he briefly dropped his eyes that Laine believed Compton had the pouch. A mere flicker of life clung to her, because she thought she would already have heard if he'd looked inside it. He would believe it filled with worthless trinkets, and if he hadn't thrown it away, had tossed it aside somewhere.

Talon got to her feet and skirted Nightwing. When she sat on her cot, he arose and turned silently toward her. "Why do you think he lied about loving me?

"He say he do that much with women. Never serious."

She had begun to remember going to Laine in the guardhouse, how Laine's confession of love had chased her fears into a realm far beyond her reach. He had said he wanted to marry her. And now, Nightwing was telling her that everything he'd said was a lie. Or was the astute Nightwing lying? The way he looked at her, caring and thoughtful—as though she were precious to him—she didn't want to believe he was capable of it. And she saw by his dark, furrowed brows that her silence troubled him a great deal. So, she tried her best to smile. "I am sorry for being such a pest."

He had hurt her deeply, but it was necessary. "Being pest what woman do best."

Her heart was on Laine's betrayal, on the treasures contained in the small pouch that most likely was in Compton's office somewhere. She trembled at the thought of Compton opening the small pouch, of her mother's locket and the small curl of her hair spilling forth before his eyes.

So deeply caught up in her anxiety, Talon didn't realize Nightwing had settled to the cot beside her until his arm slipped across her shoulders. She awaited his noticeably lingering thought. "One morning, not too long ago, you much mad, kiss your chief in front of all Apache." His dark eyes turned fully to her. "Did you put feeling into kiss?"

No matter that Laine had lied, she loved him, and did not want to discuss with Nightwing the kiss given only to humillate him. So she disguised her affection for him in the harshness of her response. "If there was feeling in my kiss that morning, Nightwing, it was that my lips would be poison to you."

He laughed pleasantly, withdrawing his arm. "Not

poison...sweet like honey."

His voice was soft and warm, and Talon fought her own biting recollection of that morning. "That is not a particularly good memory for me...and your reminder makes me mad."

He touched his cheek to her temple. "I love fire in eyes when you mad with me, Talon." Then, "I am much sorry about pebbles that morning, about my cruelty. You right. I jealous of Taylor."

Talon accepted that final declaration with mixed feelings. "I eased off those pebbles when you turned your back."

"Hoped you would. When you faint, I feel much shame."

Talon withdrew from Nightwing's gentle embrace. "You do not hate me nearly as much as you did when I first came here, do you?"

"Fire and defiance in front of Apache anger me much, but did not hate you." He could not yet admit that he loved her, since her feelings for the white officer were so strong. Arising, he approached the door. As he turned to look down on her a final time for the night, she surprised him by rising and closing herself into his arms. "What I do to deserve this sweet hug?"

"What have you not done, Nightwing?" she whispered. "You have taken care of me, and worried about me. As much as I hated you, as often as I have wished you dead—if not spoken to you, then spoken softly to myself—I believe I have learned to love you as deeply...as a brother," she added hastily, lest he misunderstand.

Her final words quelled the joy he felt in her confession. He wanted her sentiments to be those of a woman for a man, not of a sister for a brother. "Tomorrow, if you feel up to it, we ride into bluffs for one—two hour. Wish make sure strength back."

"I would like that." She pushed back to smile. "Days of darkness have left me pale as death."

"Talon golden like sunbeam." In a quiet moment, Nightwing imagined that Taylor had watched him come to Talon's quarters, and that he might even lurk in the shadows to see how long he stayed with her. "Walk outside with me." When they stood at the top of the steps, Nightwing noticed a faint stir on the porch of Taylor's quarters. Turning so that Talon would be visible to him in the shadows of evening, he drew her into his arms, keeping his voice soft. "Glad week is over, you recover spirits. Apache want you back."

She looked toward Laine's quarters, longingly, and yet with animosity. How could he have lied to her, watched her face for the radiance his confession brought, then turned from her so abruptly? She looked to Nightwing, his hand tightening painfully across her shoulder making her aware that he'd said something she didn't catch. "Sorry, what did you say?"

He knew her thoughts had drifted to Taylor. "It not important, Talon." He drew back, the whisper of a kiss touching her forehead. Then he heard a low grumble nearby and noticed several of the new Apaches loitering at the front of the scout barracks. "I must find way to get rid of Apaches. Rude—no discipline." Across the parade field a door slammed, Taylor venting his anger, Nightwing supposed. Halting a smirk of satisfaction—of triumph— Nightwing added, "You keep door locked until I know how new Apache treat woman. In morning, I saddle horses. Seven too early?"

"I will see you then."

"Will not leave till you enter quarters—lock door."

Pushing herself up, she complained without feeling, "You are just a bear, Chief, always worried about its cubs."

She glanced again toward Laine's quarters before entering her own. Nightwing hated him, hated the hold he kept on Talon. Hearing the lock click at the top of the door, he turned toward the scout barracks. Just as he skirted the Ft. Bowie Apaches, the short, darker one in a group of three barred his entrance and insulted him in Apache.

Nightwing raised a dark brow, noticing that the Apache speaking to him with such anger reeked of whiskey. He drew his hand casually to the big Bowie knife at his waistline. The two others nearby laughed as their friend backed down.

* * *

Compton had come down to his office to retrieve a decanter of brandy, but a wash of moonlight catching a glass left there earlier drew his attentions to his desk. Drawn again by curiosity, he eased into his chair, pulled open the bottom drawer and felt for the deerskin pouch he had tossed there almost a week ago. Settling back, he twisted it between his fingers, feeling a smooth oval object inside, a stone, perhaps, the Comanche carried for luck. There was little else inside, perhaps a twist of cord and tiny pebbles, and he sat for a moment, thinking about the strange effect Talon had on him. Punishing her so consistently for being Comanche had caused him agony, stirred his mind into nightmares during his sleep, and locked him into moments of guilt and shame so that he could hardly function during the day. Something about her tortured him, mind and soul, and slowly eradicated the hatred that had clung to him for two and a half decades. Every time he closed his eyes his lovely fair-haired Julia Rose flashed across his thoughts, and every time he saw her face, he also saw Talon's. Had his very personal hatred of this young woman who had never done him the first moment of harm, interwoven into his memories of his daughter as a sadistic form of vengeance? He couldn't see one face without the other, and that in itself was a persistent and unbearable torture.

Suddenly, the strange language of the Apache wafted through an open window, followed at once by a cacophony of wicked laughter. He had received daily reports throughout camp of the Bowie Apaches, complaints of debauchery, drunkenness, petty thefts, and crude comments to dependent wives and daughters. Not to mention the very intoxicated scout who had shot the blue-eyed mare. Though the wound was minor, Major Harris had yet to shut up about it.

Throwing the small pouch back into the drawer, Compton rose, retrieved the brandy that had brought him downstairs, and closed himself in his large, well-furnished quarters.

* * *

Boyd Teakle teetered on the brink of his worst drunk ever. Sgt. Mulroney was drunk enough to talk crazy, and Boyd just listened without interest. "Ya know, Muley, we should ought'a jus' get that stuck up Injun bitch out behind them mesquites in the bone yard and fix 'er good. That whippin' I gave her in her quarters—hell, that just made everybody mad...specially that old gen'ral what got the blame."

"I can't be hurtin'er, he says. That whoopin' was good enough...ya really gave it to her. I ain't touchin' that squaw."

"You scared of 'er, Muley."

"Naw...but I sure am scared of that ol' gen'ral." The bartender, the contracted civilian who operated the sutler's bar and store, approached the two men. He had never liked the sergeant, and his choice of friends didn't much surprise him. "I'm closing down, boys. Sarge, you know the regulations, and you, muleskinner, you smell like a rotting corpse."

Boyd Teakle smiled widely. "Why, thank ya much, Sir. Them compliments is few and fer between, so I 'preciate ever' las' one of 'em."

The man turned from the table, suppressing a sneer. "Sarge, get your friend out of here," he ordered across his shoulder, "and don't bring him back till you drag him through a river with a wagonload of soap."

The two men purchased a last bottle and left the sutler's bar. Minutes later, they dropped beneath a mesquite in the post cemetery, took turns swigging from the bottle, watching the swirling smoke of campfires at the Apache wickiups, and the occasional stir of women settling their camp and their brown kids. Mulroney mentioned that he'd like one of those squaws right now, and both men laughed at the vision he aroused.

Half an hour later, they emptied that last bottle for the night. In the deepening shadows of midnight, Mulroney pointed out one of the younger Apache women moving toward a low crease at the foot of the bluffs that usually held a foot or two of water. Most of the soldiers in camp knew they took baths there and respected their privacy.

Mulroney had often climbed the ladder and sat atop his barracks to spy on them. Poking Teakle in the shoulder with his elbow, he stirred him from a light snooze. Soon, the two men crawled stealthily into the darkness, following the smaller footsteps leading to the waterhole.

Leaning over a smooth rock, they watched her shed several

layers of earth-colored clothing. As she sank into the shallow water, Mulroney was on top of her, his hand clamped over her mouth before she could utter a first cry for help.

* * *

The brandy had failed to relax him for sleep, so Compton had gone to his office, intending to write a letter to his aunt who would turn ninety on her birthday in June. He owed a great debt to her, as she had taken Julia Rose into her home when he was sent to Texas. Failing to find stationery in his desk, he picked up the lamp and made his way to a small back room, where he found writing implements, and settled at a small table there.

A few minutes later, the silence was rudely disturbed, a door opening nearby, though he couldn't ascertain the distance to the source. At once, a low band of light appeared below the door. Though no footsteps echoed, he easily detected the sounds of drawers being opened in his office. Rising and approaching the door, he assumed that Taylor had come to search for Talon's pouch. Hearing the intruder's movements on the far side of his office, he opened the door a crack, intent on catching this culprit in the act of rifling through his personal things.

Talon had pulled the dark shades at the office windows and lit one small kerosene lamp she had found on a table. She stood at the mantel for a thoughtful moment and stared at her mother's photograph, sliding her fingertips onto the image in fond reminiscence. Then she began moving stealthily through the room, opening drawers and cabinets. Her grandfather was very organized, and the items in the drawers neat and orderly. Now at his desk, she had just pulled out the top drawer when the door to the corridor eased open.

"Talon, what are you doing here?"

She had no time to answer Laine.

"I'd like to know that, too." Compton stepped from the back room. "What is so important that you would rummage through my office, scout?" Talon was caught between the two men. Compton closed the distance to his desk and shoved Talon aside. At once, the pouch she had lost lay against his palm. "Is this what you want?"

210

A breath of control returned as she eased forward to take the pouch. When he withdrew and snapped his fingers shut over it, she whispered, "Sir, I do want that back."

"Talon, why would you take this chance?" She looked to the man she loved—the man who had lied about loving her in return—but did not answer.

Compton opened the pouch. "Let us see what a Comanche female treasures enough to invade her C.O.'s office for it."

Horror rippled in Talon's whisper. "Please, Sir, don't do that."

Laine fully intended to halt Compton's bold encroachment into Talon's privacy. But it was too late. The contents spilled into his hand. A long, intimidating moment of deep silence followed, and an almost strangled cry as Compton fell heavily into his chair. Talon's fingers were at her mouth, her closed eyelids pressing tears onto her cheeks. She felt sick and weak, and there was nothing she could say as the tarnished chain of her mother's locket fell between her grandfather's fingers. The shorn lock of once golden hair, now gently yellowed by the passage of years, curled gracefully against his palm.

"Where did you get this locket? My wife and I gave this to our daughter on her sixth birthday. Her aunt said she was wearing it the day she left Boston." Then he uttered with sickening disbelief, "And my daughter's hair? You Comanche bitch!" His heart quickened, a multitude of accusations twisting inside his gut. "Did your butchering father present you these tokens of my dead daughter? Did that Comanche bastard murder my daughter?" When Laine's eyes contemptibly narrowed, Talon cringed in utter horror that he would believe the brutal charges her grandfather slung at her. "Get out of this camp," Compton bellowed. "If you return I'll shoot you myself."

Without argument, Talon fled from the building, then halted abruptly and drew her trembling hands to her temples. Hardly aware that she'd crossed the parade field, she had little memory of the minutes that had passed as she pulled Shadow Dancer from her stall. She wanted only to hide as deeply in the mountains as she could get.

Fifteen

A quietly weeping Julia Compton had found a secluded spot on a garden bench newly constructed by one of their more industrious brothers. She had dreamed of Talon Rose, her heart heavy with longing for her. This little niche in the garden was her favorite, where a statue of St. Francis, his marble skirts surrounded by woodland creatures, would soon guard carefully tended flowers. Moonlight had caught his weathered features, beckoning to her from the window of her sleeping chamber some minutes ago. She had answered the summons without pause.

"Julia?" Brother Jeremy's concern reflected from the darkness of his cowl. "I was reading when I heard you pass by. Something troubles you?" He sat beside her now, his hand covering hers in comfort. The sheen of tears told him all that her trembling mouth could not. "You were thinking about your dear daughter again."

"Yes, my sweet *peta*, my Talon Rose," she whispered. "I can't shake the feeling that she needs me. She's a grown woman now, but I feel so strongly that she needs her mother."

"Children always need their mothers, no matter their age. You know we'll never stop looking for her, Julia."

Jeremy had never told Julia about the poster he had seen on a tree outside Powder Wash, that a woman named Talon was a felon, running from both the law and the Army, and had a reward of five hundred dollars on her head. He had also heard a rumor that she might have been hanged at Camp Casey. But he didn't put much stock in that rumor. If this was the same Talon—Julia's daughter—he hoped she never heard any of these rumors. Since she seldom left the mission grounds, it was unlikely that she would. When Brother Jeremy opened his arm, Julia moved into his warmth, knowing that, as always, his unconditional love would soothe her wounded heart.

* * *

Talon couldn't remember passing through the narrow valley she loved, or seeing the moon reflect among the swift passage of clouds. Dismounting the bareback Shadow Dancer, she moved on a deliberate path through the small stand of young trees toward Moonlight Stream, pulled off her boots, and stepped toward the wide, clear ribbon of water. Removing her shirt and chemise, she threw the latter to the bank and crouched to saturate the shirt in the cold water. Drawing her knees up, she eased the wet shirt across her back and sat in silence. Absently watching the movement of the water, she began tossing small pebbles into the stream.

When Laine came upon her an hour later, Talon wasn't sure how she felt about his nearness as he stood back in the shadows of the forest and simply looked at her. Casually she eased the damp shirt from her back and pulled it over her, ever mindful of the intensity of his eyes following her every move. Only when her movements ceased did he emerge from the cover of darkness, the moonlight catching the golden luster of his hair captivating her so completely that she almost forgot how he must feel about her right now.

Dancing reflections of light scattered around Talon like a fleeting ghost, as Laine wondered how she could be so nonchalant about the suffering she had caused tonight. His words tumbled forth in quiet accusation. "Have you no sense of shame Talon that you sit here soothing your wounds? God Almighty! You carried the trophies of a beloved daughter...hiding them...*flaunting* them before a man you criticized for despising you." Noticing her personal agony—her guilt, he supposed—pooling below her eyes, he spat, "Tears, Talon? Hardly suitable to you now! You've revealed your true nature, and I feel betrayed."

You lied about loving me, and you feel betrayed? "What is my true nature, Laine?"

Without pause, Laine was on his knees before her, his slim hands firmly clutching her arms. "You're a cruel, heartless fiend disguised in the gentle cloak of a woman who has broken an old man's heart." Then he shoved her to the grass, his body pinning her down even as she fought desperately to escape his weight.

Immense pain seized Talon as tiny pebbles dug into her back through the damp shirt. She could not suppress the new tears rolling into the hair at her temples. "Please, Laine, don't—"

"Your wounds, Talon, cannot hurt nearly as much as Compton clutching a lock of his dead daughter's hair. It's the most pitiful thing I have ever witnessed." Shamed by the pain creasing her fine, dark brows—pain he was causing—he released her. Sweeping to her side, he raked hair back from his forehead. "I'm sorry." Then, "Damn you, Breed, for your treachery!"

It had been a very long time since he had called her *Breed.* Sitting forward, her hand went to his arm as she whispered, "I beg you, Laine, to trust me. Trust that this is not as it seems. I do not even care right now that you lied about loving me."

Surprise took away his voice for a moment. "What the hell are you talking about?"

"You said you loved me, but you did not mean it."

"I *do* love you, Talon. That has nothing to do with what happened tonight."

Concentrating on whether Laine—or Nightwing—had lied to her made her grandfather's pain seem trivial, but only for the briefest moment. So, she was on her knees beside Laine, her hand easing across his shoulders, which grew instantly rigid beneath her touch. "Do you remember that first night we came here together? I sat right down there, and you whispered to me that there was nothing I could say or do to make you distrust me. I have never asked you for anything, but I ask you now to keep the vow you made that night. I ask you to trust me." When he still didn't shrug off the intimacy, she moved against him, her arms circling to draw him into her embrace. He didn't seem to care that her shirt was dripping wet.

Talon didn't want Nightwing to be right about him, and would rather believe the Apache had lied to her than Laine. His words, spoken that morning at drill, flew through her brain...*Taylor will turn his back on you...I never will.* "Believe in me, Laine. Believe that I would never deliberately hurt General Compton. I tried to retrieve the pouch tonight so he would never know what it contained—"

In one swift move, Laine pulled her forcefully to him. "Believe in you, Talon? If you want trust from me, I'll need something in return. Not the theatrics—the tears—but something substantial...and sincere."

"Anything, Laine."

"The truth! Explain how you came by Julia Compton's locket...how you got a lock of her hair to carry in that idiotic pouch. It is her hair, isn't it?"

Her answer came without hesitation. "It is." Stroking his cheek, her mouth sought his own, set tightly at first, then responding to her soft caresses with traitorous need. She knew he would accept nothing but the truth, and that was something she dared not give him. Because Compton loathed her, he could never know she was his granddaughter. He would survive the discoveries of the pouch much more quickly than he would the knowledge that the rest of his life was saddled with a breed Comanche granddaughter. "Every deceitful thing you think I have done has been to protect him, and to prevent the kind of pain he feels tonight. You *must* trust me—"

Laine despised himself for accepting her caresses, for wanting to feel the heat of her golden flesh penetrate the barrier of his clothing. And just as he might have surrendered to her magic, a thief broke into his thoughts, the image of her as a child, gleefully accepting the tokens of a dead white captive from her father flew through his mind like a carefully aimed arrow. He rose so swiftly that Talon was knocked from her knees.

Resting on her hip, she held herself up from the ground with both of her palms. "Stay with me, Laine. Let me convince you of my sincerity."

He gulped the smallest trace of soldierly control, pivoted, and walked away. Putting a dozen feet between them, he turned, though he didn't meet her pleading eyes. "You're not to return to Camp Casey. Your services as a scout are no longer required."

"And who are you to make that decision?" she shot back vehemently. "You are no longer Officer of Scouts! I have a binding contract, and I *will* return."

"Compton will have you killed."

"There is not a man at Camp Casey who would kill me. Even he knows that." Her voice had maintained the scorn, even as she wanted to beg his forgiveness for what he thought she had done. "Nightwing said he would bring me back in chains if I ever left camp, and I believe him."

Laine's voice became soft with regret. "Don't return, Talon, for the good of everyone. No matter what you've done, I don't want you hurt. And there is one man...no, not Compton...who will hurt you." Noticing the bewilderment in her eyes, he explained, "The only reason I was free from the guardhouse was because Compton made me swear to stay away from you. He also said he'd hired a man to kill you if we were seen together. So you would be wise not to return." Then he resumed the short walk to his horse.

Right now, Talon didn't care about her grandfather's threats as she hurried barefoot through the trees. By the time she caught up to Laine, his left foot was in the stirrup of his saddle. "Please come into the cabin. I will tell you as much as I dare about Julia."

His mocking eyes turned to this woman he loved, because he had hoped to get away from her with a shred of composure. "As much as you dare?" he responded with minimal control. "Or will you pause at the proper moment to save your own tidy reputation, Talon?"

"I have no tidy reputation," she reminded him flatly. "I am a thief...a criminal." He simply couldn't leave, believing her nothing more than the coldhearted daughter of a Comanche butcher. All of a sudden, Talon felt weak and sick, and oh, so desperate to keep him here. As her fingers tightened over his sleeve for support, she folded gently to the ground.

Pulling her into his arms, but with little charity in his features, Laine carried her into the cabin. When he settled her onto the cot, one knee lightly pressed to the mattress, he looked down on her as if she had wasted valuable time. "I must get back to camp." Turning, he withdrew the one match he always carried for emergencies and lit the lantern on the mantel. At most, the vessel contained enough fuel for an hour of light. "Compton will need to talk."

If she allowed him to ride away, she might never see him again. Thus, she sat forward, took his hand when he passed near her and held it in a nervous grip. "I knew Julia Rose, Laine, and if it means anything, I was ever so fond of her. She lived in my village, and gave me the locket herself when I was just a girl—"

Laine freed his hand, his voice harsh with anger. "That's a lie, Talon. Julia's remains were found in Texas. So she couldn't have given you the locket when you were a child."

"Before I continue, I must know how much of this you will tell General Compton."

"Not that I'll believe you, but I'll tell him everything you say. He has a right to know."

Talon had hoped for his discretion, so that she would be able to speak with him openly. Compton could not know that she was his granddaughter. Laine had known Compton a long time, and his loyalty was strong, no matter the improprieties he had committed, and that had personally offended him. "The woman who died was not Julia Rose."

Laine was furious that she continued to lie. "Compton himself purchased her dress and sent it to her for the journey to Texas. The same dress was on the corpse!"

Her mother had told her the story so many times that it was one of the few things about her she'd committed to memory without fault. "There were three women taken from the coach that afternoon. On the march to their village, the Comanches made them strip at a stream to bathe. In their confusion and distress at being naked in front of the Comanches, the two younger women pulled on each other's dresses, which were of a similar style and color. The next day, they all tried to escape, Julia's cousin Lydia fell from a ridge and died. The Comanches allowed Julia to cover her body with rocks to keep the vultures from getting to her. Julia and the older woman reached the village of my father."

There was no way she could have known the name of Julia's cousin, or that the rotting fabric which had led to the gruesome discovery had protruded from a mound of rocks. Laine dropped to the cot beside her. "All right, Talon, you have my attention."

His softly spoken declaration gave her hope. "I remember that Julia's eyes were blue like her father's, and she spoke with a soft, educated voice. Weeks later, the man who would become her husband fought for her in hand-to-hand combat. Though she was a captive, she adjusted well to village life and was happy. Her husband was good to her, loved her deeply, and she thrived. When I returned to my village at age fourteen, I did not see Julia then."

Laine drew a long breath to settle the pain easing along his spine. He hated what he was about to ask her, simply because if her answer was *yes*, then it meant she had never trusted him. "Talon—" She turned anxious eyes to him. "Was Julia your mother?"

She kept her features free of emotion with great effort, even as she wanted to scream, *Yes, she was my mother*! But he had said he would tell Compton everything, and her grandfather's hatred alone compelled her to keep their affinity a secret. "I wish I could say she was, Laine, but the truth is I never came face to face with any child of Julia's." *Except, many times, in the still surface of a pond.*

"The older woman then, taken from the coach along with her?"

"No, she was not my mother. She was traded to another village, I understand."

"Then who was, Talon?"

A tremble settled lightly against her mouth. "I only knew her as White Swan." Her husband's sister had not allowed her to use her *white* name.

"What did your mother look like? What kind of woman was she?"

Talon shrugged. "I scarcely remember." *Oh, but she did*

remember. Every detail of her mother's beauty, her gentleness, and her unconditional love, not only for her only child, but for her father, as well. "I was so young, but I remember that I deeply loved her. And she loved me."

He had to accept that she was telling the truth. "Tell me more, Talon."

"There is nothing more to tell."

Laine abhorred the secrecy lingering in her eyes, and felt strongly there was more she could tell him, even as he could see that she would not. He had to consider, too, that she was just a child last time she saw Julia. Somewhere in her short narration, Talon had entwined her fingers among his, and where they were cool and moist just moments ago, they were now dry and warm. Laine felt that his entire being was being swept helplessly along, through the complex veins of Talon's life. God forgive his betrayal of Compton, but that she had carried the tokens of a man's kidnapped daughter did not diminish the love he felt for her.

Her knees pressed into the cot, her mouth against his ear with sensual, deliberate passion. "Remember that night in the stable, Laine, that we came so close to making love? You said we would resume what we had started next time we were alone together...make love to me now."

His anger died in the sweet, softness of her eyes...in the words she whispered so casually, and so sincerely. He knew she owned him body and soul, and no loyalty bound his heart beyond what he felt for her right now. Even if he resumed his loathing for her tomorrow, he knew that, tonight, he must claim the prize she offered. "I despise you for what you've done, Talon. You must know that."

"I do," she whispered. "But you despise me for what you *think* I have done."

Laine gripped her arms and gently pulled her against his iron-hard body. "I have never wanted anything in life," he growled with husky emotion, "the way I want you now. Hell...I would have taken you that morning you shot me if I hadn't been so mad...and if you had been willing! You were so pretty—so scared. I feel guilty about that."

The manly aroma of him made Talon's senses reel with pleasure. His cool, sweet breath whispered against her temple, his lips, warm and moist, and oh, so slightly trembling, caressed a tender trail across her forehead and down the bridge of her nose. When their mouths met in the fiercest of kisses, Talon knew how this night would end.

How slim and lovely she was in the dim light of the lantern, Laine thought, her skin soft and golden, her dark hair like onyx, held back in her thick braid which he deftly untwisted, so that he might draw the soft strands against his mouth. When his hands slipped beneath the fabric at her shoulders, she caught a small breath. "I've hurt you."

He had caused a stir of pain in her wounds. "No," she deftly lied. "I just want you."

The fabric slipped along her smooth arms, and she instinctively caught it at her breast. "You didn't mind me seeing you at the stream," he reminded her, taking her fingers to gently kiss them. A virgin's moment of apprehension darkened her eyes, even as her silence and her parted mouth spoke so eloquently of her desires. Her beauty was an awakening innocence...her body a captivating temptress, and as she quietly allowed him to bare her soft, sensual breasts he knew he was her prisoner, body, mind, and soul, as completely as if she had thrown an iron cage around him.

Then his hands eased beneath the tumbling masses of her hair and felt the weals left less than a week ago. As she recoiled, his hands lowered to her hips to draw her very tenderly to him. "I can't hurt you like this," he mumbled, burying his face into her dark hair. "I should leave."

Drawing back ever so slightly, Talon cupped his face and lifted it to her. "I need the memories we will make, Laine. I can bear the coldness of your hatred, as long as I have this night to remember." Even as she spoke, Talon knew she wanted him bound to her, not only their bodies, but their hearts, so he would forgive her...and he would trust her.

Moving upward against him, she allowed him to caress her

throat, his kisses trailing over each of her shoulders in turn, and to her breasts, which tingled beneath his caresses. No man had ever touched her like this, and for one long moment, their gazes met and held passionately. When his fingers eased beneath the waist of her skirt and the single button slipped loose, his palms traveled against her bare hips and drew the fabric downward.

As his lips claimed her own, and he probed the depths of her willing mouth, his strong hands moved deftly, confidently, massaging the flesh of her hips and thighs. Instinctively, she parted for him, waiting for him to find the treasure he sought, and when he did, caught her breath as a hot flush crept through her, her own trembling hands wandering beneath the fabric of his shirt. Then she moved against his strong, virile chest and shoulders to close the breath of space separating them.

Wondrous pain swelled beneath the tender probing of his fingers, and when his mouth trailed over her hot flesh, an exquisite sensation of pleasure shot through her veins. She wanted him free of his clothing, and when her hands lowered to the buttons of his trousers, her awkward efforts brought a small chuckle to him. Withdrawing his caresses from her most intimate place, he whispered, "Let me do that," then drew up and shed his trousers and boots in one swift move.

For a moment that seemed to go on forever, his eyes alone tormented her. Seeing that part of a man's body that she had never seen before—and so well endowed—Talon felt renewed fear of their joining. She recalled the women of her father's village speaking boldly of the pain of a first joining.

But she would not let a fearful childhood memory stop her now. Kicking off her skirt, she covered his body with her own, her palms pressed to the cot on either side of him. His maleness was against her, and yet he did not move to enter her. His hands, their oh, so wicked motions, had found her breasts again and she offered them in turn to his mouth, the strong desire in his eyes catching moonlight through a paneless window in glistening rhapsody. Reveling in the exquisite heat coursing through her body, she lowered her mouth to his and enjoyed the deep, searing, intimate probing of his tongue that seemed to go on forever.

Laine could no longer bear the agony his body felt for her molten womanhood and he captured her hips to position her over him. Against her—there—he eased into her with intoxicating skill, and when her body shuddered in anticipation, he pulled her face down to his kisses. "I don't want to hurt you, Talon, but if I do, it will be only for a moment." With fear trembling in her golden features, he arched his body, entering her with sudden strength, and then one final thrust that made her completely his own.

Tears slipped from Talon's eyes as she caught her lip in the moment of pain, even as her hips pressed firmly over him, and the full length of him was within her. With their joining, Laine ceased to move, his hands circling her shoulders to draw her close.

As quickly as the burning pain had ricocheted through her hips, it was now gone, and Talon enjoyed his passion darkened eyes, and his hands stroking her arms in comfort. Now their joining became exquisite, and the quick, hot fullness of him inside her elicited the smallest moan, even as she had not yet recovered the strength to move against him.

"I could stay like this forever," he murmured against her hairline.

"Good...for I must take a moment."

Then her body rose up from him, even as they remained intimately joined, and he began to trace a soft line along her waist and hips. As his fingers spread over her breasts, he stroked them with total concentration. "You're beautiful, Talon. I could put you on a pedestal and just look at you." Though he knew she needed a longer moment to adjust to this newfound sensation, he was in agony for her, his throbbing against her most intimate depths begging for release. When he rocked forward, his legs straddling the narrow cot without interrupting their joining, her long legs circled him and her smooth heels pressed into his buttocks as she writhed against him. Her most intimate muscles contracted around him, and he moaned in intoxicating passion. Holding her close, thrusting almost with greed into the heated depths of her, his kisses covered her face as she began to match his rhythm and pace. His breath hot and quick, his mouth hungrily found the tempting peaks of her breasts, again kneading their dark nubs to hardness. But her hot, parted lips were like a siren, and he almost impatiently trailed kisses there, to probe the molten depths of her mouth.

As he drove against her hips, a river of no return coursing through their entwined bodies, it took only moments for their spasms to blend and culminate. She knew as he gasped and stiffened, then buried himself deeply inside her, that he filled her with his seed. Their bodies remained joined and they held each other until their ragged breaths slowed in unison. She did not want to part from him, nor did he, and they remained joined for a time that seemed to course into forever, until he fell to his back in exhaustion, and brought her with him to continue the intimacy.

Laine groaned at their separation as she eased to his side, to rest her head of tangled locks against his shoulder. The exquisite pain remained in his loins as her fingers played among the coarse, curly hairs of his chest.

"I feel like a woman tonight," Talon whispered, still inflamed against him.

"You *are* a woman tonight, Talon...my woman."

"Then you do love me?"

"How can you doubt it?"

Savoring his claim for a moment, she enjoyed the musky, manly scent of him, and the gentleness with which his arm folded over her. "You say I am your woman, Laine, and that you love me. But will you trust me? Will you allow me to return to camp to be near you?"

It took the briefest of moments for her words to fully sink in. He sat forward now, raking back the unruly locks that clung to his dampened forehead, the aftermath of exquisite exhaustion strengthened by suspicion. "Is that what this is about, Talon? A seduction so that I will allow you back at camp?"

She was horrified that he would think such a thing, even as she silently questioned her own motives for making love to him—here and now. Only when he rose to his full height and began pulling on his clothes did her voice return to her. "Why do you mistake my words, Laine? I want only to be near you." Clutching her skirt to her, she rose, and he quickly shrugged off her efforts to regain the intimacy.

"Do I misunderstand you, or have I simply learned to read you like a book?" As he dragged on his shirt and began tucking it into his trousers, he answered her question, "No, you're not allowed back on post." Before she might issue a protest in her defense, he had pulled on his boots and grabbed up his belt and holster. The door closed with a heavy thud and, momentarily, the clip of his horse's hooves disappeared into the hills.

Sixteen

So stunned by Laine's departure to even move, Talon half expected him to return, fold her into his embrace, and apologize for leaving her. When he did not, she realized her first act of complete love to this man had ended with him turning his back on her—as Nightwing had said he would. Grabbing up her clothing she ran to Moonlight Stream, where she sank into the cool water to wash all evidence of Laine's body from her own. Then, the stench of marigolds smothered her senses, tears pooled and she sat in the cool water for a long while, hugging her knees, closing off all her senses so that she failed to hear the rustle in the trees all around her, and the hooves of many horses muffled on the grassy ground.

But the commanding male voice certainly caught her attention, and she swiftly grabbed her dress from the bank and held it to her. She had no chance to pull it on as a single horse closed the distance, and masculine boots fell to the grassy earth to take long strides toward her. Slim, brown hands closed over her shoulders, and black facial hair grazed a path to her cheek, to be instantly replaced by a light kiss. "Little *chica*, who hurt you like this?"

Hearing Manolito's voice for the first time since early February refreshed Talon's tears. When she'd fled the Powder Wash area after Shepperd's death, he was the first person in Arizona Territory who had befriended her, who had protected her. Turning as she covered herself with her dress, she soon turned back into his arms.

"You miss this bad, greasy bandito, *chica*?"

"I did, you rogue devil. But you shouldn't be so close to the soldiers. The Army and the U.S. marshals have rewards on your head. Most of your men, too."

There was no part of Manolito Menendez that didn't physically react to the beautiful nakedness lurking beneath the wild black tresses, even as he had politely turned his eyes while she pulled her clothing over her head. "The gringos try, but they will never catch Manolito. Or his *hombres*. I am too clever for them. They should thank me, *chica*, because we kill more Apache bucks than they find. Now—" He took her hand. "Tell Manolito who hurt you and we will kill him very slowly for you."

"I do not want him killed, Manolo."

"Army men did not do this...it violates their laws. Rancher do this?"

"Not the Army...a general who hates me. I was forced to scout with the Apache at Camp Casey, or else be hanged—"

"I hate Apache," Manolito vowed for the thousandth time, cutting off the explanation she was about to give. "I wish them all dead!"

"I know you do. But a few are close to my heart."

"Be careful of Apache, *chica*, even scout." Then, "What you do so bad to be whipped?"

Manolito's men began to close in on them. "The new C.O. arrived at camp. His daughter was taken by Comanches many years ago, so he turned his hatred to me."

"I will kill him for you."

"No—you will not. And if you do, I will put a bullet through your head."

He was angry that Talon had been so cruelly treated—and would not allow him to avenge this terrible wrong against her. Yet, an easy grin spread Manolito's full mouth. "Come, *chica*. We rest at little cabin this night, then you come with us to Manolito's camp. We will not let anyone hurt you there. You know Manolito loves you—" *as a woman,* "as a daughter."

Talon moved against this friendly bandit who had always treated her with respect, even as she suspected he had hoped for a different kind of relationship between them. "You know I do not want to be with you when you kill, Manolo."

He loved for her to call him *Manolo*. Reproof shaded his black, piercing eyes. "*Chica*, do we not honor your wishes when you are with us? *Si*, we keep our guns silent. Our whips—now that is a different story."

Pulling on her boots, Talon moved among the dark, familiar faces with Manolo. Renewing old acquaintances, she turned back to their swarthy, very handsome leader, a man old enough to be her father. "Manolo, I will ride with you for now, but you must promise you will kill no soldiers, no settlers...no white people. And certainly no Indian scouts. You will kill no one."

Manolito eased his arm across her shoulder as they moved through the trees. "Only mean Apache bucks that threaten us...*Si,*" he replied, turning to his *hombres*, "You heard our Comanche *chica*. We will keep our guns silent while she is with us."

* * *

A rippling tide of crimson ascended with the sun the following morning, scattering shards of rainbow hued lights over the tight rectangle of military buildings embraced by the Huachucas. Nightwing had risen before dawn, and now stood outside, sipping strong coffee, and admiring this gentle wonder dancing over their little camp. He had waited a good half hour for a light to come on in Talon's quarters. Thinking she should have risen by now, he set his cup aside.

Failing to find her at her quarters, he thought she might be at the post corral. He was more concerned that Shadow Dancer was missing, though her saddle was still in the tack room. Fear leaped into his heart, and he went at once to Major Reisner's office and reported her absence.

"Damn," Reisner cursed. "Billy just came to me to report a missing wife, and some of your scouts are out searching for her now." He leaned forward from his desk. "Should we have them search for Talon, too?"

"Her horse gone," Nightwing replied, "but her saddle in tack room."

Reisner came around the desk. "If she left camp, it was not reported by the sentry."

"Sentry sometime sleep on duty," Nightwing reminded him.

227

He was right, of course. It had been a problem at camp since the Bowie Apaches had arrived and sleep was often disturbed by their rowdiness. "Talk to Taylor. He might know where she is. I'll talk to the guards who were on the gate, and try to pin down any of the Bowie scouts who can't account for their actions last night. I don't trust that lot."

"Apache not hurt Indian women."

Reisner grimaced. "The complaints have been sifting back, so I wouldn't be so sure about that. The way white women are barring themselves in their husband's and father's quarters, you'd think we had a case of bubonic plague."

"Big difference between rude comments to white women and hurting, killing." The white captain was the last person Nightwing wanted to talk to, though he advanced to the door for just that purpose. "I will go to Taylor's quarters now."

Moments later, he found the front door to his quarters ajar, noticing at once his stockinged foot and one hand dangling from the settee in the front room. No lights glowed, and Nightwing discovered an overturned liquor bottle, its contents seeping in a straight line between the floorboards. He lightly nudged Taylor's hand with his boot; he didn't stir. Then he slapped his cheek several times with the back of his hand, and he lurched forward. "Talon, I warned you."

Nightwing drew a breath of surprise. Taylor's outburst from the brink of sleep left little doubt he knew where Talon was. Dropping to one knee, he withdrew his Bowie knife, settled the tip of the ten-inch blade against Laine's jaw, and spoke his name until his eyes opened.

Laine froze when he felt the knife, his gaze ripping demandingly into Nightwing's unflinching features. "What the hell—"

"Where Talon?"

He thought if he moved so much as a muscle, the knife would cut him. "She's gone."

"Where Talon?" Nightwing repeated, pressing the blade just enough to draw blood.

"I told you, she's gone...and won't be back."

Nightwing savored his noticeable fear. "Why?" The knife drew slowly along his jaw and neck without cutting him, settling at his jugular. "Answer me, Taylor—where Talon, and why she not come back?"

"Nightwing!"

Reisner had startled his Chief of Scouts. "We talk privately, Sir. Please leave."

Since their mutual animosity had become camp gossip, Reisner had thought twice about sending Nightwing to talk to Taylor. "Sheath your knife, and *you* leave. This is *not* a request." A moment of silence, with the knife still at his throat, continued to feed Laine's fear. Because Reisner took a firm step toward him, Nightwing sheathed the knife and drew slowly to his feet. He now faced his Officer of Scouts with straight, unblinking eyes. "If Taylor fails to bring charges against you," he threatened, "I may possibly do so."

Nightwing said nothing as he skirted him and left Taylor's quarters.

Easing to a sitting position, Laine wiped the trickle of blood from his chin. "I won't bring charges against Nightwing, and I'd request that you don't either, Sir. He has every right to be mad as hell at me."

"He doesn't have the right to put a knife to an officer's throat. Now—where the hell is Talon?"

Laine's fingers plunged into the hair at his temples, his elbows firmly against his thighs. "I know where I last saw her, but not where she is now. I can only tell you she won't be back."

"Yes, Captain Taylor, she will," Reisner responded assuredly. "She has a two year contract with this camp, and that makes her a deserter. As soon as I can spare him, I'll send Nightwing to bring her back."

Slightly narrowed, bloodshot eyes turned to Reisner. "Don't, major. Just let her go."

"I absolutely will *not* do that. Whatever happened between you and Talon has nothing to do with her duty as a scout for this Army camp." The full flood of dawn illuminated the large room, exposing the drunken, disheveled state of this Army officer

Reisner had thought impeccable in every detail. Only a woman could do this to a man. "What the hell happened, Captain Taylor?" Then he spied the fallen liquor bottle. "It must be serious if you're in this godawful state. You have the respect of this camp, Sir, but if these soldiers saw you like this—"

Laine felt sick, his head hurt, and his strength had left him. He couldn't even stand in respect of this senior officer dressing him down. "Sir, I can't talk to you right now."

"This morning, Captain Taylor, after you've cleaned up. I'll be in my office." Then he left, slamming the door soundly enough to rattle the demons inside Laine's skull.

* * *

Just before nightfall, Billy's wife was found hastily buried beneath rocks half a mile from camp. A preliminary post mortem indicated she had been repeatedly raped, beaten, and smothered by a man's large hand. Based on the condition of the body, the camp physician put death at around midnight.

Outside camp, the women wailed their death songs throughout the night, while the Ft. Bowie Apaches were individually taken into a small room of the guardhouse and grilled. Thirty-two of the forty were eliminated as suspects, the other eight, who couldn't account for their time last night, locked up until the investigation was complete.

At three o'clock the following morning, the Apaches who were not locked up, fearing their friends would be put under the lash as the Comanche scout had been, swarmed the military prison, held guards at gunpoint, and freed their eight comrades. They fled camp on their ponies just as the bugler sounded alert. In the melee of running soldiers and fleeing Apaches, several were shot by sentries, two falling dead from their ponies just a dozen feet from the guard tower. One of the dead was Bayani, their chief. Another Apache was found two miles away, beneath stones less than a dozen feet from where the Apache woman had been buried the night before.

Later that morning, Teakle confessed to Mulroney that he was real scared, and would politely harness his team and slip away if camp wasn't locked down by order of HQ. And there was still the matter of the rest of the gold pieces Compton owed him for lying to the captain.

Mulroney was just reporting to the duty desk when soldiers and scouts left camp, headed into the bluffs in pursuit of the Ft. Bowie Apaches. Dribbling tobacco juice to the breast of a jacket soiled by weeks of wear and meals, he grinned with pleasure that he and Muley had created all this ruckus.

* * *

Nightwing and fourteen scouts rode with K Company, Fourth Cavalry, to the northeast. Dako and the other eleven scouts rode eastward with D Company, both units following well traveled trails to Fort Bowie. The campaign kept them out for the next ten days, and K Company was the first to engage Apaches, though not the Bowie bunch. During that first day of fighting in a deep crease known by the locals as Sweeping Gorge, they lost eight soldiers, one officer, and two scouts. Twenty-seven Apache hostiles were also killed. The ambulance wagons left the security of camp on a daily basis, returning with corpses and injured men...and the chapel was kept busy conducting funeral services. Taps, played several times daily over camp, drifted into the hills like death knolls. By the time both units returned to camp, ragged, weary, wounded and mad as hell, eighty-eight Apaches had died, twenty-seven soldiers, and five of Nightwing's scouts, including Billy Haigo and their old storyteller, Gad. The Fort Bowie Apaches had evaded them at every turn. Wires between Camp Casey and Fort Bowie determined that the Apaches, losing Bayani, their leader, had fled to the Sonora Mountains in Mexico, to join forces with Geronimo's band and other hostile Apaches gathering for their war against the white man in the Southwestern plains. Their white Officer of Scouts was furious that his Apaches, who had never wanted to go to Camp Casey to begin with, had been accused of a crime they didn't commit. In his opinion, Camp Casey's haste to determine guilt was solely responsible for the new sting in the Apache's war bonnet, and for the men whose lives had been lost.

Now back at camp, Nightwing allowed two days of

mourning for his fallen scouts, the days and nights filled with their songs, prayers and chants. Then a tense silence fell over the region, the soldiers rested for the next campaign, and the Apache troublemakers, for the most part, kept well out of sight. Though the campaign would likely continue, Nightwing had just one thing on his mind.

With the eye of the storm over the little camp—courting it with its deceptive calm—it was time to bring Talon back. Late that evening, Nightwing left Dako in charge, mounted his big bay, and rode into the hills.

* * *

Laine did not question Nightwing's destination as he watched him ride away from Camp Casey. Two weeks had passed since he'd left Talon alone in the bluffs, since he'd held her, loved her...listened to her soft pleas for his trust. He recalled her sitting on that little cot, clutching her clothing to her, watching him leave with all the pain and bewilderment of a scolded child. She had asked for his trust, such a small thing, and he had refused to give it to her.

Then the ambulances began making their daily treks along the bluffs, returning with dead and injured soldiers, dead scouts, and every time they came in, he was glad Talon wasn't out there, getting killed with the rest of them.

The morning Nightwing had come to his quarters and held a knife to him had been the first clear indication of his love for Talon. He had suspected for weeks that he wanted Talon, but that morning, he had seen all the clues in his black, unwavering eyes, in the barely perceptible tremble in his voice and the light touch of that damned knife to his throat.

Tonight, he wasn't riding into the hills because Talon was a deserting scout...but because he loved her.

"Where the hell is that Apache son-of-a-bitch heading?"

Laine turned his eyes just as Compton emerged from the absolute darkness of the parade ground. "I imagine he's going after Talon."

"He's a damned fool for leaving camp alone, and in uniform." Pausing below the steps, Compton crossed his arms as

232

he watched the final stir of dust settle beyond the northeast gate. "Could we talk, Laine...friend to friend?"

It had been a very long time since Compton had wanted to have this kind of talk. Trying to recall the prior occasion for it, he drew up, then retrieved his brandy glass from the porch rail where he'd set it earlier. "I suppose about your daughter...and Talon?"

"Yes...I would have been here sooner if not for the upheaval caused by the Bowie Apaches."

The last two weeks, amidst the gloom of death and daily funerals, had been hectic. Morale was low, moods explosive, and the paperwork overwhelming. Major Hiram Stahl chose a bad time to add to this stir. Laine had heard just today at the postmaster's counter that he had sent a package—rumored to be a chronology of Compton's daily activities at camp—off to the War Department in Washington. "It has been busy around here, Sir," Laine finally conceded.

Compton rose slowly up the steps. "Tonight, I'm not Sir, or general—" Cool, glassy eyes turned to Laine. "Tonight I'm Salem, and I need to talk. Will you listen?"

Since Compton had arrived at camp—had begun his incessant persecution of Talon—Laine had found it difficult to consider him a friend. "No matter that Talon carried tokens of your daughter...Salem...I'm still mad as hell that you whipped her."

"And I am telling you for the final time that I didn't! I will find out who did!" Compton cleared his throat. "Right now, Talon's is the only forgiveness I would openly solicit, were she here for the way I have treated her. Not yours."

Swinging open the screen door, Lane smothered an argument. Talon said he whipped her, and there was no reason for her to lie. "Come in. I'll pour you a brandy."

"God knows, you're the only man at this camp still willing to talk to me." Then, "Are you too drunk tonight to be a friend?"

"I've had a few. A little drunk I suppose." Compton had already settled onto the divan by the time Laine turned with the filled glass. Handing it to him, he took a chair nearby, and dragged his boot onto his knee. "What has brought this on? Two weeks ago, you ordered Talon away from camp, and now...second thoughts?"

"Seconds thoughts, hardly. A thousand thoughts, and as many regrets. I want that woman back here."

Laine misread Compton's vein. "Are you planning to punish her?"

Compton's glance carried surprise. "Punish her? God, no...if she told you the truth that night you went after her, that Julia gave her the locket, she must have liked Talon. It's all I've thought about the last two weeks. Hearing about my little girl...hearing the things that only Talon can tell me. Is it possible that Julia is still alive? Is it possible that Talon didn't tell you the truth? Could Julia be her mother? Talon's second name is Rose, just like my daughter."

"She said no. I don't want to believe she lied to me about that. And if Julia gave her the locket, she might also have given her part of her name. Indians have a different way of doing things. They can go by one name for years, then suddenly take a whim and choose another name. The Sioux do it all the time. Crazy Horse wasn't always known by his famous name."

"I don't care about Crazy Horse. I care about my daughter. I care about what Talon knows. No matter how mundane it might be, I want to hear everything—everything!—about my Julia Rose after the Comanches carried her off. Talon has that knowledge. If Nightwing is going after her, I pray to God Almighty that he finds and brings her back here."

Lane had listened quietly, and in a moment of silence, turned his eyes to Compton. "If anyone can find her, it'll be Nightwing."

"You say that with regret."

"I believe that damned Apache loves her and I don't know how I feel about that."

"I can make no comment in that regard. I regret that I have not treated either of you men any better than I have treated Talon."

"A little better. You didn't whip us." Laine stood. "You've

been a real bastard, sorry to say."

Rather than the reprimand Laine expected, Compton quietly replied, "I know." His gaze slid up. "Do you think Talon will ever forgive me for the way I have treated her?"

"I don't know why she would."

"I can't believe I was so cruel to her for so long. That I—" Compton stopped short of confessing that he'd brought false charges against Talon. Shame compelled him to drop his eyes, his hands trembling so violently he could scarcely take a sip of brandy. And—damn—he needed it.

Fairly certain he knew what Compton held back, Laine allowed a moment to pass. "That day out at Rock Bluff...did Talon defy you? Did she call you a fool and threaten your life?"

"I don't want to talk about that day. I want to talk about Julia...about Talon's relationship with her."

"But, Sir—"

"I *said* I don't want to talk about it!" Grinding his teeth, he cut savagely narrowed eyes to Laine. Then, as if a driving rain had suddenly quelled the fire, he whispered hoarsely, "Have you remembered anything else Talon might have told you that night?"

Returning to his chair, Laine settled back. "What she told me I've related to you. Perhaps in the time that's passed she's remembered other things. When—if—Nightwing brings her back—perhaps the two of you can have a heart-to-heart talk. Talon is aware that you loved your daughter deeply. If there is anything she can tell you to relieve your pain, she will."

"I don't think she'll want to do much talking to me after the way I have treated her."

Boots echoed lightly on the porch. Laine arose, both men looking toward the door as Troy Reisner paused and looked through the screen. Laine invited him in, but Reisner declined, instead directing his comment to General Compton. "Nightwing goes after Scout Talon. When he brings her back, what charges do you want lodged against her? Is she to be locked in the guardhouse or can she be confined to her quarters?"

If she was brought back, Compton did not want her to have

any chance of escaping again. He replied almost reflectively, "Charge her with desertion, confine her to the guardhouse, and make sure she's treated well."

Reisner hesitated to ask, "Will she be court-martialed?"

Of course not, you fool. "The Judicial Office will make that determination, but I shall recommend that she is not."

Compton was hated by every man at Camp Casey, including the staff of the Judicial Office. They would hardly entertain his requests, even in behalf of Talon. Hoping that Compton's guilt over his relentless persecution of her might generate leniency, Reisner had told Nightwing not to return to camp without her. But now—and not being a religious man—he prayed she had fled Arizona Territory and that none of them ever saw her again. "Good evening, General...Captain Taylor."

When Reisner retreated, Laine turned livid eyes to Compton. "All that talk about regrets was bullshit!" He slung the accusation. "You ordered Talon out of camp, and now you will allow the Judicial Office to possibly bring her up on charges of desertion?" Approaching, holding open the screen door, he ordered, "Get out...Salem...this friendly chat is over."

Compton arose. "You let me explain—"

"You have no explanation!"

"I simply want to make sure Talon stays when she returns. I will not bring formal charges, nor will I allow the Judicial Office to do so, and she will remain in the guardhouse only until I'm sure she'll stay." Pivoting sharply toward Laine, a bony finger snapped the air in front of his face. "I'd knock the hell out of you, Captain Taylor, for speaking to me in that manner if you weren't bloody drunk!"

Seventeen

Caution amassed in Nightwing's dark eyes as they scanned the high ridges of Rock Bluff. Though the tracks were many days old, the flaw in Shadow Dancer's front right shoe, preserved in the hard, dry earth against a boulder, told him Talon had come this way, and with many riders. He would have to pass through this treacherous, closely confined canyon to stay on her trail. It was not something he would normally do alone.

Halfway through the gorge, the distinct snickering of a horse reached him, its exact location muddled by its echo among the rocky outcroppings. A dozen Mexicans slowly descended from the west side of the canyon. Backing his horse, a dozen more men stirred behind him, and he eased his right hand toward his holstered Engfield revolver.

A single shot rang out, pain piercing Nightwing's left shoulder as the Mexicans closed the distance to him. As blood spread rapidly through his shirt, his right hand moved out in surrender. He knew he would be dead if he went for his revolver again. A tall, very thin Mexican, with thick, neatly cut hair and a full moustache, broke the line of men and approached him. Staring at him from the shade of a big brown sombrero, he flashed a line of straight white teeth in a menacing smile. "I think, Senor U.S. Army *Apache* scout, you should step down from your fine, fat, grain-fed horse."

"You have no quarrel with me," Nightwing stated flatly.

Menendez pulled a big Colt revolver and rested it across his wrist. "I said...off your horse, Apache!"

Nightwing cautiously stepped down from the saddle, and Menendez, reholstering his sidearm, rode up to snatch the fatigue hat from his head. "Now, take off that holster and place it over the saddle horn." Nightwing obeyed the order, even as his eyes swept for an escape route. "Throw me that fine rifle and knife. If it cuts me, Apache, my hombres will cut you down where you stand." Nightwing did as he was told, then a Mexican took the reins of his horse and led it away from him, relieving him of all his weapons. Another short, heavy man lumbered down from a black horse and bound his wrists with hemp.

Nightwing had recognized Menendez, a notorious Apache hater, from the wanted posters. He was in a hell of a lot of trouble, and today he might even die.

Manolito remembered his promise to Talon to keep his guns quiet...but she had said nothing about Rio's whip. This Army buck deserved to suffer and die for the whipping Talon had endured. Besides, he was angry at his Comanche *chica*. He had finally admitted his love for her, and she had placed her gentle hands to his cheeks and vowed her love for him, too...as a *father*. That was *not* the kind of love he desired. Having her in his blankets, willingly, had become an obsession these past two weeks she'd been with them again.

Half an hour later, the Mexicans dragged Nightwing by his bound wrists into their encampment deep in the rock bluffs. His shirt was blood-soaked as a young bandit called Rio shoved him down with such force that a small, sharp rock laid open his left palm in a ragged cut. Removing his bindings, Rio circled to Nightwing's back and ripped his shirt from him, the buttons landing in the dirt between his parted knees.

Rio was proud of his expertise with the bullwhip, a skill he had learned from his *padre de familia*—Manolito's brother who had been head of the family—and who was murdered by Apaches last year. He uncurled the fancy length of black braided leather, then stepped back and laughed, "Look at buck Indian, Uncle Manolito. He is smooth like baby, not one scar, like no Apache we have killed." Then he said to Nightwing, "Thought you crazy Apaches hold ceremonies of manhood, carve yourself up to prove your bravery, eh? You not brave Apache?"

Nightwing replied soberly, "You have this Apache confused with fool."

Manolito approached, slicing the air almost playfully with Nightwing's pearl-handled Bowie knife. "This is a fine weapon you have here, buck. Army issue?" He paused in front of him.

"Is it sharp? It looks sharp—" He propped the tip on Nightwing's left shoulder near the bullet wound, and slowly drew the blade down, cutting a shallow gorge six inches long in the flesh of a man who never flinched. "*Si*, it is very sharp." A line of blood slipped from the wound, through Nightwing's sinewy muscles, spreading along the snug band of his trousers. Menendez circled, leaning into him as he spoke. "Buck Indian never feel sting of whip, but that will change very soon. What you think 'bout that?"

"I am not *Buck*," Nightwing replied with a great deal of patience. "I am John Nightwing. What you want me to think?" He hated that these Mexicans spoke English as well as he did, and imagined that Talon had been responsible for it during the months she had been with them.

Manolito hated that this Apache's face was a mask of fearlessness, that he spoke English so well. When he killed Indian filth, he wanted him to be afraid to the last breath. "Nightwing? That is nice name, but not very Apache, ch? I think you are mongrel. What you have, little of this, little of that, in your blood? That why you speak so good English, eh?" Without warning, he slammed his fist into the small of Nightwing's back, the Bowie knife at his throat as quickly as he gasped in the instant of pain. "We not like rude Indian bucks." Pulling the knife away, Menendez made a subtle motion, and Nightwing was dragged between two trees twisting from the boulders. Bound by his spread arms, he faced a deep crevasse in the rock wall, and Menendez fell lazily against a boulder to watch his men toy with him. He hated Apaches, because one had killed Carlos, his favorite brother. Torturing and killing them gave him a great thrill, better than making love to a beautiful woman. But this Apache, he was different...much taller than Apaches they had killed. Rio occasionally popped and whirled the long, cruel whip while he made a wide sweep at Nightwing's back, filling the air with short yelps.

Nightwing's stoic silence annoyed the hell out of Menendez. He had hoped the tall Indian's first cry of pain when the whipping began would draw Talon from her afternoon nap.

But he imagined this stubborn Indian might die in silence. Watching Rio pop the whip, he thought this Nightwing showed great courage in the face of a certain and painful death. Would he break when Rio's whip began to lay him open, or would he die in stubborn resistance?

"You very brave for buck soon to be shredded by the black snake—" Menendez remarked, coming up from the rock. "Do not worry. The whip will not be silent until you die. That should bring you some comfort, eh, that you will not have to suffer later? But I should not be so rude. I do thank you for the fine *caballo,* and the weapons. What is fine horse's name, eh? Or do Apaches name the beasts they get tired of and eat eventually?"

"His name *Mageedu*...I have no plans to eat him."

"Mageedu...*Cowboy*...that is nice. Perhaps my hombres will eat him later. What you think about that?"

"When I dead will not think anything about it." Nightwing's right hand closed tightly over the hemp at his wrist. Pain threaded through his left arm and he couldn't move his fingers. Blood flowed from his cut palm, diverted by the tight rope at his wrist, and dripped to the rocky ground.

Talon chose that moment to emerge from a blanket-covered lean-to across the clearing, responding to the men's loud voices and the familiar popping of the whip. Too often these past two weeks she had heard the men vying with one another to see who could snap the whip the loudest, and was a little tired of their horseplay, especially when it disturbed her rest. For a minute or so, she sauntered among several Mexican women cooking over an open fire, and briefly exchanged small talk.

Nightwing instinctively cut his eyes to the tall, slender woman, wearing a full, brightly colored skirt and peasant blouse. No matter what these bandits did to him, he felt a great deal more pain that Talon had returned to her old ways and the company of these brown-skinned bandits...especially since he didn't know what had happened to bring her here.

Approaching the men now, Talon demanded, "What the hell is going on, Manolo? You woke me from my siesta." Then she saw Nightwing, horror filling her completely. Her eyes, like those of a rabbit searching to hide from the fox, shot between the Mexicans and the bound, bleeding Indian. Hastening her pace, she approached Nightwing, quickly ducked beneath his outstretched arm, and stood face to face with him. Only then did she notice his wounds.

They were all aware of the engagements between the soldiers and the Apache in the region, and that many had been killed. She was happy to see this tall, commanding Indian still alive, but very distressed that the Mexicans had wounded him, and apparently intended to kill him. When she lifted her fingers to his smooth chin, he eased from her gentle caress as if he found her touch repulsive. "This is a fine mess you've gotten yourself into, Nightwing. Why are you away from camp, alone and in uniform, and without your scouts?"

Talon surely knew she was the reason, so he didn't answer.

Menendez chuckled, "We caught him at Rock Bluff, *chica*. Do you wish to kill him?"

"Why would I want to kill one of the best men I have ever known?" Talon and Nightwing locked gazes as she reminded Manolo, "You promised not to kill while I was with you."

"I change my mind, *chica*."

Removing her bandanna Talon carefully pressed it to the wounds at Nightwing's shoulder in an effort to staunch the bleeding. "Manolo, you remember about a year ago, you and your hombres were camped in West Texas and I rode forty miles in a hot dust storm to bring news that a garrison of soldiers had been sent out to round you up?"

"I remember, *chica*. I still wonder how you got that information."

From a drunk, flirtatious soldier who didn't know my identity. "Never mind how. All of us got to Mexico safely, and you said you owed me." Her cautious eyes lifted to Nightwing. "I want this Indian. Give him to me, and our debt will be cleared."

Menendez slowly shook his head. "He dies today, *chica*. You must collect my debt to you another way."

Trembling with fear for Nightwing, Talon drew her hands

to the back of his neck and pressed herself as closely as a lover. "If you do not want to die today, you must not protest, Nightwing, no matter what happens in the next few minutes. God knows, I do not want you to die."

"Why, Talon, do you care what happens to this Indian?" He asked as if it was a very reasonable question.

Rising on her tiptoes, she gently pressed her mouth to his, and was somewhat surprised at his soft, sensual response. As throaty laughter howled among the Mexicans, she didn't notice Manolo's angrily set features, and his cruel eyes sweeping among his men to silence their laughter. Talon drew back from Nightwing, and touched her fingertips to his lips to savor the warmth and quiet mystery of his kiss. "I do care, you gentle-hearted Apache rascal. And I will do anything to save you. *Anything*!"

As precarious as his situation was right then, Nightwing wanted only to hear the coveted words come from Talon's lips...that she loved him. "Tell me why you care, Talon?"

Her eyes widened, her lips parting as though a reasonable explanation eluded her. "You are my chief, Nightwing, and you have been good to me."

"That is *not* good enough. Do not bargain with Mexican bastards for this Indian?"

"I must...because..."

When she paused, he demanded, "Because why?" *Say it, Talon...say that you love me!*

Talon's mouth pressed defiantly. "I do not know what you want me to say. Damn you...just let me take care of this." she ordered, furiously turning away from him.

He was weak, the tightly pulled hemp—and his love for Talon—holding him upright. "What will you do, Talon, to save this life?"

Looking back at him across her shoulder, she replied, "Whatever I must."

"If I do not approve, you will *not* do it."

Defiance rushed into her features. "You are bound and bleeding, Nightwing, hardly in a position to do anything but die.

And..." She tossed her thick braid arrogantly. "I do not need your approval...not today...not here." She turned from him then, pausing when he softly spoke her name. So much pain reflected in his dark eyes that she returned and gently covered his cheek with her palm. "I asked you a couple of weeks ago what I could do to repay you for taking care of me after Compton whipped me."

He had heard the rumors that Compton wasn't responsible, but said nothing.

"Do not—" He searched for the right word—one he had learned not too long ago in English class. "—compromise honor, Scout."

"Right now is my chance to help you—to repay the debt I owe you." Then she left before he might issue another protest. Boldly lifting her eyes, Talon stood face to face with Manolo, prideful and stubborn, even as a tremble in her jaw betrayed her nervous torment. "You said last week that you wanted me, Manolo, not as a daughter, but as a woman. You give me Nightwing's life today so that I might set him free, and in exchange, I am yours, to do with as you please."

A grin crept onto his face, even as his brows furrowed into a frown. Slim brown fingers rose gently to her cheek, and he was aware that she cringed from his touch. "You say few days ago that Manolo is like father to you. For this Indian's life, *chica*, you will now be my lover?"

The tremble strengthened. Talon caught her bottom lip between her teeth, fighting back tears. "Yes, Manolo, I will."

"He is that important to you?"

"I owe him a great debt."

A face almost black from the sun darkened even more. "*Chica*...I want you to want me. Not to agree to be with me to save this Apache. How can I accept such a bargain as this? And for how long? One hour? One day? One week?" Manolo's voice grew hoarse with anger. "How much are you willing to give for him? A lifetime as my lover? To save one Apache buck from a death he deserves?"

"No Apache I've ever met deserves death less. And yes,

Manolo, if you want a lifetime, I am willing to give it. As long as Nightwing leaves here alive."

Manolo had continued to stroke Talon's cheek, aware of her anxiety as she anticipated his reply. "Manolo will not give his lifetime, *chica*, to a woman who does not love him as a man. But for this Indian's life, I will take one hour with you."

Talon drew a deep, calm breath, trying to soothe the tremble easing along her spine. Right now, she would rather be dead than to make love to a man she looked to for the affections of a father. But she could not make that decision for Nightwing. He was virile, vibrant, deserving of life, and she would not be the one to take that from him, no matter what it cost her. "Very well, Manolo...but you do realize when that hour passes I will not feel the same about you." Talon hesitated to add, "I will leave here with Nightwing and hope never to see you again."

"*Chica*...I do not believe you mean that."

"Yes, Manolo, I do mean it."

He would take that chance. Opening his hand, Manolo waited until Talon's trembling, and very hesitant, one slid against it. Then he turned toward the barrier of blankets where he slept each night after a hard day of raiding—and killing when necessary—where he often dreamed of her lying beside him. He noticed the tears sheening her beautiful eyes as she looked back at Nightwing, struggling desperately against his bindings as his dark, angry eyes followed their retreat.

As Talon entered the blankets ahead of Manolito Menendez, Nightwing yelled hoarsely, "No, Talon!"

Half-shoving Talon toward the pile of blankets, Manolo pointed a finger at Nightwing. "If Apache says one more word, Rio, whip him."

Manolo entered the blankets to face Talon's tearful eyes. "Manolo, I beg you, don't let Rio whip him. I will hate you for that."

Annoyed as hell at Nightwing's interference, and wanting only to be with Talon, Manolo pulled back the blanket and yelled, "Let him scream, Rio...our *chica* does not want him whipped." Then he turned back, closed Talon's shoulders between his hands, and coaxed her down to the blankets with him. "*Chica...*" Again, his fingers brushed her cheeks. "You are very beautiful. I have waited a long time for this pleasure—" Unable to halt her emotions, Talon burst into tears, immediately cupping her hand over her mouth to mute her sobs. Her deep heaving as Manolo pulled her against his shoulder almost dragged consciousness from her. His hand settled against the back of her hair, his fingers tunneling into their thick depths. "Am I so bad, *chica* that your heart would break like this? Is the thought of being with me this way so terrible for you?"

"No, Manolo...it's just that...I have never looked at you like this. But—" She drew back, prideful determination halting her tears. "If this is what you want in exchange for Nightwing's life, it is a small price to pay." As her violently trembling fingers eased beneath her blouse at her shoulders to draw it down—to get this over with—Manolo took her hand and halted its movements.

Manolo, do not let her tears get to you. You bandito, bastard, without conscience. Take the treasure she offers you. But even as his mind screamed the fervent admonitions, his lips whispered with a mind of their own, "No, *chica*...as much as I want you, I cannot let you do this. Not if it means I might never see you again. Not if it means your thoughts of me will bear only hate—"

"But...Nightwing—"

His hands closed over her shoulders again. "I will give you Nightwing's life in exchange for—what the gringos say—a white lie?"

"A white lie?" she repeated.

A grin sharpened his mouth. "You stay here with me for—say—one-half hour, and let my hombres think we had a *very* good time behind Manolo's blankets. For that little lie this Apache's life will belong to you."

Throwing herself against Manolo hard enough to rock him from his knees, Talon's hands went quickly to his back. "You *do* care about me."

"Of course I do, Talon, I love you. I have for a very long

time." With a lusty, almost wicked laugh, he added, "I must love you *very* much to deny myself this pleasure. But—Manolo—he cannot break *chica's* heart."

For the better part of half an hour, they talked, laughed, and reminisced about the old days. By the time Talon, anxious to get Nightwing to safety—and a doctor—coaxed Manolo from behind the blankets and among the grinning faces of his hombres, they had settled one very important issue between them. This would never happen again. Manolo knew his role in Talon's life from this moment on.

Skipping among the men—even knowing what they thought she and Manolo had done together—Talon was happy and smiling, sharing brief, personal jokes with each of them. But she wanted only to be with Nightwing, forced to remain on his feet by the hemp binding his wrists. Going to him, she saw that he was near collapse from his wounds. Yet she had never encountered so much rage—so much disappointment—in the blackest eyes that had ever stared back at her. She touched his cheek fondly, but he employed almost the last of his strength to jerk from her hand. Requesting Nightwing's knife from Rio, she caught it and cut Nightwing's bindings. As he folded to his knees, she dropped before him, supporting him against her own body. He was too weak to fight her assistance, as she caught the shirt Rio threw to her and helped Nightwing drag his arms into the sleeves.

Then, suddenly, he was on his feet, stepping away from her.

Talon rose and retrieved the fatigue hat, the familiar rifle, and knife, and handed them to Nightwing, who snatched them with a silent scowl. Ignoring his contempt, Talon turned to approach Manolo and lightly kiss his cheek. "You do not know how much I love you today," she whispered so that only he would hear. "You have shown the spirit of a true friend."

"You know I love you, *chica*, as man and woman...not father and daughter." Manolo now stood face to face with his enemy. "You belong to Talon Rose now, Apache." The fat Mexican brought Nightwing's horse.

Talon stood beside Nightwing at his saddle while he eased his gun belt from the pommel and clumsily strapped it on. His left arm was almost useless to him, but he refused her help. When she was sure he would mount his horse and ride away before the Mexicans had a change of heart, he calmly produced a pair of shackles from his saddlebag.

"I thank you for whoring body in exchange for this Indian's life, but I take you back to camp now."

The Mexicans swiftly drew their weapons. Talon gasped in astonishment at Nightwing's reckless, and very ill-timed bravado, and the unwarranted insult to her character. Her temper flared. "I just saved your hide from these men, and they would have killed you. They could still kill you!" The Mexicans closed in, but Talon's hand swept up. "He takes me as his hostage to ensure safe passage." Then, jutting her chin in a prideful moment, she extended her arms, and Nightwing locked the cold iron over her wrists. Talon asked Rio to bring her horse, and grumbled softly to Nightwing, "When you are safely away from here I expect you to release me."

He had slipped his rifle back into the scabbard and pulled into his saddle. "I let you go when I turn you over to guardhouse for desertion." Leaning toward her, he ordered, "Get horse and come."

"I hate you, Nightwing."

His fingers tunneled softly through her hair as he spoke. "If you want hate me, Talon, hate me. But come now!" Within minutes Shadow Dancer, wearing a new saddle and gear, was brought from a small corral beyond the rocks.

"You will never make it back to camp with me," Talon spat. "And do not expect me to help you get there, you dumb, ungrateful Apache! I hope your bones bleach on the desert! Damn you!"

A grimace claimed Nightwing's lean, sun-darkened features, his voice patient and soft. "This dumb, ungrateful Apache trust you to help make it back."

"Do not trust me. I do not deserve it."

"I know that, Talon" he replied matter-of-factly. "I am not

reasonable man sometime, but I know true heart of Scout, even if Scout do not."

Shamed by his compliment, Talon pivoted to address the bandits. "You must leave Arizona territory, because he will send many soldiers."

Nightwing coaxed his horse toward the opening in the rocks to await her. When she drew into the saddle, Manolo approached her, his hand covering hers against the pommel. "Just say the word, *chica*, and we will cut down this Apache who takes you prisoner."

"I do not want him to die."

Manolo growled, "What is this buck Indian to our *chica* that you allow him to put you in chains?"

Talon glanced toward Nightwing, sitting his horse twenty paces away. When their gazes locked, he yelled, "*Yushde! You come,* Talon!"

She cut her eyes defiantly, her response to the Mexican softly sincere. "He is important to me, Manolo. I am not sure why."

"You in love with this buck Indian?"

"I trust him, and do not trust the one I love, the captain I told you about. Love with this Indian is not a complication between us." But even as she spoke, her heart warned her that wasn't quite true. He was very special to her, though she didn't believe it was love.

"You know, *chica*, if we take this buck Indian another day, we will kill him."

"You have given me his life, and graciously—" She looked to make sure no one was nearby, "without the payment you demanded. I promise you now, Manolo, and I hope you will listen carefully to me. If you ever catch him out alone again—if Rio's whip spills one drop of his blood—no matter where I am or what I am doing, I will send the authorities to take you. I know your habits and it will not be difficult."

He shook his dark, heavy hair, his eyes tenderly admonishing. "*Chica*, you talk very big for a little *senorita* surrounded by two dozen armed hombres. I have much respect for your bravery...but you know Manolo loves a challenge." His fist fell to his heart. "Your words to me I take *here* as a challenge. If I ever catch this buck alone, I promise you, *chica*, the black snake *will* tear him up." Withdrawing his hand, Manolo addressed Nightwing from across the clearing. "Remember that we let you live today because our *chica* wants you to live, though now she must regret that decision." Then softly to Talon, "My hombres must *never* know I did not have the pleasure of your sweet body. Manolo will *not* be laughed at."

Touching his dark cheek, she replied, "It will be our secret. *Hasta la vista*, Manolo." Reining her horse, she joined Nightwing. Their gazes met—firmness and fire—man and woman—in a bitter clash of wills. "All right, I am your prisoner, Chief of Scouts John Nightwing! We're thirty miles from camp, so let us see just how far you can get with me."

* * *

Laine had kept absently and annoyingly busy so he wouldn't have to think about Talon. But she consumed his thoughts, his dreams, and he recalled how sincerely she had asked for his trust. His brain had warned him to be wary, but his heart had wanted nothing more than to give her his unconditional trust.

No matter, he loved her with the fullest depths of his soul, and he wanted no other woman.

This late sunny afternoon he attended business on behalf of General Compton at the Public Relations Office. He had just settled in the front office when a man named Reynolds McFee, who billed himself on the side of his wagon as a *Traveling Photographer Extraordinaire*, entered with a large portfolio tied in twine. Laine had noticed his neat, wood-paneled wagon and healthy team at the front gate upon entering the office. He was, most likely, offering his services to homesick soldiers.

This Mr. McFee made clear with his opening remarks to the Public Relations Officer, Second Lieutenant Robert Smith, immediately after introducing himself. "Sir, I travel through this territory taking photographs for posterity. I'm informed at the front gate that I need a pass from your office to solicit business

249

at this camp."

Lieutenant Smith disliked civilians immensely, but would not deny the men of this post the privilege of having their photographs taken for loved ones back home. "While the men would be pleased of your services, Mr. McFee, we're a few days short of payday."

"If I can stay a week or two, Sir, it'll take me that long to set up appointments and develop my film. Soldiers at other camps were receptive to me, and I've a fine reputation. Photographs are delivered with full warranty and approval before I require payment." McFee offered his portfolio, which Lieutenant Smith opened at once. "These are a few of the photographs I've taken in the last few weeks, so you'll see that I'm good at what I do. And I never charge more than two bits a photograph, which barely covers my cost for supplies."

While Laine patiently waited a few feet away, Lieutenant Smith fanned a couple dozen photographs on the desk before him, selecting several to better scrutinize. "My clerk will write permission for you to remain at camp for a week, Mr. McFee. If you wish to stay longer return to my office for renewal. The transportation office will direct you where to park your wagon."

From the short distance, Laine had noticed one photograph of a group of women, mostly Indian, standing against a stone wall in what appeared to be an enclosed garden. Approaching to pick up the photograph, he noticed one particular face among the half dozen staring back at him. She wore a bonnet and gloves, her hair was loose and light across her shoulders. He thought she looked familiar. "Where did you take this photograph?"

McFee came to the side of the desk. "Mission of St. Ignacius about forty miles from here. Jesuits, very hospitable."

Laine pointed to the white woman in the group. "Who is this woman? Do you recall?"

McFee smiled warmly. "Who wouldn't remember? She was as sweet a woman as man will ever meet, fussing about a fortieth birthday coming up."

"Her name?"

"Her name...hmmm—" McFee coddled a thin goatee

thoughtfully. "I'm sure I heard one of the Jesuits call her Jenny...no, no, I believe it was Julia. Yes, that's it."

Her name falling so casually from the man's lips was like a small slap. "Julia—" Laine's last conversation with Talon flew through his mind, the fact that she claimed Julia was alive long enough to have given her the locket, and that she had not been at the Comanche village when she returned years later. "Could I borrow this photograph?"

"Keep it if you wish."

Laine went straight to Compton's office, where Private Roan straightened books on a shelf. "Where is the old man?"

"Retired early to his quarters, Sir." Laine stared conspicuously at Roan. "You want me to fetch him?"

"No."

Roan sensed that Taylor wanted him out of the office, and Compton had given him free access. When he politely excused himself, Laine approached the mantel where Compton kept the portrait of his daughter at age fifteen. For a moment, he compared the two photographs...the older woman, the bloom of youth gently faded, her cheeks maturely hollow over the soft line of her jaw. But the features in both photographs were similar, even the way her smile lifted at the left. Setting aside the locket Compton had draped over the frame, he withdrew with the framed photograph. He stood at the bottom of the stairs ascending to Compton's quarters, his heart racing as he contemplated going to him with his suspicions.

But if he was wrong, and it was not Julia at the mission, Compton would only die again, as he had died twenty-five years ago, as he had died the night Talon fled with her secrets. Returning the old photograph to the mantel and placing the locket over it, Laine went to his quarters, threw off his jacket, and rested in a chair, his boots drawn to a matching stool. He looked at the group photograph a very long time, set it aside to get a glass of brandy, then returned to resume his study. The more he looked at it, the more he was convinced the fair woman among the Indians was Julia Rose Compton. She would have celebrated her fortieth birthday in just a few weeks. The woman at the mission had fussed about hers approaching.

A mere coincidence?

Unaware of the passage of time until the lamp flickered, casting him into a prison of darkness, Laine's thoughts and suspicions reeled through his brain, leaving him with only one conclusion. He had to see the woman for himself. Returning to Compton's office, he wrote a hasty note and secured it to his desk with a paperweight, the sign between them that the matter was a priority. Then he went to Major Daniel Harris of K Company, and to the scout barracks, where he roused Chief First Sergeant Dako from a frenzied game of dice.

He wouldn't wait until the first light of morning and take the chance of having to explain to Compton. So he departed with K Company and ten Apache scouts, just as absolute darkness descended over Camp Casey.

Eighteen

Twenty feet from the spreading branches of a Paloverde, Nightwing dropped from his horse. Scrambling from her saddle, Talon grabbed her canteen and drew his head onto her lap, dread grounding into her gut when he didn't respond to the water trickling onto his lips. "Nightwing—" A few seconds passed before he coughed, forcing the water from his mouth. "You crazy, confused mixed blood. Do not die on me." When he looked to her, she harshly ordered, "Give me the keys to these shackles so I can help you to that tree."

Nightwing saw only the glimmer of tears caught by a sudden shaft of moonlight. "No key."

"What do you mean, no key?"

"I not bring from camp." He tried to stand, but could only brace himself with his right forearm. His left hand, held against his waistline, was swollen twice its size.

Capping and throwing her canteen the twenty feet to the Paloverde, Talon struggled to help him up, then half-dragged him toward the wide, low branches of shelter. Exhausted and on her knees, she tried to catch her breath. "I should get on my horse and leave you here."

Nightwing drew his sidearm and held it against his leg. "Think I will not shoot?"

"I *know* you will not shoot me," she challenged wrathfully. "You think you know my heart. I know yours just as well. You would not have nearly gotten yourself killed just to shoot me now."

"True, will not shoot you—" The gun slowly lifted, falling again for lack of strength. "But I *will* shoot horse you love. *Mageedu*, too, if I must."

She glanced toward the finest horses ever to inhabit the post corral. "You would not."

He wouldn't, of course. "Help me reach camp, and you will

253

never know."

"I suppose you do know my heart," she pouted, turning to sit beside him. "Even if I was not shackled, and you did not threaten to shoot the horses, I would not leave you to die." Retrieving the canteen, she took Nightwing's injured hand and poured water onto it. "This must be tended." When she began to look closely at the wound, he jerked his hand away. "What the hell is wrong with you?"

"Angry at what you did in exchange for Apache life."

With a small laugh, Talon placed her hand to Nightwing's cheek. "Listen to me carefully, you brute of an Apache. I did *nothing* with Manolo. Because I wept he did not touch me. And because he loves me, he let you live today."

Doubt settled to Nightwing's pained features, but only for a moment. "He did not...touch you?"

"He did not."

Nightwing's dark eyes reflected like black pools. "Is truth, Talon?"

"I swear, Nightwing. All Manolo asked of me was that I let his men believe we had made love. That was a very small price to pay for your life."

His fingers rose, pressing hers into his cheek. "Forgive me."

"For what?"

"I say you whore body."

"Because you did not know otherwise I took no offense."

Nightwing drew her hand down, settling it against his chest. "Tell me, Talon, why you desert? Did something happen?"

"Compton ordered me out of camp. Taylor told me never to return or I would be killed."

Nightwing's dark gaze grabbed her own. "Must be joke. Why you leave because Compton—Taylor—tell you to, when you not leave to avoid whip?"

"I went to Compton's office to get back my pouch and he caught me. He was very angry and poured the items out. Inside were a lock of hair and a silver locket that had belonged to his daughter, Julia."

Condemnation was written in Nightwing's glare. "You had things of daughter?"

Talon turned from him in shame. "He said I was wearing the tokens of his dead daughter, and that my father was a butcher."

"Did he butcher Julia?"

"No," she replied shortly, and left it at that.

"Then where you get trinkets?"

"We will save that story for another time." Easing her back against the tree, Talon's shoulder touched his. "And you were wrong about Taylor...he did not lie to me that night. He does—did—love me."

"Then why he send you from camp?"

"He no longer trusts me."

If Taylor no longer trusted her—no longer wanted her in camp—he would not want her for his woman. "Must tell...in recent fighting, five scouts die."

Tears quickly gathered, because Talon had special feelings for all the scouts, and especially Dako. She did not want to hear his name. "Who?"

"Young Billy, Dayahago, Cho, Lichoo, and Gad. And woman of young Billy die, too...murdered."

Talon had gasped at the sound of each name, and drew her hands over her ears at the last bit of news he gave her. "Who did this terrible thing to her?"

"Officers think Bowie Apaches who fled camp. I think very bad man still there."

Talon was thinking about the dead scouts, trying to remember the expressions on their faces last time she saw them. She recalled the beautiful prayer Gad had spoken in flawless English that day before they went out to play lacrosse. Saddened, Talon quickly diverted her attention. "I'm really angry about these shackles."

"When I put on wrists, I mad with you...with mean bandits. You know how I feel about you in heart."

"I know you care about me, as you care about all the

scouts."

Nightwing's mouth pressed as he withdrew his arm. "You must know I more than care for you, Talon. My heart much heavy many long days you gone."

"How can you more than care for this rude Comanche thief without actually lov—" Her sentiment terminated abruptly, and Talon turned her eyes into his hard shoulder. She didn't need the complication of his love, not now, while her life was so torn. So she rose to retrieve their horses before they decided to wander off, and so that Nightwing wouldn't see her tears.

When she returned to him, he appeared to be asleep. Talon looked for a single flaw in him—his lean, sharp features, full, masculine mouth, dark brows like the wings of an eagle, exquisite in every detail. Her hand instinctively rose, but withdrew before touching his cheek. Forcing her eyes from his face, she eased the fabric from his shoulder, and saw that he had finally stopped bleeding, though the flesh around the knife wound was red and swollen.

Settling against his right shoulder, she kept alert to the dangers, listened to the sounds of the night, and the far away howl of coyotes among the bluffs. Fireflies danced against the purple band of the horizon in the cool, dry air, and she drew comfort from them. Nature's lanterns, her mother had called them.

Nightwing moved ever so slightly against her, and Talon lifted her cheek to see if he was waking. Touching her lips to his forehead to check for fever—as her mother had done in her childhood—the heat of his skin tingled against her mouth. She had once seen a small cut on the foot of a Sioux child fester, poison his blood, and kill him within three days. The memory instantly stirred fear and she awakened Nightwing, cursing the shackles encumbering even the simplest movements.

Moments later, he couldn't get into his saddle without her help. He slumped, and would have fallen had she not steadied him. Talon threw a rope over Shadow Dancer, drawing up behind Nightwing's saddle to hold him against her on the journey to camp. The horses lumbered across the hot, sandy plain and into the bluffs, and her mare followed without pulling on the rope. Somewhere around midnight, the air became a little cooler, though without the flutter of a single breeze. The hours crept by beneath the purple Arizona night, and by the time the little camp came into view from the high ridge of Cimarron Bluff, Nightwing was barely conscious.

Talon was tearful from fatigue, and from holding him and reining the horse for these long hours in the saddle. When she pulled up to the guard station, both she and Nightwing fell to the ground. Despite bloody, chafed wrists, Talon pulled him onto her lap, shouted for the guard, then watched both of their horses, refreshed by familiarity, scramble toward their corral.

Within minutes, the medical orderlies on duty brought a stretcher for Nightwing and they were both in the infirmary being treated for their wounds. Captain Calloway was roused from a short sleep on the cot in his office and Nightwing was readied for surgery. Andy Wilson brought keys to remove the shackles that had been shoved out of the way so Talon's wounded wrists could be cleaned and dressed, and now stood by to learn what Nightwing wanted to do with her.

Sitting in the physician's small, tidy office, Talon dropped her head to the smooth wood of his desk. Private Wilson sat on the bench across the room, his eyes closed tiredly, propping himself on a Winchester rifle.

An hour passed. Dako and several scouts responded to the news of Nightwing's injury. One of the orderlies came out to inform them the bullet was lodged between the delicate bones of his shoulder and would take a while to extract. Another hour passed. Major Reisner, the proud father of a firstborn son, showed up to grill Talon on what had happened. She explained about the Mexicans, and though he hotly stated she should be locked up at once, as Compton had ordered the night Nightwing rode out, allowed her to stay during Nightwing's surgery. Dwelling on both her shame and her worry for Nightwing, Talon rested her head on the desk top and sought sleep. Roused a couple of hours later by the distant cacophony of the camp rooster, she was instantly aware of the time that had passed.

Captain Calloway emerged from surgery, a reassuring smile barely there. Now he dropped the large caliber slug, slightly flattened, to the desk in front of Talon, commenting that if it had exited it would have torn a hole the size of a cup in his back. "He wants you to take charge, Dako, until he's back on his feet."

"Did he say anything about Miss Talon, Captain Calloway?"

Calloway looked to the friendly guard, a favorite among the men in this small camp. "She's to be locked in the guardhouse on charges of desertion, Wilson, as General Compton ordered. Nightwing did tell me, Talon, that you saved his life yesterday, and wants it taken into account."

Talon looked to Major Reisner as if he could—would—overrule General Compton's order. Looking to Calloway now, she commented, "I cannot leave until I see him, Sir." When Major Reisner nodded his consent, Talon entered the long, narrow infirmary where a dozen cots sat neatly down a wall. Nightwing was in the farthest cot. Talon approached and looked at him, then dropped to one knee. Her cheek eased onto his bare chest, and she listened to the comforting sounds of his breathing. Almost immediately, Nightwing's hand fell to her head. "I had to be sure you were all right before I went to the guardhouse." Her tone was completely without malice. "I wish you trusted me to go to my quarters and stay."

"I do trust you, Talon, but decision Major Reisner's, or Compton's. Not mine." He rested on the brink of sleep induced by chloroform and exhaustion. "Be safe guardhouse. I not want Compton to shoot you." His fingers grazed the gauze a medical orderly had wrapped around her chafed wrists." "Much sorry about shackles."

Talon looked into his dark eyes now, thinking how handsome this Indian was who spread confusion through her like a sultry wave. "What will become of us, Nightwing, you and me?"

He didn't hesitate to answer. "What I want is to be first in Talon's heart. Not second to Taylor, not second to any man.

When you speak name in sleep, it should be this Indian's name."

Tears settling on her lower lids, Talon pressed her cheek to his warm forehead, her fingers tunneling through the thick, dark hair at his temples to caress him lightly. "You have cared for me unconditionally, Nightwing. No matter what I do, you do not desert me. You risked your life yesterday to bring me back, and if Manolo had killed you, I would not want to live either. But Nightwing—" She pushed back now, so that she might see his eyes and be sure he understood her. "I love Taylor. Though he does not love me now—does not want me—I still love him. I cannot help the way I feel, and I will need time to get over him."

He studied her pretty face for a full minute, as though the very sight of her gave him strength. "I am patient, will change Talon's heart."

Rising, she pressed a kiss to his damp forehead. For a few minutes after he had closed his eyes, she watched his lean, remarkable features, free of pain, almost strengthened by the love he swore for her. Then she made herself leave, because she remembered her love for Laine.

Camp Casey stirred to wakefulness, and as a golden haze settled over the horizon in its prelude to dawn, Talon was processed through intake and settled into a solitary confinement cell. She had so much pain in her heart that she forced herself to sleep, just so she wouldn't have to think about either of the men in her life.

* * *

Salem George Compton awoke the following morning, peeved, grouchy, and in true character. Roan ran late, his orderly was ill and abed, and he had to light the lamps along the corridor and in his office himself. Then he found Taylor's note carelessly tossed atop his desk with a paperweight indicating its priority. Instantly maligned by both his unscheduled absence and his failure to request permission for the excursion through proper channels, he thought he should start reining in the camp's upstart adjutant with more firmness.

Hearing Roan enter the clerk's office, Compton yelled for him. "I expect you to know where Taylor went in such a hurry last evening."

"All I can tell you, Sir, is that they were heading for the Mission St. Ignacius northwest through the Huachucas."

"What the hell for?"

"Sir, forgive my bluntness, but other matters are more pressing. Chief Nightwing returned early this morning with a bullet wound in his shoulder. Ran into the Menendez gang. Major Reisner, a number of scouts, and D Company just rode out in an attempt to catch up to them." Roan paused conspicuously as he added, "And Scout Talon is in the guardhouse."

Compton's gnarled fingers covered his chin thoughtfully. He had been obsessed with details of Julia's life with the Comanches, details that Talon might be able to provide. He had prayed that Nightwing would find her. "So, Nightwing brought her back?"

"Scout Talon brought *him* back, Sir. An' he would'a bled to death if she hadn't."

* * *

By the time Talon awoke a final time that day, darkness had gently covered camp. Her still warm supper tray sat untouched on the small ledge by the door, and she vaguely recalled one of the guards thumping the door when he left it. Upon every awakening, she had received a report of Nightwing, his wounds showing no signs of infection, and the swelling in his hand reduced considerably.

An overbearing shadow claimed the wall outside the door. Talon glanced that way just as Mulroney paused and looked in, his gaze skittering both ways in the corridor. Lifting her cheek from her drawn up knee, her heart quickened as he slipped a key into the lock. When the door opened, Boyd Teakle also stepped into view from the darkened corridor. Instinctively fearful, she stood on her cot and pressed herself tightly into the corner. She knew at once that both men were very drunk.

Pushing open the door, Mulroney stepped inside. "You ready to die, uppity Injun gal?"

Teakle pulled a bottle of whiskey from the back pocket of

his trousers and took a long, noisy gulp. His bloodshot eyes swiped both ends of the corridor.

Talon's noticeable fear fueled these vicious men, and she consciously mustered a moment of courage. "Leave or I will scream, Mulroney."

"Nobody in the building but me an' ol' Boyd here, an' these walls'er two feet thick." Sarcasm surrounded every word he spoke. "Before you die, you need to be reminded you ain't no fine white lady. I remember how you treated me that first mornin' when ol' Money brung you here in chains. Pullin' away like you was better'n me. Well, gal, you sure ain't no better'n that squaw we got a coupl'a weeks ago—rottin' in the ground now. An' them welts on your back...well, you can thank me for that, too."

For a moment, her fear was forgotten, as she horrifyingly remembered how she had blamed the general. Then the men approached, and Talon's fear flooded back and she instinctively searched for an escape. She lifted her foot to kick Mulroney when he approached, but he pulled her heel from under her. She hit her head on the wall as she fell to the cot, catapulting her at once into a spiraling tunnel of murky shadows.

* * *

Major Reisner crawled down from his horse with a hearty round of curses. The Mexicans led by Menendez had abandoned the area Nightwing had pointed out on the map, leaving nothing more than the debris of their encampment drawing flies in the heat. Encountering Private Wilson on the parade field, they walked to the guardhouse together, and were joined by Hiram Stahl. Mulroney was missing from the duty desk.

Andy had a real bad feeling as he recalled the way his sergeant had glared at Talon that morning. "Would you accompany me to see Miss Talon?" he asked of Major Reisner. Right then, her screams pierced the stillness of the guardhouse, the men breaking into a run toward her cell. Teakle emerged at the echo of running boots, instinctively grabbing the old Remington percussion pistol tucked into his beltline. Andy quickly dropped to his knee on the stone floor, raised his rifle, and fired pointblank at Teakle. In the fracas the madly cursing Teakle had managed to get off a single round.

"Ya little bastard," he cursed. "Ya gut shot me! Ya stinkin' little bastard!" Reisner kicked the pistol away from Teakle, writhing and cursing across the stone floor toward the intake office, gold half eagles given to him by General Salem George Compton spilling from a leather pouch at his waist. Reisner left him to the flurry of guards and soldiers responding to the shots.

Limp and clumsy from drink, Mulroney had passed out on top of Talon, whose vain struggles to be free of him had brought her near hysteria. She became aware of the other men only when Mulroney was slammed to the floor, an aggression that brought him from his drunken stupor at once.

Andy Wilson clamped his hand to Talon's shoulder. "It's all right now." Before she might respond to his assurances, he withdrew his bloodied hand and folded to the floor at her feet. Talon was instantly beside him, the crimson tide on his shirt growing larger at mid-section. His youthful eyes were filled with more fear that she had just about ever seen.

Her words tumbled in frantic spurts. "Major Reisner...get a stretcher...get Captain Calloway! Andy has been shot—oh, God—"

As Reisner rushed past Teakle, Wilson looked into Talon's wide, tearful eyes. "You all right, Miss Talon?"

She pulled her head back to smile for him. "Do not worry about me, Andy. Major Reisner's fetching Captain Calloway, so you just stay still and let me baby you for a moment." With hardly an interlude, the pillow she'd grabbed from her cot was completely saturated with blood, and she searched for other linens. Major Stahl had fetched towels from a pantry in the guardroom and now handed them to her. Talon brushed Andy's youthful face with the back of her hand, encountering a few soft hairs along his jaw. "I think you need to start shaving, Andy." He smiled and tried to sit up. "You be still now...Captain Calloway will be here soon." She had to be calm, because if he saw how scared she was right now, he would be scared, too. "Andy, you remember when Mr. Money first brought me to camp? Though you did not say so, I think you were really mad at me when you thought I would let them hang me."

"I was real mad," he whispered. Guards swarmed over the military prison now, someone yelled orders to shackle Teakle, and Mulroney was thrown into a cell. With the last dregs of his strength Andy reached into his pocket and withdrew a slightly crushed red rose. "I snuck it from Sgt. Huck's greenhouse. You won't tell him, will you?" Wilson liked that she smiled for him. "Miss Talon—" Blood trickled from the corner of his mouth. "You know you're about the finest lookin' gal I ever seen in my whole life. Why, if I was just a tad older—"

Then he coughed, eased his head down, and very gently died against Talon's shoulder.

Talon pressed a series of small, frantic kisses to his forehead as if they alone would bring him back. Major Stahl, who had a special fondness for the friendly young guard, wept openly, and the news of his death traveled swiftly among the guards in the corridor outside. Their collective grief echoed in tormenting waves.

Suddenly, the sweet fragrance of the rose swept into Talon's senses, remaining for the briefest of moments.

* * *

Compton had kept Roan at his desk well into the night, for no other reason but to keep him company. Left to his own thoughts throughout the day, he had fought the urge to see Talon, to demand everything she knew—no matter how mundane—about his daughter. He didn't want to believe his girl had thrived in her captivity, and hoped that Talon would contradict the testimony she had given to Taylor in the hills. In all the raids he had led against the Comanches, how could he have missed seeing Julia? He wanted to believe nothing but that Julia had been persecuted and enslaved by the Comanches, and that Talon had worn the tokens of a terrified captive deprived of her meager belongings. Agonizing that she might have been alive over the years that he had thought her dead—and that she had felt utterly abandoned—he had wished these past two weeks that it had, indeed, been Julia's remains discovered in West

Texas. He wouldn't have all these lingering doubts to torment him. Then to have met Talon, a half-Comanche, and allowed her to fester within him like blood poisoning—

Yet there was something about the young woman...

Tortured by his thoughts, he was half-asleep in his chair when Major Stahl charged into his office, slamming his hand down on the desk to get his immediate attention. "Had you not persecuted the Scout Talon for no reason other than her Comanche blood, I wouldn't have a dead guard lying in the post morgue awaiting burial. Mulroney said he was the one who whipped Talon—he confessed that to Talon, also—and that you were the one who ordered the whipping!" He now slung several sheets of paper across the desk. "There's a written account of what happened tonight. Your actions over the past few months are being recorded by my clerk, including the whipping you ordered for Talon, and will be sent posthaste to the War Department in Washington. And your *friend* Teakle is dying over in the infirmary. Damned good night, you sorry, no good son-of-a-bitch. May you rot in hell!"

Then Stahl withdrew, loudly banging every door he came to in his retreat. Compton never had the first chance to defend himself against the accusations.

* * *

Reisner pressed his folded hands to his mouth, waiting for Nightwing to awaken, so that he wouldn't receive the news of Andy's death through unfeeling gossip. Annoyed by Teakle's groans and curses a wall away from this open ward, he wished he would die and get it over with. The post physician had said death was imminent. Having closed his eyes for a moment, Reisner now opened them to his chief's dark, silent scrutiny. "I see much trouble in eyes," Nightwing said softly.

"We had a tragic incident at the guardhouse tonight."

Fear jumped into Nightwing's features. "Talon not hurt?"

Reisner took only a few hasty sentences to tell him what had happened before he quietly announced, "The dead guard is Andy Wilson."

Nightwing's dark eyes coated with emotion. "Skinny

Whirlwind die in Talon's arms?" Reisner nodded. "And Compton responsible for this attack?"

"Mulroney said he was, and also that he ordered him to whip Talon. An official inquiry will be held on Wednesday. We know how Compton feels about Talon."

Nightwing threw off his blanket and started to rise. "I must go to her."

Reisner's hand settled to his shoulder. "Be patient. She is coming to you."

Teakle's groans started up again. He cursed and banged his fist several times against the wall, the sound reverberating through the large, airy ward. A soldier with a bandaged foot released a torrent of curses mixed in with death threats.

"If that is Teakle," Nightwing commented acidly, "He need die now." Shadows scurried over the wall of the infirmary. Stahl entered with Talon, wearing a clean blouse and skirt Dora had collected from her quarters. Nightwing preferred the defiance and fire, not the quiet sorrow glazing her eyes. Reisner gave Talon the chair, and both officers quietly withdrew. Talon dropped her cheek to Nightwing's bare chest, the moist heat of tears pooling against his skin.

"Weep, my rude Comanche thief. As I weep."

Talon's fragile emotions shattered. "He rushed to help me, Nightwing, and he is dead because of me. Why do I hurt people? God knows, I never mean to—"

Nightwing lifted her chin so that he might see her tearful eyes. "He cared deeply in his heart for a friend he willing to die for. Be proud of him, Talon. Honor him, and remember his bravery. I, too, have lost a friend this night, and my heart grieves."

Major Reisner slipped back into the infirmary and mouthed to Nightwing across Talon's shoulder that Teakle was dead.

Nightwing now motioned to Captain Calloway. "Let Talon sleep here tonight, in cot beside me. She does not need to be alone in guardhouse."

Calloway checked with the wounded soldiers in the ward, who were almost too enthusiastic about Talon staying. Reisner had no objection. An orderly prepared a cot for her, placing it so that she would be within Nightwing's reach during the night.

Nightwing held Talon for the longest time, felt her tears, the quiet sobs and her oh, so gentle breathing against his skin. She was content to be comforted by him. Closing his own tearful eyes, he enjoyed a fleeting vision of Andy's laughing face as he won yet another game of checkers.

* * *

The following afternoon at two, Talon sat quietly in the front pew of the small post chapel, watching the soldiers file past Andy's standard military issue coffin. The chaplain, Captain Lindley, prepared to give a short eulogy, but had scarcely taken his place before all eyes turned to the double doors at the back of the chapel. There stood Salem Compton, in full military regalia, quietly removing his hat as he prepared to enter. Roan was with him as he moved up the narrow aisle and turned toward the soldiers in the small chapel.

Looking to the chaplain, Compton announced, "I need to have a word with these people." Then he noticed Talon, sitting quietly on the front pew, her eyes downcast.

Compton started to speak, but was drowned out by taunts of the soldiers. He was visibly humbled and embarrassed. When Talon rose and turned to face the crowd, silence fell at once. "Though this is hardly the time or place for anyone to be making speeches, I wish to hear what he has to say."

Talon returned to her seat, her gaze never lifting so that Compton could politely acknowledge her intervention. "It is reported to me by a good source," he began, glancing toward Major Stahl, "that I am rumored to have paid Boyd Teakle to harm the Scout Talon, which directly led to this young soldier's death. I'll admit I gave Captain Taylor the impression I kept Teakle here to hurt her, but it was not true. I also shamefully admit I have not been generous of heart to the Scout Talon—but, as God is my witness, I did not take a whip to her or order any man to whip her. Mulroney did that strictly on his own, and I am sure fresh interrogations will draw a confession from him." Grumbles of doubt stirred among the soldiers. "I would never

266

have her killed. That is all I have to say, except that I am truly sorry we lost this young man. He and I had words not too long ago, he let me know what he thought of me, and I respected him for that. I thought he would make a fine soldier."

"He *was* a fine soldier," a corporal in the back promptly shouted.

"I stand corrected." Compton, followed by Roan, left swiftly, and Captain Lindley resumed the service.

* * *

Later, after taps had sounded, and the soldiers had left the graveside service, Nightwing approached Talon, standing alone while the burial detail filled in the grave. His arm slid across her shoulder. He thought about her sleeping in the infirmary, hardly an hour of restless sleep passing before she left her cot, then lay along his right side to snuggle against him. "Could not let friend go to Spirit Father without this Indian's farewell."

Talon pressed her face into him, her fingers lifting to stroke his cheek affectionately, but briefly. "I am sorry I got into your cot last night. You should have chased me off."

"I be a fool to do that," he replied, lightly kissing her forehead.

"Does Captain Calloway know you left the infirmary?"

"He will be much mad that Dako help me sneak out." He drew her to him, his mouth lightly against her temple as he spoke. "Trust you to return to guardhouse alone. Feel too woozy to walk with you."

"Let me go to my quarters. I promise I won't run away again."

Nightwing was firm. "You *must* go to guardhouse, because General Compton ordered it. Major Stahl, his guards keep you safe from him. Perhaps, when I am released to duty by camp physician I can talk to general—"

"Compton said he did not pay Teakle to hurt me. And being in the guardhouse did not protect me from Mulroney."

"Nothing like that happen again, Talon. And do not trust Compton." As the last shovel of dirt was tamped into place, Nightwing approached Andy's grave and eased to one knee,

267

gently opening his hand over the dirt. Then he murmured, "*Hananyol...you rest,* Andy." Talon saw that Nightwing's offering was a black and a white checker. Then he stood, held Talon's hand briefly, and withdrew to the shade of the ash where Dako awaited him.

As Sgt. Huck, supervising the men in the burial detail, retreated, Talon stood for a long, long while, recalling each moment with the friendly young guard, each smile, each sweet word he had spoken to her. Then she looked to the sweeping hills just the other side of the fence surrounding the cemetery, and thought how easy it would be to run and hide in those hills. But Nightwing trusted her to return to the guardhouse, and she wouldn't disappoint him.

Taking a few steps forward, her cheeks caressed by a sudden stir of wind, Talon lowered gracefully to her knees and placed the faded rose Andy had given her beside the pair of checkers. Then she pressed her palm to the mound of dirt. "Farewell, my sweet young friend." Drawing a deep, steady breath, she turned toward the guardhouse, and the cell standing open for her. She slept the rest of that day and through the night, aware that no one had come to lock the door.

* * *

Nightwing was back with his scouts the next morning, barking orders from atop his horse. His left arm was held firmly against his chest by several lengths of gauze, as Captain Calloway had prescribed, and the scouts affectionately referred to him as Chief One Arm. He went to Talon that afternoon after dismissing the scouts, carrying a small box containing items from her quarters: books, clothing, and other personal things he thought she might need. Then he sat and kept her company, they talked, laughed, and reminisced about things Andy had said and done, and shared a meal, which Major Stahl brought from the officer's dining room.

"Mulroney confess," Nightwing offered the news matter-of-factly. "General not make him whip you. He do it because he have much hate."

Talon was greatly relieved, but there was enough bad blood

between her and Compton that she would always dislike him immensely. "It pleases me that he is not responsible."

When Nightwing prepared to leave sometime around midnight, he drew Talon into his arms and held her. "No matter what time of day or night," he ordered, "you need me, send word and I come. After all—" He drew back now, his smile almost mischievous. "This Indian belong to Talon now." Then he left the cell without awaiting her response, or looking back at her own gentle smile.

Much later that night, Talon was aware of a stir of unusual activity. Guards rushed back and forth in the corridor, and Captain Calloway's firm, questioning tone echoed among the nervous gaggle of voices. Within the hour, the silence returned and the swarthy guard, Ragin Black, stopped by her cell. "Thought you'd like to know Mulroney hanged himself in his cell." For all the response he got, he could have told her it would rain tomorrow.

Talon couldn't sleep the rest of the night. As the guards settled down, the corridors in the predawn hours snaked with shadows, the macabre stillness spooking her completely.

By Friday, she had spent four days and nights in the guardhouse since she and Nightwing had toppled from his horse. That afternoon, Laine Taylor and D Company, Fourth Cavalry, returned to camp.

Nineteen

Laine assisted a silent and thoughtful Julia Rose Compton down from her saddle. He had spent four exhausting days convincing her to come here, and even as she settled her feet to the ground beside him, Laine saw that she regretted the decision. She feared her father would condemn her for loving and marrying a Comanche. There were many things he had wanted to question her about, including Talon, but having seen her tattoos, and aware that she had lived a life not of her own choosing, he had not brought up painful or controversial subjects. All he cared about right now was reuniting this very gentle woman with the father who had never stopped loving her. "Do you wish to freshen up, Miss Julia, before you see your father?"

Coated in a layer of trail dust, the odor of her horse permeating her clothing, Julia had come this far—reluctantly— and saw no point in delaying the reunion. If it was meant to be, her father would have to accept her as she was. "I prefer to go to him now," she responded, shaking off the bonnet covering her light, dusty tresses. "I am very angry that I let you talk me into this. I am no longer suitable to be my father's daughter."

"I hope his warm reception will chase away both your anger and your doubts." Laine had told no one in D Company, nor the scouts, who Julia was, and had seen the inquiry lingering in Major Daniel Harris's eyes these past four days that the Mission St. Ignacius had been a hospitable host. Laine was aware that Julia had solicited the discretion of her friends at the mission—because he'd overheard Brother Jeremy in prayers. She had even suggested to them that she might return, if her father judged her poorly, or condemned her outright.

As Julia joined Laine on the walk across the parade field, she tried to shake as much dust as possible from her clothing. But it clung like brittlebush and she gave up the toil.

Nothing stirred inside HQ but an arid Arizona wind through an open window, rustling papers skewered to a brass peg. "Let me see where he is," Laine said. A lamp in Compton's office threw a warm rectangle of light onto the corridor floor. Returning to the front office, he motioned to Julia, and pointed to the light. "Your father's in his office. I'll wait here while you go to him."

Julia was almost too nervous to move. So many years had passed since she'd last seen him. She recalled the long nights in their tipi that she had told her beautiful little daughter about her toko—her grandfather—only once identifying him by name and forbidding Talon to remember it. He was just a few feet away, believing her nothing more than a cherished memory. Only when Laine's hand closed over her elbow to encourage her was she able to take the first step. Approaching the doorway, she looked to the back of the chair, and the rich crop of silver hair standing above it.

Her father had grown older, as she had grown older. Would she even recognize him when they came face to face? Would they recognize each other?

Compton had pivoted toward the window to watch the troops dismount. Having noticed Taylor help a woman down from a horse, he was annoyed as hell that troops, scouts, and four days might have been spent rescuing one woman from a peril. He patiently awaited the explanation of an officer who had given him a fair bit of trouble these past few weeks.

A slight movement drew his attentions. "Is that you, Taylor?" Julia froze at the familiar sound of her father's voice, husky with age—a voice she had heard thousands of times in twenty-five years of memories. Her slight breathing trembled as she walked into the room, paused just out of her father's line of sight, and stepped to the front of his desk. Noticeable bewilderment filled her father's features. "Madame, are you lost?"

There was very little Julia recognized about this worn face, except his eyes. "I came to see Salem George Compton, once a sable-haired captain at Fort Davis, Texas."

Blue eyes narrowed slightly. "Did you know me there?"

"I never made it to Fort Davis." Weak with nerves and fear, Julia asked quietly, "You don't know who I am?"

"Forgive me, but I do not."

Julia took a single step toward his desk. "Do you remember a night your little girl had a frightful nightmare, Sir? You entered her sleeping chamber with a pretty new doll, frocked in peacock taffeta, and pressed it into her arms to soothe her tears. It was supposed to be a holiday gift, and you had to rush out to buy something else for her Christmas morning delight."

A tremble settled into his jaws. "How could you possibly know about that?"

"You must know how, Sir."

Compton came slowly to his feet. A moment of quiet anger eased into the painful memories reawakened by this woman. "If you know me, then you must know my little girl died."

"No, Sir, she didn't. She just became a middle-aged woman many hundreds of miles away from her beloved papa." Then, so softly, even she barely heard her own words, "I am Julia, your daughter."

Compton stared at this pale, slim woman long enough to notice the similarities—the smile turned up a little more on the left, eyes as blue as his own—hair the color of winter wheat, so gently frosted with gray it was hardly there at all. Still, he accused, "You are *not* my Julia Rose."

Julia had the full account of the mistake that had left her father·believing her dead for the past twenty-five years. Captain Taylor had told her many things about him to convince her to come here, and yet each time she had felt he left something out. Convincing her that her father would love her unconditionally was the one thing that had brought her here today.

Skirting his desk, Julia Rose removed her gloves, revealing the circles of tattoos at her wrists and across the knuckles of both hands. "These are the marks of my Comanche abductors, and this—" Now she showed him a long, thin scar on her right forearm. "I tore my arm on a nail when I was pitched from the horse I was riding with my mother. I was only seven, and when she died of her injuries, you completely took over my care, until you were transferred to Fort Davis. Then you sent me to live with my great-aunt, Clara Forsythe, in a big white house on Charter Street in Boston."

Shivering with disbelief, Compton drew his girl into his arms. Sobs wracked his body as Julia's hands pressed to his back. She lifted her eyes when Laine came into view, though he quietly withdrew, leaving them to their tearful reunion.

* * *

Talon was aware of the secretive mumblings of the guards the moment she opened her eyes the following morning. In the guardroom, she poured a cup of coffee and settled into a chair near Ragin Black. She had always found this swarthy guard strangely quiet, a gossip, and something of a rattler, waiting to strike when one least expected it. So she only slightly reacted when he said, "Did you hear the news, Miss Talon?"

"You told me about Mulroney last night."

"The news about Old Iron Ass."

She deeply resented the frequent derogatory remarks about this man who was her grandfather. Her lips left the cup from which she had absently sipped. "Do not tell me he hanged himself, too?"

"Rumor is he has a woman up in his quarters."

"Whatever for?"

Ragin Black came to his feet, poured another cup of coffee, and resettled in the chair. "What do you think for? He's a man, ain't he?"

Perhaps he was a man, but he was also her grandfather, and a C.O. with a certain moral code that shouldn't allow his buck soldiers to make sport of him. "He would not have a woman in his quarters for lewd purposes, if that is what you are implying."

Ragin Black laughed. "Hell, Miss Talon, was Taylor what brought her to him. He went out with the troops, and come back with a woman for Old Iron Ass. Likely thought that was the only way to restore sanity in camp, give the old lecher some quim to prick—"

273

Talon slung out her cup, the coffee splashing to the floor in a semi-circle and soiling Ragin Black's trousers and boots. He was much too surprised to protest the mild assault. "I may be nothing but an Indian squaw to you," she shouted, flinging the empty cup onto the spill where it shattered into pieces. "I do not appreciate your vulgarities any more than a white woman would, or the complete lack of respect this entire camp shows its C.O. I generally keep ugly rumors to myself. You might try doing the same." Then she stormed toward her cell.

When Major Stahl entered the guardroom seconds later, Ragin Black sheepishly explained that he had spilled a cup of coffee. *Quite a spill,* the major thought, noticing the remnants of a cup and a wide stain across the stone floor seeping into the mortar...notwithstanding the full cup still in Black's hand.

This looked suspiciously like an Indian assault to him.

Talon had tossed herself onto her cot and tucked her palms beneath her head. Swinging to a seated position the moment Major Stahl entered the cell, she fully expected to be reprimanded for her tantrum. "How are you this morning, Talon?"

The softly spoken greeting kept her silent for a moment. "I am all right, Major Stahl."

"You didn't like your first cup of coffee this morning?"

She made a small face bearing some degree of apology. "I suppose I was a bit impulsive. I must have awakened on the wrong side of the cot this morning." He said nothing, allowing her a moment to refocus her thoughts on her grandfather, though she wasn't quite sure how to put a totally inappropriate question to him. "I understand General Compton has company. Do you know who she is?"

"There's a good bit of speculation, but no one who might know is talking."

"I understand Captain Taylor brought her to camp. Have you seen him?"

"I caught a glimpse of him yesterday. Do you need to talk to him?"

"No." She had responded much too briskly, and color

flooded her cheeks. "I just wondered."

Major Stahl patted her hand. "I know you care about him, scout. Don't worry, the captain appeared well, and he knows you're back at camp."

"Oh—" was all she could manage. Then Nightwing appeared, Major Stahl withdrew, and she thought this tall Indian was a bit moody this morning. Because she suspected he had overheard her ask Major Stahl about Laine, she went quickly to other subjects, managing to draw him from his brooding silence. When he sat on the cot beside her and opened his arm, she tucked herself into its protective wing.

She wondered if the stir she felt was for Nightwing...or a product of her lingering thoughts of Laine.

* * *

The day passed gently into history, nothing left in Julia's life as a captive of the Comanche that her father hadn't heard...except that she had a daughter. Compton had accepted news of her marriage to the Comanche Toya Ruhku—and her confessed happiness with him—with mixed feelings—and Julia hadn't pressed any further details of her married life on him. Julia, her father, and Laine, settled at the dining table in his quarters, awaiting the orderly and Private Roan, who were bringing dinner trays.

All day long, Laine had tried to think of a gentle way to pose the subject of Talon to this former captive of the Comanche. He ached to go to her in the guardhouse, but didn't know what he would say, or if there was anything he could say. He had heard that she'd joined up with the Mexican gang, had saved Nightwing's life, and had given the bandits fair warning so they could scram from the area before the soldiers came down on their encampment.

A clatter of dishes startled him from his thoughts. Julia laughed, "Captain Taylor, your meal is in front of you."

"Sorry, too tense to sleep much last night."

"I've heard that a man who cannot sleep often has a woman on his mind."

Hostility flared in Compton's eyes as he looked to Laine,

though he smiled at once. "Let's enjoy our meal, and—" He paused, looking to Julia. "Do you wish to say grace?"

"We haven't shared grace over a meal since that last night at Aunt Clara's before you left for Texas. I would like that." Taking her father's hand, and Laine's, she bowed her head and said a short, sweet blessing, ending with, "Enough, Lord, amen, and I'm famished." The pleasantries during dinner chased away all the ghosts and painful memories for the moments they enjoyed their meal. Later, they sat and talked, and when the orderly cleared away the trays, retired to Compton's office for an after-dinner brandy, and for Julia to choose a book to read.

While the men talked, Julia absently scanned the shelves of her father's books, recognizing many from her childhood, some of which she pulled down and looked through, to see if the little notes she had tucked into them for his enjoyment so many years ago were still there. They all were, and by their worn condition her father had read them many times over the years, always returning them to the page where she had left them. Then, spying the familiar portrait half tucked behind a lamp, the last taken of her before her capture by the Comanches, she smiled in sweet remembrance of the sitting.

Julia's wandering fingers disturbed the silver locket, its discolored chain chinking over the frame. Horror rolled through her like a black wave as she recalled the morning she had dropped it into Talon's little pouch and whispered to her, *Your heart will tell you when it is time to look at what I have given you.* Clutching the locket, Julia gripped the mantel for support. "Where did you get this, papa?"

Compton thought at once that the locket had awakened painful reminders of her years as a captive. "I should've put that away."

Her features were pale and moist. "Just tell me where you got it."

"It was taken from an Indian—"

"What Indian, father?" she demanded, closing her violently trembling fingers over the lapels of his jacket. "I must see this Indian."

"There's plenty of time for that—"

Tears pooled thickly, streaming over her pale cheeks. Only her desperate need for answers kept her from fainting with fear and dreaded anticipation. "I must see him. Is he here? I must speak with him."

Her reaction frightened Compton a great deal. Turning his eyes to Laine, he ordered. "Bring the Indian here at once."

Torn by dread that her beloved *peta*—her daughter—was dead, that this small treasure was taken from her by her killer, Julia began to sob. At Compton's order, Laine helped her up the stairs. "Bring the Indian here," she wept, covering her father's gnarled hand. "I must speak with him right away."

Neither of the men had corrected her...that the Indian was a woman.

"I'll wait in my office until Captain Taylor returns. He'll come upstairs for you." Compton had been visibly jarred by his daughter's grief. "Taylor, you are to stand by while Julia speaks to the Indian."

Laine left HQ, and swiftly crossed the parade ground to the guardhouse.

* * *

A few minutes passed before Talon tossed aside the book she'd been reading, and stretched out to listen to men's voices reverberating through the chambers and cells of the small stone prison. Swinging her feet to the floor when Ragin Black stepped into view, she felt the stir of renewed anger toward him, so settled her gaze on the book she had cast aside. "General Compton wants you in his office." His tone was apologetically polite. "Captain Taylor is here to escort you."

Her heart leaped, in fear, bewilderment, at the thought of seeing him. A minute later, she was in the intake office, noticing her name in the daily log with Laine's next to it as dispatch officer. He stood near the door, his back turned. Ragin Black approached her with irons. "Why do you shackle me? Has my status changed?"

Her softly spoken inquiry forced Laine's attention. "There's no need of restraints." It was the first time in three weeks Talon had heard his voice, not warm, loving and teasing, but cold and flat, almost rude. He had managed to suppress his southern accent as he'd spoken those few words. Crossing the parade field, he kept an even pace with her, and didn't speak until they were inside Headquarters. "Let's go on back."

Talon entered the C.O.'s office and approached her grandfather's desk. His glance carried strange indifference. "If this woman was in the guardhouse, Captain Taylor, she should be shackled. Or have regulations changed?"

These few minutes of silence between them had taken a small toll on Laine's nerves. He had wanted to take Talon in his arms and tell her how much he loved her. But she hadn't even looked into his eyes, and the hardness in her features halted any show of warmth. "She's been gracious and obliging. There was no need of restraints."

Talon didn't want Laine to say anything nice about her. "Why am I here?"

"Because someone wishes to see you." Compton's gaze merely brushed Laine. "Captain Taylor, bring the lady down from my quarters, if you will."

As Laine ascended the nearby stairs, Talon wondered why this woman rumored to be in Compton's quarters wanted to see her. Now, a rap echoed toward her in barely audible waves, then an exchange of words between Laine and a woman. Her gaze turned instinctively as two sets of footsteps approached.

Julia Rose Compton was faint with apprehension as she halted beneath the pale lights of the corridor. She had expected the Indian to be a male, and hearing Talon's few words from upstairs—the words of a woman—she'd held onto the slim hope that the voice was that of her daughter. Her heart tumbling at sight of the tall, slim, young Indian, Julia watched her for recognizable signs. She couldn't see her eyes in the shade of evening, but knew they were as green as spring, as her own mother's had been.

Talon's eyes.

No matter that she had been just eight years old last time she saw her, she would know her no matter the time that had passed. This was her daughter, grown into a fine, beautiful woman. While Laine remained in the corridor, Julia hesitated noticeably. She stood a dozen feet from Talon, an emotional bundle who feared she'd collapse before she held her daughter again in her arms.

Across Compton's shoulder, Talon met the gaze of a woman she had not seen in fifteen years, older, more fragile, with wisps of gray in once brilliant golden hair, but whose eyes were still shockingly blue. And filled with love she remembered so well.

The love of a mother.

She remembered weeping in the muleskinner's wagon for many days, weeping for her *pia.* Then she had resigned herself to the loss of her mother, and never wept for her again that anyone could see. Talon couldn't move, or think, or coax her heart to regain its life-affirming cadence, because she had been told her mother was dead.

Then her feet found a will of their own, though they felt like lead. She approached Julia, her tears caressing pale cheeks, her mouth turned up in the saddest—the happiest—of smiles. Talon's trembling palms rose to her face as she prayed they might touch warm, living flesh. Her mother's cheek pressed lovingly against her hand. With a barely audible, "Is it really you, *Pia*?" the two women fell into a tearful embrace for the first time in fifteen years, for the first time since both their hearts had been wrenched away by one Comanche woman's treachery, jealousy, and loathing.

A thought snatched Laine from his surprise, floating just outside his power of recall. *Pia.*

He was almost sure he'd heard the very small word before. But where? When?

Compton watched in quiet astonishment as the women wept in each other's arms. Laine had approached the doorway, because he thought he had been ordered to stand by to prevent a catfight between a half-breed Comanche and a terrorized former captive of her village.

"Talon Rose, oh, my heart, my soul," Julia whispered, now

covering her tearful face in a succession of tiny kisses.

Talon's knees buckled, a faint moment grabbing and pulling her to the floor. With a gentle laugh, Julia folded with her, and they continued to hold each other. Words were not necessary; their hearts spoke all the necessary sentiments.

"Julia, what is this woman to you?"

Her absolute joy radiated as she looked to her father. She thought of the long days and nights that Captain Taylor had spent convincing her to return to her father, and the fear of his condemnation at learning she had borne a child by a Comanche. But, how could he ever turn his back on his granddaughter? "This gentle beauty is the heart of my heart, papa." With her palms warmly against Talon's face, Julia confessed softly and proudly, "My daughter, my only child."

A dozen feet away, Laine whispered, "God..." remembering that he had asked her directly if Julia was her mother. He recalled Talon's words that night as she had cunningly stepped around the question. *I never came face to face with any child of Julia's—*

So much horror quaked through Compton that he thought his heart would shatter. Then Talon's hate-filled gaze locked to him, and he fled past Laine, the guilt and shame at his back like a thousand bullets, refusing to let him escape. Julia looked to the corridor where he had fled, her moment of bewilderment as readable as the love she felt for her daughter.

Laine was only able to utter, "He's stricken with emotion."

Julia would have gone after him, but nothing in the world—not even a tearful father—could coax her from this long awaited reunion with her daughter. Then Laine looked to Talon across her mother's shoulder, and he wasn't sure what he saw there. It was neither love nor loathing, and there was nothing he could say to either of these women, and especially to Talon. She had begged him to trust her, and he had walked out on her just minutes after they had lain in each other's arms in the aftermath of passion.

Filled with shame—and anger that she couldn't have trusted him—he quietly withdrew.

Talon and her mother moved to the large, comfortable divan in an alcove, where they continued to reflect on the past. "I want to know everything, every day of your life, Talon, as we get to know each other again, no matter how difficult they were for you. Thank heavens for this friend of yours, Mr. Shepperd, who so lovingly continued your education. Your English is flawless."

"He was like a father to me." She laughed, adding, "As for my English, he told me I was never to use contractions, that they were lazy English...and I never have."

"He helped mold a beautiful, gentle woman I'm so proud to have as a daughter."

Talon dropped her eyes in a moment of shame. "I have done things that will disappoint you."

"The darkness of disappointment passes in the sunlight of love." Julia was swept helplessly along in her happiness and the completeness of her life once again. "You have your grandfather now, Talon. He will love you as Mr. Shepperd loved you, even more, because you're his family." Drawing back, her expressive blue eyes lifted. "When did you look in the pouch and learn he was your grandfather?"

Talon managed some semblance of a smile that bitter memories quickly dimmed. "I learned just recently, but I did not tell him." Her mother's eyes reflected a thousand questions, so she carefully composed her words. "But I do hope you will understand. I'm the only Comanche—the only female—in the Apache scout troop, and acceptance would have been much more difficult had they felt I would be granted special privileges because I am the C.O.'s granddaughter. He learned only tonight that I am his granddaughter—that you are my mother."

"You do love him?" The smallest pang impaled Julia as she anticipated her reply.

Talon had been told that Mulroncy, not General Compton, had wielded the whip against her that night. Even so, and because Compton had tormented her from the very beginning, the demons were still strong. The three of them would never be family, and their lives would always be separate. Taking her mother's hands, Talon quietly reflected on an appropriate explanation. "Love does not come easily to me now, not like when I was your little girl. If I never love him, please know that I will honor your love for him above all else."

"Talon Rose, my sweet baby—" Julia drew her into her arms, the wash of unshed tears like fine diamonds. "One day you will tell me the reason for this new pain. And perhaps when you get to know my father, you'll love him the way I do."

Talon rose instantly, though she continued to hold Julia's hand. She needed to leave before she contradicted a mother's sentiments nurtured by decades of fond remembrance and love. "I should see where he went off to. We must both be a profound revelation for him."

"Shall I walk with you?"

Talon desperately needed to speak to Compton alone. "You stay here and think about all the things we shall have to talk about in the days ahead."

Julia pulled her into a parting embrace. "I just know you and your grandfather will have a close and loving relationship one day."

Talon turned so that Julia wouldn't notice the contempt she had by instinct for Compton. When she began her retreat, Julia pressed the silver locket to her palm. "I believe this is yours, Talon. One day you must tell me how my father got it without learning who you were."

Talon didn't want Compton's name near her heart—not now, not ever—and quietly pressed it back into her mother's hand. "You keep it." Then she slipped from her view, and Julia, holding the locket sadly, resettled to the divan.

Talon knew any affinity glowing with affection was not possible with her grandfather, a revelation she could not express to her mother without breaking her heart. Moving quietly through the darkness, she saw Compton standing quietly beneath the only tree in camp, his shoulders trembling with emotion. Talon attempted to maintain her cover in the darkness.

Compton stilled his emotions at once and, for a while, looked toward a clear night filled with stars. "You have your maternal grandmother's eyes, Talon."

Her tone was cold, chastening, and yet, strangely courteous. "I prefer to hear such remarks only from my mother."

The intractable hatred in her voice was like a sword. "I remember the morning in my office that you said I would have regrets. I do, Talon Rose."

"Your regrets make no difference to me, Sir."

Shame would not yet allow him to face her. "When I caught you rummaging through my office that night, and I accused you of wearing the trophies of my dead daughter, you said nothing in your defense. Tell me—" Now he turned to hold her closely, "When did you first know I was your grandfather?"

"When I saw my mother's photograph in your hands. Only then."

"That same day you asked how I would feel if my daughter had given birth to a Comanche child and you were that child. Why didn't you just come out and tell me you were my granddaughter? You damned stubborn girl. Taylor said he asked you if Julia was your mother, and you lied to him."

The politeness behind her words suddenly went the way of a heady wind, and Talon didn't bother with the nuisance precautions of tact. They were well beyond that in their relationship. "Not lied, Sir, deceptive, perhaps. But I had no choice, because I could not let a monster like you know he had a breed Comanche granddaughter. After the way you treated me— punished me almost on a daily basis—you have the audacity to ask me why I never told you?" Then, calmly, "I hate you, Sir."

He visibly cringed at her words. "You wrote a false confession to protect me, Talon. That is not something you do if you hate a man." Then, "Will you tell my daughter how I treated you, or have you already told her?"

"Still worried about your own relationship with your daughter! If she finds out what you did, it will not be from me. But I may change my mind about that if you ever try to keep me from her."

Pivoting, he snapped, "I will never keep you from your mother."

"She has suffered greatly in her lifetime and if you ever hurt her—" Talon left the threat hanging. "I ask only that you treat me with respect in her presence. She loves you, and I will not do anything to change that...not for you, but for her." She immediately cut off any sentiment he might utter. "I assume I am allowed to return to my position as a scout, and to my quarters?"

"There's no reason for you to work as a scout. And I'll arrange better housing for you."

"My quarters are fine, and you will not take my job as a scout from me as you have attempted to take everything else, including my dignity. Tell my mother that life for a Comanche scout in a rank of Apache has been difficult. It will be better for all of us if no one here knows I am her daughter. And you, Sir, do not need the humiliation of a Comanche breed in your bloodline."

That last statement cut as deeply as his regrets. "I can't promise no one will find out."

"I assume that only Taylor knows, so you *will* manage the confidence."

"If that's what you want, I'll do my best."

Talon retreated into the darkness, halting at once. "Never forget, Sir...as a scout I will respect that you are my C.O. But you are never to call me *granddaughter,* even if my mother is the only other person present. Good evening, Sir."

Twenty

Feeling the salty wash of tears against her cheeks, Talon closed the distance to her quarters. Having just set foot on the top step, she was startled by the soldier who suddenly stepped into the moonlight from the dark side of the scout's barracks. Brushing away the tears, she did not face Laine Taylor.

"Is there anything, Talon, I can say to you right now that you might want to hear?"

Talon kept her eyes turned from him. "I have stated my position to your C.O., Captain Taylor, and would request that you speak to him before any other man."

The chill of her voice did not match his memories of that night she had fled, the warmth and passion of her body as they had become one. "Captain Taylor...are we back to formalities now?" Then, "I will speak to him first, Talon." He had heard her talking to Compton, the anger and the regret, but not their quiet words. "Is that all you wish to hear from me, Talon?"

"Yes, Captain Taylor." Rushing down the steps, her fingers eased beneath the wood handle of the door as she sought to escape from him.

"Talon—" He had her attention, even if she didn't look at him. "If you'll hear nothing I have to say, is there anything you wish to say to me?"

A fragment of silence, distilled by the warm night wind, drifted painfully between them before she spoke. "You should have trusted me. That was all I asked of you that night—that you trust me."

"I am truly sorry." When she started to enter her quarters, he added very softly, "No matter what happened between us, Talon, I love you. That has not changed."

She looked to him, the hatred as strong as the love she felt. "Love, Captain Taylor? You do not know the meaning of the word." She wanted to hurt Laine as he had so deeply hurt her, even as she fought the urge to rush into his arms. "Go to hell," she uttered, "go now," and entered her quarters, quickly closing the door between them.

* * *

Compton went straight to the livery. Hearing the steady pounding of metal against metal, he closed the doors to the livery and followed the sound to a narrow corridor. Wearing a canvas apron, his sweat-drenched back turned to him, Matthew Money shaped a horseshoe against a large anvil. He looked around, a little startled when Compton stepped into view. "I want you to take a whip to me!"

Mattie grimaced. He would have taken a whip to this menacing bastard without a second thought after what happened to Talon that night. "Sir, you must have me confused with a son-of-a-bitch. I don't whip, not even a horse that kicks me in the shin."

Hard blue eyes glared threateningly. "You'll take a whip to me, or you won't be at this camp long enough to sneeze."

"I'm under contract and here to stay." Mattie wondered what had brought this on. "I ain't whippin' you, so leave me to my chores."

Drawing himself erect, Compton quickly shed his uniform jacket, his suspenders and shirt, folding them neatly and laying them over a stable partition. Then he dragged his undershirt down, letting it fall loose from the waist of his trousers. Compton pivoted, grabbed a supporting post, and harshly ordered, "I ordered you to whip me...now whip me!"

With a slow, deep breath, Mattie threw the horseshoe and anvil aside and rose. Before Compton could be aware of his movements, Mattie had shoved him hard against the support post and was angrily tossing his clothing at him. "Ain't goin' to happen, Sir, an' I don't know why the hell you think I would do this in the first place."

He had to hurt deeper than his soul, if that was at all possible, so he wouldn't keep seeing his granddaughter's tears every time he closed his eyes in sleep. But he knew this iron-hard former deputy wasn't going to give him the pain he

286

deserved tonight. After he had restored his clothing and buttoned his uniform jacket, trying to maintain some dignity, he sat down and admitted everything that had happened tonight, and how he had learned that Talon was his granddaughter.

Matthew had heard about the return of the general's daughter, and he was somehow not that surprised that Talon Rose was his granddaughter. He listened as a friend might listen, and when General Compton finally left him, Matthew Money knew one thing. He had a hell of a lot of respect for him that he never thought any man at Camp Casey would have.

The man was truly repentant, and ashamed. He almost hoped that Talon would forgive him one day. Almost—

* * *

Nightwing stood against the dark, watching Talon enter her small room as Taylor, with whom she'd exchanged a few abrupt words he hadn't heard, stormed off. Entering her quarters without knocking, he found her weeping against the wall with her knees drawn up. "Why can I not be left alone, Nightwing? Damn you!" Then she rose and fled into his arms.

"Major Reisner said Taylor took you to Compton's office. What did he want?" Her emotions crumbling, she slumped to her knees, her palms pressing into her eyes. Nightwing was on his knees with her, drawing her hands from her face. His touch was gentle, even as his voice grew hard. "Taylor made you cry?"

"No," she replied, though Laine was certainly part of the reason. "Compton...and the woman with him, his daughter Julia Rose."

Nightwing's hand moved smoothly onto one shoulder to shake it a little roughly. "You do not like woman?"

"I like her very much," she whispered, taking his bandaged hand tenderly between her own. "She's my mother, Nightwing, and I love her dearly."

Nightwing's breath caught in surprise. Her tears were like a twilight-darkened stream, and as sad as any he had ever witnessed. "But you said mother dead."

"That is what I was told at my village. But Compton's daughter *is* my mother."

"Then he your grandfather!"

His statement evoked instant rebellion, anger blending with her strong emotion. "I will never call him grandfather."

"He *is* Talon's family. You *must* forgive what he did." Nightwing lowered his voice to reason with her. "One day you will not have grandfather, Talon. You regret you did not forgive him. And you not be able to take back what you did not do. Forgiveness not only for him, but for you."

Nightwing's gentleness took away any new arguments she might present. "I know you and Major Reisner plan a scout recruiting excursion. Let me go with you. It will give my mother time to spend with her father. I promise I will not run back to Manolo."

"You swear on this Indian's life?"

"May vultures gouge out my eyes if I lie, the sun dry my wretched flesh, and the wind scatter me like dust."

He smiled at her very colorful vow. "I check with Major Reisner before I say yes."

"I will see my mother before we leave."

His fingers went roughly beneath her chin, forcing her to face him. "Then go now, while Compton away from her. I saw him go to livery." His touch relaxed, his mouth slightly parting, as though he would share a small secret with her. "Apache bucks in village might want to be scout when they see beautiful half-blood riding among us."

When he stepped from her, Talon delayed his departure. "No person at Camp Casey is to know I am his granddaughter."

"He and mother will tell...Taylor will tell."

"No, they will not. And you mustn't tell either. You do understand?"

He did not want her life mired in secrets. "Understand." Then he was gone, and the clip of his boots across the planks, muffled at once by the sandy soil, left her in quiet solitude.

* * *

Compton wanted only to confine himself to bed. But he could not yet face Julia, so went to Laine's quarters, where he found him nursing a goblet of brandy. He hardly stirred as the

288

door opened, allowing an uncomfortable breeze to waft in with Compton. "Is this a social visit? Or should I get on my damned feet?"

Compton dropped to a chair. "I've done an abominable thing." Laine swung to a seated position, the half-empty goblet finding a place on a small table. "I didn't know she was my granddaughter, Laine, and she will never forgive me."

Laine could count on one hand the times Compton had referred to him by his given name. It was always *Captain* or *Taylor,* and then with insipid military flair...or anger. "Did Talon *ever* disobey you, Sir?"

The usual sounds of Camp Casey subsided in the moment of silence before he answered. "I posed silly hypotheticals at Rock Bluff and she was courteous and respectful." Regret ground into his voice. "Why the hell didn't she speak in her defense and tell them I was a liar? Why did she write that damned confession?"

"Because she wouldn't disgrace you in the eyes of this camp," Laine retorted crossly, rising. "And she wrote the confession because she knew you wouldn't back down! She thought it would make you look like a fair man to the soldiers you command!"

"I persecuted my own granddaughter, simply for being Comanche!" Reeling with grief and pain, he again dropped to the chair. "I would rather put a gun to my head, pull the trigger, and die in my shame, than face my daughter...ever again."

Laine poured a brandy, which he roughly handed to Compton. "The shame belongs to both of us, Sir. I should have trusted her." Boots echoed on the porch, and Reisner stood in the open doorway. "Come in," Laine said. "Enjoy a brandy with us."

Reisner would shoot himself in the foot before he had a social drink with Iron Ass Compton. "Thank you, no. I saw the C.O. come this way and need a word with him, Captain Taylor." Laine stood aside, and Reisner entered the dimly lit front parlor. Compton didn't rise as Reisner addressed him. "Sir, as you know I'll make a recruiting excursion tomorrow to replace our dead scouts, and add several more as you suggested. I request permission for Scout Talon to accompany us."

Compton eyed him coolly. "Is this something she wants to do?"

"I understand it is, Sir. I need to know that she'll be allowed to return to camp."

Laine didn't want her to go, but imagined that it was because of him that she was willing to ride away from Camp Casey for a few days and put distance between them. Laine stepped forward. "Major Reisner, of course, Talon will be allowed to return. She's his—"

"Captain!" Compton came to his feet, Laine's near blunder temporarily restoring his strength. "Talon will get no more opposition from me." Reisner withdrew, and Compton looked to Taylor. "She doesn't want anyone to know she's my granddaughter."

Laine would question him on that later. Right now, he needed to catch Reisner, and halted his retreat thirty paces from the porch. "Does Nightwing also go on this recruiting excursion?"

Reisner gritted his teeth in a moment of silence. "When we hire scouts, Sir, Nightwing approves the final cut. Of course, he goes." Reisner was well aware of Taylor's fondness for Talon. Tonight, John Nightwing had confessed that he loved her, and if it was up to him to decide who was best for Talon, there would be no hesitation in naming that man...John Nightwing. "Is there a problem?"

"No, sorry to have held you up." Laine reentered his quarters to find that Compton had emptied his goblet and was now refilling with the last dregs from the bottle. "Don't let Talon leave the post."

Compton had heard the inquiry put to Reisner. "Or don't let her leave with Nightwing?"

"If you demand specifics, don't let her leave with Nightwing."

"If Talon loves you, she'll return to you."

"Talon despises me, but I hope to change that, which I can't do if she isn't here."

"And off with another man?" Compton sipped the brandy, which did little to numb the pain he felt tonight. "I would suggest, Captain that my grand—that Talon could use these few days to sort out her own feelings. If she doesn't return to you, then it wasn't meant to be."

"Talon and I are meant to be," Laine growled, venting his moment of rage by kicking over a small table destined for storage. "And she can't leave with that black-hearted Apache bastard!" Storming past Compton, he yelled, "By your leave, Sir. See yourself out."

* * *

Talon gently tucked the combs Laine had given her into her hair, feeling the curves of delicate filigree against her fingertips. She deeply regretted her anger as she had spoken to him. Though she and Laine couldn't be together, she didn't want him to think she hated him.

The door open with a loud thud, and Laine stood against the darkness. "You are *not* going off with Nightwing when there are issues to be settled between us!" The words flew from his mouth. "When we've had a chance to talk, Talon, if you still want me to go to hell, I'll don my finest blues and go in gentlemanly style!"

Each word he'd spoken—yelled—pounded in her pulse. "I believe, Taylor, that you need to sober up," she replied, removing the combs from her hair before he might notice them.

But he did notice, and was instantly against her, drawing her into his arms, even as she fought to keep distance between them. "You love me, Talon. Don't go on this excursion," he whispered, his mouth caressing her soft, loose tresses. "Stay here and let's work out the problems between us." Before she might break his grip, his rough, demanding mouth covered her own. Forcing the smallest space between them, she struck him with her fist hard enough that he reeled from the blow.

Laine attempted to right his footing, even as Talon was against him, pummeling him with both of her fists. Her eyes were filled with tearful rage. Managing to capture her flailing wrists, he crushed her body against the stone wall. "Forgive me,

291

Talon." Regret rippled upwards from the pit of his stomach. "Forgive me for not trusting you. Without you, I'm a shambles."

Talon felt her resolve slowly drift. She wanted to be angry with him, even to hate him, and yet his nearness stirred her to quiet passion. A wild, uncontrolled river flooded her, forcing her to gasp air, to still the intense flutter of her heart. But even as she tried to force him back with her body, her hands went to his shoulders to draw him sensually close. The rippling play of muscles beneath his shirt enraptured her so completely that when his hands went beneath her blouse, boldly rubbing her flesh until it was moist and hot, she couldn't force her mind to regain her sanity, to revile and curse him for not trusting her.

Small, panicked gasps rushed into her lungs as his hands were suddenly at her breasts, his mouth holding her own prisoner, the deep probing of his tongue taking away her breath. Then his hands moved lower, popped the stays of her skirt and before she quite knew what was happening, his finger had roughly invaded her womanly flesh. She wanted to hate him—to curse him for this violation—but her thighs instinctively parted, allowing for his deep, aggressive probing. When his kisses trailed hotly over her neck, between her breasts, across her stomach, and paused...there...where the pain of passion erupted like a flame, she couldn't believe what was happening to her...how weak her body felt beneath this act that she could never, in her most passionate dreams, have imagined. As he took her to the depths of a hunger so great she couldn't open her eyes, her fingers dug into his shoulders, one knee lifting high as she accepted the tempestuous caresses that tore through her body and tumbled her into the clouds.

Deep within her abdomen the spasms tormented her, small moans escaping her lips as he suddenly rose and unfastened his trousers. He was swiftly inside her, the seizures of her ultimate pleasure surrounding him. As she molded against him, he turned from the wall, eased her onto her cot and maintained their intimate joining, his face separated from her own so that he could see the crimson passion flooding her features, continue to taste the honeyed depths of her mouth, and watch the betrayal of her desire wash over her. Freeing her breasts from her blouse, he kept them captive beneath his caresses, his hips grinding against her own as the warm cavern of her femininity caged him below.

Talon hadn't planned for this fiery violation of her body, but was powerless to halt it, unwilling to deny herself the passion he awakened. As he rocked against her, she wrapped her long legs around him, arching to accept him fully. Then, when she was sure she would scream in her torment, her thighs trembled with weakness against him as his legs and hips jerked with explosive release. An almost animal passion ground from the depths of his throat as he collapsed above her. His breath shallow and quick, his cheek eased alongside hers. She lay very still, silently berating her body for this betrayal, and him for causing it.

When the weakness of passion washed away from him, he drew up; one knee pressed to the bed between her thighs, and casually refastened his trousers. Then he propped himself atop her with his palms to her sides, a half-mocking smile catching his mouth. "You *are* mine, Talon, just as I am yours. You will *always* be mine, just as I will always be yours. You're going to stay here with me to work out whatever problems you think we still have."

"Nothing has been solved, Laine! This does not settle the trust between us that has been lost!" Talon quickly pulled the fabric of her blouse together and refastened the buttons. Then she raised her foot and would have kicked him out of her way if he hadn't suddenly moved. Restoring some order to her clothing, she got to her feet and put floor space between them. "No matter what just happened, I might love Nightwing!"

A reckless hand flew out and captured her shoulder. "Your body is aroused only by mine. You don't love Nightwing!"

"You are an egotistical bastard, Taylor!" Removing his hand as though she would caress it, she merely threw it away from her. "You will *never* again touch me without *my* permission."

"You didn't exactly fight me off!" Since they had just made love so completely—and he had done for her what he'd never done for another woman—he didn't want to think that she might actually love Nightwing. He remembered all the times the Indian had been deceptive, had wrongly translated the words Talon had spoken to him in Sioux that night in the guardhouse, though he still had only a vague idea what she might have said. "And I don't want you leaving with Nightwing. I couldn't bear losing you to *any* man and especially him!"

Talon turned from Laine to sweep up the combs she had carelessly tossed to her bed. "What happened tonight can never happen again. I cannot be with a man who does not trust me." When she handed the combs to him, he refused to take them.

"I'll take them only when you tell me you no longer want me. If you keep them, I'll know you love me." Again, she tossed the combs aside. "Maybe I didn't trust you, Talon, but you're as much to blame for that as I am. At any time you could have told me Compton was your grandfather. So the lack of trust here is mutual." When she turned her back to logic she wasn't prepared to hear, his slim hands covered her shoulders from behind, his mouth easing against her hairline. "I made a mistake, and I'll go to the ends of the earth to make it up to you. But, Talon, if you leave tomorrow with Nightwing—"

She spun toward him now, her hostility reignited. "I'm a scout! If I leave with Nightwing, what will you do?" Her eyes darkened with spite, with a need to fling accusations. "Turn your back on me again? Then come to me only when you want a woman's body against your own? Come to the Indian with her loose morals, fondle, molest, and defile her?"

He gripped her shoulders, ignoring her wince of pain. "I want you to be my wife! And I don't want you going off with that son-of-a—!" His words halted at once. He couldn't scorn his rival without driving her into his arms. Right now, he could either regain her trust, or lose it altogether. Releasing his grip, he half-turned from her. "You go with them tomorrow, if that's what you want. When you return to me, the matter of Nightwing will never again be an issue between us."

"*If* I return to you!"

Opening the door, he paused, his head resting against it in a moment of rueful thought. "Yes, Talon...*if* you return to me."

Despite his lack of trust, she had never questioned his love for her. "Thank you for bringing my mother back to me. She told me how you found her."

He smiled sadly. "You'll want to say goodbye to her before you leave. Compton is at my quarters, ashamed to face her." Drawing up, he added, "Ride safely tomorrow. Oh, and—" He turned quiet, glassy eyes to her, "I'm really sorry about Andy. I know you were fond of him." Pain erupted where she had struck him and he rubbed his chin. "You do pack a punch."

When he left, Talon leaned against the closed door, the lingering passion of him still vividly flooding her body.

* * *

Half an hour later, Talon crept up to Laine's quarters and peered in the window to make sure Compton was still there. She didn't actually see him, but heard his voice, so eased toward HQ, entered the front office and ascended the steps to his private quarters. Her mother sat quietly at a small table, mending a tear in the hem of a dress.

Talon kneeled beside her, as she had so often done as a child, Julia's hand settling to her hair. "I still cannot believe you are here. I expect to wake up, and it is all a dream, a terrible trick that the—" She halted the derogatory remark she had been about to make, by instinct, against Compton. "A terrible trick of the night," she quietly amended.

"Did you find your grandfather?"

"I did, and we had a little chat. He is talking business with Taylor now and should be back in a while."

Silence tensed between them, her mother still gently stroking her hair. "You don't like him, do you, Talon?"

Her mother would know if she lied. "The fact that I am half-blood Comanche started us out on the wrong foot when he first came here."

"I need to ask you something." Julia's fingers easing beneath her chin, Talon instantly feared her question. "Has my father *ever* hurt you?" Talon's lower lip trembled before she caught it between her teeth. "I see that he has, and I want you to

295

tell me how he hurt you."

Talon attempted to shrug off the inquiry. "I was sassy and rude to him one night. He lightly slapped my cheek," she fibbed. "It was nothing."

"A light slap on the cheek? That's all?"

"That is all. He apologized for it later." Nerves—guilt that she had lied to her mother— brought Talon to her feet. "Do not worry so much about my relationship with him. Think about all the things we shall have to talk about when I return."

"From where?"

"That is what I came to tell you. We are leaving early in the morning on a recruiting expedition. We should return within two weeks."

"I don't want you in this kind of danger?"

"I'm a scout, it is my job."

"You're my daughter."

Pulling a chair up Talon took both of her hands and held them warmly, keeping her eyes downward. "I need to talk to you about that. I reminded your father of the difficulty I had being accepted by the Apaches when I came here. We both agreed that it would be better if no one else knows I am your daughter—that he is my grandfather. If the Apaches think I might be favored among the scouts, it will make things more difficult for me." She had expected and dreaded the emotion now sheening her mother's eyes. "When the time is right, the whole world can know I am your daughter. But for now, it must be a secret between the four of us—actually, the five of us—since I told my Chief of Scouts tonight."

Julia couldn't prevent the disappointment shading her eyes. "As long as you can be my daughter when we're alone."

Talon touched an almost childlike kiss to her cheek. "Thank you for understanding." A door closed within the building. Anticipating the general's return, Talon climbed to her feet, holding her mother's hand warmly. "You start making that list of all the things you want to know about my life, and all the things we can talk about when I return. When I enter that gate in a couple of weeks, you come straight to my quarters." A man ascended the stairs, Talon's heart leaping with dread at seeing him again tonight. "I had better get going. Nightwing wants all the scouts to get a good night's sleep before we leave in the morning. You take care, get to know your father, and I will see you when I return." With a brief hug, Talon turned just as Compton entered the roomy parlor. Moving past him, she said politely, "Good evening, Sir," and quickly descended the stairs.

Compton was at once distracted by his daughter's tears. "What troubles you, Julia?"

"Talon is leaving with the scout troop tomorrow, and might be gone a couple of weeks."

"Oh—" Relief filled him completely. "She'll be back soon enough."

"She told me what you did to her."

The statement left him pale with dread. "What do you mean?"

"That you lightly slapped her cheek when she was sassy and rude to you."

He gave her a thin smile. "Oh...that," he replied, and wondered what had come up to require such a response.

"Promise me now that you won't slap her again, lightly or otherwise." Then she hugged him, very long and very tightly. "I am so happy, Papa."

Twenty-one

Ten miles from his home village, Nightwing sent two scouts ahead, to warn them of the approaching soldiers. Then he began telling Talon, who had ridden beside them for the duration of the trip, all about his mother, Hanhanna. Not only was she the tribal medicine woman—her powers bestowed by Goddess Earth—but also the unofficial leader of the village, a rarity in an Apache society where man was dominant.

Lagging behind the troops, they drew their horses up where the trail began its descent from Black Wolf Bluff, and looked over the scattered tipis and hogans of Nightwing's camp. Children played, women were at their looms, old men smoked their pipes, and horses paced restlessly in a small corral. Talon recognized the painted mare and wondered to whom Nightwing had given it. Almost as if he had read her thoughts, he remarked, "You see mare you gave this Indian, Talon. It belongs to mother now. Her pony grew old."

When they finally entered camp several minutes behind the troops, the children scampered to Nightwing. Talon watched with deep admiration as he took a brown bag from his saddlebags and spread the hard candies and jujube paste among the eager hands. Not only was it evident that the children loved Nightwing, but he loved them as well. Then she remembered his little son—and a warm night in the bluffs that he had told her about the night he'd been kidnapped from their village.

Watching him now, his eyes lit with pride as he watched the children scamper, she thought what a wonderful father he must have been to his son.

While the troops settled down just east of the village, Nightwing took Talon to meet his mother. Hanhanna's light golden skin was smooth and unlined, her hair only slightly peppered, and Talon scarcely believed she was forty-eight years old. She had never seen eyes so bright, youthful, and alive, as she shared a brief moment of affection with her son. Then she turned her attentions to Talon, and those same eyes became narrow and critical. Even as she continued to stare, she invited them both into her tipi, where she offered cups of Mormon tea, sweetened with a little sugar she had gotten from a Navajo tradesman friendly to the village. Talon was sure Hanhanna had given Nightwing an unspoken signal, for he suddenly set his cup down and said he would leave them to talk alone. Hanhanna sat and looked at Talon for several minutes. During this close and somewhat unsettling scrutiny, Talon had quietly sipped her tea.

"Son tells truth," Hanhanna eventually said. "Comanche half-blood very beautiful." She paused, drew a small breath, and settled her hands on her knees. "I see something inside you, deep as love you have for white soldier." Hanhanna usually spoke a strange mix of Apache and Sioux, but now relied mainly on the language of the white man that she had learned at the Mission St. Ignacius.

Talon looked up from her tea, a little surprised that Nightwing had mentioned such intimate details of her life to his mother. "Oh? What is that?"

Hanhanna leaned slightly forward, her voice soft and polite. "Love for Hanhanna son," she replied, and continued to study her intently. "Indian man, Indian woman belong together, no matter tribe of birth. White man, he like Indian woman because she different from pale woman he see all time, and he like warm Indian body in blanket. You be wife of Nightwing...not white officer who grow tired, look to woman of own kind."

Talon cowered beneath Hanhanna's bold eyes, and the words she spoke with deliberate cruelty. "Did your son put you up to this little talk with me?"

"He much mad if he know what mother say. But she see heart of son. She see how much son love Comanche. You be wise choose Hanhanna son."

Nightwing had spoken of his mother several times these past few months, but had failed to mention that she was rude, brazen, and boldly spoke her mind. "Would you be pleased if I told Nightwing about our little talk?"

Hanhanna shrugged, as if it didn't make much difference one way or the other. "If you tell him what mother say, she deny it. She want son happy. Tell me, Comanche woman, what it cost me for you to choose Nightwing?"

An incensed Talon gulped a quick breath. "Cost you? You would be willing to pay me to choose Nightwing?"

"We make deal. You want ponies? I have men bring ponies. I send south, bring fine *Espanio* ponies...strong stallion cover good, strong mare, many as Comanche want. You tell me. I make happen."

Nightwing must have told his mother she'd been a horse thief. Drawing a long, slow breath, Talon attempted to still her moment of ire. "You know, Hanhanna...I do not think I like you very much." Hanhannah just smiled.

Finishing her tea, Talon announced that she needed to see to her horse and withdrew from Hanhanna's tipi as hastily as good manners allowed. By the time she reached the shallow dip where the soldiers and scouts were setting up camp, she was almost too angry to breathe. Combing Shadow Dancer, she cursed quietly. Nightwing approached a few minutes later.

"You—Hanhanna have talk?"

"We finished talking, Big Mouth," she growled, her burning sense of outrage stronger than ever. "Now I am grooming my horse. Do you have a problem with that?"

Nightwing closed his hands over her tense shoulders. "She say something to upset you," he laughed. "What she say to bring such fire to eyes?"

Talon spun toward him, shaking the currycomb just inches from his smiling features. "Your mother wanted to know...she asked me...she said she would...she said—" Grappling for words that eluded her, she reeled toward Shadow Dancer, nervous beside Talon's moment of ire, "Oh, never mind. It does not matter!"

Nightwing walked off, laughing softly to himself. In response to one of the soldiers, he said his mother must have *walked into Comanche's tipi and made off with moccasins.*

A little later, Talon settled her head on her saddle and

thought about Hanhanna's outrageous "deal." She felt in her heart that Nightwing knew nothing about it, that he would never have proposed such a thing. It was strictly Hanhanna's idea, and though Talon tried to fault her, she had to admire her great love for her son. But to be blatantly told, as Nightwing himself had done several times, that a white officer would want her only because she was different hurt her a great deal. Later, when the soldiers and scouts joined the villagers for a meal of desert pig and boiled bread root, Talon was too upset to eat more than a couple of small pieces of meat.

Later in the day, Reisner and some of the scouts talked to a group of men about the rewards of scouting for the United States Army. By nightfall, they had picked up two confirmed recruits, with three others strongly considering it. Nightwing was pleased with the men who showed interest, with the exception of a young buck who was a bit wilder than he liked his scouts. Haldani wasn't a bad Apache, but tended to mimic the troublemakers.

The next morning the soldiers and scouts left to visit other friendly camps spread over a fifty square mile area. Always when they were within a few miles, Nightwing sent scouts ahead to warn of the visit. As they spent those first long hot Arizona days traveling between the camps, they knew the watchful eyes of renegade Apaches stayed on them from the bluffs. But beyond Reisner's horse boldly stolen from the string one night, little trouble ensued between the soldiers and hostiles.

* * *

The Overland Stage pulled up to the Mullins-Adair Way station three miles from Camp Casey. Lieutenant Colonel Paul Heitman, who had spent an exhausting eight days traveling from the War Department in Washington, ate a small noon meal, and rented a horse for the short ride to camp. Before he drew into the saddle, he thought that good Arizona soil beneath his dusty boots sure felt good.

With a slightly mocking salute to the coach driver, pulling away after changing out the team, Heitman turned the horse toward camp. Entering a familiar trail through the Huachucas, rather than the direct route over flat ground, he thought about the charges that had brought him back here. He couldn't help thinking of that lazy afternoon he had spent in his quarters at Fort Foote, Maryland, when the missive had arrived from the War Department. The charges against the new C.O. were serious, but none had affected him as deeply as the report on Talon. That afternoon they had talked in his office, before his departure from Casey, she had sworn she would stay out of trouble and be a good scout.

Upon arrival at camp, he would set up an office at the judiciary, take depositions and make a recommendation to Washington. If all affidavits were fully supported by depositions, formal charges of malfeasance and abuse of authority would certainly be brought against this Major General Salem George Compton.

Halfway into his journey through the Huachucas, Heitman met up with a small troop of soldiers, many of whom he knew, on their way to the way station to meet him. Their officer, a stuffy man and a recent transfer from a more northern post, admonished him for leaving the way station alone, before falling in to escort him the rest of the way to camp.

The familiar military post soon stood serene in the valley below. Pulling up to the main gate minutes later, several soldiers welcomed him back. Tired enough to nap, he fought the urge to settle into his temporary quarters, and reported instead to Hiram Stahl's office. After a brief, mundane chat about the trip Heitman had made from Fort Foote, Hiram reiterated his written complaint, with the necessary postscripts, and the news that another man had been responsible for the attack on Talon. Heitman laid his head back, keeping his eyes on Stahl across his cheek for no other reason than exhaustion. When Hiram concluded, Paul ordered, "How can you be sure this bastard in charge did not order the whipping? Send for the Scout Talon, and the camp photographer. I want photographs of these whip marks."

"As I said, Mulroney confessed...he said Compton had nothing to do with it. Still, had it not been for Compton ordering the whipping in the first place, Mulroney would not have thought to do this." Hiram Stahl withdrew a large envelope from his desk drawer and slid it across the desk toward Paul. "I had these taken in her quarters the same day. They show the extent of this scout's suffering, and I only wish color photography was possible. New photographs seven weeks afterward will show how slowly the marks are fading. And, no, I haven't seen them recently. Nightwing mentioned this concern to me." Then, "Talon is on a recruiting expedition with her troop, and not expected back for another eight to ten days." Disappointment washed Heitman's swarthy features. "Should I send soldiers to bring her back?"

Paul slipped the photographs from the envelope and turned them over. "God!" Placing them down for a moment, he blew out a long breath, and resumed his study. "Talon is a handful—but she did not deserve this."

"Every person at this camp agrees that she did not deserve it...I will have Talon brought back if you wish it."

"I plan to be here a month, longer if my recommendation to the War Department results in formal charges against the bastard, so I'll wait. What about Taylor? Will he cooperate in this investigation?"

"I'm really not sure, Colonel. Though he and Compton have been friends for a number of years, there's been a great deal of animosity between them over the subject of Talon. Should I send a guard for him?"

"I would like to talk to him."

Hiram rose and opened the door. Private Black was changing guard. "Go over to the adjutant's office before your duty ends and ask Captain Taylor to meet with me here."

For a few minutes, Hiram and Paul discussed the Apache unrest, and the implication that the lock down of the Bowie Apaches might have been a leading factor. Paul had to concede its responsibility to a certain degree. By the time Laine stood in the doorway, their discussions had gone on to domestic matters of camp.

Laine politely addressed the former C.O., a man greatly

admired by the soldiers at this camp. He had heard it often since his arrival, confirming that Compton was a sad contradiction to this efficient, stable, and well loved officer he had served with only two weeks before his departure.

Heitman stood, extending his hand in greeting. "Good to see you again, Captain Taylor," he said, returning to his chair when Laine settled beside him. "I understand you've tried to keep matters sane around here."

"I wouldn't know about sane, Colonel Heitman. Things haven't been sane since I arrived."

"Tell me, Sir—this commanding officer who replaced me—"

Laine cut him off in mid-sentence. "General Compton has not adjusted well to this camp. I'm aware that complaints were forwarded to the War Department."

"I've been sent to investigate."

Recalling Heitman's signature on Talon's contract, Laine was stiff with disapproval. "Why you, Sir? Shouldn't Washington have sent a man without personal involvement? Without history here?"

"I was sent *because* of my personal involvement, Captain Taylor. And I know this camp. It was home for twenty years."

"I feel a certain degree of loyalty to Compton," Laine confessed. "Since his daughter returned, he has made an effort to amend his bad behavior."

"Whipping a scout simply because she's half-blood Comanche is hardly bad behavior. It's damned criminal."

"It was criminal...but he wasn't responsible for it!" Laine's reply was abrupt to the point of rudeness. "Sir, the information I give you now should go no further than this office." Laine paused as he gathered his thoughts. "Compton is Talon's grandfather."

"What?" This was the first Hiram Stahl had heard of it. "Preposterous, Captain Taylor. What kind of game do you play?"

Seeing that the door was slightly ajar, Laine rose to shut it, and continued to stand as he spoke. "His daughter, Julia Rose, is

Talon's mother. He didn't know this until his daughter returned. Certainly, and with good cause, Talon is reluctant to have a relationship with her grandfather. Though most of the charges against Compton are valid, this is just a really bad time."

Heitman turned his chair toward the tall, pale-haired adjutant. "Then, Sir, I'd strongly recommend you cooperate with me in my investigation, do what you must to restore the integrity of this maligned general officer, and let's reach some conclusion the War Department will accept without quarrel."

"You speak of him, Sir, as maligned, but you're the one who threatened to hang Talon so that she had no choice but to sign a contract and work against her will as a scout."

"And I like to think that little scare saved her life. If I hadn't threatened to hang her, some bastard without my sense of humor would've strung her up before she'd had a chance to say her prayers." Stroking a stubbled chin in need of a shave, Heitman added, "Do I have your cooperation, Captain Taylor?"

With only the slightest pause, Laine replied, "You do, Sir," making a mental commitment to help Compton get through this investigation with some grace.

* * *

Nightwing liked the spreading brow over Wolf's Bluff where he had often ridden to as a boy to sleep beneath the mysteries of the open sky. High above camp, the rocky outcroppings echoed every sound for miles, above the snores of soldiers snug in their bedrolls below. He had expected, perhaps, the haunting glide of an owl or a flurry of bats claiming the night, certainly not the stir of feet toward him on the treacherously narrow rise of this particular brow. Against the backdrop of a pale yellow moon, Talon rose from the rocky trail. She stood and looked down on him before turning away. She'd hesitated because of his lack of clothing, and the fact that he wore only a loincloth. Because he wanted her to stay, he pulled a blanket across his hips, whispered her name, and put his hand out to her.

Lowering to her knees, her warm cheek pressed into his bare shoulder, her fingers easing onto his chest. "I needed to see you, Nightwing."

He spoke almost lazily. "I always here, Talon, when you need me."

Nightwing drew her close, and the vow this gentle Indian had just spoken jumped into her thoughts. She felt too guilty to respond, a small sigh betraying her deep reflections. "I saw Taylor before we left camp," she said softly. "He wants an answer from me. I do not know what to do."

Nightwing's fingers tightened over hers, relaxing as she stiffened against the light pain. "What answer he want, Talon?"

"He said he wants to marry me. But, Nightwing, you are so strong in my heart. I know that I love you. I am just not sure what kind of love it is."

Her confession dangled in a moment of silence. This was the first time she had admitted she might love him the way he wanted to be loved by her. He was pleased, but angry that Taylor kept a stronger hold on her. He had never hated the way he had grown to hate him, and thought he might even like to see him dead. "Do you feel in heart, Talon, that you love me as woman love man?"

"I do not know," she admitted quietly. "I just know that I smile when I think about you, my blood races when you are nearby. Is it possible for me to love Taylor, and yet feel more secure when I see you?"

Nightwing closed his eyes and drew a deep, long breath, to quell the hunger Talon stirred in his blood. "You know this Indian love you, Talon—want you—"

Her fingers quickly covered his mouth, her eyes moist with tears. "I do not deserve to hear that right now, Nightwing."

Propping his head on his raised palm, his dark eyes glistening like dark pools, he continued to hold her hand against his hard chest. "Listen, Talon, to sound of night, stir of life, pale wind that is Arizona Territory. This desolate land, beloved by Indian whose moccasins tred its path many generations. It pulls from beneath moccasins. Soon, only thing left of Indian way of life is memories. With each generation they pass." The hunger in his blood for Talon remained with him. "Sleep here beside me, my rude Comanche thief, beneath this gentle sky, for it will always belong to Indian. White man cannot claim that."

Quiet and thoughtful, she closed her eyes and listened to the rhythmic drumming of his heart. But even as it was Nightwing's life pulsing against her ear, her visions were of Laine Taylor, as she remembered the moments they had spent that night in her quarters. For that reason only, she sat up and said, "I should not have disturbed you."

"I came up here to sleep beneath beautiful sky, to enjoy silent night," he whispered, "You add to beauty, Talon. Stay." Sitting forward, pressing his cheek lightly to her forehead, he murmured, "This Apache need you."

"Nightwing, you know I love Laine."

Raw pain trembled in the vow Nightwing spoke. "Yes...I hate him for it." Leaving her suddenly, he crouched at the edge of the bluff. When she approached him, he said, "A man want for nothing with woman like you, Talon. I want you enough I could drag knife across that—" *bastard's throat.* Though he didn't actually say the words, they spread upward from his very soul.

Talon's hands closed over his shoulders. "If you ever hurt Taylor in any way, I would never forgive you, Nightwing. And I would never want to be with you."

This beautiful half-blood saw into his soul, for she had heard his threat as clearly as if he had spoken it. He would not insult her with denials, so drew her to him almost desperately, his hand roughly tangled through her dark hair. He breathed the sweet fragrance of her as though it had to last a lifetime. Moments later, he pulled her down to sleep beside him, though he didn't seek sleep himself. His heart churned with a love for Talon as strong as his hatred for Taylor. He would never have her as long as that white bastard was alive.

※ ※ ※

They returned to camp just after midnight nine days later, with sixteen new scouts, including a half-blood trapper named Chester Man Alone, who spoke English, Spanish, and Apache, and understood four other Indian languages to some degree.

Though he was somewhat nefarious—and his placid tone of voice tilled suspicion—Reisner thought he would be a good translator between the tribes and the soldiers.

A ton of Arizona dust stirred from horse and rider as they dismounted. Reisner, complaining the last two weeks about sitting a hogbacked horse after his own was stolen, went to the post infirmary to secure an ointment for his brutally chafed thighs. Mattie, still at his anvil at this late hour, took a few moments from his work to inform Talon that the formal hearing on Andy Wilson's death had resulted in no charges against Compton. She accepted the news with mixed feelings.

Entering her quarters, she quickly shed her filthy clothing and settled into the tin tub of lukewarm water. She had scarcely worked up a good lather when her mother's voice sifted into the narrow silence.

Julia was unaccustomed to her daughter being full-grown, when she continued to think of her as a child to be cuddled and soothed. "I heard the troops ride in," she said, politely turning from Talon's bath. "And you said I could come to you as soon as you returned. I'm sorry to disturb your privacy."

With a small, nervous laugh, Talon replied, "I am a quick bather...and very happy to see you, *Pia*." Quickly washing away the layers of dust and pouring water through her hair, she listened to her mother's small talk for several minutes, then rose, wrapped herself in her large towel and stepped from the tub. She made sure the towel covered the fading marks on her back. Dropping to the bed beside Julia, she noticed the pretty blue dress she'd seen hanging in Dora's sewing room and remarked how nice it looked on her. "Tell me about the last two weeks. You and your father got along well?"

"He was ill and in bed the first week you were gone. Strange mood he was in...spoke only to Mr. Money, whom he sent for each day. I think he finds he can confide in Mr. Money, but no one else, even Captain Taylor. My father has acted very strangely."

Matt Money was a friend to everyone. It didn't surprise Talon that he was willing to befriend the general. "He's all right now?"

"Much better, but hardly allows me to leave his quarters alone, except to visit Dora."

He doesn't want you to hear how he treated me. "He worries he'll lose you again...you like Dora?"

"Very much." Softness echoed in Julia's voice. "I am none too pleased that I can't embrace you as my daughter. Can't I be free to see you whenever I wish, and the soldiers believe we are just friends?"

"I think that will be just fine." A sigh coaxed Talon's curiosity. "And what else is in your heart that I should know?"

Julia's eyes shone as innocently as a young bride. "It's Mattie, such a gentle giant of a man. We have grown quite fond of each other. Yesterday, we sat for a long while in the shade of the ash and just talked. He thinks a great deal of you, Talon, and since he didn't know I'm your mother, told me about the occasion you two first met."

"You could never meet a better man than Mattie." Then, "I suppose he told you I got into a bit of trouble before I became a scout?"

"I heard all about it!" Julia laughed. "And I know the charming rogue saved your life."

Rising to grab a sleeping gown from atop her bureau, Talon pulled it over her head, tossing the towel aside in the same moment. "I'll never be in trouble like that again, *Pia.* I promise you that."

"Another thing, Talon...an officer has been sent by Washington to investigate your grandfather's improprieties, though I can't imagine what such a gentle man could have done. My father won't discuss the matter with me, and requested that I not talk about it with Dora. What could such a dear man have done to draw the attention of Washington and this Colonel Heitman—"

"Lieutenant Colonel Paul Heitman?"

"You know him?"

Talon laughed tiredly. "He is the previous C.O. who ordered me to be hanged a few months ago, before I sweet-talked him out of it. I do not really think he was serious about it though."

Julia Rose came to her feet as gracefully as a sparrow. "Come to supper tomorrow night, Talon. The three of us—you, me, and your grandfather—can have a nice chat."

Talon stiffened, the contempt she felt for Compton like ice in her veins. "Let me see what is planned for tomorrow," she replied, even as she knew she'd find a way to avoid the dinner date.

Withdrawing to the door, Julia resettled a thin shawl over her shoulders. "I'd better return before father sends his orderly for me."

When her mother left, Talon tried to settle down to sleep at once, but a thousand thoughts stirred through her. She was back at camp, listening to a light breeze whistle down from the bluffs, the familiar beat of sentry's boots on the dusty earth, and the soft echo of pain in her heartbeats.

She couldn't make the decision Laine had demanded upon her return. Just as she made up her mind that she would go to him at dawn, and tell him she needed more time, a note slipped beneath her door. Looking at it for a moment, knowing without seeing his handwriting that it was from Laine, she retrieved it and sat beneath the pale glow of the lamp. Unfolding the small bit of paper, she read the few abrupt words: *I await your decision, Talon, if not now, first thing in the morning. I will not be put off beyond that point.*

* * *

Laine had watched Julia go to Talon's quarters, and fifteen minutes later, had watched her leave. These past two weeks he had done nothing but think about his Indian princess, the gentle echo of her voice, long for her lithe, golden body beneath his own, remember their last wildly passionate moments together. His heart fluttered with fear and dreaded anticipation, because he couldn't bear the thought of Talon not returning to his arms.

The thought of her being with that lying Indian bastard made his skin crawl. Since he feared he'd not be able to sleep tonight if he didn't know her decision, he had waited another

310

half hour for her to make an appearance. When she didn't, he ordered the duty guard, passing on his rounds, to slip the note beneath her door.

Now he had waited another fifteen minutes, and she still had not come to him.

Stepping off the porch, he slung the brandy glass he'd just emptied, heard it smash against the stone base, and took several awkward steps toward the parade field and Talon's quarters. Then he paused. He couldn't force her...couldn't demand her answer...couldn't push her toward Nightwing. He would have to wait for the morning. Pivoting before he might change his mind again, he entered his quarters, quietly shut the door, and ripped his shirt from his sweating body. Wanting to go to her so badly, he paced the floor for half an hour, then threw himself face down on the divan, managed to drag off his boots at a clumsy angle, and forced himself to sleep. If Talon chose Nightwing, it would take every shred of military dignity to keep from killing him.

Twenty-two

The two halves of Talon's soul had struggled within her throughout the night, one compelling her to overlook Laine's lack of trust and believe in his love, and the other fueling her determination that she could not live with a man who turned his back on her. Despite a lifetime of struggles in those few short hours she'd been unable to sleep, the cool pre-dawn moments before sunrise came too quickly. Talon stood on the porch, listening to the stir of Laine's boots inside his neat one-story quarters. The darkness of early morning kept its grip on the sky, a gold and lavender haze settling over the ragged horizon of the mountains. Concentrating on the snickers of horses she couldn't see in the post corral, she waited what seemed an interminably long time for Laine to come to the door after she had lightly knocked. Then he stood there, still tucking his shirt into his uniform trousers, his golden hair not yet seeing a comb this morning. Just for a moment, her thoughts returned to the darkened corral, to the music of a band growing worse as the players frequented a spiked punchbowl...to a magical waltz that had filled her heart with love for this man.

What had happened to that first memorable touch of happiness between them?

Now, Laine's eyes swept almost rudely over her, snatching her from her thoughts. Yet a sensual softness echoed in the sound of her name coming from his lips. Rebelling against the passion spreading through her flesh, Talon forced hardness into her eyes as she held a lightly clenched hand out to him. One of the silver combs eased onto Laine's outstretched palm, Talon promptly pivoting to put distance between them.

In those few seconds, Laine thought of the last two weeks, his mind constantly forming Talon's image, hearing her voice, his heart longing for her to return to him, to tell him she loved him and would give him nothing less than the rest of their lives together. Now, the answer he wanted lay in his hand—just one of a pair of matching silver combs—and damned if he knew what it was.

Talon had just left the last step when he halted her with softly spoken words. "What is the message here, Talon Rose?"

Her cold stare was tantamount to a lie, for heat spread through her like a fever. "You said when I returned you wanted an answer, and you gave me two choices. If I love you I will keep the combs. If I return them I no longer want you. I must keep one of the combs because I will always love you, Laine. I must return one, because I cannot make a decision today—as you demand." Her passions for him struggled with her need for detachment. "You must give me a week or two." If he hadn't forced a decision today, her feelings might have changed tomorrow, or the day after, or the day after that, because she knew she could never love another man as she loved Laine. "I am sorry...this is as it must be."

She had put another few feet of distance between them when he crossed the porch and again stopped her. "You chose Nightwing, Talon? You say you'll always love me, but you chose him?"

Talon wanted to walk away without complications, but nothing seemed rational here. So, she turned, ascended the steps and closed herself into Laine's arms, not because she felt he needed it, but because she did. Her mouth touched his in the briefest, the sweetest, of kisses, as she enjoyed his embrace for a twinkling that seemed like eternity. "I will always love you, Laine, but right now I cannot commit to a man who does not trust me. And no, I have not chosen Nightwing, though it may be that I love him in a special way. It is still my intention to make a decision in a week or two, and I will not let either of you rush me." She wanted only to escape, which Laine seemed intent on preventing.

"Left to make the decision on your own terms, what are my chances?"

"I will not answer that, Laine." *Oh, but she knew the answer. She wanted no man the way she wanted Laine Taylor.*

"That is *not* acceptable. You're not choosing between a pair of good riding horses. You're playing with the lives and emotions of men. Men, for God's sake! If you leave now without telling me your heart, I won't take you back tomorrow, or the day after, or the day after that. I won't be a pawn in this game of yours. "

Those last few contemptible words tore through her, shredding her composure. "Laine, if you think our lives have been a game, perhaps you are not the man for me."

His hand went out to her, his voice softly persuasive. "Talon, come inside and let's talk. Give me half an hour of your time this morning." When she hesitated, he added quietly, "Please, Princess?" She returned, paused at the bottom of the steps, and followed him into the parlor. Dropping to the divan, he patted the cushion next to him, smiled, and said, "Come on...I won't bite you." Scarcely had she settled beside him when the back of his hand gently brushed her cheek. "Tell me again, Talon, that you love me?"

As hard as she tried, she couldn't keep her love for him from shining like a beacon. "I should not have to say it."

"I need to hear it, Talon. Say the words...then tell me, without glancing away, that you think you love Nightwing." Again, she hesitated, and he swung his boots over her head and lay on the couch. Then he patted his shoulder. "Put your head here while we talk."

"I do not think I should do that." When she started to rise, he grabbed her arm and kept her from completing the move. "Let me go, Laine."

"Whisper to me those Indian words I first heard in the guardhouse."

"I do not recall them."

"Perhaps if you lie beside me, you will."

The way he aggressively held her arm, Talon knew he wouldn't let her go. So she drew her legs up to the divan and settled her head against his shoulder. She allowed a few seconds to pass before she murmured, "Sorry—I still do not recall them." His hands closed over her shoulders when she started to arise, his mouth against her temple. "Laine, please—"

"Anything for you, Talon—"

"Then let me go."

"Anything but that." His forearm against her upper chest pinned her against him. "I told you, I just want to talk."

"I talk better standing up."

"I don't."

Turning to reprimand him, to demand that he release her, his hot male smell suddenly assailed her senses. Then his mouth was against hers, not in a kiss, but rubbing lightly, enticingly, allowing no room for her to withdraw from him. "A man could want for nothing with a woman like you, Talon."

The breath rushed from her. Nightwing had spoken those same words to her on the crest of Wolf's Bluff, the memory compelling guilt as she thought that he wouldn't like her being with Laine like this. But Laine wouldn't allow her retreat, his hands now boldly sweeping over the fabric of her blouse. Her breaths came in soft gasps, as he continued to rub his lips over her warm features. "Laine, please—"

"I told you, Talon, anything for you."

"Then let me go."

His caresses ceased at once, and he half-shoved her from the divan. "Go...run to that black-hearted Apache son-of-a-bitch. You Indians stick together like sweat. Does *he* arouse your passions better than I do?" As she drew to her knees, her tearful eyes lifting at once, he pulled her roughly against him. "Talon, forgive me," he whispered, embracing her so tightly that she nearly lost her breath.

Talon was sure eternity passed before he broke contact, his cheek sliding to her moist one. Even as she wanted to flee from his cruel words, desire held her in his arms. "You are the only man I have been with, Laine. Despite what you think of Nightwing, he has respected my love for you too much to touch me in that way."

"And I want to remain the only man you've been with— made love to. Short of letting you leave me this morning, is there anything I can say...anything I can do...to convince you of that?

To win your trust again?"

Drawing back so that she might see his eyes, she replied, "Yes, there is something you can do."

"Anything within my power."

"Do not rush me into a decision this morning that I may regret in an hour."

Almost as though he were about to lose her forever, Laine pulled her close, rested his cheek against her dark hair, and whispered, "I can't wait an hour, I've got to know now, or I won't be able to function as a human being, let alone a man. What can your heart know in an hour, in a day, in a week that it doesn't know now?" His hands closed over her shoulders as he forced her to face him. "If you leave without giving me an answer, I won't be here for you in an hour. You tell me yes, now, Talon, or it ends now."

The breath Talon pulled in trembled with disappointment...with quiet rage. "Rich white officer, accustomed to having his own way...and having it now." Steadily, she rose and put a few feet of floor space between them. "Not this time, Laine. I told you, I need time to think."

When she turned her back to him, he spoke her name sharply. She paused but did not turn back. "Leave now, Talon, and we are finished."

Without pause, Talon replied, "Then I suppose we are finished, Laine," and left before he might have responded.

Tears flooded her, and it was the worst moment to encounter her grandfather moving toward Laine's quarters. Ducking past him just as Laine stepped onto the porch, she did not acknowledge his hasty greeting as she kept her eyes turned from him.

"How can you treat her so casually?" Laine snapped. "Your own granddaughter."

"It's as she wants it," Compton reminded him, and with only a second's pause, "I need to talk to you about this colonel who arrived from Washington, and these depositions he's taking throughout camp."

He had lost his heart, the love of his life, and this selfish bastard was worried about a reputation that already slithered with the reptiles. "Permit me to finish dressing...Sir...and spend some time alone. I'll come to your office at some point during the day...at my convenience, not yours."

* * *

Concerned about the reliability of some of the new scouts, Nightwing had just emerged from the scout barracks to talk to Reisner when he saw Taylor and Talon talking at his quarters. Their few words kept halting Talon's retreat from him and, even from this distance in the dark morning he felt the stress in their exchange, even as the clarity of their words failed to reach him. Just as he was sure Talon had told the white officer she had decided against him, she entered his quarters. That alone conveyed the message Nightwing had dreaded. She would be Taylor's wife.

When Talon rushed from Taylor's quarters, Nightwing drew farther into the shadows until the door to her quarters closed behind her. Reveille abruptly swept over camp, and he stood reverently until its conclusion. Then he was keenly aware of the commencement of activities generally following this announcement of morning, the drone of soldier's boots stirring toward mess halls, horses plodding the hard earth of the post corral, and dependent children flowing from quarters to play marbles or skip rope, until the morning grew too hot for outdoor play. All the sounds he loved.

Knowing he wouldn't awaken to Talon's voice each morning, to her vows of eternal love, made it all so unimportant.

Across the parade field a familiar figure emerged from the guest quarters. Leaving the darkness of the barracks now, he crossed the parade field to meet Lieutenant Colonel Heitman. Broadly smiling, Heitman took his proffered hand at once. "I suppose you know why I've returned, Nightwing?"

"I know you investigate Compton and take depositions." A notice had been slipped under the door of Nightwing's quarters during his absence. "What can this Indian say important enough for deposition?"

"A great deal, I'd imagine," Heitman replied. "I'm on my

way to see Talon if she's up. Walk with me?" Reckless humor entered his eyes. "I suppose you and Talon managed to get along after I left?"

Nightwing glowered almost menacingly. "We managed, but it was not easy at first. Comanche rude and defiant."

"I thought the way you two treated each other, you'd fall in love."

The tightness of an insincere smile struggled onto Nightwing's lips. "Scout Talon is up." A minute later he and Heitman stood at the bottom of the steps. Talon called, "Enter."

Though she'd been crying, Talon managed a smile when she saw Heitman, her eyes sliding briefly to Nightwing. "Colonel, I thought we'd seen the last of you when you left in February."

Heitman approached, firmly gripped her shoulders and turned her from him. "Drop your shirt, scout."

Talon cut Heitman a stiff look across her left shoulder. "I will not do that."

"Drop your shirt, scout. That's an order. Or do you defy the authority of your superiors despite your personal pledge to me that you wouldn't?"

"Do as the colonel requests," Nightwing ordered brusquely.

Talon reluctantly unfastened the buttons of her uniform shirt, and held the garment to her as she shuffled it from her shoulders. Heitman roughly drew the fabric all the way down, so that her entire back was exposed. The well-healed marks remained sharply red against her golden skin. "How many lashes was this, scout?"

Talon suspected he already had that answer. "I am not sure, Sir," she replied, attempting to pull up her shirt even as Heitman held it down.

"And how many did Compton order before he backed down?"

Vexation jumped quickly to her tongue. "Criminee, Colonel. Twenty-four, and I am sure you knew that!"

Heitman did not attempt to mute the sarcasm. "At least the old bastard had a smidgen of compassion when he called off a public whipping!"

Talon drew strength from his remarks and forced her shirt up, refastening the buttons before turning to him. Rage splintered from her eyes. "I would think, Sir, that you have been told the old bastard is my grandfather. So let us forego the insults to his character."

"I fail to understand why you care about this man, grandfather or not, when he subjected you to persecution on a daily basis."

"I do not understand why such a big fuss is being made."

Withdrawing to the door, he said to Talon, "I'll want photographs of your back these seven weeks afterwards to show the slowness of healing. I already have the photographs Major Stahl had taken that same day—"

Talon questioned harshly, "What photographs?"

A shaggy eyebrow shot up inquisitively. "Didn't you know about the ones taken the next day, Talon, when you were returned to your quarters?"

"I did not. And I consider that an invasion of my privacy and dignity." Her attention flew furiously to Nightwing. "Did you know about the photographs?"

"Yes."

The colonel wasn't in the mood for an argument. "I need them for my report to Washington, so you prepare yourself for the photographer."

Talon became tearful and upset. Not only would strangers in the nation's capital see photographs of her beaten and half-naked, but Colonel Heitman was here to bring down a man her mother very much loved. "Is this investigation about a stupid whipping, colonel that the general had nothing to do with? I cannot believe the War Department would spend any amount of time investigating something so inconsequential, especially where it concerns an Indian."

"It is not inconsequential, scout. And no, I'm not here just because of a flogging. It's also about a civilian kept on this post to intimidate and to kill, a young guard who needlessly lost his life, both an officer and a Chief of Scouts locked in the guardhouse on insane whims, and almost every action your grandfather has taken since the day he arrived at this camp, actions I might add that bloody well could have directly led to an Apache uprising in this territory. My understanding from the men I've talked to is that this man began a personal crusade against you the very day he arrived here. Now, I'd suggest you keep your tone respectful when you speak to officers. I'll advise you of the appointment with the photographer. Good morning, scout."

"Colonel Heitman, please—" His seething gaze returned to her, almost daring her to continue her arguments. "I do not want my mother to learn of her father's actions."

A frown darkened his entire face. He had met Julia Rose Compton, and she was a fine, decent woman. "I don't see how that can be avoided, scout. I'm surprised she hasn't already heard about it." Heitman quickly withdrew.

When Nightwing turned to join him, Talon caught his hand, his features hardening beneath her scrutiny. But his dark mood withered her at once, and she wondered if he, too, was angry that she had gotten cross with the colonel. "We need to talk, Nightwing."

Denying her even the smallest glance, Nightwing wasn't ready to hear that she had chosen Taylor. "I have no time. We talk later."

"But, Nightwing, I—" Her protests were left short. Wanting him to know that Laine's ultimatum had ended any hope of a relationship between them, Talon was very let down that he couldn't make time to hear it. She also desperately needed to tell Nightwing that she did not love him as he wanted to be loved, and her heart would always belong to Laine.

* * *

Laine had brooded throughout the day, emptied a decanter of brandy, and mentally kicked himself for being so hot-headed. What would a week or two have mattered? He loved Talon enough that he would have given her a year, had she demanded it.

Nightwing! That Apache bastard made his blood boil.

Late in the afternoon, reeling from the effects of too much brandy, Laine needed food to quell the nausea. Deep in thought, he didn't realize he was on a collision course with Nightwing until he stood face to face with him thirty feet from the officer's dining room. Either could have stepped aside in the unencumbered space, but a challenge of wills rooted them, their hatred for each other as strong as their love for Talon. Neither gave an inch.

Laine despised this Indian who might possibly wake every morning to Talon's warm smiles, to the passionate heat of her golden flesh, to ebony hair lying like thunderclouds against his shoulder. Clenching his teeth, he refused to budge. Let this mixed blood bastard step aside.

Nightwing despised this white officer Talon had chosen over him. He instantly recalled the night he had startled her from his arms in a darkened corral. He remembered that first night they had ridden into the hills together. Wondering if they had made love had consumed him that weekend. And just this morning, Talon had chosen him. Instinctively, Nightwing's hand rose to the pearl handled Bowie knife. "Move now, Taylor."

"You move." Laine heard the big blade slide along the rough interior of the sheath. Lifting his hand to his sidearm, he instantly found that he had not strapped it on before leaving his quarters. Lacking a weapon, he still didn't back down.

Blood would have been drawn if Major Daniel Harris hadn't appeared from the darkness. Wading through the tense hatred emanating between these two normally sensible men, his hand dropped to Nightwing's arm, forcing his attention even as his dark eyes continued to hold Taylor. It aggravated the hell out of him that grown men acted like spoiled children. He didn't know Taylor well enough to judge him, but expected better from the Chief of Scouts. "Boots and saddles, Nightwing. Get a dozen of your scouts together. Civilians report a gathering of hostiles."

Nightwing loosened his grip on the Bowie. Believing Taylor would go to Talon the minute he rode away, he took a single step back, and pivoted toward her quarters.

She sat reading at the table as he burst in without knocking.

"Boots and saddles, scout! Dress! Now! No time to waste!" The orders left his tongue in short, angry bursts. "Major Harris need dozen scouts. I saddle your horse. Ten minutes." Then he withdrew before she quite knew what had hit her.

* * *

Laine went to the officer's dining room, threw together the makings of a roast beef sandwich, and headed for the adjutant's office. Sitting at his desk, absently shuffling both his boot and papers needing his attention, he half-heartedly ate the sandwich, washing it down eventually with water that was only slightly cool. He had just thrown the last morsel aside when Roan entered. "The C.O. wants you in his office posthaste, Captain Taylor."

Laine huffed rudely. "You tell Compton if he wants something at his beck and call to get a spaniel. I've got better things to do."

Roan stepped back. For several seconds, he said nothing. Then his tone was laced with contempt. "You know, Captain Taylor, I got better things to do, too, than play arbitrator to a pair of snarling dogs wearing officer insignias."

Laine showed his first smile today. "Tell him I'll be there in a few minutes."

A little later, he sat in Compton's office, his boot drawn lazily to his knee, while the old warrior ranted and raved about Colonel Heitman's investigation. He offered to mediate talks between them. By the time Laine escaped, tension crawled along his spine. So he returned to his office to write a letter to his sister, Analisse Amelia. She already had a dozen of his letters awaiting her return from New Orleans, and they were about Talon. He wished he could fly across the distance and snatch them back, so he wouldn't have to explain what had happened between them.

Night fell like a slowly descending mist, wrapping the little camp in a colorful aura left over from the sunlight. By the time Laine sealed the letter, the envelope bulged with a dozen pages, and he hadn't even mentioned Talon. Perhaps that written silence would be all the explanation his sister needed. Pressing his

322

palms to his eyes, he was just about to retire to his quarters when a stranger entered the office, quickly introducing himself as Chester Man Alone, a newly hired scout.

"I don't know many of the officers on post," he announced dryly, "an' I cain't find Major Reisner or Major Harris, the ones I do know. I seen your light on, Sir, an' the sentry I spoke to jus' now said if I had somethin' to report, I could see you, since you're the camp adjutant."

Wanting to escape to his quarters, Laine grimaced instinctively, even as he invited the man in. "What can I do for you?" His strangely bright eyes didn't settle on him—not shifty or sly—but like a man who might have been made to feel all his life that he wasn't quite good enough.

"Well, Cap'n—" Chester Man Alone's gnarled fingers nervously twisted the brim of a blackened leather hat against his waistline. "I speak Apache and I overhe'erd a coupl'a them new scouts talkin' a while ago. They was sayin' as how a bunch of the scouts and soldiers got called into the hills on a false report of hostiles. They was real 'ti'cler 'bout one scout, Chief Nightwing, an' said the first arrow'll be for him. I jus' thought, Sir, that somebody should oughta know 'bout this, an' maybe them scouts out there need to be warned real quick like."

Laine had heard that the scouts would be checking the bluffs around the cabin on Moonlight Stream. Through his mind ran a tormenting image of Talon lying dead on those grassy hills they had once enjoyed together. "You said Major Harris is not at camp?"

"He's out in them bluffs with the scouts."

"Hostiles would be crazy to hang in the bluffs this close to a military camp and, frankly, I didn't trust the information when I first heard it. I'll ride out there."

Very dark, thick brows rose into a deeply lined brown forehead, an unexpected softness easing into the roughened voice. "Now, you don't need to be goin' out there alone, Sir. I'll get some of the other scouts together."

"I'll go alone."

"Sir, I don't—"

"We won't argue about this, scout." Rising, Laine snatched up his jacket and hat. "Ask Mr. Money over at the livery to saddle that big roan for me while I retrieve my sidearm and rifle."

"I'll saddle the horse for you but, Cap'n Taylor, Sir, you ain't thinkin' clear."

"You just keep a watch on those Apaches you overheard until I get back."

Outside, the two men parted, Chester Man Alone going to the post corral to saddle the horse, and Laine to his quarters. When he emerged minutes later, he had strapped on his sidearm, his rifle held lightly against his shoulder. Chester Man Alone was just leading his saddled horse from the corral. "Let me ride with you, Sir...a few of the other scouts, too."

Laine sheathed his rifle and pulled into the saddle. "Keep an eye on those scouts as I requested," he ordered, reining the horse toward the front gate.

The guard halted him at once. "It's against regulation for *any* man to leave camp alone, Sir, even an officer."

"You can report my insubordination in the morning." Then he heeled the horse ahead, ascended the trail on Cimarron Bluff a few minutes later, and halted, looking back on the small military post sitting peacefully in the valley below. Turning his eyes soon enough to the bluffs, he continued his ride toward the narrow trail that would descend into the crease of the Huachucas, take him through a couple of valleys, over a hill, and up to the banks of Moonlight Stream.

Keeping the horse at a slow pace, he lost his thoughts in the night and the solitude, the far away sounds indicating life in the dark skies over Arizona Territory, the scampering of small creatures into the bluffs. He ignored the sounds skittering away from him, toward him, beneath and below him.

Quietly ignoring the shuffling in a rocky outcropping above him, he turned his horse into the narrow pass. The wide, low stretch between the boulders was the last leg of this journey before he descended into the swath of lowland ribboned by the iridescent stream where he had come upon Talon, just moments before they had lain together in a passion that held him in her grip, even now that she no longer wanted him.

* * *

Major Daniel Harris sent twenty soldiers to the southwest, twenty to the northwest, and ten each to the north and south. If there had been Apaches—or anyone—around the cabin recently they found no trace of them now. They had found evidence elsewhere in the bluffs, indicating recent encampments. Major Harris had instructed his soldiers to return within two hours, to have all hands available to burn the cabin. It abutted a rock bluff, and there was virtually no air stirring to spread the fire. Gathering every item from the cabin that could hold water, Harris ordered a line of men to the stream fifty feet through a stand of young trees. The cabin was then set afire to eliminate it as a haven for outlaws and Apaches.

Talon sat atop her horse at a distance of forty yards and watched the fire calmly sweep up the dry logs of the cabin, taking less than five minutes to break through the roof. Listening to the crackle of flames and hissing of logs, she recalled the night she and Laine had made love on the small cot just inside the door, their passions as hot as the flames now consuming the place where they had lain. Tears of remembrance, of the love she had felt before he left her, swept through her as calmly as the fire.

A horse eased up beside her. Nightwing looked stoically ahead, the darkness of his mood lingering into the night. Turning her head slightly, Talon brushed the tears from her cheeks. "I must have gotten smoke in my eyes," she explained, returning to him with a smile.

"Not smoke in eyes...tears," he roared out roughly. "You bring Taylor here that night?"

His sarcasm snatched her with the speed of a devouring cougar. All day long and through the night she had wanted to talk to him, but he had avoided her. Once, when she eased to his side, he quickly heeled his horse and joined Dako on the trail ahead. "And what night are you talking about?"

"That night you say I am dirty minded, foul-mouthed son-

325

of-a-bitch, and you ride off with Taylor."

Drawing a deep breath, Talon regained an ounce of control, even as her chest fluttered with anger. "Why do you bring up memories that will simply infuriate us both? Why have you been so cross today—and so aloof? You haven't allowed yourself to be alone with me for a minute—until now."

"Do not know *aloof.* This bad word for dirty minded, foul-mouthed son-of-a-bitch?"

"No. And it doesn't matter what it means."

"Then do not use words if it not matter."

"Nightwing, please—" Her hand crossed the space between them, settling on his arm. Her gaze softened, even as anger continued to grapple within her. "Could we talk for just a minute?"

He kicked his horse lightly, coaxing it away from her side. His voice remained brusque and rude. "I must speak to Major Harris."

Talon was terribly bewildered by the hostility he had shown today. She watched the tall, slim form of him, sitting atop the big gelding beside Major Harris, thinking that he looked like an unreachable illusion against the flames leaping into the air.

Twenty-three

Sending most of the other scouts ahead just moments after Company D, Fourth Cavalry, returned to camp in the predawn hours, Nightwing and Talon, with Dako and Black Jake riding fifty yards ahead, ambled almost lazily along the familiar crease from the cabin where they had expected to find Apaches. He had decided to let Talon speak her mind, but she hadn't uttered the first word.

He couldn't stop thinking about yesterday morning, as he had settled into the darkness to watch her go to Taylor. Her actions had clearly shown that she had returned to him. He needed to hear her confession now.

They had just left a narrow, treacherous trail winding through an outcropping of boulders when Dako galloped his horse back to him, speaking excitedly in Apache while he pointed down the canyon. Nightwing heeled the big gelding into action, with Talon close behind.

Above an outcropping of bear grass splattered with blood, a man hung upside down against the rocks, wearing only his blood-saturated uniform trousers. His wrists were tightly bound behind his back with rawhide, and strapped to his neck, his hair matted with blood. Black Jake remarked that he looked scalped, though he wasn't. Apache arrows protruded from his right thigh, hip, left shoulder, and left rib cage. He had several deep knife cuts in his legs, upper arms, and shoulders. Two small cuts along his jaw had streaked blood through the contours of his face and pooled in his eyes.

The men quietly speculated why a soldier was out alone, when it was clearly against camp regulations. Dako stood under him while Black Jake, knife clutched between his teeth, climbed the rock to cut him down. Nightwing looked on silently from atop his horse. Talon had turned away. No experience in her life had prepared her for this.

Dako laid him on the ground. Nightwing threw him a canteen, so he could clean the blood from his face solely for the purpose of identification. Black Jake remarked that he had probably only been hanging there a couple of hours. Dako had just trickled water onto the soldier's face when he suddenly took a very shallow breath. Sidling from him in surprise, Dako yelled, "He still lives," and quickly crawled back to the soldier, wet his bandanna, and squeezed a few drops of water onto his lips.

Nightwing was almost certain it was Taylor. He hated that this had happened to him, but was angry that his rival for Talon remained alive. Because he was sure he would die soon, and should do so beneath a familiar hand, he yelled back to Talon, "He still alive. I think it is Taylor."

Jolted by his dispassionate declaration, Talon was quickly off her horse. Dropping to her knees beside this half-naked, scarcely recognizable human form, she pulled him onto her lap. Blinded by dried blood, he could not have opened his eyes had he tried. He took short, hard breaths, with just enough strength that he struggled to free his hands. Talon cut the rawhide binding his wrists, and his breathing instantly relaxed. Then Dako wiped the last bit of crusted blood from his face, and Laine's familiar blue eyes slowly opened.

Horror spiked along Talon's spine. "Laine, can you hear me?" Looking to Dako, she calmly ordered, "Ride to camp and bring an ambulance wagon."

Nightwing coaxed his horse toward them. "I go. Dako...Black Jake, remove rifles—watch for hostiles." Then he reined his horse toward the southeast and disappeared over the rise of the hill.

Laine's deathly pale features resting against her, Talon talked calmly to him. He didn't respond to her for many minutes, until she whispered, "Always will I remember the night you danced with this rude Comanche. I fell in love with you that night." The smallest smile struggled onto his mouth.

The time passed. Talon continued talking to him, trying to elicit even the smallest response. But none came, and the sun began to lower in the sky, indicating the passage of too much time since Nightwing had ridden to camp.

Dako approached. "Maybe Nightwing not send ambulance wagon."

"He will send it." Dako walked off, his dark eyes scanning for hostiles. Occasionally, Laine stirred, and pain grabbed his features. She wished she could take back the words she had spoken to him yesterday morning, especially now that he was likely dying.

Laine's hand moved, ever so slightly at first, then easing along his chest, his blood-encrusted fingers searching for hers. Clasping them lightly, he struggled to speak. "Talon, I love you—"

"And I love you, Laine...I always will—" When he tried to speak again, she touched her trembling lips to his cold ones, seeking the gentle stir of his breath against her cheek. Then he grabbed the arrow in his chest, and she frantically wrestled his fingers from it. Frustrated by the time that continued to pass, she growled her frustration, "Where the hell is that wagon?"

* * *

As he'd closed the distance to Camp Casey, Nightwing got to thinking about a burly, fast talking sergeant named Clarence Brogan. The same day—four years ago—that his first Officer of Scouts, Major John Campbell, was killed—a half-dead Brogan was brought back to camp in the ambulance wagon. He'd been shot nine times, six bullets and three arrows, in a fierce skirmish with renegade Apaches just beyond Rock Bluff that had also claimed the lives of four other soldiers. Nightwing remembered the ambulance driver—Corporal Dant, still a fixture in Casey's infirmary— joking that we *ought'a jes' call this a hearse, too, cause this ol' sarge is goin' in the ground by nightfall.* His fallen Officer of Scouts in the second ambulance wagon with the other dead soldiers, Nightwing remembered halting the ambulance team, looking squarely in Dant's face to tell him that one more word and he'd be the one in the ground by nightfall.

They'd reached Camp Casey just past six in the evening. Sergeant Brogan was taken to the infirmary and immediate surgery under the skillful hands of Captain Calloway. Despite

329

the odds, Sergeant Clarence Brogan not only lived, but last he heard, was up in the Dakotas dealing with the Sioux.

Pulling up Mageedu at the crest of Cimarron Bluff, Nightwing patted his sleek, strong neck and looked over the little Army camp. If Laine Taylor arrived at the infirmary still breathing, chances were that Captain Calloway might save his life.

Quietly easing Mageedu down the bluff, Nightwing knew he couldn't let that happen.

Later in the afternoon, he wasn't sure how much time had passed since he cantered his big horse by the guard gate and closed himself in his quarters at the back of the scout barracks. But he was very aware that the half-empty whiskey bottle had been full when he took the first drink. He was not too drunk to feel the gut-wrenching guilt of Taylor lying out in the bluffs, with Talon trusting him to send the ambulance wagon.

But Taylor had to die if he was to have her.

He would send the ambulance wagon when he was reasonably sure the life had left Taylor's body.

* * *

Hours passed for Talon and the scouts, in silent vigil over a fallen Army officer. By the time the sun indicated the hour of four, Talon's legs were numb beneath Laine, and pain ricocheted through her spine. She had refused to move—even to stir the circulation in her legs—because if he died, she wanted it to be in her arms, against her body. Then, when she had almost given up hope, wagon wheels rising on rock suddenly echoed in the near distance. "Thank God...thank God—" Within minutes, the familiar ambulance wagon halted a dozen feet from her. Two medical orderlies hopped down from the seat and pulled a stretcher from the back. "Where the hell have you been? It's been hours since you were summoned."

The orderlies dropped the stretcher beside her. The man named Dant quipped rudely, "We left camp as soon as Nightwing notified us, scout, at three forty-five." Roughly grabbing Laine's chin, then forcing one eyelid open, he said with little sympathy, "We'll be puttin' him in the ground by nightfall."

Reproachful green eyes cut to the orderly. "He can hear everything you say."

The two men roughly dropped Laine onto the stretcher. "He don't hear nothin', scout," Dant said after a moment.

Talon rode with him in the ambulance. Despite the rough terrain, the ambulance made good time, and at five fifteen, Laine was taken into the post infirmary. A quiet, shaking Talon entered the post physician's office and sank into a chair, hardly stirring as Major Reisner sat beside her. But when his hand covered hers, she looked to him with quiet puzzlement.

"Nightwing rode back to camp before noon to fetch the ambulance. The orderly said he did not get word until quarter to four."

Reisner patted her arm in a gesture of comfort. "I'll find out why the ambulance wasn't sent right away." Quietly slipping from the infirmary and into the descending day, he encountered Chester Man Alone, the new Mexican-Apache scout. "I'm really busy, scout," Reisner impatiently announced.

"This is about Taylor." Reisner paused to listen to a man who never once looked into his eyes. Chester repeated the story he'd told Laine the evening before, concluding with, "I went to Taylor's office, an' he said he'd go out an' warn Nightwing that he an' the scouts was in danger. I told him I'd ride with him, some of the other scouts, too, but he said I should keep an eye on those two bucks. That's the last time I saw him, when he rode out of camp last night."

Reisner had crossed his arms while he listened. "Why didn't he go to the Officer of the Guard so these Apache you overheard could be confined, and then to a company officer so a detail could be dispatched?"

"The cap'n didn't say. He weren't in a good mood so I didn't talk to him long. I'm real sorry, but I did offer to get some scouts together."

Reisner proceeded to the scout barracks. Nightwing, who lay on his cot with his arms crossed against his chest, opened his eyes to stare at him almost rudely. "You arrived back at camp this morning before noon. Why did you wait until almost four to send an ambulance wagon for Taylor?"

Sick from intoxication, Nightwing was slow to react. He clumsily settled his boots to the floor. "Did Taylor die?"

"Is that why you delayed? So he would die?" Reisner spied the empty whiskey bottle in the shadows beneath the cot. Alerted now to Nightwing's drunkenness, he noticed that his eyes were bloodshot; his hand trembled as he raked back his hair, and the odor of whiskey permeated his clothing. "I asked you a question, and I expect an answer."

Nightwing lifted furious black eyes. "And I ask you, Major Reisner, Sir, if Taylor dead. Answer, and leave me alone. I feel sick at gut."

Reisner had never imagined the savagery and hate reflecting in Nightwing's dark eyes. It would be useless to talk to him without quarreling—or dying. And he didn't have time to do either. "No, he's not dead, but likely will be before this night is over. For your information, Taylor rode into the bluffs last night to warn you because he heard you and your scouts were riding into an ambush. You think about that while you wretch your whiskey-sotted guts out, mister."

* * *

Captain Calloway had three medical orderlies carefully cut away Taylor's trousers without disturbing the arrows. In the preparations, Dant chloroformed him—though he hardly needed it—and stood at the ready in case he came to during the surgery. Calloway was worried that he'd lose this one. One open, gaping wound gushing blood and other bodily fluids was enough, but this man had four that would likely saturate this small surgical antechamber with whatever was left in his veins.

While an orderly cleaned and stitched the knife wounds, Calloway focused his attention on the more serious wound in his chest. Since Apache shafts were generally thirty-three inches long, he estimated that the arrowhead itself was very close to his back. Determining the direction of the shaft, he had the orderlies turn him over, and made a T incision in his back. Once he located the tip of the arrow with his index finger, it was so twisted and bent that a great deal of manipulation was necessary to loosen it. He cleanly cut the shaft three inches from Laine's chest, and with a large cleaver, shoved the arrowhead through the incision, withdrawing it and the rest of the shaft through his back. Blood gushed from the wounds on both sides of him. Calloway didn't detect lung fluid with the blood, which was his first sign of hope for this gravely wounded officer.

An hour had passed.

While the chest wound was being stitched and wrapped, Calloway concentrated on the arrow wound in his left shoulder. The tendons fitting the arrowhead snugly to the shaft had probably swelled and stretched in his bodily fluids. After he had made a large incision on each side of the shaft, he dilated the wounds with a bistoury, and used a wire loop with a long stem, which he inserted into the hole, splitting muscle and fascia, and easing between the small bones of his shoulder, along the arrow's pathway into the flesh. After he had determined the location of the point, he threaded the wire into a Coghill suture twister and shoved closer to the embedded arrow. Then he carefully manipulated the wire loop so that it encircled the point. Rocking the wire back and forth, he was able to loosen the arrowhead and withdraw it.

Going through the clavicle bones near his shoulder without breaking them had taken a full two hours.

Calloway was exhausted, covered in blood, and now had to concentrate the same procedure on the thigh wound. An orderly stitched the bloody wound at Taylor's shoulder and wrapped it in gauze.

Extracting the arrow from the thigh would possibly take another hour, and he stood for a moment, close to the point of collapse, whispering a small prayer that clumsiness produced by exhaustion would not result in a severed artery

The wound in his hip proved to be more complicated than he'd initially thought. After making a T incision, he inserted the wire, went through the procedure a third time, and just as he loosened the arrowhead, it broke, leaving the tip in his thigh as the shaft and most of the arrowhead emerged from the bloody wound. He tried to feel for the tip with his finger, but it was firmly embedded in the ball joint of his right leg. Since Taylor had already lost so much blood, he made a decision to leave the tip in. Perhaps a more skilled surgeon would be able to extract it at a later date, but he wasn't going to risk it now.

Another two hours had passed.

Dropping to a chair, Calloway hung his hands over his knees and watched Taylor's blood drip to the floor between his boots. One of his orderlies handed him a small white towel, but he was too exhausted to reach for it, let alone wipe his hands.

"Captain Calloway?" He managed to lift his head just enough to look at Dant, who had only now withdrawn the chloroform. "He ain't breathin', Sir."

* * *

Talon had failed to settle anywhere for a patient wait, and had even crept around the corner of the infirmary several times to cry. Now, she rested on one of the little benches, while her mother and Compton sat in the post physician's office quietly talking. She had thought Nightwing would have the decency to make an appearance tonight. His delay in sending the ambulance wagon might mean Laine's death, and she wanted explanations.

Nightwing entered the post infirmary just after nine o'clock. To the left was the physician's office, from which the voices of Compton and his daughter sifted lightly toward him. To the right were two small benches against a wall. There, Talon sat alone, absently rubbing the sole of her boot on the planked floor. When she lifted her tearful eyes, he exited the building, because he knew she would follow him outside to say whatever was in her heart.

Beneath the cloudless night, he awaited the approach of her light footsteps. Then he slowly turned, and had not completed the move when the full force of her palm struck his left cheek. He looked into her agony and disappointment, her mouth pressed tightly, and yet still trembling.

"You know what is so hard to accept about what you did today, Nightwing?" she whispered. "I went to Taylor yesterday morning and told him I needed more time to make a decision. He told me if I did not make a decision right then, he would not accept me tomorrow, or the day after. When I walked away from him, it was over between us, and *he* had made the final decision. I tried a number of times to get you alone yesterday and last night to tell you, but you were angry and short-tempered. Finally, you managed to make me so mad I did not want to talk to you."

"Talon, I thought—"

"I do not care what you thought!" Then she was in Nightwing's arms, weeping against his shirt, even as her fist drummed faintly against his shoulder in her frustration and rage. "I told you that night on Wolf's Bluff, Nightwing, that if you ever hurt him I would not forgive you and would not want to be with you." Nightwing had no response. Then Talon's mother appeared at the door to announce that the surgery was over. Talon stepped away, her gaze lifted to him. "If he is dead because you did not send help right away—"

When she fled into the infirmary, he stepped up to the door but did not enter. His cheeks burned with tears.

* * *

Captain Calloway was almost too exhausted to speak. He sank to the chair at his desk, his hand dropping onto a stack of papers. Julia and Talon had settled into the chairs in front of his desk, and Compton stood slightly back from Julia.

"He's alive for now." In absolute relief, Compton sank into the nearest chair. Julia took Talon's trembling hand and held it against her lap. "But this is a gravely injured man, and the only encouragement I can offer is that if he lives three days he has an even chance of surviving."

"I wish to stay with him," Talon offered quietly.

"I do want you to be aware that I hold out little hope for the survival of this man."

Talon hesitated to ask, "Would his chances be better if he had gotten here sooner?"

"Not really."

She was almost relieved by his noncommittal answer. Covering Julia's hand for a moment, she went to speak to Dako and Black Jake. Before turning toward the infirmary, she heard

335

Compton announce that he would send a wire to Laine's family.

He was in a small antechamber to the right of the open ward, a curtain partially drawn. Talon entered, and the orderly withdrew. Pulling up a chair, she settled beside him, her fingers gently brushing his ashen cheek. She detected only a light, sporadic flutter in Laine's abdomen, the only evidence that he breathed at all. His hair had been washed, and was damp and darkened, a few wayward strands resting against his cool forehead. His body was mottled and bruised, hardly an inch of flesh left unmarred by the Apaches who had so brutally attacked him. Picking up his lifeless hand, she held it against her cheek. "It seems that Indians are always shooting at you, Laine."

Then she rested her head next to his on the pillow and quietly wept, because he had a tremendous struggle facing him.

* * *

Nightwing entered Compton's office at seven the next morning, where he faced Compton, Reisner, Calloway, Chief First Sergeant Dako, the half-blood scout Chester Man Alone, the guard who had been on the north gate yesterday, and the medical orderly Dant. All in attendance, he supposed, to confirm facts and time line. Private Roan sat at a small table, preparing to take notes of the meeting. There was nothing these men planned to say to him that he didn't deserve.

Compton spoke grimly. "We're investigating events yesterday, Chief Nightwing, surrounding the delay in getting a gravely wounded Army officer back to camp. Do you understand that is why you're here?" When Nightwing nodded, Compton demanded, "I don't read sign language! You *will* answer me!"

"I do, Sir, understand."

"Then we will set forth events as a matter of record. Leaving with the main force of Company D, Fourth Cavalry, you, Scout Talon, Scout First Sergeant Dako, and Scout Black Jake, leaving the area of Moonlight Stream, came upon a grievously injured Captain Laine Taylor. You volunteered to ride to camp, a distance of three miles from your location, to get help for Taylor. You entered the gate at eleven thirty-three

336

hours, as attested by the guard's log. At three forty five hours you went to the post infirmary and notified Captain Calloway of the situation, and an ambulance was dispatched at three fifty hours. Do I have my facts straight so far?"

"You do, Sir."

"You delayed over four hours before having the ambulance dispatched. Why?"

"To give Captain Taylor time to die."

Reisner mumbled, "God." He had expected some semblance of this answer, but hearing so calloused a confession from this man simply stunned him.

"And for what reason, Chief Nightwing, did you want Captain Taylor to die?"

The answer was shallow, inadequate, and the greatest shame he would ever bring on himself. "I did not want Talon to marry him."

Though the answer didn't matter, Compton demanded, "Do you love Talon?"

"That not your business, Sir."

"Do you love Talon," he repeated vehemently.

Nightwing's thoughts struggled for a moment that felt like an eternity. "I do, Sir."

"And you think the love of a woman is a good enough reason for a rival to die?" Compton's old eyes blazed with a bright new fire. "Captain Calloway advises that the delay in getting Taylor back to this post had little effect on his chances of survival. But for your actions yesterday, John Nightwing, you are deemed insidious of character and untrustworthy to continue as a scout for the United States Army. You are hereby relieved of your position as Chief of Scouts and will surrender your uniforms, military weapons except for one sidearm, collect your personal items, take one horse of your choice, and leave this camp within the hour. Chief First Sergeant Dako will assume the position of Chief of Scouts. Take notice that you will never again work as a scout for the United States Army." Then, "Major Reisner, as Officer of Scouts, do you concur in my decision?"

Clearing his throat, Reisner went pale and tense with anger.

"Under the circumstances, I do concur." He now spoke to Nightwing, who kept his dark eyes turned from the man he respected above all others. "You have been Chief of Scouts here for seven years, four of which I had the pleasure of working with you. In that time, you developed a scout troop this camp has been proud of, certainly with little help from me. It's best that you leave this camp at once. That I called you a friend sickens me."

Nightwing stiffened against the weight of Reisner's words. "Is that all, General Compton, Major Reisner?"

"You are dismissed."

In his departure, Nightwing touched his hand briefly to Dako's shoulder, and removed his hat insignia—the crossed arrows centered by a feathered bonnet—pressed it into his hand, and left the C.O.'s office.

He went straight to his private quarters. The items he would take with him, clothing, his fatigue hat which he had purchased himself, his sidearm, a couple of boxes of ammunition, the scout wages he had saved over the years, and the little bow broken years ago by his scampering son, were all packed and ready for his departure.

He changed, and neatly laid out his uniforms, rifle, and accoutrements. Slinging his saddlebags over his shoulder, he was just about to leave his quarters when Lieutenant Colonel Heitman entered. Nightwing was too ashamed to face him.

"I don't know what to say, Nightwing." Heitman looked deeply into his shame, remembering all the times he had been proud of him. "I read the minutes of the meeting this morning, and I must concur in the decision. But this camp will not be the same without you." Then he offered his hand.

Nightwing still had not faced him. "I not deserve to take your hand, Sir."

"Yes, you do, Nightwing." With slight hesitation, Nightwing took Heitman's hand. "I'll always consider you one of the best men I've ever known."

Nightwing could not answer as he withdrew. Entering the scout barracks, he saw that the new recruits had left, giving him and his scouts this private moment together. They said their farewells, some stoic and silent, others tearful and promising. But all swore to continue their long friendship, no matter the time and distance that passed between them. After a brief, private conversation with Dako—and a solemn moment in which Dako returned the hat insignia to his friend to keep as a memento—Nightwing continued his walk to the post stable. Drawing the big gelding to the rail, he retrieved his saddle and tack and prepared for travel. By the time he was ready to mount, soldiers had silently lined the parade field. Pulling into the saddle and turning to their line, Nightwing was respectfully saluted.

Then Reisner stepped forward from the line of soldiers and stood beside him. "I was angry and disappointed. I said things in Compton's office I did not mean. Memorable journey, my good and faithful friend, John Nightwing." Extending his hand, Nightwing took it at once. Reisner held his strong grip for a long, silent moment, before withdrawing his hand and turning abruptly from him. The soldiers maintained their salutes as Nightwing, staring straight ahead, allowed his big, gaited horse to prance gracefully toward the front gate.

Then his name drifted softly on a wisp of air, and he pulled up, to watch Talon run toward him from the post infirmary. He wasn't sure what to expect from this woman he loved, but owed it to her to listen. Now, she pressed against his leg, her cheeks flushed and pretty, her raven tresses tumbling to her waist. Drawing her fist to her heart, Talon raised tragic, tearful eyes to him. "I will always carry you here, John Nightwing. Always."

Bending, he touched a light kiss to her forehead, his fingers caressing her chin. Though he knew her answer, he had to ask, "Come with me, Talon."

Surprise delayed her response. "You must know I cannot leave him."

Taking her hand, he murmured, "It is just as well. I love you too much to take you with me." His fingers easing beneath the masses of her hair, he bent and touched his lips to her forehead. "Find your happiness where it waits for you, my rude

Comanche thief."

Drawing up, he coaxed his big horse ahead, leaving the familiar camp settled among the Huachucas that he had called home for the past seven years. As he ascended the trail to Cimarron Bluff, he never once looked back.

Talon slowly dropped to her knees on the dusty earth. Aware of the sorrow rushing through her soul, no man approached her. Her nervously snickering mare leaned across the corral fence a parade field away, and one of the soldiers opened the gate. The graceful, high-stepping Shadow Dancer trotted to Talon, pressing her soft muzzle into her left shoulder. As soldiers looked on, horse and woman remained still for moments that seemed like eternity, lifelike statuary speaking sorrow as eloquently as poetry.

Twenty-four

By the time Talon had regained enough composure to whisper words that magically sent Shadow Dancer back to the corral, Julia's hands had closed over her trembling shoulders. Talon rose into her comforting arms and the two women, silent and tearful, returned to the infirmary. Julia settled her daughter onto one of the small benches in the front entrance, her fingers easing lovingly among the strands of Talon's dark hair. In the embracing warmth of her mother's arms, Talon listened to her silence, solaced by the wisdom flowing into her heart and soul as surely as if she spoke the words.

Then she went, without parting words, to Laine's bedside, dropped her head against his on the pillow, and quietly wept. How long would it be before she heard his voice again...how long before the tremendous ache—and her love for both men— freed her to the simple chore of just living from day to day?

Laine was lost to a fading distance Talon could neither touch nor reach. He didn't awaken by the third day, or the fourth, and in the late evening of the fifth day, Captain Calloway reaffirmed his first prognosis. It was just a matter of time before Laine Taylor slipped away from them.

As Talon struggled, virtually without sleep and with little food, into the sixth day since the attack, she continued talking to Laine as though he heard every word. She saw to his personal needs, made sure to shave him every morning, and kept his skin clean, cool, and dry. Only twice had she allowed an orderly to relieve her vigil, so that she could bathe and change into fresh clothing.

Dropping her head to the pillow beside him, Talon's hand settled onto his chest. She felt his weak heartbeats beneath her fingers, his cool, dry skin, his erratically drawn breaths, almost like small sobs, indicating that life clung to him despite the physician's prognosis. Closing her eyes, her long, virtually sleepless days and nights brought her close to twilight dreams, in which she heard Laine whisper her name..."Talon." She was almost asleep when again he drew a small breath, opened his eyes, and her name, "Talon," came languorously from his lips. "Thirsty —very thirsty—"

Thinking her mind played tricks on her Talon touched her fingertips to his mouth. He stirred ever so slightly, and she ran to the door to yell frantically for Captain Calloway. He stirred several rooms away, and she rushed back to Laine to pour water into a cup. With her palm beneath his head to hold him up, her violently trembling fingers managed to lift the cup to his lips while he took a very small sip. Captain Calloway, thinking he had died, and he'd have to comfort a grieving woman, was slow to arrive. Just as he prepared to console her, she gave him a very big hug. "He's awake."

Impossible, he thought, forcing Laine's right eyelid open. His pupil contracted from the light for the first time since he had been brought in from the bluffs.

In the twilight moments of his awakening, Laine had felt and heard the soft rush of Talon's voice, tumbling through many hours of darkness. As he looked to her now, her features almost like a light glowing before him, his memories rose from the vast depths to which they had plummeted. He recalled their last conversation at his quarters, her confession of love for him whispered in the same breath as her vow to leave him. As her hand slipped over his, the first string of words he had spoken in six days quietly left his lips.

"I don't want you here." Talon's smile faded. Thinking his mind still foggy, she swept hair from his forehead, but he turned from her. Then he repeated, "I don't want you here, Talon." Calloway's hands settled over Talon's shoulders, urging her from his bedside. She slipped from the room, too stunned to form a single argument. Laine's eyes settled on the post physician, who had now dropped a very cold stethoscope to his chest. His voice was hoarse and sore as he spoke. "How long have I been out?"

"Six days, Captain Taylor, and that young lady you just sent away hasn't left your bedside for more than a few minutes in that time. To the detriment of her own health, I might add."

"She shouldn't have bothered."

Calloway had noticed the cold detachment of a man who might have spent days nursing animosity, rather than hovering on the brink of death. "Perhaps...but she did."

"Just tell me if I'm going to live."

"I can probably answer that in a minute or two," he responded matter-of-factly. "I didn't think that arrow grazed your heart, but I might be wrong about that. If it hardens much more, we might need to inject a healthy dose of tolerance and appreciation."

Laine closed his eyes, to stay a moment of argument he was too weak to nurture. "Don't make judgments, Sir, without the facts. I don't want Talon here again."

"Fine, Captain Taylor. When your face is slowly covered by a rough beard, with none of my orderlies as patient as Talon to keep you shaved, and when you start smelling like a horse, because they also won't keep you clean and cool the way she did, maybe you'll think about just who you're hurting here. In the meantime, yes, likely you will live. And, frankly, I don't know how I feel about that." Whipping the stethoscope across his shoulder hard enough to cause pain, Calloway added in parting, "If you need help, call an orderly. I'll be getting some sleep, since I've also been up most of the last six days and nights, trying to see that your ungrateful ass lives."

* * *

Talon went straight to the post cemetery and knelt beside Andy Wilson's grave. Here, in this quiet place, with the sounds of the post muted by the short distance and the lingering souls of some very good soldiers, she could whisper her thoughts and unload her troubles.

And now, especially, she could cry.

The gathers of her skirt had scarcely settled before her name was spoken. Talon turned her eyes just as her mother stood beside her, her questioning eyes fully, and lovingly, upon Talon. "He woke up, and did not want me there."

"Dr. Calloway told me," Julia replied, dropping to the

343

ground beside her. Her cheek was against Talon's dark hair at once, her words soft and sincere. "Why do you weep, daughter? Is it because he didn't want you there...or because you didn't leave with Nightwing when you had the chance?"

"Oh, *Pia*...no...I will always love Nightwing in a special way, but no matter what has happened, my heart is truly Laine's."

A gentle silence settled over the cemetery—sending the routine din of camp on a far journey beyond her sensation—weeds fluttering against a fence post the only sound to be heard. "When you would like to tell me what happened, Talon, remember I am always willing to listen."

"Do you have time now, *Pia*, to hear my heartache?"

Taking Talon's hands Julia clutched them against her lap. "I always have time for my daughter."

While she spoke, Talon lightly rubbed Julia's fingers, noticing that she'd finally forsaken the gloves she had used to hide the tattoos. "The morning before Laine rode into the bluffs, I told him I needed more time to make my decision about returning to him. He was angry and hurt, said he would not play my games, and I could not return to him if I did not make a decision right then. We talked inside his quarters for a little while, and when I left without giving him the answer he demanded, he said we were finished. I can only think now, in retrospect, that Nightwing must have been watching. I tried all day and into the night to tell Nightwing that Laine did not want me now, but he would not listen. Then that night Laine rode into the hills after getting the report from the new scout, and when we came upon him the next morning—well, you know what happened with that. Nightwing did not send help straightaway because he thought I was returning to Laine. When he said today that he does not want me with him, I felt I could die." She looked to her mother now, a single tear caressing her cheek. "When I thought I would lose him, I realized how much I loved him...and I knew there was no other man in the world for me."

"I truly don't think he meant it, Talon. He must love you very much."

"He is too angry now to love me."

"Perhaps he's angry, but he hasn't stopped loving you. In the meantime, your grandfather and I will be here for you."

Talon drew a small sigh, filled with many hours of deep thought. "About your father—may I ask a very important favor?" Julia looked expectantly to her. "No matter what you hear during Colonel Heitman's investigation, you will not turn your back on him. A child is blessed to be loved as much as he loves you. Promise me that you will stand by him always."

Julia drew Talon into another embrace. "What a strange thing you ask of your mother, Talon. But, yes, that should be an easy promise to keep. He's such a good man." Rising now, Julia continued to hold Talon's hand. "Walk back with me?"

"You go ahead. I would like to sit here a while longer."

Julia had noticed the checkers on the grave, now faded by the harsh Arizona sun. "If your young friend here wins every game of checkers, do be a good sport about it." Then she turned from her sadly smiling daughter.

* * *

Dako and several of his scouts left camp about the same time each evening. For days Talon had made a practice of going to the window of the infirmary to watch them ride out, assuming that Nightwing was being kept apprised of Laine's condition. This last journey from camp, witnessed from the stoop outside her quarters, had kept the scouts out all night. Only Dako had not returned by morning reveille. Talon had seen to Shadow Dancer's grooming, and was returning to her quarters when Dako rode past the guard station an hour behind his scouts. She was beside him as he began rubbing down his horse.

"How is he, Dako?"

He grinned across his shoulder, his right hand furiously attacking the horse with a damp square of feed sack. "How who, Scout Talon?"

"Nightwing."

Her inquiry wiped the smile from his mouth. Dako lowered his eyes for a moment before speaking. "He much glad Taylor live. He say you always in heart. Now...go. Do not bother Chief of Scouts. He much busy." The grin returned, he waved his hand, and only half-heartedly ducked her kiss against his temple.

Throughout the day, Talon thought about her future at Camp Casey. She thought of all the reasons she should stay, and all the reasons she should go. She had been brought here as a prisoner—had it been only a few months ago?—and forced into an all male Apache scout troop against her will. She had ruined the lives of two very good men and, perhaps, the life of a white grandfather who hated her for being Comanche. The only good thing that had come of the last few months was finding her mother again. Though she didn't want to leave her, she couldn't stay at Camp Casey, where she would be a constant, painful thorn to Laine Taylor, and her grandfather. She prayed that her mother would understand.

So, she dressed in her uniform for what she thought would be her last official act as a scout, and went to Reisner's office, where he absently tapped the blade of a big knife against his palm. "Nightwing gave this to me four years ago, when I became Officer of the Scouts. It's just like the one he carries." He shoved the knife into the top drawer of his desk. "What's on your mind that this lamentable soldier can help you with?" When she continued to stand, his hand swept out a little impatiently. "Sit, please."

By the time she settled into one of the chairs, tears had spread along her lower lids. Clearing her throat against her curled fingers, she gained a moment. "Major Reisner, without giving you a reason, I request that I be released from my scout contract."

He was not surprised by her request, and had even expected it. "I hate to lose you, Talon, but Compton must agree—"

"He will allow me out of my contract, Sir...he's my grandfather."

He'd heard the rumor, but hadn't place much stock in it. The fact that Compton was unaware of the affinity at the time he ordered this lovely young Indian whipped—an act he did not carry out, but someone else did—did not diminish the severity of his act. "I wouldn't believe that rumor until I heard it directly from you." Pulling open a desk drawer, he withdrew his copy of Talon's contract, tore it up, and handed it to her. "When Compton hands you his copy, you're free. But if you're thinking of going to Nightwing—"

"I'm not going *to* any man," she interrupted, only mildly indignant, "but I cannot say I am not running *from* one."

"Will you leave Julia—your mother, Talon?"

"I will probably leave camp, Sir, but I will certainly keep in touch with her." Gathering up the pieces of the contract as she stood, Talon managed a smile, brief and a little sad. "It has been a pleasure serving with you."

"Likewise, Talon. You will be hard to replace." Reisner came to his feet as she withdrew.

It had been one hell of a week.

Talon wasted no time going to her grandfather's office. The front office staff, who had also heard the rumors, paid her little mind as she moved past their desks and entered the corridor. Moments later, she stood at Compton's door, where a spread of papers on his desk reflected that he might be preparing his own tidy package of denials and defenses for Washington. "May I have a word with you?"

"What is it, Scout?" Then he looked to her as if she had intruded on an important meeting.

"I wish to be relieved from my scout contract. Major Reisner has given me his copy, and said when you give me yours, I am free to leave."

He was surprised, certainly. "You're not leaving your mother, Talon?"

"I will never lose touch with my mother."

"After all I've put you through to make you leave. Why now?"

"I do not wish to share my reasons with you."

Compton turned an ear of regret to the contempt that time might never erase. "It is because of Taylor, isn't it?"

"It is, Sir."

"I don't want you to leave, Talon."

Her tone did not change. "Too much pleasure tormenting

me, Sir?" His features darkened with shame. "If I am released from my contract, I would ask that you tear it up and hand it to me."

How staid and angry she was. He would not waste his breath asking for her forgiveness, though there was nothing he wanted more. With only the slightest pause, he withdrew her contract from the top drawer.

But as he started to tear it up, Talon saw the heavy ink blotch where part of her name should have been. "May I look at it first?" Compton handed it to her without delay, confirming that he had obliterated the name she shared with her mother. "When did you do this?"

"Before I knew you were my—before I knew who you were, Talon Rose."

"When exactly?"

"The day I arrived...while Nightwing was in my office."

Quietly, she handed the document back to him, he tore it up, then slid it across the desk to her. "If you must go, Talon, do so with my profound respect."

She almost snorted her surprise as she swept up the pieces. "I will leave my uniforms and military issues in my quarters. When I leave camp, I will take my horse and saddle. She was mine when I came here. The saddle and tack were given to me outside this camp." Talon began her withdrawal.

He had been told the Mexican saddle had been given to her by Manolito Menendez. "You won't return to Menendez, will you, Talon?"

She turned to glare at him. "Will I return to a life of crime? No, Sir, I will not. I can manage just fine without resorting to larceny."

"Will you let me help you settle somewhere?"

"You are offering me money, Sir?" He nodded. "I have sixteen dollars left of my scout wages since February. I need nothing from you."

* * *

Analisse Amelia Taylor had never imagined there could be so much dust in any one place. Stepping down from the stagecoach at the Mullins-Adair Way station, she thought that all of it had settled into her skirts and slipped beneath her bonnet to make a dust mop of her hair. She spoke to the lady at the way station, then gathered up her skirts and went to the livery thirty paces to the north. There, she arranged for transportation to Camp Casey, and settled at the way station to await the buggy's preparation. While the driver loaded her bags, she made a necessary stop at a small outhouse behind the way station.

Emerging and rounding the building, fussing beneath her breath about spiders clinging to a web in the corner of the primitive outhouse, she came face to face with the first Indian, and the tallest man, she had ever seen. Her mouth gaped as her eyes lifted to his dark, steady ones.

John Nightwing was aware that he had startled the white woman, absently flicking dust from a cascade of fiery copper tresses that had tumbled from her bonnet. Her eyes were very blue, her cheeks sun-kissed against the palest skin he had ever seen, and she was tall, willowy, and as graceful as an unbroken filly running free on the desert. She was, unquestionably, the prettiest white woman he had ever seen.

"Pardon me, Sir," she whispered, just now recovering her voice. "I wasn't watching where I was going."

Nightwing's big horse had thrown a shoe, and since he was familiar to the family who ran the way station, he thought he would get a bite to eat while the shoe was being replaced. Despite a heavy heart that had lingered for a week now, he managed a smile for a woman clearly traveling in an unfamiliar land. She had a pleasing drawl, like the soldiers who had been raised in the south...like Taylor. "I not watching my step, too," he said, politely standing aside for her.

Analisse was surprised that the handsome Indian spoke English. She resumed her walk, her eyes turning to hold him as the distance spread. She would have run into a post if the driver hadn't called out a quick warning. Momentarily, she settled into the buggy, her bags stacked on the seat and floor beside her, and began the last leg of her journey to her critically injured brother. Her eyes cut shyly to the Indian standing in the door of the way station. As she lost sight of him, Analisse forced her thoughts back to Laine.

It had been more than six days since she'd set aside the last of her brother's newsy letters to accept the wire that arrived at Shady Grove. With their mother remaining in New Orleans for the season, convinced that an old voodoo woman might cure her ails where a college-educated physician could not, Analisse had not hesitated to make travel arrangements. The plantation overseer kept abreast of the news and had warned her that Indians were causing trouble in Arizona Territory. She and their mother had never wanted Laine transferred to this desolate region of savage Indians, dusty bones, tarantulas, and death. All her information had been culled from the books she had read about the Southwest since his transfer here, and not one thing she'd read had been hospitable. Her imagination had run wild as the distance had closed, and now she'd encountered her very first Indian.

She had not, however, imagined that these indigenous men, justifiably peeved that the white man had invaded their lands, were so terribly handsome.

* * *

Laine sat against several pillows long enough for Dora Huck to spoon-feed him a bowl of beef soup. Both his arms were too sore to lift, and every breath he took caused considerable pain. Annoyed that this chatty, smiling woman insisted on force-feeding him, he wanted only to talk to Calloway about the expected delay in full recovery. But Calloway was still angry enough that he hadn't spent any more time than necessary checking the progress of his recovery. Calloway had accepted his humble apologies—and his thanks—with little more than a grump.

Finally setting the empty bowl aside, Dora remarked, "There now, Captain Taylor, don't you feel better?"

His thoughts vanished. "I do actually, thank you," he replied, watching her tidy the bowl and utensils on a small wooden tray. "Would you mind asking Nightwing to come see me?"

"Nightwing?" Confusion swept over her features. "He was dismissed as Chief of Scouts and left camp a week ago."

"Why the hell was he dismissed?"

"No one has talked to you about this, Captain Taylor?"

"No."

"He waited four hours before dispatching an ambulance wagon into the bluffs when you were found. He was dismissed the following day."

"I didn't know. Talon and I had parted ways. He didn't need to see me dead."

Dora had no time to respond. A swishing of skirts and a lively bounce brought a very pretty young woman up to Laine's bedside. She had also brought in a fair amount of dust, which settled around the bed like a suffocating mist. With hardly a "how do you do," she began kissing Laine's face with her hands pressed to his cheeks. He seemed very surprised by all this.

Dora quietly withdrew with the tray.

"What are you doing here, Analisse?" Laine wished he could take her hands to still her excitable movements. "You're the craziest female I've ever known to travel here with Apaches stirred up. You're lucky not to be tied to a stake somewhere."

"I saw only one Indian," she pouted in her smoothest drawl, "who hardly showed interest in tying this Louisiana peach to a stake." *Not that I would have minded so much,* she thought, beginning a new series of kisses over Laine's face. "I received a wire from General Compton, and made travel arrangements right away. Now show some appreciation for your loyal sister's efforts."

"If I could lift my arms, I'd hug the hell out of you, little Annie."

"Oh, I hate it when you call me that. And look at your pretty face, Laine Taylor. Who cut you up like that? Those damned Apaches?"

He managed a slight grin. "I cut myself shaving."

While they talked, she about their mother's extended stay in New Orleans, and he with assurances that, yes, he was going to live, it took only an hour for word to spread through camp that

Captain Taylor had a beautiful flame-haired Southern belle at his bedside.

* * *

Hearing about the presence of Analisse, Talon remembered teasing Laine about having *an anxious white lass fretting over him back in Louisiana.* Though he had promptly denied it, she wasn't surprised that one had answered Compton's wire.

Talon had decided to leave Camp Casey sooner than expected. Nothing would be gained by staying, and she and Laine running into each other on a daily basis would make life awkward for them both.

She'd been packing her personal things, but at mid-afternoon stretched out on her bed for a short nap. She'd scarcely fallen asleep before alert sounded over camp, and pulled open the door just as Companies D and K were mounting up. All the scouts were falling in, dust stirring like a storm as they left camp. Standing in thoughtful silence, she noticed a green-clad woman, lugging large traveling bags, emerge from the post infirmary. Even from this distance, she saw that she was very pretty, hair as bright as flames leaping from the sun. When she disappeared into Laine's quarters, Talon reentered her own small sanctuary.

Again, she sought sleep, but was kept awake by tears and memories. Daylight held onto the skies longer this time of year, and the one small window overhead afforded too much glow for sleep. So Talon lay there, her eyes lightly closed, Laine obsessively fixed in her thoughts.

Finally, she felt the lightness of sleep overcome her. In her dreams, she walked the swirling sands of the Arizona dustlands, beneath the smooth yellow gold bluffs caressed by a receding sun, felt the stir of hot wind through her hair. She wasn't sure how long her sleep lasted, but when she awoke, night had descended, and yet a lamp, which she had not lit herself, glowed softly from the corner of the room. The pretty woman sat at the table, reading one of her books of poetry. She'd had to be as stealthy as an Indian to settle in without awaking Talon.

Analisse smiled when their eyes met. "You're Talon...I'd

know you anywhere."

Swinging her feet to the floor, Talon felt miserably underdressed in her loose drab gown. With her long, dark hair messy and uncombed, she imagined she looked like a wild Indian savage to this tidy white woman. "You are Captain Taylor's young lady from the south?"

Analisse Amelia laughed sweetly. "He's been known to deny he even knows me! I'm Captain Taylor's young *sister* from the south," she corrected. "If he has a young lady back there, he certainly kept that a secret. He avoided those haughty belles like they had cooties." Rising, she dropped to the bed beside Talon, her hand slipping into the large pocket of her gown to withdraw a bundle of letters tied in a yellow ribbon. "I don't know what happened between you and my brother, because he's not talking much beyond regrets, but I want you to read the letters he's written home to mother and me since he came here in early February."

"The letters are not intended for me."

Analisse insistently pressed the letters into Talon's hand. "While I know my brother sent you away from his bedside after you had so patiently sat with him for six days—that doctor over there is just seething about it, by the way—you have to know how he feels about you. The kind of love he wrote in his letters doesn't just go away."

Talon saw so much of Laine in the woman's bright eyes, in her warm, sincere smile. "As long as you understand he sent me away, was not the other way around. For that reason, whether he loves me should not matter much."

"It does matter. So...please read the letters."

Talon wasn't sure how she felt when this young white woman she didn't know suddenly embraced her, and was relieved when Analisse put several feet of floor space between them. When a few seconds of awkward silence passed, Talon thought she should say something. "I will leave the letters on Captain Taylor's front porch."

"Promise you'll read them." Talon only nodded. "You're as beautiful as Laine said you were. And he's right about something

353

else. That sweetness settles all around you like a pale, heaven-sent cloud. I'm sure those are the words he used." With an almost wicked laugh, she added, "He's even glad you shot him first time you met. He might not have fallen in love with you otherwise." She had reached the door, her hand disappearing into her pocket again. Returning to Talon, she dropped the comb to her lap. "You must keep them together. I purchased them, and make the rules in their regards." Launching another hesitant withdrawal, Analisse looked to Talon for a long, silent moment. "I heard General Compton tell my brother you've resigned as a scout. Are you leaving camp?"

Talon lied. "I have not made that decision yet."

"If you do, I hope you plan to tell Laine."

"He does not want to see me."

"Don't you *want* to tell him you are leaving?"

"No, I do not. I just wish I could see him one last time, even if he is sleeping."

A mischievous grin swept across Analisse's very pale features. "Leave that to me. I'll send word when he's asleep. Tomorrow?"

"All right." Then Analisse was gone, and Talon sat for a moment, absently caressing the tidy bundle of letters.

* * *

The cavalry of K and D Companies returned to camp just after midnight with four wounded soldiers, one dead second lieutenant, and seven Apache prisoners. They also had the roan Laine left camp on last week, and his military weapons and hat. With the exception of one Apache, who said he had stopped at the encampment for a meal, Dako had identified the other six as men from his village.

Compton was notified of the capture, and issued orders that Taylor view the Apaches at first light. He was anxious to hang them and get them out of the way. Turned over to Major Stahl and his guards, the Apaches were put in irons and settled down in general confinement. Three extra guards pulled duty that night.

354

Stahl had the chained Apaches taken to the infirmary at the conclusion of reveille the following morning. Two guards escorted them into the front office, while Stahl accompanied Captain Calloway to Taylor's small, private room. He had just eaten a light breakfast, and was struggling to raise his arms a few inches off the sheet for the ten minutes of exercise Calloway had prescribed.

Before Stahl could make known the reason for his visit, Laine remarked, "I understand you have Apaches for me to see."

"I do, Captain Taylor. Are you up to it?" Laine had hoped he would never again see the faces of the Indians who had attacked him. When he nodded, Stahl turned and ordered, "Private Black, have the prisoners brought in." Within moments, seven Apaches, shackled hand and foot to each other, were brought into the room, several visibly startled to face the officer they thought they had killed.

"They're so young, Major Stahl." Laine looked at each face separately but quickly, and when he reached the last stony face, restored his gaze to the left of the line and studied them again, slowly and more deliberately. He recognized the ones he had faced that day in the ravine, heard again the echo of their taunts, and the cruelty of their hands ripping his uniform and boots from him. He remembered the one in particular, the second from the left, keeping his hands together while the one next to him tightly bound his wrists with rawhide. Another, short of stature and very dark, in the middle, stabbed him several times while his hands were wrenched painfully up his back and strapped to his neck. He recalled that the first two had dragged him up the bluff by his rawhide bound ankles when he was too weak to remain on his feet, the shorter one stabbing him several times again as his back scraped up the bluff. He recalled those moments when he knew he was about to die, as each of these young bucks, foolish from whiskey, clumsily drew their bows tight while he watched in the most frantic fear he had ever known. When they leisurely released their arrows, four broke against the rocks to the side of him, while the other four had shot through him with an all-consuming fire, so swiftly that he never had time to react to any one distinct pain. Even believing him dead, these Apaches were about to release their lances on him when horses clipped on the other side of the rocks. The last thing he saw before he was grabbed by merciful darkness was his attackers running to their ponies and riding away.

Though he wanted them imprisoned for what they did that day, he would not be rash now that he faced them. And a third time, he studied their faces, youthful and sharp like mountain ridges, fiercely dark, and as lethal as the poison of hatred they had for all white men.

Stahl whispered to him, "Do you recognize these Apaches, Captain Taylor?" startling him from his brutal reminiscences.

With a slightly raised finger, Laine singled out the third Apache from the right. "The one in the red shirt—he wasn't there."

"The others?"

"Yes, and there were two more I don't see, the one I heard called Haldini, and another, shorter, not as dark as these."

"Those two were killed during the capture. You're sure these Apaches, with the exception of the one in the red shirt, are the ones who attacked you?"

"I'll never forget their faces. I'm sure."

Stahl flicked a glance at the two guards. "Take them out. I apologize, Captain Taylor, for having to make you face these mean young bucks again."

"What will happen to them?"

"The scout will be court-martialed. Compton wants the rest hanged this morning."

Horror sprang to Laine's features. "Son of a bitch! You're telling me these Indian boys have to die for an attack on one white soldier?"

"Compton ordered it."

"Tell him I demand to see him at once."

"I'll send word, but you know Compton." He quickly withdrew.

The guards retained the Apaches outside the infirmary to await Stahl, who now exited to continue with instructions. "Release the one in the red shirt, give him back his pony, and let him leave. Lock the scout in a segregation cell. Take the others to the side of the building until I talk to Compton."

"I'm here, Major Stahl," Compton announced flatly. "And you *will* address me as *General* Compton." Then, "Taylor identified them as his attackers?"

"He did, *General* Compton, except the one in the red shirt."

"Hang them all now."

"Taylor doesn't want them hanged, and demands to see you."

"Taylor is *not* the commanding officer of this camp, and no one makes demands of me. Hang them all."

"I won't hang the one that didn't take part in the attack on Taylor, and the judicial office advises that the one hired as a scout is entitled to a court-martial."

"Which one was hired as a scout?" Stahl pointed out the one farthest to the right. "I don't give a damn about the scout's rights, or what Taylor wants. Hang all seven."

"No, Sir, I won't. We'll hang the five, if you insist, but not the other two," Stahl argued hotly, his bravado reinforced by the presence of Colonel Heitman on post. "Private Black, do as I ordered, and send a guard for Dako so he can tell these bucks in their own language they'll be hanged for the attack on an Army officer. Then dispatch six guards to the scaffold to await me."

Salem George Compton calmly unholstered his large caliber sidearm.

One of the Apaches yelled, and the guard, Ragan Black, leaped across five feet of space to knock Compton's sidearm from his fingers. One of the big caliber bullets he had intended for the Apaches discharged into the air as the weapon hit the dirt. Guards swarmed from the direction of the military prison, soldiers from their barracks and mess halls, the Indians swiftly subdued and forced to their knees. At some point in this confusing fracas, a fretfully angry Salem George Compton had retrieved his sidearm and calmly reholstered it.

"Damn you, private," he growled, then at Stahl, "I said I want all seven of these bucks hanged."

"For that abominable act, *General* Compton, the judicial office will be consulted before any of these Apaches are hanged."

A furious Compton pivoted, huffed a few obscenities, and returned to HQ.

Compton's attempted execution of the Apaches outside the infirmary became an addendum to Lieutenant Colonel Heitman's almost completed report for Washington. That evening, Heitman organized his reports, packed them, and put them on the mail coach for the first leg of its journey to the War Department in Washington. He also wired Washington that it was on its way, and requested extended assignment to Casey until the final recommendation was made. If Compton was forced into retirement—or court-martialed—Heitman requested that he be appointed interim commanding officer.

* * *

Later that day, Laine couldn't bear to look at Compton when he approached the bed and laid his hand on his arm to gently shake him. "I'm awake...but I don't know how I feel about you right now. If you had killed those Apaches—"

"A year or two of imprisonment won't mellow those bucks. Given their freedom, they'll do the same thing again. Savage tendencies do not diminish, Captain Taylor." When Laine failed to respond, Compton added, "Will you do anything about Talon leaving camp?"

"What can I do?" Then, "Do you know where she's going?"

"No...I pray she'll tell her mother."

"Miss Julia has a lot on her mind. I think she's worried about the relationship between you and Talon."

"Yes...I know she is." Compton pulled up a chair and sat down, his fingers linking nervously. "There is no part of me that doesn't want Talon's forgiveness for the vicious way I treated her when I came here, for slapping her so viciously for no fault of her own. If not for me, she would not have been so brutally whipped. I don't hold out much hope for it. I wish I could go back, listen to the clues she dropped that she was my granddaughter—listen to my own heart that there was something special about her. I was too bullheaded."

Laine had not been able to lift his arms more than a few inches in the past two days, but now his right arm moved with new energy, his fingers closing over Compton's wrist. "God—" Beside the curtain stood Julia Rose, her tearful eyes betraying that she had heard her father's confession.

Absolute horror drained Compton's features as he saw his daughter. "Julia, let me explain—"

But she fled at once to the livery, and the big, friendly arms of Matt Money. He was, as usual, at his anvil this late hour, and a tearful Julia threw herself at his knees. "Oh, Mattie," she whispered. "My father hated Talon...he was brutal to her! He was responsible for her being whipped! Oh, dear God, beautiful Talon..."

"Christ, Julia...who told you that? He wasn't responsible for that whipping. He had nothing to do with it!"

"I heard my father say it. Tell me my ears were deceiving me."

"I can't do that, sweet little lady...but he didn't have her whipped. I swear, Julia—"

Julia placed her cheek against his thigh, Mattie's hand resting comfortingly on her hair. Then she cursed beneath her breath—cursed her father—and her daughter—for so casually lying when she had asked her if he'd ever hurt her. "Was she hurt bad, Mattie?"

"She was hurt real bad, Julia...but she's strong." He wondered why she was this distraught over a young woman she had so recently met. But then, he had lost his own heart to Talon first time he met her. "Is it Talon you're worried about, Julia? Or that your father is capable of brutality?"

Talon entered the livery to talk to Mattie, surprised to find her mother there. Then Julia's tearful eyes swiped the smile from her. Julia got to her feet, approached, and firmly gripped her upper arms. "Why didn't you tell me the truth, Talon?"

Nervous ticks struggled against the corners of Talon's mouth. "The truth about what?"

"I asked you if my father ever hurt you." Julia gritted her teeth to gain a moment. "Show me your back, Talon."

Though she'd expected it to happen eventually, she was horrified that her mother knew about the whipping. "He was not responsible for this. And you must remember your promise that no matter what you heard you would not turn against him. He loves you so."

"Let me see where you were whipped!"

Talon instantly drew her into a solid hug. "He did not do it. Please, *Pia*...forget this."

"*Pia*! Awe, hell." Mattie had spent time in Texas back in the early 70's and knew enough Comanche to get him out of a scrape. "That's the Comanche word for mother." Both women spun as Mattie came to his feet. "You telling me, Julia, that Talon's your daughter?"

"Yes, she's my daughter, Mattie."

That sure explained Compton wanting the whip laid to him that night. "Dadgum, gals—" Mattie's big, strong hands went across each of their shoulders. "I wish one of you would'a told me."

"I said let me see where you were whipped," Julia repeated. When Talon turned pleading eyes to Mattie, Julia's fingers dug into the fabric of Talon's light blouse and ripped it down her back. "Let me see what my vicious father was responsible for."

Talon reluctantly turned her back to her mother. "He was not responsible, I swear to the almighty—" At the sight of the fading red marks so strongly indicating the severity of the whipping, Julia sank, sobbing, to the floor, her palms pressed firmly against her face. Mattie roughly took her shoulders and drew her into his arms. Talon was instantly at her back, one hand going to Mattie's arm, and the other smoothing the loose, curly tendrils of hair at her mother's cheek. "Listen to my words, *Pia*," she began, recalling the events Laine had related to her one night. "A very long time ago a brilliant young Army captain waited nervously for the arrival of his fifteen year old daughter by stagecoach. Before her arrival, he received news of an Indian attack on the coach she was riding in, and several women, including you, were taken captive by Comanches. He began a ten-year campaign to wipe out the Comanches, all the while believing you to be dead. Finally, his atrocities compelled his transfer to the east, where he worked tirelessly to become the best officer in the Army, moved up through the ranks, but never did he forget the daughter he had lost. And all those years, the hatred grew inside his heart. To know my father loved me like that would bring such pride. This man did terrible wrongs, but the one thing neither of us can deny is that he loves you. The fact that he was brutal to me at first has *nothing* to do with that love. I have been angry enough with him for both of us, and if you love me, you will not turn your back on him. I must insist that you honor your promise to me."

"Listen to her, Julia," Mattie whispered with husky emotion. "And take it straight from me that your pa's livin' with a lot of guilt...a lot of regret. Nobody knows that better'n me."

"How can I face him, Talon—Mattie—knowing that he...hated and tormented you?"

Mattie's statement had evoked bewilderment in Talon, taking her thoughts for a moment. He had never told anyone that Compton came to him, wanting to be whipped the way Talon had been whipped.

"He knew only that I was Comanche, not your daughter." Talon managed the smallest laugh. "I should be angry with you for tearing a favorite blouse. Now...do you honor your promise, or do I assume I cannot trust your word?"

Julia drew back, sharing a look between Mattie and Talon. "Both of you ask me to forget that I'm your mother."

"That is the last thing I want you to forget, *Pia*. But this grumpy old warrior has lost everything. He has exposed himself to a great deal of shame, and an ugly smear on a long military career, all because of me. If he loses you, too, I will never forgive myself."

Julia conceded with a shrug. "I can't treat him as if nothing has happened."

"Do not make your anger another complication in our family."

Hugging her daughter gently, Julia looked to the man she had so quickly grown to adore these past two weeks, to his kind, compassionate eyes. "Only for you, Talon...and Mattie." Her hand swept out, and she waited for Mattie to gently take it.

* * *

Compton went straight to his quarters after leaving the infirmary. He thought Julia would go to Talon, but felt confident she would do what she could to quell the situation. Most likely, Julia would never again settle into his gentle hugs to whisper, *I'm so happy, Papa,* and already he missed the absence of her sweet affection.

The door opened downstairs, delicate feminine footfalls ascended the steps toward his private quarters, free of the bounce he had listened to so often these past few weeks. Then Julia stood in the semi-darkened parlor, quietly looking at him. He noticed the change at once, the usual gaiety shaded by melancholy, the crisp blueness of her eyes faded with disappointment. Though there was none of the hatred he deserved, he couldn't think of a single word to say to this daughter he loved so deeply.

"I'm tired, Father. I'll retire to my room now." Julia made a wide swing around him, and went to her bedchamber without the customary hug and kiss goodnight.

Not Papa...but Father. No hug...just blunt departure.

Salem George Compton sank into a chair and quietly wept. He had lost everything.

* * *

Later that night, Analisse waited for the light to go on in Talon's quarters, and slipped down the short length of stairs to slip a note beneath her door. She was halfway across the parade field when the door opened, and Talon searched the darkness. Slipping into the infirmary, she looked out the window until Talon withdrew to the inside. Her note had said simply, "He always sleeps between nine and ten in the morning. Come then."

Analisse had to look out for her brother's interests now. Although the letters she'd pressed into Talon's hand were tied exactly as she'd received them when she found them on Laine's porch, she had no doubt that she'd read them. Talon simply had to understand how deeply Laine loved her, because Analisse would not allow him to go through life denied the love he deserved.

When her own short-lived marriage at age nineteen abruptly ended two days later with the accidental death of her new husband, Laine had journeyed home from his post in Florida to be with her. She had lost her clumsy husband to the hooves and wheels of a mail coach, so angry with him for dying that she had immediately returned to her maiden name. She was determined that her brother wouldn't chase off the only woman he had ever loved, and spend the rest of his life regretting it. Besides, she could barely tolerate him when he was miserable, even when miles of distance separated them.

"You're plotting something."

Until he spoke, Analisse hadn't realized Laine had awakened. "I was thinking you really should let me shave you."

"And have you cut my throat? I don't think so."

"I'll be careful."

"Don't think so. Hell...I deserve to look bushy."

"If you hadn't run Talon off you'd have a smooth jaw line, and I wouldn't have to complain when I hug you."

His mouth pressed, his eyes admonishing. "You've nagged me unmercifully. All right, I was a little hasty."

"You were a *lot* hasty. Talon truly loves you."

"She wouldn't commit to me."

"Oh, well! Spoiled and pampered white soldier from the great State of Louisiana! Talon hesitated to make her decision when *you* felt she should. How long will you pout about that before reason sinks into that Yankee-sized brain of yours?"

Laine looked to her with a crooked smile. "You're real mean to a man who almost died."

"Taylors don't have time to die!" Rising from the chair to

which she had settled, Analisse put distance between them. "I might go over to the dining room and get some breakfast. Want anything?"

"Eggs, bacon, biscuits, and brandy."

"Perhaps everything but the brandy, brother."

He grinned boyishly. "Thanks, Little Annie...I'm glad you're here. And...be nice to Major Harris. He visited me yesterday, and all he talked about was you."

Analisse shook her finger several times, a habit she'd picked up in childhood from their old nanny. "I swear, honey chile', don't you go fixin' me up with a spoiled Army officer. One in the family is quite enough." Then, grinning, she danced through the sick soldiers in the open infirmary in a wave of flirtatious small talk and laughter.

* * *

Analisse spent the morning visiting around camp, and enjoyed tea and pan-dowdy with Dora Huck on her front porch just after nine o'clock. From her perch her eyes swept the entire camp, and though Talon's small building was partially obscured between the barracks, the dark hole descending to the bottom of the stairs was clearly visible. She had just told Dora of her plan, and now waited for Talon to emerge from her quarters, so that she could put it into action.

Talon made an appearance at twenty-five past nine, attired in a long white fringed deerskin dress, its bodice and lower skirts decorated with bright bead work. A single feather emerged downward from a rawhide tie to the right side of her headband. Her black hair was long, full and loose, hanging well past her waistline. Analisse thought she was like an Indian princess in a treasured painting.

Talon had struggled with the decision to go to Laine, but knew his feisty sister would likely hogtie and drag her if she didn't go voluntarily. She shared a few words with Dora and Analisse across the rail of her porch, then entered the infirmary and peeked around the door to Captain Calloway's office. Seeing only the back of his chair, and a head of peppered hair poking above it, she slipped past his office without detection.

For a moment Talon stood behind the curtain, listening for the telltale signs of Laine's sleep. Then she stole a glance around the thick fabric and saw that his faced was turned toward the far wall. Easing to his bedside, she stood and watched him sleep for several minutes. Instinctively, her fingers rose to that little lock of hair that always settled on his forehead, but withdrew before touching him. She whispered a few words to him, to be sure he wouldn't awaken, and quietly spoke all the sentiments that had settled in her heart since the first time she had met him. She was unaware of Analisse standing on the other side of the curtain.

Earlier that morning, Annalise had taken the biggest book Captain Calloway had on his shelves and hidden it near the curtain. She listened to Talon, almost a breathy whisper so that she wouldn't wake Laine, then lifted the book to the height of her head and let it fall to the planked floor.

A cannon fired beside her wouldn't have made a more effective bang.

* * *

Laine lurched from his sleep as if his breath had been swept away. The light within the room, offered by one long window, glowed like a heaven-sent halo around the angel who gained clarity before him. He thought he was still dreaming of his lovely Talon. Divine in her state of surprise as she looked to him, the fingers of her left hand pressed anxiously to her mouth. Because of the harsh words he had spoken to her three days ago, he imagined she sought an escape route.

Seeing Analisse's feet beneath the curtain, Talon was furious that she had deliberately awakened Laine. "I know you did not want me here. I am so sorry I went against your wishes, but I had to see you before I leave."

Laine took her hand, barely able to hold it in his weak grip. He had been chastised unmercifully by his sister. Now, before him stood his faithful Talon, her thick, tumbling hair freshly washed, held back from her temples by the beaded headband matching her fringed dress. The color in her cheeks was pinker than usual, and she almost blossomed beneath his scrutiny. But the anxiety—almost a fear—in her very poignant sea green eyes

365

tore at his heartstrings. "Where are you going, Talon?"

"I have resigned as a scout," she replied at once. "I was thinking I should leave camp, and wanted to see you a final time."

"Tell me why, Talon, you didn't leave with Nightwing when you had the chance?"

"Because I do not love Nightwing, not as a woman should love a man. I do hope you will keep in mind that, no matter what he did, he is a very good man."

Her confession that she did not love Nightwing brought joy to his heart. "I do know that, Talon. But...why would you return here after the way I treated you?"

"To say farewell. No other reason."

From some invisible source, Laine found the strength to tighten his grip on her hand. "Before you say farewell, rest your head against me and tell me something soft and sweet about Talon, the Comanche daughter of a chief. Just for old times' sake."

A thousand memories flew through Talon, their wonderful talks, in which he had asked her the very same thoughtful question, his sweet sentiments, the rush of love she had felt for him. Slowly approaching, drawing his hand gently to her, Talon dropped her head beside his, her lips trembling against his jaw, brushy because she hadn't been here to shave him the past three mornings. "Something soft and sweet about Talon," she echoed his words. "I suppose the softest, sweetest thing I can tell you about Talon right now is her cherished memory of a heartless Officer of Scouts, all decked out in his finest blues, with a legion of military medals pinned to his chest like a pompous barnyard rooster, brandy sweet on his breath, strolling boldly into a corral where the woman who had shot him first time they met absently groomed her horse in the light of a single lantern." Lifting her eyes, she saw the sheen of moisture settling over the deep, azure pools that had so often smiled at her, saw his mouth press tightly to keep from trembling with the emotional memories she had stirred in him. "Where is the love I felt that night, Laine? The love of that reckless soldier who made me feel like a princess?"

Tears fell gently to the pillow beside him. "You were always first in Talon's heart...but that night in the hills, when I begged for your trust and you denied it to me, even after you had loved me so completely, I knew then that love wasn't enough." Touching her trembling mouth to his cheek, wet from the tears he had shed while she spoke, she whispered, "Why did you not trust me, Laine? Such a small thing to ask, but I would always have treasured it." Then she pulled back, so that she might see his face more clearly. "I must go."

Weak with emotion, Talon tried to flee from his bedside. But when he called, "Talon—" she paused, her fingers clutching the curtain separating the room from the open ward. "Will you ever forgive me?"

"I do forgive you."

"Do you love me, Talon?"

"I stayed with you when you were hurt, Lane, because I love you. But the fact that I stayed did not resolve the trust that does not exist between us."

He did not hesitate to confess, softly and sincerely, "I want you to be my wife. I promise to trust you, to love you and make you happy."

"Why would you trust me now, when you would not trust me when I asked for it? I am sorry, but I must go," she said, and fled from him before he might halt her.

Just outside the infirmary, Analisse Amelia snatched her arm to end her flight. "You're not going to leave him, Talon. You read his letters home and know how much he loves you. I wasn't nearby when you were together just now...but I imagine he confessed that he still loves you."

Talon's trembling fingers spread over the silky sleeves of Analisse's pretty dress. "He deserves better than me...better than a Comanche thief and rabble rouser."

Analisse laughed outright. "If that's what you are, Talon...then no, he doesn't deserve better. I grew up with him. He roused more rabble than you could ever dream up."

"But he did not trust me—"

"Poppycock. If he trusted you completely, Talon, he

wouldn't be a man." Softness flowed into Analisse's voice as she drew an arm around Talon. "Give him a chance to undo the wrong he's done. Because if you don't, so help me—" Then, before she might finish the threat, she pulled Talon into an embrace and whispered, "Please...please, don't break the heart of a brother I love so dearly." Pushing Talon back a little roughly, she ordered, "Go to him now and tell him you will be with him always."

Taking Analisse's hands, she whispered, "I'm so torn—"

"You're stubborn, Talon. Pure female. Give him a chance to turn that trust thing around. Give him a chance to prove how sorry he is."

Analisse was right. She *was* stubborn. She had admitted just this week that Laine was the only man she would ever love...and now, she was willing to spend the rest of her life alone than to truly forgive him. And she was partly to blame, because she had not confided in him that night in the hills. He had asked her outright if Julia was her mother, and she had not trusted him enough to tell the truth.

Feeling petty and stubborn, Talon knew she'd be a fool to walk away from Laine's love.

Halting only a moment, she softly smiled, left Analisse, and returned to Laine's bedside. His eyes were closed, and she remembered the days that she'd watched the bruises and wounds on his face slowly heal, even as she thought he wouldn't survive. When he opened his eyes and looked to her, she pressed her cheek to his warm one. "Your sister would have driven me back in here with a gun if she had one."

"She probably has a derringer hidden in her skirts," he said. "I won't even ask you where you ran off to."

"Not very far."

He breathed the sweet fragrance of her skin as she rested her head against his own. "I may be too weak to stand, Talon, but I'm persistent. Before I make a complete fool of myself and ask you again to marry me, I should mention that Calloway thinks the arrow I took in my hip might leave me lame."

"Heavens forbid," she said with feigned indignation, "that

Talon's man should walk with a limp! Not an issue for me, paleface."

"Marry me, Talon. And if you need time to give me an answer, I'll wait...no matter how long."

"I really do not need a lot of time." Talon's emotions swept between joy and astonishment. When she hesitated to continue, his lips lightly touched her forehead, his fingers lifting her chin. "But there are still issues we must work out."

"See the clock on that wall? You have until it chimes the hour of ten to tell me how long you need."

"That is only two minutes, Laine."

"Long enough." Talon began to watch the clock. "What are you waiting for, Talon?"

"For the clock to chime the hour of ten." Drawing his hand to her mouth, she held it for a moment, watching the clock, the little hand moving so slowly, and she knew that Laine watched it, too. In the interlude of silence, she realized she was about to tell him she would be his wife. Then the little hand was straight up and the clock began to chime, shutting everything out of Talon's mind but her happiness. When the chimes halted, she whispered against his cheek, "I do not need any more time. I will marry you, Captain Laine Taylor." Laughing, she added, "Because I don't want your sister to kill me."

He grinned. "Didn't this spoiled white man warn you he always gets what he wants? Especially when he has a homicidal sister." His kiss was soft and gentle. "I'll love you always, Talon. Never will you be in doubt of that."

Talon pressed her cheek to Laine's, his promises soaring, like a legion of doves caught in the sunlight. Closing her eyes, enjoying the warmth of his arms around her, she saw two men in her thoughts...but one had slipped quietly into the shadows. She knew he might occasionally reach a hand to her across time and distance to touch her heart with fond memories...but the man in her arms now would share her life, protect and cherish her, and—she prayed—smile on the children born of their love.

Epilogue

Seven weeks into the Summer

Talon and Laine sat patiently in the chapel with Major Lindley this late Thursday afternoon, congratulating him on his recent promotion before getting to the matter that had brought them here. He would perform the wedding ceremony on Saturday afternoon, just two days away, and had called them to chapel because he felt the need to counsel them on their diverse cultures and the problems they might face adjusting to life together.

In all his years he couldn't recall a stronger, more determined or sincere woman than Talon. He had no doubt that the union of this man and woman would last a lifetime and beyond. Dismissing them from his counsel within the hour he watched them leave the chapel, he supporting his leg on a cane, she tucked protectively beneath his arm for extra support.

They had agreed to dine with Compton and Julia in the officer's dining room that night, made available after evening repast for their private dining. As a result of Colonel Heitman's investigation, Compton had received official notification from the War Department of his forced retirement, with full pension, to take effect the end of August. Talon didn't wish to add to his woes by declining his invitation, since they were all acutely aware of the tension that had settled between a father and his daughter.

Talon knew there was so little time left to make things right between them again. And it had to be done before Compton left Arizona Territory.

That night, Laine, Talon, and Analisse met General Compton and Julia in the officer's dining room. He had paid several orderlies to work overtime and prepare a feast for them, and had even obtained an excellent bottle of California

Bordeaux through the commissary to toast their upcoming wedding. After their plates had been cleared, General Compton withdrew an envelope from his pocket and presented it to Laine and Talon. Inside was a draft from a bank in Boston for a rather sizeable amount. Laine immediately handed it back. "We can't accept this."

Hurt reflected in Compton's eyes. "It isn't just from me, but from Julia's Aunt Clara in Boston." He also had an identical check for Julia, but would present it to her at the appropriate time, perhaps at announcement of her anticipated marriage to Mattie. "I suspect you won't stay in the Army with that lame leg, Laine. That'll buy you and your new wife a nice spread here in Arizona Territory, or wherever you might wish to live."

When he looked to Julia, she said stiffly, "She and Laine won't live in Boston, if that's what you're hoping for. And neither will I."

Talon gained closeness to her mother and whispered very softly, "He's living with a lot of regrets. Please don't be one of them."

Julia rose at once. Though she had kept her promise to Talon to remain civil with her father, she hadn't forgiven him for his persecution of her. "You don't need a wet hen at this little gathering, so I'll tell you all goodnight." She withdrew before anyone could protest.

Talon looked to Laine, to see what he would do about the wedding gift from her grandfather. He had already tucked it into his pocket. "Thank you, General Compton, for the wedding gift," she said politely. "I promise we will put it to very good use."

"General Compton," he repeated. "Will you ever call me Grandfather, Talon? Or Toko?"

Before Talon might give an awkward response, Analisse arose. "I need to get some sleep. I have a world of preparations tomorrow. You!" She playfully shook a finger at Talon. "Soon-to-be sister-in-law, come to Dora's promptly at five for your final gown fitting."

Talon teased her about the amorous attentions of Major Daniel Harris, and promised that she would be prompt for the fitting.

The next afternoon, however, Laine interrupted her walk to Dora's to read her a wire from his mother in New Orleans, wishing them much happiness, and sending her regrets that she wouldn't be able to attend the wedding.

Analisse disapproved of Talon's tardiness by—heaven's forbid—five full minutes. For the next hour, Talon allowed herself to be fussed at and smothered by Dora, Analisse, and her mother, who tugged and poked and snipped and pinned, until Talon was so happy to escape that she ran straight to the stable to see Shadow Dancer. As the eve of her wedding approached, she led the spirited mare into the corral and spent a full hour grooming her until her coat shone like the sun, untangling her flowing mane and tail, and telling her how happy she was.

A veil of late evening shadows had fallen over the little military post when the corral gate opened, and Talon became aware of a man's footfalls approaching her. Then her beloved whispered, "Dance with me, Talon. I'm sure your horse won't mind," and Talon turned, threw her arms around him, and kissed him with fierce need and passion.

The hours until their wedding passed so quickly Talon scarcely believed the hour had approached. Standing in front of a cheval mirror in Dora's sewing room the next afternoon, a very nervous Comanche bride still tasted her betrothed's kiss, as though they had shared it just seconds ago. By the time she got a round of approval from the women in her life, Talon had settled her nerves enough to think she might be ready to be a wife. As the women left to take their places in the chapel, Talon said a small prayer, counted her many blessings, and imagined all the wonderful years that lay ahead for them.

But issues needed to be settled before she walked into that chapel and became Laine's wife.

Just before the hour of two, Talon stepped from Dora's porch, and was about to lift her skirts for a run across the parade field when she suddenly looked into the bluffs far above camp.

She didn't see Nightwing, but knew he was there, watching her. Lifting her hand, she whispered, "Always will you be in Talon's heart...but I belong with Laine now." Then she resumed her journey to HQ, and entered the darkened offices and corridors. Spying the glow from her grandfather's office, she moved to the slightly ajar door, at once horrified to see him sitting in his chair with a pistol held lightly beneath his chin. She was angry that he planned to do this terrible deed at the exact moment of her wedding.

Compton caught sight of his slim, golden Comanche granddaughter, elegant in her wedding finery of cream silk taffeta, her veil tossed carelessly back from her loose raven hair. He lowered the pistol to his lap. "I can't bear what my life has become."

Talon dropped to her knees beside him, her fingers closing lightly over the sleeves of his dress blue jacket. "Before you pull that trigger, will you first consider coming to the church to give your only grandchild in marriage?"

Placing the gun on the desktop, his glazed eyes turned to her as if he hadn't heard her correctly. His trembling fingers eased beneath her chin, so gently that Talon scarcely felt the pressure. "After what I've done, Talon, you want this hateful old man to walk you down the aisle on your happiest day?"

She smiled. "Look at you, Sir, all dressed up and thinking you have no place to go. But you do now." When he tearfully drew her into his arms, she whispered, "Ask me again, Toko, to forgive you. Ask me now while I am so happy."

Salem George Compton could barely find his voice. "Will you, Talon, forgive a vicious, brutal old man, and allow him to be your grandfather?"

Tears settled on Talon's flushed cheeks, her mouth trembling ever so slightly. "In all fairness, Sir, you must know that I will never forget how you treated me. But yes, I will forgive you. I forgive you today because I am happy, and I am so in love. I cannot have the animosity between us spoiling all of our lives, not now, when the future stretches before us like a golden dream. It is time to put our differences behind us. Come with me, before my handsome groom thinks I have changed my mind."

Moments later, a quiet Talon, escorted by her grandfather, crossed the parade field, his hand firmly clamped to the many medals on his chest to keep them from jingling. When the guard saw them coming, he opened the door to the chapel and announced the arrival of the bride. At once, the young soldier at the piano began playing the wedding march.

A warm stillness fell over the filled church as Talon entered, her arm tucked gently through her grandfather's. Compton was so proud right then that any animosity lingering in soldiers' faces went without his notice. All eyes turned, and Laine, in his formal parade uniform, turned to watch his adoring bride approach on Compton's arm.

He had never seen such a heaven-sent vision. Dora and Julia had lovingly sewn the rustling taffeta dress with its front-fastening bodice and skirts settled over stiffened muslin, snuggly fitting her slender frame, such a lovely contrast to her golden skin. Her wedding veil was finely appliquéd bobbin lace, and an orange blossom wreath settled around her flowing ebony hair like a halo.

Talon was happy to see four pews to the right filled with their Indian scouts, and waved her fingers to them as she passed by. When she and her grandfather paused at the front pew, Major Lindley asked, "Who gives this very beautiful young woman in marriage?"

Compton patted her hand with rough emotion. "Her proud grandfather, who doesn't deserve this great honor."

"I beg to differ, Toko...and thank you." Talon kissed his cheek, approached Laine, and turned to watch her mother slide closer to Mattie, allowing room for her father to sit on the pew beside her. Talon lifted her eyes to her bridegroom only when her mother's hand softly covered her father's. She had prayed that her own forgiveness would allow her mother to forgive him, also.

Laine whispered to her, "How proud I am of you."

Their hands met, fingers gently linking, and sharing a

loving look between each other, turned their eyes together to the man who would seal their union.

Only later, with the ceremony over, the festivities and gaiety of a lavish reception in the officer's dining room being cleaned up by a bevy of orderlies, did Talon even remotely recall some of the words Major Lindley had spoken. But the most important announcement, *I now present Captain and Mrs. Laine Taylor,* echoed softly in her thoughts as she shared a last dance tonight with her less than graceful new husband.

Then, nagged by the single ladies, Talon tossed her bouquet, which was quickly snapped up by a bouncing, giggling Analisse Amelia, who had consumed a little too much wine during the evening toasts. She joked that she had met the man she wanted at a way station three miles away, but would give no further details. Major Daniel Harris overheard and remarked to Troy Reisner that he was going to have this flame-haired belle before any other man put his brand on her.

While Laine settled into a chair to rest and chat with Mattie and his new mother-in-law, Talon moved lovingly among the scouts, hugging them all. Dako had shyly stood off to the side. Approaching this friendly Apache who had been her friend from the beginning, Talon waited for his eyes to turn to her. "When you see Nightwing again, Dako, tell him how happy I am. Tell him I will always think of him with warmth in my heart."

Dako promised that he would, stopping short of telling her that Nightwing had said he would sit atop Cimarron Bluff to watch her go to her wedding.

Colonel Heitman stopped her as she crossed the floor, gave her a big hug, and chuckled, "You know, Comanche Talon, you look a helluva lot better in a wedding dress than you would've looked in a noose." They laughed together, and Talon, knowing that her grandfather sweltered still in a cloak of routine animosity among her wedding guests, felt a need to spend more time with him.

As she moved in his direction, Julia and Mattie stepped into her path. Mattie smiled widely, taking her hand to hold it warmly. "Gotta tell you again, Talon, what a dandy bride you make. An' I figured—" His arm went across Julia's shoulders, "since you was too young for me, I'd take your ma. If we got your blessin', girl, I'd like to marry her."

Talon threw her arms around both of their necks, nearly butting them together. "You have my blessing a thousand times over. When?"

"I'll travel to Boston with my father to see Aunt Clara at the end of August," Julia replied, glancing to Mattie with love. "We will marry when I return. We've set a date for November 12th. You'll come, won't you, and your new husband?"

"With bells on," Talon laughed, hugging them both again. Then she watched them walk into the warm night to sit somewhere and look at the moon, as they often did. Her mother had found happiness at last, and that made Talon's wedding day even more special.

When her grandfather announced that it was time to retire from all this excitement, Talon offered to walk with him. As they crossed the parade ground toward HQ, she allowed him to rest his arm across her shoulders as they walked. "Grandfather, about that pistol you had in your hand when I entered your office this afternoon—"

Halting at once, Compton pivoted to Talon, taking both her hands to hold them warmly. "I thought it was the only way, Granddaughter. Regret that I hurt you so deeply will remain with me always, but what I don't regret is you walking into my office this afternoon and giving me reason to live. I'll always hold your kind words to my heart, simply because you gave them to a man who did not deserve them. Nothing I can ever do will make up for what I did, but I promise you and your family will never want for anything. You need only let me know."

"Laine and I do appreciate the generous gift you and Great-Aunt Clara gave us, but it just simply isn't enough."

"Indeed?" A thick, white brow shot abruptly up. "And what would be enough, Talon?"

"I was thinking, Grandfather, something along the lines of...another sweet hug?"

With a throaty laugh, Compton drew her into his arms. "A

hug," he whispered huskily, "does kind of warm up the coldness of money. Thank you, Granddaughter...thank you for making my remaining years a little easier to live."

His hug tightened, a moment of silence passing between them. Then he spoke with fond reminiscence. "One day you and your young man will have children, Talon. I remember when Julia was born, how proud her mother and I were of this tiny human given so casually to our love and care. Since she was born in summer, we would fancy her up in silks and laces, bundle her into her pram and stroll through our neighborhood, stopping to let everyone admire our precious angel. Those strolls would last for hours, we were so sure our neighbors lined up to see her." Tears settled into his voice, so he roughly turned Talon, continuing the walk to his quarters. Pausing in front of HQ, he took her hands again. "May you and Laine be blessed as was Julia's mother and I."

Later, as Talon and Laine lay together in the big bed in his quarters, their gently entwined bodies sated by lovemaking spoke so eloquently of their commitment to each other, and the many blessings in their lives. They shared their secrets, their hopes, and their dreams, laughed as they spoke of the sweet Analisse, who had decided to spend the week on the divan at Dora's, so the lovers could have Laine's quarters to themselves. They even found an appropriate moment to speak of Nightwing.

"You know, Talon, I don't think we've seen the last of that Apache." Snuggling to her new husband, Talon settled her tangled tresses against his shoulder, her fingers lightly tracing the scar along his chest where the arrow had been removed. She would always have a special place for Nightwing in her heart. "I won't say he and I don't still have our problems, but—" Laine left the sentiment hanging, turning to take Talon in his arms in a loving embrace. A kiss adorned her forehead, teased the bridge of her nose and settled against her full, moist lips. He loved that her firm, full breasts scorched his flesh, her fingers spreading along his waistline and easing to his back to draw him oh, so close. "You know, my bride...that sweet lovin' we had just a few minutes ago? I sure could go for a second helping."

With a gentle smile, Talon whispered a special vow to him in the language of the Sioux.

Laine's eyes glowed in gentle reminiscence. "You spoke the same words when you came to me that night in the guardhouse. You must tell me what they mean."

"I said, my husband, with every shred of my being, every beat of my heart, the fullest depths of my soul...I love you." Then with a slightly wicked smile, "If you want me, take me now, before I fall asleep."

Covering her body with his own, capturing the sweet kisses she offered him, he smiled, because he had always known that Nightwing had lied about the words he had overheard Talon speak to him that night.

The rascal had loved her even then.

But as he held his woman, his wife, and loved her completely, he decided not to hold Nightwing's deception against him. He had truly loved Talon and there was no fault in that.

"And I love you, Talon," he murmured against her dark hair. "Always will I treasure you, always will I trust you—" Then the splendid Arizona night just beyond the window sent shards of golden light into the window, and the passion they held for each other covered them like a misty blanket.

"Always," his new bride whispered. "Always Talon's heart is yours."

Caroline Bourne was born in Southampton, England to an American father and an English mother. Spending only seven months in England, she grew up in the small southern town of Lecompte, Louisiana, in between transfers to Army posts in Texas and Arkansas with her Army father. She was an avid horse lover and spent many hours on horseback, riding with a group of friends on weekends. Graduating from Lecompte High School in 1965 she went on to spend two years in the United States Marine Corps, being honorably discharged as a Corporal E-4 in 1967. Returning to Louisiana, she went to work for a local newspaper, the Alexandria Daily Town Talk, eventually married and had two daughters, Kristen and Kimberly. Her first novel was published in 1984 by Kensington and twelve others, plus a co-authorship and two contributions to anthologies followed. As the years passed, she worked for lawyers and judges, and eventually moved to Indiana to be near her sister. For the past fifteen years she has worked for a Southern Indiana police department. Today, she is the grandmother of six granddaughters and one great-grandson.